PRAISE FOR MESSIANIC MARRIAGE

Sam led a two-day marriage conference for our church that covered many of the insights included in this book. The feedback from couples was extremely positive, with many expressing that understanding the Lord's original design—beginning in Genesis—and His intent for marriage helped them see their roles and responsibilities in a whole new light. The spiritual truths and prescriptive guidance were both strengthening and encouraging in ways the couples did not expect. I highly recommend this timely resource and believe wholeheartedly it will bring scriptural understanding, help deepen and protect marriage relationships, while bringing glory to Jesus Christ!

—Pastor Tim White,
Senior Pastor of Calvary Chapel, Richmond, Virginia

This book and its teaching are really for everyone! Whether married, engaged, or single, your life will be enriched. Beginning in Genesis, Sam guides his readers through Scripture to understand God's perfect design for relationships and how to practically apply these principles in everyday life. Messianic marriage does matter, for through it God's redemptive heart is revealed to the world. We've been so thankful for this teaching in our lives and highly recommend this book, as it will be a blessing for both married and single people alike.

—Tim and Laurel James

The Messianic marriage relationship is a lifelong process of discovery. We have been married for over thirty-six years, and we are still like babes learning about one another and about God through our marriage. We need continual renewal in our understanding to keep our eyes aimed toward God's foundational purposes for us in marriage. This book gave us new insights that ministered to our needs as we attempt to align our marriage to a Biblical framework. We came to see how the principles lived out in the garden of Eden are timeless—from God's covenant, to the innocence of man and woman coming together as one flesh, to innocence lost, to the consequences of rebellion, and finally to the hope of redemption that is ultimately fulfilled in Yeshua HaMashiach.

—Jerry and Michelle Shelfer

My husband and I took the Messianic Marriage Matters seminar twice and loved it, particularly the foundation for marriage teaching found in Genesis. There was also tons of practical take-away information. We are so excited about the publication of this book!

—Carolyn Phillips

Taking Sam's Messianic Marriage Seminar showed that we are never too old to learn new things to apply and strengthen the marriage. Sam's teaching reinforced that God must be included. There was great insight into how caring, sharing, and respect for one another in the marriage are crucial. Even after fifty-five years of marriage, my husband and I continue working to keep our marriage strong, healthy, and focused on the Lord, and without Him we would only falter. Sam has shown how all things in a marriage must center around the Messiah, and that the Scriptures help us to reinforce and stay focused.

—Shari Belfer

MESSIANIC MARRIAGE MATTERS

Restored to Our Original Design

Sam Nadler

Charlotte, North Carolina
2019

Messianic Marriage Matters
Restored to Our Original Design
by Sam Nadler

Copyright 2019 Sam Nadler

ISBN: 9781098714796

Scriptures marked SN are the author's own translations.

Unless otherwise indicated, Scripture is taken from the NEW AMERICAN STANDARD BIBLE®, Copyright © 1960, 1962, 1963, 1968, 1971, 1972, 1973, 1975, 1977, 1995 by The Lockman Foundation. Used by permission.

Scripture quotations identified as TLV are from the Tree of Life translation of the Bible. Copyright ©2011, 2012, 2013, 2014 & 2015 by the Messianic Jewish Family Bible Society. Used by permission of Baker Publishing Group. All rights reserved. www.bakerpublishinggroup.com.

Scripture quotations identified as CJB taken from the Complete Jewish Bible by David H. Stern. Copyright © 1998. All rights reserved. Used by permission of Messianic Jewish Publishers, 6120 Day Long Lane, Clarksville, MD 21029. www.messianicjewish.net.

Capitalization and punctuation has occasionally been modified from the original.

Editor, Cover Design, Interior Layout: Michelle Shelfer, benediction.biz
Cover photo by Daniel Taylor, used by permission

No part of this publication may be reproduced, stored in a retrieval system, or transmitted, in any form or by any means — electronic, mechanical, photocopy, recording, or otherwise — without prior written permission.

Independently published.

MESSIANIC MARRIAGE MATTERS

DEDICATION

I want to dedicate this book with a heart filled with thanksgiving to my Lord, Yeshua the Messiah, for providing my wife, Miriam, who has been His greatest encouragement and instrument of grace for me to know that His Messianic Marriage Matters!

ACKNOWLEDGMENTS

My Deep Appreciation
In writing this book, there are so many that have both assisted and supported this endeavor. Without question, my greatest thanks is to my Lord, Yeshua the Messiah, who gave me new life, a deep appreciation for the Messianic marriage, the truth of the ministry of marriage in His Word, and the gift of the wonderful marriage to my wife, Miriam. Miriam has been a biblical example of a godly wife to me and a loving mother to our two sons, Josh and Matt. Matt also helpfully edited an early draft, but the final editing was handled by Michelle Shelfer, who greatly encouraged me to persevere through the rigorous editing process, and expertly advised me on my use of illustrations as we waded through the voluminous material.

Early on, Carolyn Phillips was also helpful on transcription of my notes. But then even more supportive is Shari Belfer, my administrative assistant and a choice servant of Messiah, who handled the majority of the transcription from my Messianic Marriage Matters seminars, administrative details, correspondence, collecting various kinds of materials, and also the printing details. Whew!

The Messianic Marriage Matters seminars were taught in different locations, but every few years at Hope of Israel Congregation. The input from the members there helped direct the content to be more applicable to a wider range of families and thereby more helpful to the many couples who were involved.

I want to thank Dan and Lauren Taylor for the use of their marriage photo for the cover (and thanks to Tim James for helping us find it!).

Sam Nadler

CONTENTS

Dedication . . . . *vii*
Acknowledgments . . . . *ix*
Introduction *1*

PART I: The Foundation of Marriage *5*

Chapter One
The Principles of Marriage *7*

Chapter Two
The Process for Marriage *53*

Chapter Three
Foundational Priorities in Messianic Marriage *93*

Chapter Four
Foundational Precautions for Marriage *115*

Chapter Five
The Tanakh's Take on Marriage *177*

PART II: The Restoration of Marriage *211*

Chapter Six
The Spirit-Filled Life *213*

Chapter Seven
Restored Leadership in the Family *233*

Chapter Eight
The Triumphant Spouse in a Troubled Marriage *245*

Chapter Nine
Divorce and Remarriage in the New Covenant *267*

Chapter Ten
Faithful Wisdom for the Marriage Condition *283*

Appendices *301*
About the Author *331*

INTRODUCTION

Scripture teaches that, of all human institutions, marriage is the relationship that God speaks of as most representing His relationship with His people (Isaiah 62:4–5; Ephesians 5:31–32). From Eden until today, marriage is, therefore, the most attacked and misunderstood institution, resulting so often in frustration and failure, as well as being the object of mockery in a cynically divided and defiled society. Nonetheless, marriage remains the most important of relationships to anchor a wholesome and growing society from generation to generation. Society becomes community when it is made up of healthy marriages and families. But it takes spiritually healthy individuals to have spiritually healthy relationships of any kind, and healthy relationships are essential to having a healthy community. The more intimate and committed the relationship's nature, the healthier the individuals must be in order to attain that healthy relationship. God's desire when He created us in His own unique corporate image was for us to be eternally committed and joined with Him and with one another in His covenantal bond of shared life and love.

To understand marriage, and relationships in general, we therefore need to understand them from the point of view of the creation of marriage by the Creator in the book of Genesis. Yeshua utilized teaching from Genesis several times in His ministry, as did the writers of the New Covenant when they spoke of marriage. We need to understand the importance of this biblical foundation for all relationships in society, and especially the most important, most intimate relationship—marriage.

The health of the Messianic marriage has impact far beyond the home. Messianic congregations are built on the solid foundation of its member marriages. A congregation—Messianic or otherwise—is made up of families and can be no stronger than the families that make it up. Strong marriages in Messiah are necessary for strong Messianic homes and a strong Messianic congregation. And regardless of the Jewish—or any other—cultural expression of the marriage, the relationship must be built upon Yeshua the Messiah and must be lived by His Scriptural values to be a testimony of His faithful love for *"the lost sheep of the house of Israel"* (Matthew 10:6) and to guard the unity of Jew and Gentile within the community (John 17:20–23; Ephesians 4:1–6). Healthy Messianic communities must have committed, grace-filled Messianic families that reflect God's redemptive plan and perfecting love relationship with His people. To become healthy individuals, let's go back to the "Owner's Manual" to discover just what it means to become healthy individuals engaged in healthy relationships for a healthy community.

For those in good marriages, my prayer is that this material from God's Word will further mature you into an even greater testimony of His love for us all. For newlyweds, this will provide a firm foundation for your marriage. And, for those in struggling marriages, it will point you to hope and healing as you apply His Word to your lives. Indeed, there is hope for any of our marriages if we will sincerely turn from unbiblical values, attitudes, and practices and then by faith obey His Word regarding our marriages. So, it will not be marriage—or life—on our own terms; God didn't create marriage to work that way. Instead, we must understand that marriage was invented by God for His purposes. Only when we're in alignment with Him will we be in alignment with our spouses, friends, or anyone else.

For those who are unmarried, this book will prepare you for your marital calling, if that is what the Lord has in store for you. In most congregations, anywhere from 10 to 20 percent of the attendees are single. We need to understand that being single is a blessing. Being married is a blessing. Any calling through which you serve God is a blessing, for, all of God's blessing for your life is in Messiah (Ephesians 1:3). And sadly, marriage can be a curse, as can being single, when you are not living for the Lord. Being single is not the curse, and neither is being married. Both singleness and marriage are a calling blessed by the Lord.

Single people need to know about marriage and the biblical values involved with it so they can both pray for and counsel married couples. Some may wonder if single people can counsel married people. We need look no further than Scripture for the answer to this question. Paul was single; Yeshua was single, and being single didn't seem to hamper them from authoritatively teaching on the subject. Being married is not a qualification for marriage counseling, and being single doesn't disqualify a person from being a counselor to those who are married, any more than a heart surgeon would be disqualified for not having heart disease. Effective counseling requires a proper biblical understanding, not merely having experience in a marriage. Experience in marriage may give you compassion for other couples but doesn't necessarily give you the skills to teach on marriage. There is a great need for single people to be enabled and prepared to understand the issues of marriage from God's Word, even if they are never called by God to be married.

Regarding the "Messianic" terminology in this book, the word "Messiah" (Hebrew: Mashiach) means the Anointed One, and is the dynamic equivalent to the word "Christ" (Greek: Christos). Thus the word "Messianic" is the equivalent of the word "Christian" as commonly understood. "Messianic" believers express their faith in a more Jewish (or biblically Jewish) frame of reference. "Christian" believers express their faith in a more Gentile frame of reference, as is common in churches.

Furthermore, by "Messianic marriage" I refer to those couples that not only trust in and follow Yeshua as the Messiah, Lord, and Savior and fully accept a whole-Bible view of the truth, but also embrace God's faithfulness to Israel by praying for the peace of Jerusalem (Psalm 122:6; Romans 10:1), as well as all people (1 Timothy 2:1). They are a witness "to the Jew first," as well as equally to the Gentile, and therefore live out a lifestyle that is not only Messiah-centered, but a clear Messianic witness to Israel. This Messianic witness utilizes the celebration of the biblical and Jewish holidays (as opposed to Gentile-cultured holidays such as Christmas and Easter), and it refrains from social matters that would distract the Jewish pre-believer from the Good News message (religious lingo, religious symbols, etc.). In short, the Messianic witness expresses fervent faith in the Messiah in a way that communicates to the greater Jewish community that Yeshua is God's faithfulness to Israel (and therefore to nations by promised extension). Because of the thoroughly biblical approach, all believing "Christian" couples in Messiah will find the material edifying and helpful, and the book does not seek to exclude anyone who embraces a more Gentile-cultured expression of faith. There are already many marriage books available for "Christian" couples, but this is especially written to help strengthen "Messianic" couples.

"Yeshua" is the actual Hebrew/Aramaic name of Jesus. In this book, we use that name, since it reinforces that He is the true Jewish Messiah.

"Assembly" is used as the translation of the Greek word *ekklesia*, which is what it actually means (unlike the Gentile term "church," which is derived from a different word altogether and communicates to the greater Jewish community a non-Jewish place of worship).

"Torah" literally means "instruction," and it is used in reference to the first five books of Moses, or by its literal meaning, to the whole Bible. It is commonly translated "law" (*nomos* in Greek) because the authoritative nature of God's instructions are not meant to be merely His suggestions. "Torah" is a helpful word to better appreciate what Paul meant when he referred to the "Law" of Messiah (Galatians 6:2, etc.). The "Torah" of Messiah refers to Messiah's commandments (John 13:34–35, etc.) and teachings (Matthew 10, etc.), which are His authoritative instruction for all His followers.

"Tanakh" is an acrostic for Torah (Five Books of Moses), Nevi'im (Prophets), and Ketuvim (Writings), which together make up the Hebrew Scriptures. In our witness for Messiah, Tanakh is also a user-friendlier word than "Old Testament" within the greater Jewish community.

"B'rit Chadashah" is the exact Hebrew phrase for "New Covenant" in the prophecy of Jeremiah 31:31–34. Whereas "New Testament" doesn't register as relevant to the average Jewish person, "New Covenant" at least places the Messianic faith in a more receptive context.

This book's first section is an in-depth study of Genesis chapters 1–3 regarding marriage. With this foundation, we go on to see how what follows in the Tanakh (the Hebrew Scriptures) is the result of Genesis 3, and how the B'rit Chadashah (the New Covenant) is a redemptive return in Messiah to God's original design for marriage and society.

PART I

THE FOUNDATION OF MARRIAGE

CHAPTER ONE

The Principles of Marriage

Genesis 1:26–28

What constitutes a healthy relationship? All of us want wholesome relationships, but for the most part society ends up with something else. This reveals the misunderstanding that most people have on the marriage matter. In Genesis 1:26–28, we learn that with our creation by God came principles for wholesome relationships that are intended to reveal His image and likeness through our lives and marriages. As we will be addressing marriage in the context of humanity's creation, let's first place it in the biblical context of creation itself. God sovereignly creates by making something out of nothing. God is beyond His creation, even as a painter is beyond His painting. Imagine if paintings could think. One painting might think that paintings are all that there is—how else could a painting see it? The painter is incomparable to the paintings, other than how He created them to represent Himself in some way (Romans 1:20).

In creating, God created a mature universe—that is, He created both the chicken and the egg, both the star and its light, rocks as well as mud, and trees as well as seeds. He created humanity with an ability to adapt to our changing environments. And the Creator's response to His creation is, "*Good!*" (the Hebrew word *tov*, found in Genesis 1:4, 10, 12, 18, 21, 25, and with humanity in 1:31, *tov me'od!*, or "*very good!*"). The first use of "*no good*" occurs when God describes a lack of proper relationship, for "*It's no good that man should be alone*" (Genesis 2:18 SN).[1] Today, wholesome relationships still make the difference between a life that is "good" and one that is "no good."

The Principle of a Relational Identity: Humanity Is Created in the Image of God

Then God said, "Let Us make man in Our image, according to Our likeness." (Genesis 1:26a)

Through the words *image* and *likeness*, this verse presents the principle of *representative relationship*. There are two preliminary phrases to consider before we discuss the implication of being created in God's image. These two phrases are "*God said*" and "*Let Us make*."

---

[1]. Scriptures marked SN are the author's own translations.

"God said"

The first phrase "*God said*" precedes His creative pronouncement in Genesis 1:26. God speaks words before He creates works. This gives us an initial principle for marriage. As with God, so also with us: communication precedes creation. To whom is God speaking? Even within the divine nature, a glorious and gracious relationship requires great communication. We'll discuss that divine relationship more in a moment. For now, consider that in any relationship, and especially in marriage, communication is vital for the God-intended creative connection that represents Him. This communication can include discussing what you experience together (kids, movies, etc.), and seeing life from your spouse's perspective. It also includes praying together, which is vital for every marriage. Regarding the intrinsic importance of prayer, we read, "*You have not because you ask not*" (Jacob [James] 4:2 SN). A prayer-less couple reveals a "*have not*" marriage. A lack of communication often results in apathetic relationships, lacking the creativity needed to triumph through all the diverse circumstances that marriages will encounter.

The Messianic couple is called to spiritual growth through all the circumstances of life. Adverse winds cause the plane to fly higher. By God's grace in Messiah, the couple grows into a deeper level of mutual acceptance as it grows by communicating through the tests of life. Couples who merely tolerate each other in their married life are not "*speaking the truth in love*" with each other and are therefore not "*growing together into Messiah*" and "*building up one another in love*" (Ephesians 4:15–16 SN). Sadly, those couples are not enjoying and reflecting the blessed intention of God's purpose for their lives.

Furthermore, "*God said*" reminds us of a vital fact for the healthy Messianic marriage: God inspired words. The Creator, of course, need not have spoken any words, and He still could have just as easily created everything by His unlimited power and sovereign will. He could also have whistled, drawn, painted, or sung—or anything else that was pleasing to Him as the Creator. But "*God said.*"

God's Word is inspired. We may think of music and art as inspiring—that is, uplifting, encouraging, and instructive. But that's not how the Bible in 2 Timothy 3:16 uses the word "inspire" (*theopneustos*, literally "God-breathed"). We may love music and art, but God inspired words. We don't know David's music, but we have his inspired lyrics in the psalms! When Paul writes, "*All Scripture is inspired by God and profitable*" (2 Timothy 3:16), the word *Scripture* in the original language is *graphe*, or "writings." In so saying, Paul is making a monumental statement: only the written Word is inspired. Some at that time, and even now, may have thought and think that the *oral law* (i.e., the orally transmitted traditions of the fathers) might also have been inspired. But no, Paul writes, only what was written is "*inspired*," and therefore authoritative, for all faith and practice. The Scripture, God's Word, is inspired and profitable, and it's as fully profitable as it is fully inspired. When His inspired Word is depended upon and followed, the profitability is revealed in a couple's life together in Messiah. This is a vital matter to having a healthy Messianic marriage. Like well-meaning advice, oral tradition may or may not be helpful. But only the written Word of God is the authoritative wisdom for a marriage and a family. His inspired words of Scripture will both instrumentally edify and spiritually strengthen the Messianic marriage. When followed, His Word is "*a lamp to my feet and a light to my path*" (Psalm 119:105) that will give the Messianic couple the guidance and direction needed through the trials of life. Our lives and marriages need to be built upon His Word, because "*God said.*"

Since words are the expressed symbols of thought, the fact that God inspired words reminds us that Adonai revealed Truth in a rational way that utilized our symbolic protocols of language so that His Truth could be comprehended by us, His creation. For me, this is mind-blowing! Here is the Almighty God of all who humbles Himself to His creation's level of communication (words), just so we can understand what He is doing and why He is doing it! This is love. And when we love one another, we desire to communicate with one another; communication helps the Messianic couple to move forward together. Without good communication, you each may grow, but beware that you don't grow apart.

The value of Scripture that demonstrates the rational work of God for our lives and our marriages is seen in another way as well. In creating humanity, God's purpose is for all people to be the Creator's representatives to the rest of His creation. So, when the Scripture states, "*Then God said, 'Let Us make'*," we see His divine, rational purpose, as opposed to random evolutionary accidents. That is why the creation of humanity came at the climax of all His creation; for all creation would be subservient to humanity,[2] and the dust of the ground would be the tool God would use in creating humanity.[3] His creation of humanity is rational, not random—by design, not by accident—purposeful, not by chance. The Creator had a plan for all His creation and especially for humanity, which is fulfilled in the Messiah.[4] You are not a mistake, and your marriage is also part of His plan. God's entire creation, including the relationship of marriage, is according to an eternal plan for all of us to relate to Himself and then for all of us to represent the Creator to His creation. Although His eternal plan may conflict with your own personal plan, all of creation is nonetheless according to His plan and purpose for you.

It is vital for the Messianic husband and wife to incorporate this truth of God's rational, Scriptural purpose into their marriage, so that they will know that the difficulties that occur are opportunities for His grace to prove sufficient for their hearts and their home. Apart from God's grace, every problem faced without the

---

2. As Psalm 8 declares.
3. As seen in Genesis 2:4–7.
4. Please read over Ephesians 1:3–14 for the biblical overview of the divine plan for you in the Messiah.

Lord will merely reinforce the fleshly fear that the marriage was all a big mistake. Problems will either make you better or bitter. If you face the problems as a Messianic couple trusting the Lord, those "problems" become what He intended them to be for you: His tools to make your marriage better. Otherwise, those same matters endured without mutual trust in the Lord will make you bitter. Without repentance, deep-set bitterness in your hardening heart can characterize your marriage. The Scripture warns us: *"See to it that no one comes short of the grace of God; that no root of bitterness springing up causes trouble, and by it many be defiled"* (Hebrews 12:15). Since we all fall short of the glory of God, beware that you don't fall short of the grace of God.

The fact that *"God said"* directs us to God's initial creative work: *"God said, 'Let there be light'"* (Genesis 1:3). John the *sheliach* (apostle) identifies with these very Genesis portions when introducing his Good News account about Yeshua the Messiah as the Son of God, who is God incarnate:

> *In the beginning was the Word, and the Word was with God, and the Word was God. He was in the beginning with God. All things came into being through Him, and apart from Him nothing came into being that has come into being. In Him was life, and the life was the Light of men.... And the Word became flesh, and dwelt among us.* (John 1:1–4, 14)

Thus, *"God said"* refers to the communicative work of God, which is the outworking ministry of the Messiah, who is the incarnate expression of God (Hebrews 1:2–3). As *"the radiance of His glory and the exact representation of His nature,"* the Son is God-expressed, and is always the manifested presence of the Father throughout Scripture, whether it be walking in the garden of Eden to fellowship with Adam and Eve, or appearing to Abraham in Canaan, or revealing Himself—to Moses in the burning bush or on Mount Sinai, or to His frightened friends at the Last Passover before He died for us. Thus, He could say to His *talmidim* (disciples): *"He who has seen Me has seen the Father"* (John 14:9).

Let's understand together how this impacts the Messianic marriage. The creative work of God is intrinsically tied to the life-giving work of Yeshua, the Son of God. Thus, a creative Messianic marriage is such because the Messiah, the Living Word, is central to the relationship of the Messianic couple. Indeed, the couple that *"abides"* in Yeshua *"bears much fruit"* (John 15:5)—love, joy, peace, and much more. Where Yeshua is relied on within the marriage, God is represented through that Messianic couple. The Holy Spirit testifies through the home where Yeshua is glorified in the heart.

What *"God said"* is His living and life-giving Word, and that Word of God is the Messianic inspiration for the marriage as He intended for it to be. So, in Messiah, marriage works from a different paradigm than the traditional marriage which society understands, experiences, and assumes as the norm. Traditional

One • *The Principles of Marriage*

marriage clichés and formulas must be reevaluated and readjusted according to both the Scriptures and the person of Messiah, whom the Messianic marriage is meant to live out in love and grace. As the individual is "*a new creature*" in Yeshua (2 Corinthians 5:17), so the married couple must likewise understand their marriage as that new creation, as expressed in their home and community.

"Let Us"

The second phrase, "*Let Us*," is composed of the words that God uses to refer to Himself. It has stirred up no small amount of controversy over the years. Who is the "*Us*"? The meaning of this plural is vitally important for marriage. Let us briefly consider some interpretations offered for God's use of a plural:

Plurality of majesty[5]

This view proposes that God, being so great, speaks of Himself in the plural, just as Elizabethan royalty refer to themselves. Since God's use of "*Us*" and "*We*" is found elsewhere in Scripture, the plurality of majesty argument is apparently a rationalization that developed long after the Bible was written.

Conferring with the angels[6]

The Bible teaches this to be an impossibility according to Isaiah 40:13, for God counsels with no one, including His created beings, the angels. His sovereign will is His own. That's why in Genesis 1:27, God states that He created man "*in His own image*" and not in the image of angels. No angels were involved in the creation process!

"A potential plural, expressing a wealth of potentials in the divine being"[7]

Though I can certainly agree that God's potential (i.e., His power) is a wealth, to say the least, and even beyond all human understanding, this potentiality would be just as true in the singular pronouns as well as the plural. So, the more natural reading is that the plural pronoun is informing us as plural pronouns normally do.

The mysterious Triune nature of God

This teaching on God's Triune nature is hinted at in Genesis and developed throughout the Scriptures. Some argue that God's reference to Himself in the plural in Genesis and the rest of the Hebrew Scriptures comes too early in biblical history for such teachings to be revealed. I would simply respond that there is but One divine Author of all the Scriptures,[8] and all Scripture is His self-revelation

---

5. Dr. J. H. Hertz, *The Pentateuch and Haftorahs* (London: Soncino Press, 1971), 3.
6. Rashi, *Pentateuch with Targum Onkelos, Haphtaroth and Rashi's Commentary* (New York: Hebrew Publishing Company, 1935), 6.
7. Allen Ross, *Creation and Blessings* (Grand Rapids, MI: Baker Book House, 1988), 112.
8. Yeshua stated, "*The Scripture cannot be broken*" (John 10:35). Paul therefore taught, "*All Scripture is inspired by God and profitable*" (2 Timothy 3:16).

to His people. Much later in biblical history, the same *"Us"* speaks again in the prophet Isaiah's call to service, in Isaiah 6:8.[9] This being said, as Messianic believers, we also declare without reservation, *"Shema, Yisrael, Adonai Eloheinu, Adonai Echad!" "Hear, O Israel! The Lord is our God, the Lord is One!"* (Deuteronomy 6:4).[10]

In God's very being, He is Triune. This is not generally accepted among the greater Jewish community. One day, I was sharing the Good News with an Orthodox Jewish man who refused to believe that Yeshua is our Messiah. When I asked him what his major difficulties in considering Yeshua as our Messiah were, he said to me, "I could never, ever believe in a divine Son of God." I said, "Really? Do you believe that HaShem is eternally Avinu (our Father)?" He replied, "Of course I do!" I responded, "If you believe He is the eternal Father, He must have an eternal Son." This Father-Son relationship is intrinsic to God's being. The love of God is eternally expressed in His Triune nature. The Father always loved the Son.[11]

This view that God is one and yet Triune in nature is the key to understanding relationship and marriage. Understanding God's nature is vital to understanding our own nature, for these truths are all Scriptural seedlings of what will develop into a solid biblical basis for all healthy relationships, a healthy society, and of course, a healthy marriage.

"In Our image"

In creating humanity, the Creator uses two phrases to describe why He is making people: we are made *"in Our image,"* but also *"according to Our likeness."* Though the words *image* and *likeness* may be considered synonyms, the phrases that contain these two words have subtle differences that influence our relationships in marriage and in society.[12] So, as we will discover, the two primary words in those phrases, *image* and *likeness*, refer to two different but vital aspects of our identity as God's creation and in relationship to our Creator.

The Hebrew word for "image" (*tselem*) means something that is derived from something else—that is, a representative of another.[13] This could be a coin with the

---

9. For further study on God's mysterious nature, refer to the author's *The Messianic Answer Book* (Charlotte, NC: Word of Messiah Ministries, 1998), 51–58; and *Messianic Discipleship* (Charlotte, NC: Word of Messiah Ministries, 2014), 68–74.
10. We accept by faith the Scripture's revelation of the divine complexity of God's absolute unity: 1) We accept the *simple singularity* of the divine nature. 2) We accept the *essential equality* within the divine nature. 3) We accept the *divine diversity* of the divine nature.
11. John 5:20.
12. In Scripture (Malachi 2:11–16; Matthew 5:14–16), the family is the basic component of society. Strengthen the family, and you strengthen society. So too for Messianic congregations. The congregation is no stronger than the families that make it up; strong Messianic families make for strong Messianic congregations.
13. R. Laird Harris, Gleason L. Archer Jr., Bruce K. Waltke, *Theological Wordbook of the Old Testament* (Chicago: Moody Publishers, 2003).

image of a king on it, as in Mark 12:16. No one would think that the coin is the actual king. The coin is a representation of the king. As we spiritually mature and are thereby "*conformed to the image of His Son*" (Romans 8:29), there is a growing imprint of the King on our lives. Also, this word *image* is illustrated by the sun's reflection on the water's surface. When you drive past a lake and see mountains reflected in the lake, you wouldn't think that the mountains are actually in the lake, but instead that their image is reflected, or represented, on the lake's surface. In this regard, all people represent God. As a drop of water or a giant lake reflect the same sun, so babies, as well as adults, represent God in their lives. And as we each spiritually mature, His image in our lives is made clearer for others to see. And so, as Yeshua "*must increase*" and Sam "*must decrease*" (John 3:30), so in Messiah's redemption, I have "*put on the new self who is being renewed to a true knowledge according to the image of the One who created him*" (Colossians 3:10). My faith and obedience to God's holy Word mature me into God's holy image. And so, as they spiritually mature together, Messianic couples reveal the Sun of Righteousness more clearly to others.

Image is a representation, and in our case a spiritual representation. This carries two Scriptural applications for our lives and marriages: 1) a *representative responsibility*, and 2) a *representational resemblance*.

First, we have a *representative responsibility* of image on God's behalf. This aspect of image is the result of God's authority delegated to humanity. Our responsibility is brought out clearly at the end of Genesis 1:26, where we are taught that on God's behalf, we are to "*rule over*" all the other creatures on the earth. This responsibility both gives us the authority to carry out the assigned task and holds us accountable for the authority delegated.[14] Our obedience to such a call is required, within the parameters that God has established.[15] Human disobedience to God's authority has had devastating consequences on humanity and on our ability to rule on God's behalf. That's why Adam is judged by God for having "*listened to the voice of* [his] *wife*" instead of listening to God (Genesis 3:17).

In Messiah's redemption first promised in Genesis 3:15, we are renewed and made ambassadors for Messiah with the authority to represent His values, decisions, and Good News to all of humanity (2 Corinthians 5:18–20). As to this representative responsibility, the image of God is renewed in a special way in the Messiah. Yeshua, as the incarnate image of God, is "*the firstborn of all creation*" (Colossians 1:15). *Firstborn* doesn't mean He was the first one physically born, but refers instead to authority in the family. This is seen in Joseph, the eleventh son

---

14. These matters regarding delegation of responsibility are more fully discussed in the author's book, *Developing Healthy Messianic Congregations* (Charlotte, NC: Word of Messiah Ministries, 2016).
15. For instance, see Genesis 2:16–17 for the Edenic Covenant, Exodus 19:5–6 for the Mosaic Covenant, John 13:34–35 for the New Covenant, etc.

born to Jacob, who receives the rights of the firstborn in that family (1 Chronicles 5:1). Though a firstborn may not physically resemble the father, he nonetheless represents the father's authority in the family. So, Messiah has the rights of the firstborn over the family of God. By faith in Messiah, *"all things…work together"* as we're being *"conformed to the image of His Son, so that He would be the firstborn among many brethren"* (Romans 8:28–29). In Yeshua's authority as firstborn we are redeemed and authorized to lead as well.

This image, renewed in Messiah, provides a renewed representative responsibility in our families, where the husbands are the designated leaders (heads) of the home. For, the Scripture clarifies the matter of image on this point of authority in the home: *"For a man ought not to have his head covered, since he is the image and glory of God; but the woman is the glory of man"* (1 Corinthians 11:7).

Men were expected to assume spiritual leadership in the marriage even in the symbolic veiling that Corinthian wives used to represent submission to their husband's headship. For, regarding *image* as representing delegated authority, husbands are *"the image and glory of God."* Wives are *"the glory of man,"* as representing delegated authority from the husband as his partner-helper (Genesis 2:18). Whether a man is properly prepared for the responsibilities of caring and loving leadership in the home may be another matter, for his spiritual immaturity may require much more grooming. Though we know that Yeshua was the perfect image of God from his conception in Miriam's (Mary's) womb, He grew in His representative responsibility, even as He was in subjection to His parents while He was young (Luke 2:51). But as Yeshua grew *"in wisdom and stature, and in favor with God and people"* (Luke 2:52 SN), He handled greater responsibilities and exercised greater authority representing the Father. Likewise, some men may require "re-parenting" (i.e., focused discipleship) before taking on the responsibilities of husband and father.[16] Though all parents are biblically responsible to prepare their children for the sacred ministry of marriage, some parents were never prepared growing up and may need some instruction and coaching on this matter. A maturing Messianic home means that Messianic parents are raising their children to be Messianic disciples who will start a new Messianic home when they marry. But foundationally, if a Messianic couple does not grasp their representative responsibility as the image of God, they will not prepare themselves or their children for such foundational and vital calling for their married lives.

In marriage, we have hierarchical responsibilities of leadership. We understand, though, that before sin (in Genesis 3) and after redemption (in Messiah), humanity was and is living for God's glory. There is a mutually submissive leadership role in the marriage (Ephesians 5:21). Mutual submission is seen as the wife respects

---

16. This should not be attempted by the fiancée or wife, but by his Messianic rabbi or elders, who have both responsibility and gifting *"for the equipping of the saints for the work of service"* (Ephesians 4:12).

her husband's position as "*head*" (Ephesians 5:23). For his part, the husband is sacrificial in his leadership, even as the Messiah laid down His life for us, His beloved (Ephesians 5:25).[17]

To illustrate, in our home, this is how I live out this principle via my own leadership responsibility. I will ask, "Miriam, would you like to go out to eat?" She will generally say, "Yes!" I will then ask, "What would you like to eat, Miriam?" She will generally say, "Fish." I will then decide and declare, "Miriam, we are going out to eat fish!" In other words, my authority in the home is never to be used by me for self-serving purposes, but always for the benefit and blessing of others. And Miriam fully supports my leadership in the home, for she knows my leadership is to her benefit. This is how God intended to bless the wife through her husband as he uses his delegated authority from the Lord for the Lord's purposes to bless the home.

This testimony of His image through representative responsibility can be damaged in two ways: first, when the wife asserts authority over her husband. She (and he) might think, "After all, buddy, I'm smarter (or wealthier, or stronger) than you—so I'm in charge, not you." This was Eve's problem—and Adam's as well—since she first ate the fruit of "*the tree of the knowledge of good and evil*" before her husband and was thereby sinfully wiser than her husband. Adam foolishly listened to his wife instead of to God (Genesis 3:17).

Secondly, God's image in the home can be damaged when the husband abuses his authority and mistreats his wife, either emotionally or physically. He might think (and she might wrongfully agree), "It's a man's world, and a man's home is his castle. What I say goes—or else!" We often hear of "executive privilege," where someone in politics is abusing their authority for self-serving purposes. This is evil, and especially so in the marriage or within the home, for the home is the microcosm for society. Executive privilege is the corruption of delegated authority in every case. In either case, repentance is needed for the home to be restored to its redemptive foundation in Messiah, so that the home may then be blessed in the Lord. Authority is divinely delegated only to serve one another on the Lord's behalf, for Yeshua taught us that "*whoever wishes to become great among you shall be your servant*" (Matthew 20:25–28). Self-serving sin distorts the image of God in society and in our homes.

Besides the representative responsibility of image, there is a second aspect to the word *image* regarding the image of God, and that is a *representational resemblance*—that is, humanity spiritually resembles God. As we will discuss later in this book, this means that a human is not a physical being that has a spirit, but is a spiritual being that has a body.

---

17. This section of Ephesians will be covered more fully later in this book.

Regarding this spiritual resemblance, since *"God is love"* (1 John 4:8), He both loves us *"with an everlasting love"* (Jeremiah 31:3) and created us to love Him *"with all your heart and with all your soul and with all your might"* (Deuteronomy 6:5). To be spiritually healthy, people need to both love and be loved. We were created in His image to both love and be loved, both at home and in our communities, in order for our essential spiritual nature to be healthy. Proper discipleship in the home and congregation is intended to assist believers to attain and sustain spiritual health as we learn to love one another.

Though God may appreciate all His creation, humanity alone was created in the image of God (Genesis 1:26). This unique image that bears God's representational resemblance comes with the due respect that His image in the world should have. As His image bearers, we symbolize His presence in the world. His image gives us intrinsic value! Each person has value because each person is created in His image. Our self-image should be based upon the image of God.

As Messianic believers, bearing God's image gives us our true personal identity. Some of us have a poor self-image simply because we don't see ourselves as our Creator sees us. Who is correct, you or God? We may take our cues from society and the media, or whatever our parents may have foolishly and falsely said about us. Who is correct, society or God? If you don't see yourself as created in His image, you will never understand His will for your life. God's will and purpose for you are contained in creating you in His image.

Your ministry to others is not even based on who they think they are but on who God says they are. You are not what your own flesh says you are. You are not what your spouse or your friends or your family say you are. You are who God says you are! You must have this fact firmly planted in your mind and act upon it. Otherwise, you are not walking with God. For, *"can two walk together unless they are in agreement?"* (Amos 3:3 SN).

This is true even if you still have not come to faith in Messiah—even if His image in you has been sinfully tarnished beyond recognition. Sadly, because of sin, we do not represent God but have misrepresented Him in our homes and in society. In this case, His only will for you is to come to faith in Messiah and be thereby restored and renewed to your original design. He works with you according to His image in you, according to His Word, which is His eternal purpose for you and your marriage.

Intrinsic human value, which all people have as the image of God, brings certain restrictions. First, there is capital punishment for murder, *"for in the image of God He made man"* (Genesis 9:6). Every person is a representative of the Creator. All matters of life take on greater significance as we consider our role as His image bearers.

One • The Principles of Marriage

What you do against people, you are doing against God. In redemption, it is written that if you say that you love God and hate you brother or sister, you are a liar (1 John 4:20). No, you're not a liar about hating your brother or sister, but you are lying about your love for God! To say that you love God and hate your spouse makes your professed love for God a sham. Therefore, if you have stopped loving your spouse, you have stopped abiding in Messiah. But if you will abide in Messiah—that is, trust and obey His Word—you will be empowered to love your spouse with God's own love for you both. As you respect your spouse's representational resemblance, you will live out your own representational resemblance to God.

Humanity, uniquely bearing the image of God, is also subject to the restriction of no "*graven images*" of God in any way—that is, all idolatry is to be destroyed (Numbers 33:52, etc.). "*God is spirit*" (John 4:24) and is not to be engraved, painted, or sculpted in any image. For, in making images, one limits God's nature to what an idol represents of Him. This demeans the omnipotent, omniscient, and omnipresent God. He is to be worshipped "*in spirit and truth*" (John 4:24). So, since we are God's representational resemblance in this world, people must be appreciated and respected, but not idolized. We are not to "worship the ground" our spouse walks on. Our sufficiency, satisfaction, and security are in the Lord alone, not in people, no matter how dependent upon others we think we are. "*Cursed is the person who trusts in people*" (Jeremiah 17:5 sn). Your spouse should be respected, but God alone is to be worshipped. All people are to be respected for their representational resemblance to God, if for no other reason. If God is properly worshipped, this will put into biblical perspective how to properly respect our family, job, and experiences without making idols of them. Again, for the Messianic married couple, regular prayer unifies spouses through their mutual worship of their Creator.

The incarnate and divine Messiah Himself bears the ultimate representational resemblance to God, made perfectly in His image. His representational resemblance is the heavenly made flesh. And in Yeshua, as His new creations, we have all "*borne the image of the earthy,*" so too, "*we will also bear the image of the heavenly*" (1 Corinthians 15:49). This heavenly image more and more resembles God in Yeshua not only through our faithful experiences that conform us "*to the image of His Son*" (Romans 8:28–29), but also as we are properly taught by the transformative "*mirror*" of the Scriptures: "*But we all, with unveiled face, beholding as in a mirror the glory of the Lord, are being transformed into the same image from glory to glory, just as from the Lord, the Spirit*" (2 Corinthians 3:18).

For, through the inscribed Word of God (the Scriptures), the light of God in Messiah (the incarnate Word) is shining out for all who can see (2 Corinthians 4:4). Therefore, as the Messianic couple faithfully applies the Word of God by faith in Yeshua, that marriage experiences and expresses spiritual transformation. This transformation reveals the enlightened couple as "*a city set on a hill* [that] *cannot be hidden*" and as a well-lit home that shines "*before* [others] *in such a way that they may see your good works, and glorify your Father who is in heaven*" (Matthew 5:14–16). This representational resemblance makes the transformed Messianic marriage God's living testimony, which is His redemptive light in the darkness. As has been often said in comparing Ephesians 2:8–9 with 2:10, we're not saved *by* good works, but we're saved *for* good works. So, this practical light of God's "*good works*" earns the couple the right to be heard regarding their Messianic faith in their community. In principle, our good works in Messiah should precede our good words about Messiah.

We must make a distinction between these two aspects of *image* that we have just explored. Though my son has a representational resemblance to me, he can't always have representative responsibility for me. So, even when he can't authoritatively represent me, he will always still resemble me. Likewise, for all of us, this representational resemblance from having been made in the image of God gives all people equal respect on account of our human identity. Whereas representative responsibility is hierarchical and requires obedience to God, the representational resemblance from having been made in His image merely requires our existence. As noted previously, this representational resemblance is true in a baby or in an adult, as a raindrop reflects the same sun as the lake. We are to respect all people, regardless of nationality, religion, or gender, for representational resemblance crosses all such distinctions. Therefore, we're each being "*renewed…according to His image,…where there is no distinction*" (Colossians 3:10–11 SN), whether Jew or Gentile, rich or poor, or whether we are male or female. We are required to respect one another simply because we are created in God's image. To disrespect people is to disrespect the One whom they all represent.

In marriage, therefore, since we each equally share the representational resemblance to the image of God, there must be mutual respect. We must respect our spouses, otherwise we are disrespecting God (1 John 4:20). This, then, is a spiritual partnership in "*the grace of life*" (1 Peter 3:7). My spouse is my equal in our representational resemblance to God, and therefore, we truly need each other in order to fully represent God through our love for each other. In this area of our image, marriage problems can occur if 1) we confuse responsibility and resemblance, where we think that equality of representational resemblance is equality of representative responsibility or authority, and therefore usurp or abdicate authority in the home. Or, 2) we think that greater or lesser responsibility means that we're therefore superior or inferior in nature to our spouse.

Though I stop when a police officer halts traffic, he still must treat me with due respect as an equal because I have representational resemblance to God, just like him. So too in the home; a husband's designated leadership through his representative responsibility in the home doesn't nullify his wife's representational resemblance equality to himself. He must always lead in the home with the respect due to those also created in God's image, whom he is privileged to serve.

This truth that we are created in the image of God impacts all our human interactions, and it is what makes society wholesome and healthy. If we don't treat each other as those created in the image of God, but rather treat others as a means to some end, we are left with a toxic society where relationships are characterized by manipulation and abuse.

"According to Our likeness"

Other than *image*, the other key word that defines who we are created to be is *likeness*. The Hebrew word for "likeness" (*demuth*) is simply a word of comparison—that is, to be alike or similar to something or someone else.[18] But unlike *image*, *likeness* is not derived from another, but is like another in some way. Two brothers may resemble each other in many ways, and may have much in common as brothers, but they are two distinct individuals. So it is for humanity. We're created to be like God in some ways, though we are certainly distinct from Him. But being made according to His likeness provides us with something wonderful!

Whereas *image* is how we represent God, *likeness* is how we can relate to God! Since *likeness* refers to comparable traits or similarities with another, those similarities are points of potential relationship with the other person. Remember that the representative responsibility that comes from the word *image* refers to our leadership role, such that God could command Adam's obedience (Genesis 2:16–17). The representational resemblance that comes from *image* means that humanity reveals God by our very existence. But with the word *likeness*, we find relationship and fellowship. Since they had so much in common, God wanted to hang out with Adam and Eve in the garden (Genesis 3:8)! By illustration, Bill and I both enjoy jazz. And though he doesn't represent or resemble me, we can enjoy jazz concerts together. To the degree we have something in common, we can have fellowship with one another.

We have been made with many spiritual characteristics (love, grace, mercy, holiness, etc.) that are *like* God. Our likeness to God in those points of similarity allows us to enjoy fellowship with God in those areas. The more we have in common with God, the more points of relating to God we will have. We develop in our commonality with God as we spiritually mature in Messiah—that is, where we have developed points of likeness to God through Messiah, we increase in enjoyment of our relationship with the Lord. But where we don't grow into the likeness of God, our ability to enjoy His presence is hindered. This matter of developing commonality is illustrated in our family life. As your children grow into adulthood, you have more in common with them and can have more points of relating to one another. But where parents and their children do not share

---

18. Harris, Archer, Waltke, *Theological Wordbook*.

commonality of values and behaviors, they will enjoy less fellowship together. Some parents will come up with common interests, just to spend time together with their children. Understandable. But a thin veneer of commonality may not actually minister the godly love that develops genuine family relationships.

The same is true in the marriage relationship. During the dating process, couples may try to identify with each other's interests to have a sense of commonality. Yet pretending only makes for a pretentious relationship where the couple will grow apart and eventually think they are incompatible. This will be handled more fully in Genesis 2, but for now, we need to foundationally understand that our relationship with Adonai and each other develops as we grow in likeness to each other.

Though people are especially created in likeness to God, because of the universal damage from sin, we all *"fall short of the glory of God"* (Romans 3:23). Any original similarities become corrupted, distorted, and sinfully substituted. In fact, our image and likeness have become so sinfully tarnished that humanity may be spiritually unrecognizable from the original image and likeness. We spiritually appear more like Gollum in *Lord of the Rings*—this pathetic creature so horribly distorted by his sinful, idolatrous love of the "precious" ring that inhumanity (or un-Hobbitness) characterizes his life. Sinful humanity is more like beasts in Scripture than like God (Psalm 49:12, 20; Ecclesiastes 3:18). Sadly, some accept this characterization of themselves and others and live in a dog-eat-dog world where dominating others validates their lives. Though brutal prison life is generally pictured this way, it is also a common enough malady in married life, where "might makes right" attempts to justify abuse.

Why are so many marriages—and much of society—like this? Though sin is the cause, sin manifests itself by substituting almost anything for God. We can foolishly substitute a love of worldly and passing pleasures, and even mere lust, for a love of God. The Scripture warns us not to *"love the world nor the things in the world. If anyone loves the world, the love of the Father is not in him. For all that is in the world, the lust of the flesh and the lust of the eyes and the boastful pride of life, is not from the Father, but is from the world"* (1 John 2:15–16).

Some may have replaced a healthy reverence for God with a spirit of fear, which God never gave us (2 Timothy 1:7). And rather than love God *"with all your might"* (Deuteronomy 6:5), we develop a *"love of money,"* which is *"a root of all sorts of evil"* (1 Timothy 6:10).

Thus, by God's grace and His concern for our welfare, as with our image, our likeness has certain restrictions, like guardrails. Idolatry is equally condemned as either the use of an image or of a likeness in worship, representing God with some attribute of Him in an image or figure. Thus, the golden calf (Exodus 32:1–6) was intended by impatient and disobedient Israel to characterize in the likeness of the strong bull idol the power of God that delivered us from Egypt. Despite their intentions, God condemned three thousand participants in this idolatry (Exodus 32:28).

Because of the corruption of sin, our prayer life can easily make idols of the likenesses of God in our minds—i.e., God in the likeness of Grandpa, since Gramps was always so sweet, and you want God to be like a nice grandpa to you. But this idolatry in our personal worship will only corrupt us further, for we must worship God "*in spirit and truth*" (John 4:24), both publicly and privately.

Here too we must praise God for His redemption in Messiah that restores us by faith into God's likeness. This restoration matures us as we "*long for the pure milk of the Word*," and "*grow in respect to salvation*" (1 Peter 2:2), and thereby continue to "*grow in the grace and knowledge of our Lord*" (2 Peter 3:18). God's redemptive goal for all Messianic believers is to be like Yeshua. And so, we read, "*Beloved, now we are children of God, and it has not appeared as yet what we will be. We know that when He appears, we will be like Him, because we will see Him just as He is. And everyone who has this hope fixed on Him purifies himself, just as He is pure*" (1 John 3:2–3).

Though by faith in Yeshua we are already *b'nai Elohim* (children of God), it does not yet appear what we, as His sanctified ones (i.e., saints), will be. Yet being "*like Him*" is God's only goal for us in Yeshua, and it will be fully achieved when Messiah appears at His return. If His return is our blessed hope, we are now purifying ourselves as He Himself is pure by "*perfecting holiness in reverence to God*" (2 Corinthians 7:1 SN) and by the cleansing and pruning through His Word (John 15:3). May His Name be blessed forever!

This likeness to God has two applications to marriage: first, for our personal relationship with God, and secondly, for our relationship with our spouse.

For our personal relationship with God.
The golden rule is the key to revealing your fellowship with God. Luke 6:31 (SN): "*Treat others like you want them to treat you.*" Treating another "*like*" you want to be treated doesn't necessarily improve your fellowship with that person, but it does reveal that you're in fellowship with God as His child. Treating your spouse in the same manner as you'd have your spouse treat you doesn't ensure that you'll have better fellowship with your spouse, but it does mean that you are in close fellowship with God, and that, in some cases, despite your troubled marriage relationship.

Besides testifying of your fellowship with God, treating others as you want to be treated also shows your willingness to accept others by grace, even as God has fully accepted you in the Messiah (Romans 15:7; Ephesians 1:6). When we do not treat our spouses as we would want to be treated, yet we want to be treated kindly, we need to repent to God and then apologize for unfair treatment of our marriage partners. These may seem like little things, but Scripture informs us that *"the little foxes"* are *"ruining the vineyards"* (Song of Solomon 2:15). The couple's mutual trust in the marriage relationship can be eroded by *"the little foxes"* of unfairness, fibs, or neglect whenever they enter the *"vineyard"* of the marriage, and more erosion occurs when no sincere apology follows these behaviors. In the same way, the "little things" like caring affection, kind remarks, and thoughtfulness strengthen the marriage bonds.

How we speak to God and one another can reveal the reality of relationships, for we read that with the tongue *"we bless our Lord and Father, and with it we curse people, who have been made in the likeness of God; from the same mouth come both blessing and cursing. My brethren, these things ought not to be this way"* (Jacob [James] 3:9–10 sn). Being made in the likeness of God, once more, refers to being in intimate fellowship with God. How can we bless God, while His arm embraces the very one we curse? If we curse an ambassador, we're cursing the country he represents. When we curse people, God also takes it personally. When you speak unkindly to your brother or sister in Messiah, the sincerity of your fellowship with God comes into question. So too, in marriage, we cannot praise the Lord one minute and then, the next minute, speak unkindly to our spouse and think that we're truly in fellowship with God. Our fellowship with God is not only revealed in our praise for Him but also in our kindness to our spouse. Whenever we speak unkindly to our spouse, we need to both repent before God and then apologize to our marriage partner.

So too, because we are made *"according to"* His likeness, our fellowship with Yeshua in our marriages is revealed when we maintain our marital duty of intimacy (1 Corinthians 7:3–4), and in our considerate relations even with spouses who are *"disobedient to the Word"* (1 Peter 3:1, 7). Our fellowship with God in our marriage is based on following and obeying Yeshua even when our spouse doesn't. Through Messiah's *"example"* (1 Peter 2:21), wives are to be *"like"* Messiah by being submissive, even to their disobedient husbands (1 Peter 3:1), and *"you husbands in the same way"* are to live sensitively, even with their disrespectful wives (1 Peter 3:7). Our fulfilled lives in marriage are not based on having perfect spouses, but on our likeness to and fellowship with our Messiah by grace through faith in Him. More on these sections of Scripture will be covered later in this book.

For our relationship with our spouse

In marriage, our likenesses are what spouses have in common with each other. And to the degree that a couple has primary spiritual matters in common, they will enjoy genuine fellowship with each other. What unites them are the primary matters they appreciate about each other. But are these likenesses eternal values, or merely superficial interests? Physical appearance, golf, kids—all these interests can change, and as they change you will thereby grow apart. For instance, the well-known problem of the empty-nest syndrome is that when children move out, the couple realizes that without the kids they really have nothing in common. But on the other hand, a couple that has prioritized eternal values will grow stronger in the Lord despite changing circumstances. By way of illustration, two tires certainly resemble each other, but are in alignment with each other only when each is in alignment with the chassis. When a couple makes a priority of their mutual commitment to Messiah's eternal values, they are moving forward with the Lord in marital alignment to Him and thereby to each other.

Preposition matters
To further understand the foundational principles for marriage in Genesis 1:26, we also need to consider the prepositional phrases that contain the words *image* and *likeness*. The prepositions "in" (*b'* in Hebrew) that we find in the phrase "*in Our image*" and the "*according to*" (*k'* in Hebrew) that we find in the phrase "*according to Our likeness*" give us further insight on *image* and *likeness*. The phrase "*in our*" is used ordinarily in Scripture to refer to something specifically localized (e.g., "*in our place*" [Genesis 29:26]; "*in our sacks*" [Genesis 43:18]; "*in our tribulations*" [Romans 5:3]). The phrase "*according to*" is used ordinarily in Scripture to refer to proportional relationship (e.g., "*according to our ability*" [Nehemiah 5:8]; "*according to our sins*" [Psalm 103:10]; "*according to our works*" [2 Timothy 1:9]). Thus, "*in Our image*" speaks of specificity, while "*according to Our likeness*" refers to a proportionality. "*In Our image*" indicates that humanity is more precisely made in God's own image, and that phrase is emphatically repeated in the next verse (1:27). But "*according to Our likeness*" indicates that though there are points of comparison between humanity and God, the likeness to God is only proportional. Therefore, it can rightly be said by the Lord, "*To whom then will you liken [damah] God? Or what likeness [demut] will you compare with Him?*" (Isaiah 40:18). Obviously, nothing can truly be compared with the eternal God.

Thus, *image* gives us a direct correspondence to God as the One whom we represent, while *likeness* gives us a relative association to God, proportional in all points of comparison. "*In Our image*" requires much more absolute obedience from each of us, as we are held responsible for ruling His world in the context of our homes on His behalf and must give due respect to others. But on the other hand, *likeness* reminds us to lower expectations just a bit, for our spouses will never be perfectly like God, and that shouldn't surprise or disappoint us. We are made merciful like God, but not nearly as merciful as He is merciful; we are made to be kind, but, once more, not nearly as kind as He always is. Where problems arise in marriage, it is because we are created in His image and have eternity in our hearts (Ecclesiastes 3:11), which can give us perfectionist standards and cause us to be dissatisfied with anything less. This manifests itself as self-loathing or judging others with an eternal "*log that is in* [our] *own eye*" (Matthew 7:3).

The purpose of God placing eternity in our hearts is to give us an insatiable *"hunger and thirst for righteousness"* (Matthew 5:6) and to encourage us to *"press on to...the upward call of God in Messiah"* (Philippians 3:14 SN). Because of sin, we're tempted to judge others (or ourselves) by the perfect divine standards that characterize God and God alone. In each other's eyes, our spouses fall short of God's glory and we can thereby see each other as having diminished value. This temptation can be overcome by His grace through faith if we remember that our likeness to the Holy One of Israel is proportional, and we must accept one another graciously, just as we have been accepted by God through Messiah, but fully respect and love our spouse, as we were all created in His image.

The fall of humanity was an attack on a marriage. The result of that demonic attack is the corruption of the image of God and the likeness to God in each of us. But in both our image and likeness, our redemption by faith in Messiah is restorative, as we are renewed in both vital areas.

We are exhorted to *"put on the new self who is being renewed to a true knowledge according to the image of the One who created him"* (Colossians 3:10). Similarly, we are to *"put on the new self, which in the likeness of God has been created in righteousness and holiness of the truth"* (Ephesians 4:24). This new self in both image and likeness is our renewed identity as a new creation in Yeshua. By our faith-obedience to His word, we are putting on the new self and living out our renewed image and likeness to God through our married lives.

Marriage continues to be attacked today by a world rebelling against God that despises His redemptive plan for society. We must therefore *"fight the good fight of faith"* by lighting a candle and not by cursing the darkness. The candle is Messiah's light through our hearts and our homes. We can now begin to truly represent Him in love and grace through our Messianic marriages. Messiah came to restore us to our creation calling, and He thereby renews the Messianic marriage according to the image and likeness of the One who created marriage to represent His love to His creation.

We are digging deep with our studies and considering some very challenging applications of Scripture. This might be a great time to take a moment and reflect on what we've covered thus far. Seventy-one times in the book of Psalms we encounter a special Hebrew word that might be useful here. It is the word *selah*, and it literally means "to lift up," or "exalt." *Selah* may have been intended originally as a musical direction, but we understand it to mean that it's time to take a pause and reflect. I suggest you take a *selah* from reading further at this point to consider just what it means to be made in God's image and according to His likeness. You may wish to discuss it with your spouse, or just ponder on your own before moving on to the next section.

One • *The Principles of Marriage*

The Principle of a Relational Identity: The Image that Rules for Its Creator

And let them rule over the fish of the sea and over the birds of the sky and over the cattle and over all the earth, and over every creeping thing that creeps on the earth. (Genesis 1:26b)

Being created in God's image and according to His likeness, we not only relate to our Creator, we also represent Him. It is amazing to think that out of all creation, only humanity is created in the image of God. Not even the angels share this trait, although they may be greater than humans in other ways. Being created in God's image and according to His likeness makes us different from any other created being, because we alone can intimately relate to Him. If you were to go outside and talk to a tree, you could lie to it and tell it you're a billionaire, and the tree would not care one way or the other. Lie all you want—the tree still won't get mad at you. But if you lie to people, they get upset. If you lie to God, it grieves Him as well, for we are created in His image and according to His likeness, and our lies impact our relationship to Him. In eternity, only a redeemed people can praise Him for His love for sinful humanity. "*He does not give aid to the angels but only to the seed of Abraham*" (Hebrews 2:16 SN). We see here that God fulfills His covenantal promises in Messiah "*to the Jew first, and also to the Gentile*" (Romans 1:16 SN). His people of faith alone understand and accept His redemptive love, His forgiveness, and His mercy in Messiah. We will shout the loudest praises in heaven because we alone of all His creation know of His redemptive love for sinners! We understand His love as no other part of creation can.

The second half of Genesis 1:26 begins with "*and let them rule.*" Humanity's uniqueness is further seen in that we are not only able to identify with God as made in His image and according to His likeness, but we are also able to identify with creation because we are made from the dust of the earth and therefore represent the Creator to His creation. We can translate His truth into the language of creation. But when you think about ruling, you may think that there must be problems in order to necessitate ruling. But this command was given before the existence of problems. Scripture talks about ruling, not as dominating, because ruling preceded sin. What was ruling like before there was sin? In a redeemed relationship and home, what is it like to rule? What would it be like if there were no sinfulness to restrain, punish, or correct? The question is best understood by seeing how God ruled before sin. God is, of course, the true Ruler and we are to rule on His behalf, representing His values in our service. There was no need for domination; the lion could lie down with the lamb. The sin-caused issues that we see today were nonexistent then.

Today, we need police officers and the military because of the corruption of humanity due to sin. But it need not be this way in a Messianic marriage. A husband need not rule his wife and family in a domineering way; they're not the enemy. Domination is not the intention of God's command to rule. Before sin, God rules to affirm His creation. In the case of everything created on those six earlier occasions (Genesis 1:4, 10, 12, 18, 21, 25), God calls each "*tov*" ("*good*"), and finally, in the case of humanity, God declares, "*tov me'od!*" ("*very good!*"). God consistently affirms and appreciates His creation.

This is very important in understanding marriage. You represent God to your spouse and to your children, though that image may take a bit of maturing to make it as clear as it should be. When we redemptively represent Him, we affirm those around us. In this regard, consider Paul's instruction: "*Finally, brethren, whatever is true, whatever is honorable, whatever is right, whatever is pure, whatever is lovely, whatever is of good repute, if there is any excellence and if anything worthy of praise, dwell on these things*" (Philippians 4:8). We are biblically encouraged to prayerfully, intentionally, and redemptively affirm what is right about our spouses. Again, we are not to curse the darkness, but light a candle of grace and love.

We were not created to come up with our own values and evaluations of others. We're not the owners; we're only His managers. For, those who have the privilege to serve will also have to "*give an account*" (Hebrews 13:17). In this stewardship role of serving others, we must understand the Master's intentions for a Messianic marriage. How does He look upon your redeemed spouse? God says *tov*! But do you?

As His redeemed people, we are called to affirm, to build up, develop, encourage, and be thankful for others. This is what it means to rule in a redemptive environment. We were created in His image in order to relate to Him so that we can then represent Him, the Ruler, over His creation. In other words, you are to represent Him in whatever area of stewardship you have. The degree to which you properly relate to God, is that degree—and no more—that you can properly represent Him. Where you're not relating to God is where you are misrepresenting Him to others. Your areas of stewardship are your areas of responsibility, whether this is in your marriage, in your home, at school, or at your workplace. In every relationship you have, you either represent or misrepresent Him. By His grace and by the power of the Holy Spirit, you get to be that one person at work or in the home who is gracious, caring, and affirming to others. Imagine that! This is the great calling God has given each of us in Messiah.

As His representatives, we need to see His creation as He does. Unfortunately, our perspective has been corrupted and skewed by our sin nature. However, in recognizing this, we can go to the Lord to ask for His help. Each time we resent others, hate others in our hearts, and inwardly curse others—these are surfaced areas where we must ask the Lord for His help in order to more fully represent Him—yes, even in our hearts. By the grace of God in Messiah, we are renewed into His image and grow to truly represent Him in every area of our lives.

The text states, "*Let them rule [v'yir'du],*" which is plural. His purpose was not to have merely one human, but to have humanity. His intention in creating each of us was that together we would rule creation on His behalf. One person or people ruling over others is the miserable consequence of sin, starting in the marriage (Genesis 3:16), then the family (Genesis 37:8), and then the nation (Genesis 42:6). God's intention is that our delegated authority will be demonstrated by our unity. In the redeemed Messianic home, this unity is vital to the wholesomeness of the family, for the parents' unity is their children's security. The divided home develops insecure children who will grow up to have dysfunctional homes, producing more dysfunctional disciples. The truth of God's intentions in creating us to live in unity should motivate us to resist and reject anything or anyone that would divide a married couple, even as Yeshua said: "*So they are no longer two, but one flesh. What therefore God has joined together, let no man separate*" (Matthew 19:6). The couple's real victory is in their restored unity in Messiah.

The designated stewardship of our delegated rulership is expressed in this verse: "*And let them rule over the fish of the sea and over the birds of the sky and over the cattle and over all the earth, and over every creeping thing that creeps on the earth*" (Genesis 1:26).

God could have stated, "over the fish, birds, cattle, and creepy things," or He could have said, "over all His creatures" if He'd wanted. Instead, we find that each species is designated relative to its proper environment, whether sea, sky, or earth. They are to be appreciated by humanity for who they are in the natural context of their particular environment. A fish swims brilliantly in the sea, but not so brilliantly climbing a tree! Every creature has a place, but not necessarily in some other creature's place. To properly rule over His creatures on His behalf is to be sure that we also protect their place—their environment—so they can thrive. This stewardship to care for their environments, and our own, fulfills the representative rule of God through humanity. Our rebellion against God is further seen in our devastation of the environment, making it unfit for His creatures, though we may think it is thereby better fit for our own desires and designs. In other words, our representative rulership requires that we properly care for the creatures and their environment on God's behalf.

Though we may love the animal kingdom, or at least certain creatures therein, it is not primarily for those creatures that we care about the environment. Nor is it because we're in a symbiotic relationship of interdependence with the rest of creation, as true as this may be. Our proper concern for the environment is always because of our love for God, and therefore "*our ambition…to be pleasing to Him*" in all things (2 Corinthians 5:9). Poor stewardship over His creation reflects our lack of love for Him and our resistance to His rulership calling for us.

Our proper rulership in the world correlates to our proper rulership in our homes. Our marriages also have their "natural environment" of love, grace, and acceptance that needs our intentional care and protection. There are corrupting human influences that can destroy our home environment, preventing it from being the safe place it should be for our marriages and our children. Ask yourselves: Shouldn't the environment in our homes be characterized by kindness, acceptance, and affirmation? To cynically think that this is mere idealism reflects the corruption of one's soul that foolishly accepts abuse in the home as a natural part of family life. If this is the reader's case, please repent before God for such corruption, and reject this evil thinking that can only further harm your marriage and undermine the welfare of the home.

The truths found in Genesis 1:26 are of vital importance in understanding His creation of humanity. We are created in His image so that we might relate to Him, and thereby represent Him in unity as we considerately rule over His creation on His behalf.

The Principle of a Relational Identity:
Humanity Is Created in the Actual Image of God

God created man in His own image,
in the image of God He created him. (Genesis 1:27a)

This truth that "*God created man in His own image*" is of such importance that it bears restating. God created humanity in His own image and therefore not in the image of angels or anything else. As He purposed in verse 26, so He did in verse 27: He Himself created humanity. (As we will see later, Genesis 2 goes into the details of the process that took place between these two verses.) It was no more difficult for God to create us in His image than it was for Him to create anything else. You may be quite difficult for other people to handle, but you're not that big a problem to God. He can handle your thorny issues quite well. Your marriage may be overwhelming you, but as you look to Him, God is able to create hope and faith in your heart and give you the power of the Holy Spirit for your married lives.

Is it not interesting that in restating in this verse that God created us in His image God does not reiterate that it was also according to His likeness? This is simply because our likeness to God is proportional and changes as we mature. But our image is absolute from creation and from our conception. It is that matter of our image—our relational identity in God—that is now vital to grasp.

Created in the image of God right from the beginning, humanity did not evolve or develop into His image. Instead, we were created in His image. Remember that though this image is something we had right from the start, we each need to grow and mature into who we are. Your marriage is likewise purposed to represent His image from the very outset—that is, from the moment you said "I do." His life and love is to be lived out through your married lives together simply because you're both already created in the image of God. If your marriage is not living out the life and love of God, then you need to pray together and rededicate your lives to honor the Lord in your hearts and home. You both can certainly mature in your faith by living out His love and life through your marriage—but only if your lives are dedicated to honor God according to His word. The longer you wait to rededicate your lives to God, the harder it will be, for your heart will grow harder and more carnal. Rededicate now in order to spiritually grow and mature from the point of dedication forward.

As we mature in the Messianic faith, we also mature in our understanding of who we are in Him. This understanding of who we are in Yeshua becomes essential in the marriage relationship. However, if husband and wife take their cues from each other rather than from God, they may forever try to manipulate one another in order to address their deeply felt individual needs. We must remember that our feelings and emotions are wonderful blessings from God, when they are the result of trusting God and His word. Love, joy, and peace, etc. are the "*fruit of the Spirit*" (Galatians 5:22–23) and not the "root" of the Spirit. This spiritual fruit is a result, or consequence, of the spiritual root, which is looking to Yeshua as you run the race that was set before you (Hebrews 12:1–2). We are rooted as we abide in Yeshua, and He causes us to have "*more fruit*" (John 15:1–5). The illustration of the choo-choo train is helpful: God's Word is the locomotive that powers the train, through the Holy Spirit. You sit in the passenger car of faith in the Word. Following after that passenger car is the caboose baggage car, with all your emotions and feelings from unbelief and disobedience to God. Don't let the caboose pull the train! If you do, you will have all your emotional baggage guiding your decisions and reinforcing personal and married problems conflicting with the Word of God. When you are, by faith, led by the Holy Spirit and thereby empowered by the Word of God, all your "emotional baggage" gets sorted out in Yeshua the Messiah, and it all amazingly works "*together for good…according to His purpose*" (Romans 8:28).

Here's a simple question for you to consider: Who are you? If you were to ask me this, I might say, "My name is Sam Nadler." But you can change your name if you wish.

"Well, I'm a Jewish man." But you can stop living as a Jewish man if you wish.

"I'm a male." But medical science can change that too if you wish.

So, the question remains, Who am I?

Who you are unchangeably is this: "I am created in God's image." This is really and essentially who I am. This image of God precedes my personal identity as found in my family name, my ethnicity, or even my gender. Who we are is only understood in relation to God's image. We need to grasp this before we ever try to understand who we are in relation to our spouse. Trying to initially understand yourself relative to your spouse will always come out wrong. For, you are created in the image of God from conception, and that will not change with marriage.

Your marriage is meant to be the occasion to live out who you are already by God's design. The cause of who you are is the image of God; the occasion for living out who you are is the marriage. Marriage is provided to live out the eternal cause of your life and God's divine purpose for you in Messiah: to live Him out in love.

The fact that we are created in God's image also influences all our other social interactions. We need to first understand who we are and who other people are, as made in the image of God. Every person we will ever come in contact with is created in the image of God, whether they believe it or not! But still, God expects us to interact with others in light of who He says they are, not who they or we may think they are. We may think they're "creeps," like one of the creeping things God gave us authority to rule over. But God doesn't see them this way. He sees each person as created in His image, and so must we. God's intention is to minister to them through you in light of who they are to Him. It is only the obscuring by sin that keeps us from seeing people this way. Our redemption in Messiah helps us to see people as God sees them. Paul understood this quite well: *"From now on, we do not look at anyone from a fleshly viewpoint. Even if we once regarded the Messiah from a fleshly viewpoint, we do so no longer"* (2 Corinthians 5:16 SN).

Before coming to faith in Yeshua, Paul has a carnal and traditional viewpoint about what the Messiah is going to do: Messiah will throw out the Romans and have Israel as chief of the nations. Though this is the eventual work of our Kinsman-Redeemer, Paul initially misses the most vital matter about the Messiah. Messiah will have to first die for the sins of Israel and the nations, and Israel will have to repent of their sin of rejecting Him before Yeshua returns to fulfill God's promises for the Jewish people (Isaiah 2:2–3; Acts 1:6). It's easily missed, for Peter also misunderstands the necessity of the Messiah dying through the hands of evil men for our sins (Matthew 16:22). This sinful confusion can continue after coming to faith in Yeshua, as we must first accept God's viewpoint on life and people and then mature into that godly perspective. Without this mature perspective, our married life can find us judging each other according to the flesh and manipulating each other to have our felt needs met, never ministering God's grace in the Spirit's power, as God intended in the marriage relationship. For it's by His grace through faith in Yeshua that we're Holy Spirit empowered to more and more live out the life and love of God.

Children are created to be like their parents right from the beginning. They will mature in this, but their DNA is set from conception. Every man is born as a male and matures into a man; every woman is born as a female and matures into a woman. This simple fact is very important in understanding what it means to be a child of God. From the moment you trust in Messiah, you are a born-again child of God. You mature as a man or woman of God just as you mature in the Messianic faith. From the beginning, you are a child of God and you mature into who you are.

The Principle of a Relational Identity: Humanity Is Created in the Relational Image of God

Male and female He created them. (Genesis 1:27b)

As we study and apply the phrase "*male and female He created them,*" we want to recognize that this phrase is a progression of thought from the first phrase of the verse, and also a summarization of verse 1:27. As a progression from the first phrase of the verse, "*male and female*" is subordinate to and a development of the image of God. This progression in the verse determines the relationship between the image of God and our genders. As a summarization, "*male and female He created them*" explains the prior phrase, "*God created man in His own image,*" identifying God's image as an image expressed in "*male and female.*"

Looking at the progression of Genesis 1:27, we see that the creation of humanity in the image of God precedes the creation of the male and female gender roles. That is because gender roles were created by God to live out the essential matter of the image of God. The essential identity of all people is that we are created in the image of God; genders are merely our divinely appointed roles through which we live out the image of God. Indeed, God was weaving us in the womb according to His will for each of us (Psalm 139:13–15). This is vital to understanding ourselves and our spouses. Since so many people only understand themselves by their gender, this primary image of God as our identity can seem strange and even impossible. But our genders are for this age—that is, for procreation in marriage, etc. In the age to come, there won't be marriage or procreation, and genders may not be an operative matter. Therefore, Yeshua said, "*The sons of this age marry and are given in marriage, but those who are considered worthy to attain to that age and the resurrection from the dead, neither marry nor are given in marriage; for they cannot even die anymore, because they are like angels, and are sons of God, being sons of the resurrection*" (Luke 20:34–37).

It's not that a person's gender is a problem or a mistake that needs to be solved or removed—not at all. But the purpose of gender is simply not for the age to come (*olam haba*). Gender is useful for the age we are in (*olam hazeh*). Our particular gender is divinely given for the purpose of expressing His image through our particular gendered calling. Our purpose as children of God is to represent Him through the divinely assigned role of female or male. We represent Him as His child through our particular gender, but He relates to us as His child, regardless of our gender. If you are female, then you represent Him as a female, and if you are male, then you represent Him as a male. Yet whether male or female, you are first a child of God, and you represent Him as such through your gender. Prior to sin, all people were children of God, and humanity lived out the image of God through their genders seamlessly.

Then sin entered the human equation and so tarnished the image of God in humanity that everything human was skewered as a result, including gender identity, which has become gender confusion for many. The initial problem that sin caused is a spiritual separation from God (Isaiah 59:1–2). All of humanity is spiritually "*dead in your trespasses and sins*" (Ephesians 2:1). This spiritual separation from God thereby horribly disfigured humanity's intrinsic image of God. They no longer identified themselves by the image of God and as His children. Without identifying ourselves based on the image of God, sin caused a self-oriented perspective, and gender identity became the default identity for a fallen humanity. But if we focus first on being male or female, we get confused about ourselves and our purpose. Our divine purpose is replaced by our now self-centered purpose to seek fulfillment apart from God.

This damage to the human soul from sin is seen in many ways, but for now we'll limit ourselves to those that help address Messianic marriage matters. Historically, gender damage manifests in two ways: gender domination and gender confusion. When gender is the primary identifier and not just a role to express our relationship and representation of God, then our gender becomes god-like to us. We are left with the impossible task of finding fulfillment, satisfaction, and completion in our gender alone. Neither gender roles nor our marital roles were ever meant to do any of that. Looking to our genders to satisfy us has the same problem found in all idolatries: they fail, and people therefore feel that their birth gender doesn't satisfy them.

The issue of gender confusion is also seen in immoral behaviors, such as womanizing, harlotry, and having numerous casual sex partners, with the assumption in our perverted sense of masculinity or femininity that they will validate our self-esteem. Similarly, those who feel invalidated by heterosexual relationships may feel validated by sexual relations with members of their own gender.

Rather than recognize that sin has caused this human dissatisfaction, people blame their genders for their lack of fulfillment. Thus, gender confusion and even gender disfigurement. This sinful human gender confusion has some people questioning their biological identity. They report that they don't feel like males though they were born as males, or can't identify as females though they were born as females. Though there are hormonal differences, there are no set "male" feelings or set "female" feelings—your personal feeling about your gender doesn't determine or alter the actual fact of your gender. Facts don't care about your feelings.

But too many men and women have no self-image apart from their gender. They can therefore tie their self-esteem to their personal sense of femininity or masculinity. This always leads to trouble, since this self-centered perception may not measure up to some socially informed male or female scale. This can lead to feelings of inferiority or gender confusion. Sadly, many reinforce these false values by going through various makeovers or surgeries to "improve" their position on a male or female index. This disfigurement is all just vanity. The process in Genesis 2 shows that within the human male there is the potential for female, as also the potential for all human ethnicities. Many of our feelings are gender neutral, and we can thereby relate to one another regardless of gender or ethnicity.

If God created you as a male, you can therefore live as a child of God as a male. If you're His child as a male, the image of God will give meaning to your being a male. If God created you as a female, your femininity likewise has meaning as a child of God. There is no intrinsic value in gender apart from being His child. When God blesses you, it is as His child, not as a male or female. He blesses his child to live out His family resemblance through your particular gender role. We each need to first become properly oriented as a child of God, and only then will our role of male or female fall into its proper place.

This proper orientation should be achieved before marriage, for our spouses are not equipped to make us feel good about our gender, or to boost our esteem or self-worth. Our spouses are struggling with their own issues as well! We are self-deceived when we think that our spouses are going to bring fulfillment in our lives and meet all our needs, even if they promise they will. We are just as self-deceived to think that we can fulfill our spouse's life. God alone can fulfill our spouse's life, and He can therefore bless and use you as His instrument. But when each spouse seeks their fulfillment from the other, they are like two fleas, each one hoping that the other is the dog.[19] The needs of the human soul are so profound, they are beyond understanding.[20] We don't even understand our own needs, so how could we possibly fully meet the needs of our spouse? Only God and His Word can properly orient us as His children through our gender roles, once we understand that our primary identity is in the image of God. Otherwise people are inventing meaning for genders that doesn't have any intrinsic grounding in fact.

Gender only has meaning and purpose when we begin with the realization that we are first and foremost children of God. Gender was created for the purposes of God in order to express His image more fully. The problem is not our gender—the problem is our sin; it's our sin that distorts human feelings, emotions, and thinking.

The Scriptural solution is to be "born again"—that is, to be spiritually regenerated. A sinful lifestyle reveals that the individual is spiritually dead and separated from God.[21] Yeshua said, "*You must be born again*" (John 3:7). And it's a "must" for all people, not only to be saved from eternal judgment, but to be in your right mind while still in this world in this age. This spiritual regeneration restores us to

---

19. I don't remember when I first heard this illustration, but it's possibly from a book by Larry Crabbe.
20. Jeremiah 17:9 (SN) states, "*The heart is wicked beyond all understanding*," which warns us against trusting in our own sincerity as any gauge of our own righteousness.
21. See Isaiah 59:1–2 and Ephesians 2:1–3.

the image of God and enables us to live out our creation and redemption calling, which is to live out His love and life through our divinely assigned genders. We, therefore, as Messianic believers, do not first identify ourselves as male or female, but as *b'nai Elohim* (children of God).

The restoration in Messiah is transformative of all we understand about who we are and how we live out who we are. Scripturally, by simple faith in Yeshua, the newborn child of God has gone from death to life (Ephesians 2:1–5) and from darkness to light (Ephesians 5:8). Your inner person is no longer living in response to fears and lusts that are not from God, but in response to faith and love that is from God. As a man, you are now God's kind of man. As a woman, you are God's kind of woman. You no longer seek to live out the world's stereotype of a male or female. But by faith and love you are being restored to your original design.

This is seen as we live out every other role as well. As an American, I am God's kind of American—my values are Scriptural as lived out through my U.S. citizenship. As a Jew, I, like Paul, can say, "*To the Jews I became as a Jew*" (1 Corinthians 9:20). That is, though I was born a Jew, circumcised on the eighth day, and became Bar Mitzvah at thirteen, "*I am crucified with Messiah and I no longer live, but the life I now live, I live by faith in the Son of God, who loved me and gave His life for me*" (Galatians 2:20 sn). Now my ambition is to exalt the Jewish Messiah in every area of my Jewish life. I am, by grace, God's kind of Jew.

Our gender, like our ethnicity, culture, and career, is another stewardship responsibility that lives out our identity as children of God. And so also, I'm God's kind of man and husband, and my wife is God's kind of woman and wife. As a Messianic married couple, we are no longer to be seeking our fulfillment for our married lives as the dysfunctional world teaches through the sin-warped lives seen on TV, movies, internet, etc. Marriages that follow such distorted images of marriage or seek non-biblical counseling to address their struggles with carnality and immaturity are futilely chasing the mirage of marriage that a fallen world offers.

We are therefore cautioned not to "*be conformed to this world, but* [to] *be transformed by the renewing of your mind*" (Romans 12:2). As Messianic believers, we must unlearn what the world has taught us, learn what the Word instructs us on how to live out the image of God through our male and female roles, and apply it to our roles as husband and wife. This unlearning always begins with faith in Messiah's atonement for our sins, and with repentance for the carnality and immaturity that offends God and others, especially our spouse. We ask the Lord to help us outgrow these unbiblical patterns. We apologize to our spouses and become members in congregations that both teach and model biblical values for the Messianic marriage. This growing application of the Word to the lives of the married couple becomes the vibrant testimony of the Messianic marriage.

One • The Principles of Marriage

As we understand this foundational truth of who we are as children of God, the question may arise, "Just why did God create us as male and female?" The summarization of Genesis 1:27 that we see in the phrase "*male and female He created them*" addresses this question. There the word *created* is used at the beginning and end of the verse—the same verb is used both times. This signifies that God created humanity with the designed purpose of making them male and female. In Genesis 2 we see the process of that creation—how woman was taken from man's side. However, the creation of male and female was simultaneous with the creation of humankind ("*man*") that occurred in Genesis 1:26–27. God didn't create man initially and then later decide He could do better, nor did He create humanity as a self-sustaining and self-perpetuating unisex and then later decide to divide him into two genders. Though some believe that God created woman as an afterthought to creating man, this summarizing phrase disproves that assertion. Two genders express the image of God both individually and, even more profoundly, together as a couple.

Through this section of Scripture, God is teaching us that gender is intrinsic to His purposes in creating us. Humanity was created to rule by representing Him as male and female. This dual representation was alluded to when God said, "*Let them rule*," in 1:26. We rule together by representing His mercy, love, kindness, and compassion. In this regard, we can begin to understand what marriage is really all about. The Messianic marriage represents Him as we relate to Him and to each other by His mercy, love, kindness, and compassion. These qualities require another person.

Because of His mystery nature, humanity was created to best represent Him in relationship to one another. We see a hint of this relationship when God says in Genesis 1:26, "*Let Us make man in Our image*." Earlier we reviewed the various options of what this "*Us*" statement could mean, and recognized that it reflects the mysterious Triune nature of the one and only God. God is love,[22] and that genuine love requires relationship. Therefore, relationship is intrinsic to the nature of God, and a loving relationship is intrinsic to His character.[23] You can't be godly without loving relationships. This matter of relationship and God's own nature must be grasped in order to understand God's purpose in creating humanity as male and female.

Because of the direct correlation between God's nature and the redeemed nature of the married couple, the subject of relationship is really a discipleship matter. Scripture teaches us that a person grows Scripturally to better understand

---

22. First John 4:8. God's love is defined in this book as 100 percent total commitment to the eternal welfare of the other person. God's love is not so much a feeling per se, but a commitment that acts on behalf of the beloved, as revealed in John 3:16: "*For God so loved the world, that He gave…*"
23. "*The Father loves the Son*" (John 5:20).

the nature of God through Messianic discipleship (2 Peter 3:18). In such discipleship, we clarify different aspects regarding His nature and our responses.[24]

The unity of God is a testimony issue. God's unity is clearly stated in our public declaration of Deuteronomy 6:4, "*Shema, Yisrael, Adonai Eloheinu, Adonai Echad!*" ("*Hear, O Israel! The LORD is our God, the LORD is One!*") This declaration of His unity identifies our faith with what the greater Jewish community and most of humanity can most easily understand of God: His oneness.[25] Regrettably, so many churches have profiled "Trinity" as their initial and unexplained identifier, that most Jewish people don't understand that faith in Yeshua is monotheistic. But for the Messianic congregation and the Messianic marriage, the Shema identifies us with God's unchanged calling upon the Jewish people.

The deity of Messiah is a salvation issue. Romans 10:9 (TLV) states, "*If you confess with your mouth Yeshua is Lord, and believe in your heart that God raised Him from the dead, you will be saved.*" Yeshua often made this a critical point of belief, for He said, "*Unless you believe that I am He, you will die in your sins*" (John 8:24). Yes, only the perfect God can provide a perfect sacrifice for our sins. And this is divine love truly expressed.[26]

The mystery of His nature is a discipleship issue. Because His mystery nature is a discipleship matter, Yeshua said in Matthew 28:19 (SN), "*Go therefore and make disciples of all the nations, immersing them in the name of the Father and the Son and the Holy Spirit* [The Triune nature of God]." For us to make *talmidim* (disciples), we must teach the biblical truth of God's Triune nature before being immersed. While an Ethiopian eunuch may be ready to be immersed upon trusting in Yeshua (Acts 8:35–38), Yeshua's Great Commission assumption is that immersion is an intrinsic part of a believer's discipleship.

When we think of the divine relationship values that guide our Messianic marriages, we can certainly discuss the vital and eternal values in God's Triune nature:

In the image of God, the Messianic marriage responds to the Father's essential nature.

The love of the Father informs us about unconditional love, since the sovereignty of God is free to love according to His own will. As that love is part of His nature, we can understand that His love is the same for everyone and is forever, as He is. This love of God provides equality for all of us, since we are all loved the same by the one true God, who loves us based on His own nature and not based on our deeds. But since love is only love as it cares for another, this divine love accepts

---

24. Once more, these matters are more fully discussed in the author's books *The Messianic Answer Book* (Charlotte, NC: Word of Messiah Ministries, 1998) and *Messianic Discipleship* (Charlotte, NC: Word of Messiah Ministries, 2014).
25. There are some Messianic Jewish people who came to faith from seeing the Triune nature of God in the Shema, since God is mentioned three times (Adonai, Eloheinu, Adonai).
26. John 3:16; Galatians 2:20; 1 John 4:9–10.

diversity, as He continually seeks to bring others in to share in His glory. When the beloved is estranged, God's own nature pours forth love, grace, and acceptance. The Messianic marriage is essentially a divine love connection that is unconditional, produces equality, and accepts the other graciously, bridging the diversity of gender and personality. The redeemed couple seeks and speaks truth in love to build up their beloved in that divine image of love.

The Father is also holy with an uncompromising holiness, since the sovereignty of God is free from all influences that could ever change the One who never changes (immutability). This holiness produces the highest expectations—it is why we press on to the mark of our high calling, why we commit our utmost for His highest, and why we will one day live in His glory.[27] This is His sanctification process that produces our holiness and righteousness in His image. In the Messianic marriage, each therefore believes the very best for their beloved spouse and holds to high moral standards, seeking together to be pleasing to God and doing Kiddush HaShem (Sanctification of the Name) to His eternal glory.

As the Father is the substance (i.e., the reality) of truth, so the sovereign, uncaused cause of all things *is truth* in His nature and character. He is the source of all that is; His creation therefore is true in that it reflects His nature in some way.[28] To the degree that something reflects God's nature, it is true. Once, we were untrue to His nature and image because of sin, for sin contradicts His nature and image. In redemption, we become true to His nature as we are renewed in His image.[29] This truth of God's nature produces wisdom. Therefore, all understanding and discernment begins with knowing His nature as truth: "*The fear of the Lord is the beginning of wisdom*" (Psalm 111:10). The Messianic marriage honors the Lord, and therefore the couple is set free by the truth, as His nature is the living wisdom of their lives together. The Messianic marriage is the application of truth, living out the redemption from sin by grace through faith in holy love.

In the image of God, the Messianic marriage responds to the Son's expressed nature.

Yeshua is divine love manifested, who becomes the saving sacrifice for others. This matter of sacrificial love is not only seen in His death for our sins, but in His incarnate life. He spoke truth to power, cared for the disenfranchised, and was willingly "*despised and forsaken of men*" (Isaiah 53:3). He had no place to lay His head, "*for you know the grace of our Lord Yeshua the Messiah, that though He was rich, yet for your sake He became poor, so that you through His poverty might become rich*" (2 Corinthians 8:9 SN). Therefore, by His love, He intervened for

---

27. "*And these whom He justified, He also glorified*" (Romans 8:30).
28. "*For since the creation of the world His invisible attributes, His eternal power and divine nature, have been clearly seen, being understood through what has been made*" (Romans 1:20).
29. "*...and have put on the new self who is being renewed to a true knowledge according to the image of the One who created him*" (Colossians 3:10).

us, taking upon Himself our judgment. And even now, Yeshua lives to intercede for us.[30] In the Messianic marriage, therefore, we love one another through the daily sacrifices that demonstrate care for our beloved. Yes, that's why the husband puts the toilet seat down, refrains from his own pleasures, and, wherever he can, seeks to please his wife, laying down his life for her, as Yeshua did for us. And she, for her part, in the humility of love, humbles herself to her husband's leadership, trusting God's blessing through her husband, though she may know that he has a long way to go. We all have a long way to go, but this is the direction we're intentionally going, to grow more and more in His sacrificial love.

Yeshua is divine holiness manifested. What would a holy God look like if He came in the flesh? The answer is Yeshua! All those who had seen Him had "*seen the Father*" manifested (John 14:9). This manifested holiness is shown in His submission to the Father's authority. Yeshua did not bend to man's corrupted religious, economic, or political power. This submission is the humility of Messiah, who, though He was God, humbled Himself to even death on a cross (Philippians 2:6–8). This is the attitude we will develop as we're being "*conformed to the image of His Son*" (Romans 8:29). Holiness manifests as submission to the will of God. The Messianic marriage is in submission to God and mutual submission to "*one another*" (Ephesians 5:21). The wife respects the authority of her husband, and the husband, in submission to the will of God in marriage, lays down his life for his wife. This humble submission to the Lord's authority is exercised in the husband's prayer life, as he does what he can to see his wife grow in the grace of God into the beauty of holiness without "*spot or wrinkle*." In the same humbleness of heart, the wife respects his position as husband, despite his inadequacies in perfectly fulfilling that high calling.[31]

Yeshua manifests the divine nature as the revealed expression of truth in human form. The incarnation therefore modeled the divine values of truth for daily living. Both in His instruction for daily application and in His good works, Yeshua manifested the living Word of God—the image of God—in both His deeds and words. This was seen in His humility at the washing the disciples' feet, in compassionately touching a leper to heal him (Matthew 8:3), in sinlessly fulfilling the righteousness of Torah for our redemption (Romans 10:4 sn), and in His service to the Jewish people, confirming "*the promises given to the fathers*" (Romans 15:8). His service revealed the truth, so that we might follow in His footsteps and example (1 Peter 2:21).

Many women may be understandably concerned regarding their husbands having authority in the home. This concern is reflected in the well-known adage, "Power tends to corrupt, and absolute power corrupts absolutely."[32] But this saying

---

30. Isaiah 53:12; Romans 8:34; Hebrews 7:25.
31. First Peter 3:1–2. This will be more fully developed later in this book.
32. The Lord Acton, in a letter to Archbishop Mandell Creighton, April 5, 1887.

is not true, as evidenced in Yeshua the Messiah, for He has "*all authority... in heaven and on earth*" (Matthew 28:18), but without any corruption. What is true is that power reveals what is in the heart of the person in power, and the more authority the person has, the more the heart is revealed. What is vital, therefore, is for a woman to marry a properly discipled man worthy of the authority of a husband. And a humble reverence for God and for his own mother is the attitude that produces a spiritually wise husband (Psalm 111:10).

The Messianic marriage manifests the holiness of love, caring for one another, and care for those around us as well. The discipled Messianic husband blesses his wife with "*the washing of water with the Word*" (Ephesians 5:26) and uses his delegated authority to sustain, protect, and encourage his wife as God's precious gift. The redeemed wife sees the Proverbs 31 woman as a model of grace. By faith, she too can cause her husband to bless her in the gates and among others. Also, the Proverbs 31 wife demonstrates that submission to her husband's authority in the home does not restrict her own creativity and initiative, as she both cares for her family's needs and builds a business (Proverbs 31:15–16). As we discuss more fully further on, her submission to her husband's authority is a functional subordination but not restrictive on her value as a child of God.

As the Son brought us into favor with God, so the Messianic couple becomes, by grace through faith, God's instrument of favor as husband and wife walk together in the truth of the image of God. The Messianic couple manifests this truth in their hearts through their daily lives. This manifested favor of God testifies of the truth, that His Word is the lamp unto their feet and that Yeshua is the true and living way for their lives and marriage.

In the image of God, the Messianic marriage responds to the Spirit's empowering nature.

The Holy Spirit is the divine instrument of God's saving love for you. By faith in Yeshua, He pours out God's cleansing and redeeming love into our hearts (Romans 5:5; Titus 3:4–5). The Spirit sent forth by the Father and the Son[33] is the Encourager, Comforter, and Helper in our redeemed lives. As the Messianic marriage is filled with the Spirit,[34] the Spirit's ministries and qualities grow in the marriage. The Spirit-filled husband and wife mutually encourage one another in what is good and true. They comfort one another and minister God's hope as His divinely appointed instruments to one another. Your spouse alone is divinely called to be God's intimate love gift to you.

The Holy Spirit empowers your life with spiritual holiness, growth into sanctified likeness to Yeshua, and transformation as you study and apply the Word.[35]

---

33. John 14:26; 15:26; Galatians 4:6; 1 Peter 1:12.
34. To learn how to be continually filled with the Spirit, see the author's book, *Messianic Discipleship* (Charlotte, NC: Word of Messiah Ministries, 2014), lessons 11 & 12.
35. See 2 Corinthians 3:17–18.

His power is tied to holiness; the impure are powerless. His purity enables His power in you. The blood-cleansed Messianic couple is empowered by the *Ruach* (Spirit) to testify in their daily lives. Holiness in the Messianic marriage can be seen in avoidance of gossip, evil media, and whatever else may threaten the unity of the couple. This threat can come through corrupted friends, a job that causes undue separation, or accumulated debt that can bring harmful stress to erode the marriage bond and trust. By the Spirit's power, we pray for each other and together, believing God for His high calling upon each spouse and the marriage itself. By the Spirit's power, when one falters, the other spouse will graciously seek to restore their spouse "*in a spirit of gentleness*" (Galatians 6:1).

The Holy Spirit's divine calling is the exaltation of the Son: He glorifies Yeshua and not Himself.[36] The Messianic couple manifests the power of the Spirit as they exalt the name Yeshua, to the glory of the Father.[37] Whether together or apart, at work or at home, this redeemed couple acknowledges Yeshua as Lord in all their ways. They are unashamed of His Good News and recognize that the power of the Spirit helps them fulfill the calling for their marriage to make *tikkun olam b'Shem Yeshua* (to make the world a better place in the Name of Yeshua) as they interact with the world around them. This is the glorifying power in their worship, walk, and witness that manifests the life of Yeshua and the image of God wherever they go.

Since a relationship is intrinsic to God's nature and image, and to be godly we must relate in love toward others, some may think that people are the problem rather than a blessing, and thus seek to be holy hermits. We may be tempted to hide behind our computer or TV screens and only come out of our man-cave once a week to worship God, but not wanting to get too close to others and the real issues of life. This hermit-like behavior is not of God! God created us to relate, and to relate with a love that represents Him through our lives. He created us as male and female in order for marriage to have a unique intimacy that lives out God's own love. Therefore, in order to mature in godliness, we must love one another, and that is especially true in marriage, since God created us male and female.

Yeshua said that His *talmidim* (disciples) will be recognized by the divine quality of their love.[38] Messianic couples are to love one another just as He loved us. This reflects upon the very calling we have as His people and upon the purpose of marriage. Marriage was created by God in order to reflect His kind of love. God's love produces His grace, which provides for His acceptance of sinners in Messiah. This divine love is required in our Messianic marriages since we're all married to (forgiven) sinners, and His grace alone empowers our acceptance of one another.

---

36. Zechariah 12:10; John 15:26; 16:14; 1 Corinthians 2:10; 12:3; 1 Peter 1:10–12; 1 John 4:1–3; 5:6.
37. Philippians 2:9–11.
38. John 13:34–35, "*A new commandment I give to you, that you love one another, even as I have loved you.... By this all men will know that you are My disciples, if you have love for one another.*"

One • The Principles of Marriage

As in all other matters pertaining to humanity, God's purpose for marriage is to prove that His grace alone is sufficient! Every other purpose for marriage is merely man-made and inadequate.

Throughout the years, I've heard all sorts of reasons why people decide to get married: "It validated me as a person," or "It was economically smart," etc. We come up with ideas about marriage and then find that none of them really works to make for a fulfilling relationship. Only in the redeemed life that we have through Messiah can we have the power of the Holy Spirit for renewed marriages that are able to reflect His life and love. As we implement His love, we graciously accept one another and therefore care for one another to the glory of God. The marriage relationship was created to be God's testimony of His redemption of a lost humanity: because He loves us, He graciously accepts us in the Messiah. Love produces grace; grace reveals love. A grace relationship reveals His great redemption.

As mentioned before, relationship is a discipleship issue, and people should not get married if they are not properly discipled and thereby grounded and rooted in the Messianic faith. In marriage, you must graciously relate to each other, which means that we are to forgive each other, be merciful to each other, and care about one another as part of our daily lives in marriage. This is a discipleship issue because marriage is divinely purposed to represent and express the life and love of God. If people do not know this, they may be getting into marriage for the wrong reasons and with far too narrow a spiritual skill set to have a blessed marriage. Strange but true: a person must get a driver's license before they can go on the road and drive; however, you can get a marriage license without knowing how to "drive"—that is, how to properly live as a spouse with your spouse. This is why there are so many marital "crashes," even among Messianic believers. People who are not properly discipled can often get married having no idea what they are doing.

Yossi and Tilda wanted me to marry them. I had started to disciple Yossi and knew what areas he was still working on. But I don't officiate at a wedding without first providing the couple with twelve hours of premarital counseling, and only after the counseling is completed will I agree to marry the couple—if I think they're ready for the ministry of marriage. At the end of our final session, I said, "I think Yossi needs six months of further discipleship before he's ready to marry anyone. He just doesn't grasp the calling of being a spiritual leader in the home. I can't agree to officiate at your wedding at this time." The couple (mostly Tilda) would not accept that. They admitted that they were already sleeping together despite my warnings against premarital sex. They easily found someone else to marry them. A few weeks after their wedding, Tilda came to me complaining that Yossi wouldn't lead in prayer or anything else! I simply encouraged her to keep praying, and, in time—Yeshua willing—Yossi would mature, if he's willing to be further discipled in the faith. It took a few tough years before their marriage began to improve.

41

Like Yossi and Tilda, many couples are merely responding to their sense of felt need or personal desire, and not to what God has for them in Messianic marriage (which is also intended by God to address their personal needs and desires). Without proper Messianic discipleship, they quickly find their needs are not being met by their spouse, who, as it turns out, is yet another needy person.

The truth is that we are to be complete in Messiah, not in our spouse. Our redeemed and loving spouses can address and minister to our needs, but they cannot meet our needs. This can be done by God alone, for we are created in His image. Men will never fully understand women well enough to meet their every need. To attempt this can seem like trying to understand an alternate universe, because men and women are wired so differently. Women have a different stewardship calling and different responsibilities than men. Women will also never fully understand men, though some may think they have us all figured out! The fact of the matter is that it is not our job to meet our spouse's every need—this is God's job. Our different wiring produces a different sense of need: men need significance; women need security.[39] The husband's desire for feeling significant, when perverted and corrupted, can become domination. The wife's need for security, when perverted and corrupted, can become manipulation. This is wholly improper in marriage and only comes about when we do not understand the purpose of marriage and how all of our needs are fully met in Messiah. In Yeshua alone are we complete[40] and able live out the completed image of God in redemption.

As you consider that relationship is intrinsic to your being, ask yourself, "Do you believe that God is love?" Do you accept that you are created in God's image? If God is love, then you are created to both love and be loved, like God. If you are not being loved, it is understandable that you feel a great sense of need. The only One who can love you fully and forever is the Lord Himself. Everyone else falls short. But by His love you can still love your spouse to the glory of God, for even apart from your spouse, you are truly complete in Messiah.

The Principle of a Resourced Intimacy: Humanity Is Resourced by God's Power

God blessed them. (Genesis 1:28a)

Thus far we've covered some basic foundational principles regarding how we relate to God and represent Him. Now we need to ask how this is going to get done. Maybe you feel like you're running on fumes in your marriage. How on earth do we get what we need to fulfill this huge calling? God answers this question, for Genesis 1:28 reveals our resource for our creation calling.

---

39. For more on significance and security, see Larry Crabb's book, *The Marriage Builder: A Blueprint for Couples and Counselors* (Grand Rapids, MI: Zondervan, 1982).
40. Colossians 2:10.

"God blessed them." First of all, what does it mean that God blessed them? The word for *bless* in Hebrew is *barakh*. Though there is also another Hebrew word translated *blessed* (*ashrei*), this word *barakh* is used in reference to God's bestowed power, while the word *ashrei* means "happy" or "praiseworthy." Its root word *ashar* means "straight," for it is a praiseworthy life that walks the "straight and narrow" with the Lord.[41] The relationship between God's *barakh* blessing and God's strength for His people is reiterated in the Scriptures. "*HaShem will give strength to His people; HaShem will bless His people with peace*" (Psalm 29:11 SN). And "*His descendants will be mighty on earth; The generation of the upright will be blessed*" (Psalm 112:2).

Whom does God empower with blessing? It is the one who is yielded to Him, for the word *barakh* is from the root for "knee" (*berekh*), picturing that a yielded believer is a blessed believer. It is the yielded Messianic marriage that enjoys the blessing of God for their lives and through their home.

Now returning to the text in 1:28 and focusing on the idea of whom God blessed, the Scripture is specific on that matter. Does this verse say that "God blessed him," or that "God blessed her"? No. "*God blessed them.*" Also, the verse doesn't say "God blessed it"—God doesn't bless a marriage per se, but the couple who lives out His image. The marriage is merely their instrument to live out His image as a blessed couple. Beware of making marriage into an idol, where you think that you will be blessed just because you're married. No way! God blessed them as a couple so they could live out His image through their marriage. He blesses a "*them*," not a "he" or a "she" or an "it." Though at times we may think we are more or less deserving than our spouses, we are blessed together, for the calling of God requires that the couple pull together, or they may get pulled apart. We see throughout Scripture that the blessing of God resides in unity and fellowship. "*Behold, how good and how pleasant it is for brothers to dwell together in unity!*" (Psalm 133:1). "*...Not forsaking the assembling of ourselves together, as is the habit of some, but encouraging one another—all the more as you see the Day approaching*" (Hebrews 10:25 SN). All the "*one another*" instructions develop out of this foundational teaching in Genesis. The basis of our unity in fellowship and in the community is found in marriage. Marriage is the cornerstone of what develops into society and community. If you want to improve society, it starts by strengthening the family, which requires having a blessed and empowered marriage.

If you are not relating well with others, you may go unblessed and powerless. We have the blessed resource of His power as we relate lovingly with one another in unity. God's power is given for His creation purposes for the marriage, not for the couple's selfish interests. Do you believe this? The apostle Paul did: "*For I am

---

41. In general, the *barakh* blessing is the cause of our faithfulness, and the *ashrei* blessing is the result of our faithfulness.

not ashamed of the Good News, for it is the power of God for salvation to everyone who believes, to the Jew first and also to the Gentile" (Romans 1:16 SN).

Messiah's Good News power fulfills His purposes for you. And from the above text, it is applied to those who believe. The unbelieving are the unblessed. This power demonstrates God's faithfulness *"to the Jew especially, but equally to the Gentile,"*[42] for His covenant promises are ultimately fulfilled to demonstrate His righteous character. So, I reiterate, His power is always for His purposes and His promises. In fact, God's promises for you are only fulfilled by His power, not by yours. The promises of God that we rely upon necessitate depending on His power to fulfill them, abiding in Him, and relating well to Him. This is evidently so in marriage, where we are called to relate well in unity with our spouse, despite being two very different people with needs neither can fully comprehend, let alone meet. God intended it this way, so that we would need to consistently depend on His blessed power to fulfill His purpose in our marriages.

Good News! In the Messiah, God has given us the power to do all that He called us to do. He teaches us that we *"can do all things through Messiah who strengthens me"* (Philippians 4:13 SN). Everything God has created me to do, He gives me the enablement to accomplish. God's blessing in marriage fulfills our calling as a couple; as we believe, we achieve! He blesses us and says, *"Be fruitful and multiply"* (Genesis 1:28). It is because of the blessing that we can now go do what God created us to do. Yeshua reiterates this point when He says, *"Apart from Me you can do nothing,"* but, *"he who abides in Me…bears much fruit"* (John 15:5). A spiritually fruitful marriage results from the couple abiding by faith in the Messiah, and from nowhere or no one else.

All that God has for our marriages is based upon the blessed power He provides for us in the Holy Spirit as we abide in Yeshua. He can give the increase to whatever He's called us to do, despite our feelings of total inadequacy. Because I loved Miriam, I almost didn't marry her. Though my dad did the best he could, I grew up without a godly behavioral model of a husband and father. As a result, I wasn't sure I could be a godly, faithful husband. Thankfully, I changed my mind when I looked at God's Word. His Word promised me that in God's will for me to marry, and to marry Miriam, He would give me what I would need to be the husband He called me to be. It bears repeating that *"I can do all things through Messiah who strengthens me"* (Philippians 4:13 SN). Although I believed this about being a husband, I still told my wife-to-be that I did not want to have children because I didn't know how to raise kids. Looking at my experiences in life, I had no idea what it would take to be a godly father. I was looking at my inadequate flesh, rather than looking to my all-sufficient God. How did David ever stand up to Goliath? David trusted One much bigger than the gigantic problem he

---

42. As wonderfully translated in the Complete Jewish Bible, by David Stern (Clarksville, MD: Messianic Jewish Publishers, 1998).

was facing! And once more, the Lord convinced me from Scripture that if I kept my eyes on my Heavenly Father, He would help me to be a godly father to my children. So, for my wonderful marriage and family, I have to praise the Lord!

It was also the divine blessing that enabled Adam and Eve to do the will of God and the work of God and fulfill the purposes of their creation in their marriage—that is, while they looked to God for the power to fulfill their purpose. If you are not trusting in His blessing and His enablement, again, you are running on fumes. Apart from His word and instruction on marriage, you are really just guessing and probably manipulating your spouse in a vain attempt to get your felt needs met, or merely distracting yourself with escapist fare. But, if you will trust in the Lord and obey His word, "the task ahead of you is never as great as the power behind you."

His grace is indeed sufficient for us (2 Corinthians 12:9), so that "*we are more than conquerors through Him who loved us*" (Romans 8:37 SN). Understand that the point of Genesis 1:28a is that both were blessed. Some of us are without the blessing because we are not relating well to our spouses. Scripture teaches us how to be a good spouse even if we're married to a not-so-good spouse. You can still do God's will by His power even though your better or bigger half isn't living up to the calling.

The Principle of a Resourced Intimacy: Humanity Is Resourced for God's Purpose

And God said to them, "Be fruitful and multiply, and fill the earth, and subdue it; and rule over the fish of the sea and over the birds of the sky and over every living thing that moves on the earth." (Genesis 1:28b)

We are resourced by His power for His purpose. We saw in Genesis 1:26 the phrase "*let them rule.*" The verb for "rule," *radah*, is also used in verse 28, but now as a result of a process of blessed obedience. The five verbs in this verse teach us how to properly rule by representing Him, governing, and handling our responsibilities.

"*Be fruitful*": be productive

This Hebrew word *parah* means to be productive and creative (as well as procreative). God enables each of us by His blessed power to be blessedly productive. You don't need to be married to be productive; you can have spiritual children. (And if your physical children are not also your spiritual children, there may be more heartache than blessing.) This command is not only for those with physical children; it has to do with the calling of God to make a difference in this world. Long before Abram had any physical children, he had 318 "*born in his house*" (Genesis 14:14); these were his disciples. Abram was impacting his pagan world with the Good News,[43] even as we're called to do. Paul was unmarried but had many spiritual children. He often speaks of his service to his disciples as his fruitful labor, and the fruit of his labor (Philippians 1:22; 1 Corinthians 16:15, etc.), and he cared for them as a *"nursing mother"* (I Thessalonians 2:7).

God has gifted us to impact this world—to be fruitful. We are called and empowered to be winning people to faith and making disciples well beyond our childbearing years. Reach out and share the Good News with the people around you. Encourage and mentor adults who may need re-parenting. Be productive by God's power, for that is His purpose for all of us. He enables us and blesses us to be productive, fruitful disciples in Messiah. Trust God's promise: if you abide in Yeshua you will bear much fruit (John 15:5). In this passage, Yeshua was not talking about physical children. Only in Him can we have the fruitfulness and productivity to be able to fulfill our creation purpose through His redemption power. In your Messianic marriage, can you think of spiritual disciples (whether they're your physical children or not) that you're mentoring? If not, please make this a matter of prayer, since the Lord's blessing on the Messianic couple is for that purpose.

"And multiply": fruitful growth

The Hebrew word for "multiply," *rabah*, means to be growing and increasing. We are to be continually growing *"in the grace and knowledge of our Lord"* (2 Peter 3:18), which will result in greater impact in our sphere of influence. Even those who are retired are without excuse, as they now have even more time in which to grow and help *tikkun olam* (repair the world). Not only are we to be productive, but, as the word implies, we are to be growing in all areas of our lives, for as the Body, we are called *"to grow into all areas into Him who is the Head, Messiah"* (Ephesians 4:15 SN). Growth is the norm, regardless of whatever limitations you may have. In Luke 19:12–27, Yeshua tells His disciples a parable that illustrates this idea. He speaks about a certain nobleman who left for a distant country, leaving his servants in charge over his resources. He commissioned them to *"do business"* until he returned, increasing the resources he gave them charge over. Through this parable, Yeshua is referring to the stewardship role He has given each of us that enables us to continue to grow His Kingdom. We are to be doing business here on earth, growing and being productive. This is how we are to live until the Lord takes us home. Our fruitfulness is to be realized in genuine growth for the Lord's sake. In other words, our children should be part of His purpose to impact the world; this fruitful growth is how we increasingly represent Him in our ever-maturing image of God. In your Messianic marriage, are you both growing *"in the grace and knowledge of our Lord"* (2 Peter 3:18)? Be very prayerful together that you will be growing together so that you won't be growing apart.

---

43. See Galatians 3:8.

"Fill the earth": be influencing

The English word "fill" translates from the Hebrew word *malah*. It means to influence, complete, and fulfill (the earth's potential). There is to be "no vacancy" for evil anywhere that we're God's stewards. God has no plan B.

This commission is repeated in Noah (Genesis 9:1) and finally became the Great Commission—Yeshua sent out His *talmidim* (disciples) to impact and influence this world on His behalf.

The idea of filling is reiterated in the New Covenant in Ephesians 5:18: "*Do not get drunk with wine…but be filled with the Spirit.*" Here *filled* refers to being under the control and influence of the Holy Spirit. This idea of being people of influence helps us understand our calling in our biblical identification as "*salt and light*" (Matthew 5:13–16). Through various Scriptural commands and metaphors, we're instructed to be influencing the people around us and making a difference in our communities. The fruitful and productive Messianic marriage should therefore be active in society, not only in caring for the poor but also upholding godly values and morals and making sure our votes count. Once more, we are not called to be holy hermits, waiting in our prepper homes for the world to end, but rather we're to be out in the world, involved and proactive. Influence those around you; impact this world; fill it to capacity with His righteousness!

The blessed power of God is to be His blessed influence as we represent Him through our families and our involvement in the world. We're blessed to be a blessing. It is for good reason that our children are described as "*arrows in the hand of a warrior*" (Psalm 127:4). If we are Messiah's spiritual warrior, then our children are our spiritual arrows impacting the world around us, even from generation to generation. The assumption on this matter of influence is that our family will be a godly influence, which once more assumes a discipled couple that can properly raise Messianic disciples to God's glory. Does your Messianic marriage make a growing impact for Messiah on your world? As a believing couple, are you praying to impact your neighborhood and community with Yeshua's Good News? Now remember, "*God blessed them,*" so one reason for a lack of "couple power" may be a lack of spiritual unity, for a divided marriage cannot influence the world if they're not under God's spiritual influence for their home first.

"And subdue it": manage your resources

The spiritual impact of this fruitful, growing, and influential godly marriage on the couple's world is to "*subdue it.*" This Hebrew word *kavash* means to manage your resources and keep them under control. The Bible tells us to redeem the time (Ephesians 5:15–16), to make our punches count, and to use our finances for the purposes of God. All this is encompassed by the truth that we are to be subduing our stewardship. Each of us is accountable for the realm of responsibility that God has given us. If I were in control of your finances, I'm sure I would be living better than I am. However, we only have control over areas of our own stewardship. In whatever "garden of Eden" God has given you, take responsibility and manage your resources properly. This is the subduing, the managing, the controlling of your time, talent, treasure, and all that you have. All the areas of our stewardship and responsibility are meant to be under our management and governed by God's Scriptural values. This authority makes us responsible, not invincible—we're defeated when we're corrupted (Isaiah 59:1–2). Apart from Him, we become predators and victims.

The very word *kavash* used here is also used in the book of Micah to explain how God treads on our iniquities (Micah 7:19). You mustn't let sin dominate your life. By the grace of God, you can take a stewardship control over all areas of your life, not just the parts that are visible. This is how we overcome the world—by our faith. You don't have to let your nasty habits and the problems of your childhood ruin your life any longer and corrupt, distract, and distort your perspective on life. No, God has given us the enablement to take this stewardship responsibility, by His grace, and to impact society as a result. In your Messianic marriage, do your possessions possess you? Subduing is the step that comes after influencing and growing fruitful. Work your way back as a couple to the unity that brings the blessing, then work forward in unity through each step to fulfill God's calling that your marriage would be a Messianic light in the world's darkness.

"And rule": take responsibility

Finally, as a result of the process of being fruitful, growing, influential, and subduing, we come to the word *rule*. You cannot rule what has not been subdued. The Hebrew word *radah* means to take supervisory responsibility.

As previously mentioned, because there was no sin in the garden when God gave humanity the command to rule, His way of ruling seems counterintuitive to us. But our true ruling has to do with representing Him. As God's representatives, we control His creation on His behalf and for His glory, never forgetting that *"the earth is the Lord's, and all it contains"* (Psalm 24:1). This is how we take responsibility for our lives within society, managing the various resources that God has given us. Let His grace rule our hearts and this world! We therefore take a supervisory role over our lives to make sure our influence in society brings glory to God.

With the presence of sin in this world, there is a need for law enforcement and armed forces. Let us not, however, see our Messianic marriages become a battleground. Do not treat your spouse as the enemy, especially if your spouse is a believer. You are allies in the spiritual warfare, where together we *"fight the good fight of faith"* (1 Timothy 6:12), for the enemy of God is still trying to destroy the testimony of God in the Messianic marriage. We are representing a God who says in Messiah to each of us, *"tov me'od!"* (*"very good!"*), and we need to understand the importance of representing His rulership as His way to affirm others through us. Through the Messianic marriage, we subdue and manage in order to rule and take responsibility for the things of God as a testimony to His all-sufficient grace in the Messiah.

But what if your spouse is disobedient? What happens if there is dysfunction in your marriage and home? We will deal with these matters in future chapters as we look at how to redeem that which was lost, and how to have a testimony now with a Messianic marriage that shows His "*power is perfected in weakness*," for His "*grace is sufficient*" (2 Corinthians 12:9). His rule through your marriage is a witness to the world that by following His Word, Yeshua's name may be glorified. Where there's disobedience in the married couple there's a lack of blessing needed to fulfill the Messianic marriage calling.

The Self-Sustaining System

> *Then God said, "Behold, I have given you every plant yielding seed that is on the surface of all the earth, and every tree which has fruit yielding seed; it shall be food for you; and to every beast of the earth and to every bird of the sky and to every thing that moves on the earth which has life, I have given every green plant for food"; and it was so.*
> (Genesis 1:29–30)

Food is an additional resource from God for humanity and all of creation for sustaining life. Prior to sin we were all vegans, since we ate only a strictly vegetarian diet. Specifically those fruits and plants "*yielding seed*" were for food. For this matter, seed, with the mist that arises to water the plants, provided a self-sustaining system, needing man's ruling oversight, but not his arduous labor, per se.

Many find it hard to accept that Genesis 1:30 clearly teaches that before sin, all in the animal kingdom were herbivores as well. Sin, amazingly, has an impact that not only made snakes part of the crawling world, but drastically changed other animals so that they became predators and prey. The promise of *olam haba* (the world to come) is that with the removal of sin from the natural order, the original harmonious interaction amongst animal life will be restored: "*And the wolf will dwell with the lamb, and the leopard will lie down with the young goat, and the calf and the young lion and the fatling together; and a little boy will lead them*" (Isaiah 11:6).

Diet is not the real point, of course. The real point is that a marriage is not based on predation, but on the harmony of grace and love, where ruling is not dominating others, but serving one another in Messiah.

"Tov Me'od!"

God saw all that He had made, and behold, it was very good. And there was evening and there was morning, the sixth day. (Genesis 1:31)

The summation of the six days of creation in a sin-free world is declared by God to be *"tov me'od!"* (*"very good!"*). As His *"new creation, where old things have passed away and all things have become new"* (2 Corinthians 5:17 SN), the Messianic couple has a new perspective—God's perspective. Husband and wife are restored by grace in Messiah to see everything differently more and more as they mature into God's perspective in Messiah. Our spiritual growth helps us see all that God has made that is now under our restored rule in the home so that we can agree with God that it is *"very good!"*

Some questions to help apply these teachings

1. What are some ways you value others (especially your spouse if you have one) as the image of God?

2. What are some ways you have affirmed and thanked those around you?

3. What are some ways you have expressed your primary identity as a child of God (1 John 3:1)?

4. What are some ways godliness can be seen in your relationship to others?

5. How do you depend on God's power for relationships (Philippians 4:13)?

6. How have you been fruitful by His power (John 15)?

7. How are you growing by His power (Romans 8:29)?

8. How are you influencing the world around you as salt and light by His power (Matthew 5:13–16)?

9. How are you managing your stewardship by His power (Ephesians 5:17)?

10. How are you representing His righteousness and love to those under your stewardship by His power (John 13:34–35)?

CHAPTER TWO

The Process for Marriage

Genesis 2:1–22

Introduction: Shabbat (Genesis 2:1–3)

Thus the heavens and earth were completed, and all their hosts. By the seventh day God completed His work which He had done, and He rested on the seventh day.
(Genesis 2:1–2)

Genesis chapter 2 opens with the day after creation, the seventh day, when God rested from all the "*work which He had done.*" God is the first person to labor in the Bible. Work is not a necessary evil, but a purposeful good, for God does no evil. Work is godly. And be assured, "*your toil is not in vain in the Lord*" (1 Corinthians 15:58). But now God's creation work is completed.[1] We call this seventh day the Sabbath, or in Hebrew, Shabbat. The Sabbath was created by God, for His work was finished. The account of the seventh day of creation is different from the other six days. With the first six days, "*there was evening and there was morning*" (Genesis 1:5, 8, 13, 19, 23, 31). But on the seventh day, Scripture does not say "*there was evening and there was morning.*" The biblical implication: there was to be no end of the Sabbath; it was to be endless Shabbat between God and His creation. God desired to have unending fellowship as He walked in the garden with humanity (Genesis 3:8–9), together appreciating all that He had made. When sin entered the human equation, however, it broke relationship between God and humanity. As this relationship was broken, the Sabbath, having to do with rest, was broken as well. But this brokenness is not permanent. Eternity will be an eternal Sabbath, restored in Messiah forever. Today, the rest that the Sabbath points toward will also be reflected in our redeemed relationships and Messianic marriages.

Since the Shabbat is mostly misunderstood in religious circles and since it plays a major role in our married lives, let's consider His finished work for our Shabbat fellowship in Genesis 2:1–3.

---

1. But keeping His creation blessed, God still works, even on the Shabbat! For Yeshua taught us: "*My Father is working until now, and I Myself am working*" (John 5:17). It is always good to do good for others on Shabbat.

*Thus the heavens and the earth were completed, and all their hosts.
By the seventh day God completed His work which He had done,
and He rested on the seventh day
from all His work which He had done.
Then God blessed the seventh day and sanctified it, because in it
He rested from all His work which God had created and made.*
(Genesis 2:1–3)

The fact that God "*rested*" doesn't mean that He was drained, tuckered out, or exhausted. Shabbat fellowship "*refreshes*" God from His finished work (Exodus 31:17). God never grows weary (Isaiah 40:28), and He doesn't need a break. Though it may seem odd to some, the Shabbat was created so that God could relate to you. Our lives were intended to be oriented around God, but also, He created us in His image and according to His likeness just so we could relate together in Him. God loves us, and He wants to be with those He loves. When God is love, why would He need to create Shabbat? Because relationships, even with God, take time to develop and mature, especially godly relationships. Messianic marriages need this Shabbat time as a couple with the Lord to mature in relationship together with one another and with Him.

Shabbat was especially sanctified so you, His sanctified people, would relate to God. Shabbat as a rest day isn't merely a day off because we get tuckered out, but because we were created to find our true rest, our spiritual rest, in the Lord. Our lives are meant to be oriented around the Lord and for our souls to be refreshed spiritually in fellowship with the Living God. This is so vital for families today. The world is so disorienting that a weekly reorientation for the Messianic marriage is essential. The couple's fellowship is based on their fellowship with the Lord. As Messianic believers, we're called "saints" (holy ones) because we're sanctified in Messiah.[2] That is, we've been set apart in the Lord and to the Lord. The Shabbat was sanctified by the Lord for those who are sanctified in the Lord. It is really the one day that testifies of our sanctified, set-apart relationship with the Lord, who wants to be resting with His people.

There are many who misunderstand the purpose of Shabbat and therefore either consider it a time for keeping rules or think it unimportant and ignore it altogether. Special days (Shabbat, the annual feast days, and the new moon) are by nature secondary matters, for no one obtains a saving relationship with God through the keeping of these special days. Though they're secondary, they still matter. They are all "*foreshadows of Messiah, who is the substance of them*" (Colossians 2:16–17 SN), that is, He is the primary matter in these secondary occasions. The Shabbat is God's chosen day for rest with His people, and through that day we get to glorify Yeshua, "*the Lord of the Shabbat*" (Mark 2:28 SN). Without the

---

2. "*We have been sanctified through the offering of Yeshua the Messiah's body once and for all… For by one offering He has perfected for all time those who are sanctified*" (Hebrews 10:10, 14 SN).

Lord of the Shabbat, the value of the day is lost, and it becomes another religious occasion for so many, and not a day of relating to our Creator, Redeemer, and Lord.

Shabbat is a creation memorial to remind us that our relationship with God and with each other is completed, rested, blessed, and sanctified in Him. Shabbat testifies to the blessed and sanctified memorial in the Lord of the Shabbat, like an anniversary of the completed relationship. Therefore, Shabbat is blessed and sanctified because our relationship in Yeshua is blessed and sanctified. Though keeping the Shabbat holy is legislated in the Torah of Moses (Exodus 20:8–11), Shabbat preceded the Mount Sinai Covenant. Moses reminds us of how much our relationship is a priority to our God and Redeemer.

Approaching the creation process of Genesis 2

Following the Sabbath portion in Genesis 2:1–3, Genesis 2:4–6 gives us a recap of day three of creation. Genesis 2:7–22 then gives us a recap of day six, detailing how God created humanity. In Genesis 1:26 we see that God is going to create us (future tense). Then, in verse 27, God has created us (past tense). Therefore, the whole portion in Genesis 2:7–22 takes place in between Genesis 1:26 and 1:27. This recap of the creation of humanity emphasizes humanity's preparation to represent God and rule creation on His behalf. As we see in Genesis 1:28, God has promised us the world—that we will be rulers over all creation. However, in this portion, we see that He first gives us a garden. God's Word in Romans 4 says that Abraham will be the inheritor of the world. Matthew 5:5 states that the meek will inherit the earth. The stewardship over the world that was lost by Adam has been redeemed by Messiah.

The Messianic couple often needs to get their married act together during the first year, before they can be a fruitful, growing, influential, subduing, and ruling couple in the years ahead. My counsel has always been that during their first year of married life, newlyweds step back from leadership responsibilities in the congregation. This counsel comes from applying the Scripture: *"When a man takes a new wife, he shall not go out with the army nor be charged with any duty; he shall be free at home one year and shall give happiness to his wife whom he has taken"* (Deuteronomy 24:5). The marriage relationship is so important to society that the newlyweds need that first year to establish their marriage and home before they can be an influence in the years ahead.

First a garden, then the world.

If we are faithful with small things, then more will be given.[3] Before woman was taken from the side of man, man was given a garden to care for. This was to prepare him to care for and provide servant leadership in his family, which can be far more difficult than caring for any garden, or any occupation. All the principles for the wholesome marriage are the same basic principles for a wholesome society;

---

3. See Matthew 25:21.

the marriage is the cornerstone and microcosm of the larger social macrocosm. We change and improve society by changing and improving the marriages that make up the greater community.

As we consider the process of creation in Genesis 2:7, the context of Genesis 2:4–6 is also vital for what our creation means to God and how our marriages are best understood and appreciated.

The Context of the Covenant of Marriage

This is the account of the heavens and the earth when they were created, in the day that the Lord *God made earth and heaven.*
(Genesis 2:4)

The phrase translated "*this is the account*" is the Hebrew phrase *eile toledoth*, a phrase that organizes ten sections in Genesis.[4] The piece from Genesis 2:4–4:22 includes the first four of these sections, explaining: (1) the process of human creation, (2) its completion, and what went wrong: (3) sin and (4) its awful results.

This Genesis 2:4 *toledoth* is about creation, but specifically about creation as the covenant work of God. The covenant name of God (spelled out in Hebrew: *yud, hey, vav, hey*), is introduced in Genesis 2:4.[5] This name is brought in to refer to His covenant work in the creation of humanity. Since the exact pronunciation of God's covenant name is disputed, we'll use "HaShem," meaning "the Name," as this is commonly used in the greater Jewish community. God as HaShem is in the very process of creating, with an eye toward a covenant relationship between God and humanity.[6] Thus, creating us in His image and likeness was to be lived out in a covenant relationship, set by the same values that God lives out in His nature. Someone who is born looking like you can only represent you well if He also acts like you, otherwise you may get blamed for the work of your evil twin. In fact, because of sin, God is misrepresented by our fallen humanity.

The importance of a covenant relationship with God and with our spouse is that we know our boundaries, promises, and provisions in that sort of relationship with God and in our marriage. Your relationship with God and representation of God in your life and through your marriage is on His terms, not yours. God's covenant relationship with all of His creation is through humanity. His covenant commitment is a promise renewed every Shabbat. If you're going to relate well with God, you enter via a (New) Covenant relationship with God through Messiah.

---

4. Genesis 2:4; 5:1; 6:9; 10:1, 32; 11:10, 27; 25:12, 19; 36:1, 9; 37:2.
5. Since this name is considered unpronounceable, it is translated in most English translations as capitalized Lord, and in some Messianic English translations as ADONAI (the Hebrew word for Lord), but I'll translate it as HaShem (the Name).
6. The covenant that God made with humanity in the garden of Eden is noted as such in Hosea 6:7, "*But like Adam they transgressed the covenant; there they dealt treacherously against Me.*"

Otherwise, you're not actually relating well to God any more than you're actually married to Barbra Streisand, just because you may subjectively feel or think you are.

Scripture has two different types of covenants between God and humanity: conditional and unconditional. Unconditional covenants reveal God's faithfulness despite failed human activities. Conditional covenants require humanity to obey the covenant terms to receive the benefits of the covenant. The covenant that God made with Adam in the garden of Eden exemplifies a conditional covenant; Adam was required to obey the covenant's stipulations to avoid suffering the consequences of breaking it.

Like a relationship with God, marriage covenants can be either conditional or unconditional. Marriages based on the conditional covenant relationships with God in Scripture will be conditional covenant marriage relationships. Those Messianic marriages based on the unconditional relationship with God in Messiah's New Covenant will find God's grace as sufficient.

The Garden Covenant, like all conditional covenants (Mosaic, etc.), demonstrates the need for God's grace and mercy for humanity to have any relationship with a holy God. Not even the paradise of the pre-sin garden of Eden is sufficient to have a blessed relationship with God and each other. Your circumstances will not determine your marriage. As nice as it is to have a lovely home, great neighbors, a good job, and an excellent school system, those are insufficient to secure your marriage. Only God's grace is sufficient for you and your spouse (2 Corinthians 12:9).

Your marriage relationship reveals your understanding of your covenant relationship with God. Thus, there are undiscipled married couples that wrongly think that just because they wed in a Messianic synagogue or a Christian church, and since Messiah's name was mentioned in the ceremony, that they have a marriage based upon God's unconditional covenant of redemption. The religious wrapping paper belies the conditional gift inside. It is God's faithfulness in Messiah that saves and secures you in an eternal relationship with Himself. It is that same faithfulness in Messiah that secures the marriage relationship, despite the personal failings of the individuals in that relationship. Is your marriage based on "three strikes, you're out" or "seventy-times-seven" forgiveness of each other? If your marriage is not based on grace through faith in Yeshua, it is on the shaky ground of the conditional, fifty-fifty relationship that may be one personal offense away from failure.

The Context of the Cultivation of Marriage

Now no shrub of the field was yet in the earth, and no plant of the field had yet sprouted, for the LORD *[HaShem] God had not sent rain upon the earth, and there was no man to cultivate the ground. But a mist used to rise from the earth and water the whole surface of the ground.* (Genesis 2:5–6)

On the third day (Genesis 1:11–12), God creates plants that have the potential to sprout and become fruitful. In Genesis 2:5, God states that the uncultivated shrubs (*siach* in Hebrew, first mentioned here) will need rain and so are not yet available. The work of humanity (as in 2:15) is needed to fulfill the potential of the cultivated plants to sprout. All creation awaits humanity.

Genesis 2:6 informs us that pre-sin, rain is not needed, since God has a mist arise for irrigation of the land. Pre-sin, the garden (and the world at that time) represents a God-blessed, self-sustaining system that needs people to care for it, but that this work is not a toil, as it will later become as a consequence of sin (Genesis 3:17). Sin will turn rain into a flood, and work into toil. With sin in the world, the land will need the special grace of God, since the much-needed rain can be divinely withheld through a drought as a judgment upon sinful disobedience.[7] Humanity's role in representing God to creation, which is meant to be an affirmation of life but is subverted by sin, makes creation *"subjected to futility"* (Romans 8:19–22) and *"the ground which the LORD has cursed"* (Genesis 5:29) by our failed leadership through that initial disobedient marriage relationship.

As a part of creation, marriage is also *"subjected to futility,"* and the work of marriage is often a toiling effort by two very flawed individuals. But there is Good News! Redemption in Messiah is meant to restore that self-sustaining system in the marriage, home, and then in the community. This is the very expectation for the redeemed home and community spoken of by Paul:

> *Speaking the truth in love, we are to grow up in all aspects into Him who is the head, even* [Messiah], *from whom the whole body, being fitted and held together by what every joint supplies, according to the proper working of each individual part, causes the growth of the body for the building up of itself in love.* (Ephesians 4:15–16)

The total dependence on the Messiah conforms us to Him in every way, if we will just speak *"the truth in love"* (Ephesians 4:15). It is not truth without love; it is not love without truth. The couple's total dependence on Messiah is seen in their total interdependence on each other (Ephesians 4:16). *"What every joint supplies"* reminds us that we need each other. What he has, she needs; what she has, he needs. In congregational life this is also the case. I need my Messianic brothers and sisters, and they need me. A Messianic congregation, like the Messianic home, reveals their total dependence on Yeshua by their total interdependence on each other.

"According to the proper working of each individual part" reminds us of the need for discipleship that makes us functioning members of the Body, whether in the congregation or in the home. The undisciped believer is the dysfunctional

---

7. Deuteronomy 11:17; 1 Kings 8:35; Jeremiah 50:38; Haggai 1:9–11; Zechariah 14:17–18.

member of the Body and the family. Discipleship should always precede membership, both in the congregation and in the marriage.

The self-sustaining nature of the community and family is the result of our dependence on Yeshua, producing interdependence on each other by what we each provide, following the discipleship-produced "*proper working,*" so that this whole process "*causes the growth of the body for the building up of itself in love.*"

Thus, Messiah redeems us to restore us to the original design of marriage, family, community, and society. This redeemed design of the image of God now has the Messianic marriage representing His love and grace to whoever looks at our garden and home. God has all that is needed for your life and marriage as you trust His grace through faith in Messiah, the redeemer and restorer of the ministry of marriage.

Marriage without the toil of worry and fear is what Yeshua taught those that would trust in Him and His Word.[8] In the redeemed life, His disciples access the needed provision for living by prioritizing "*first His kingdom and His righteousness, and all these things will be added to you.*"[9] What He created, He can keep! Don't worry, pray! Cast all your anxieties upon the Lord, for He cares for you.[10] His work includes His provision to accomplish all that He intended according to His divine will for marriage. To those Messianic couples that will trust in Him, God can give the increase.[11] Marriage works well in the Messiah!

The creation process of humanity in Genesis 2:7–25 is outlined by several principles for the marriage relationship (that apply to the larger community life as well):

I. The marriage relationship is spiritual, not carnal (2:7)

II. The marriage relationship is serving, not dominating (2:8–9, 15)

III. The marriage relationship is obedience, not arrogance (2:16–17)

IV. The marriage relationship is teamwork, not solo work (2:18–22)

V. The marriage relationship is appreciation, not toleration (2:23–25)

Each principle, when applied, will help us to approach the marriage relationship (and society) as God intended according to His original design.[12]

---

8. Matthew 6:22–32.
9. Matthew 6:33.
10. First Peter 5:7.
11. First Corinthians 3:6–7.
12. The last point from Genesis 2:23–25 will be covered in the next chapter.

The Marriage Relationship Is Spiritual, Not Carnal

Then the Lord God formed man of dust from the ground, and breathed into his nostrils the breath of life; and man became a living being. (Genesis 2:7)

As our Creator and "Former," God is the Designer. We were created by His will. We are absolutely not a product of blind chance. This demonstrates the sovereignty of God over His creation. We are formed for His purposes, not our own.

Being made from the dust of the ground, we are similar to all God's creation, and we are therefore to be representing the Creator to all His creation. The Hebrew phrase for "living being," *nephesh chayah*, is used elsewhere for God's creation (Genesis 1:21). We can identify with all other created beings and properly relate to them because we also are taken from the dust of the earth.

Where we differ from the rest of creation is that our soul reflects the image of God by *nishmat chaim*, "the breath of life." Only humanity has that. When He breathed *"the breath of life"* into man, it was that breath that provided the image of God for all humanity. We should not think of our physical bodies as being in the image of God; it is our spirit through our soul—our immaterial self—that is in the image of God.

We're not merely physical beings with a spirit—we're spiritual beings with a body! Having the image of God determines the kind of being we are, and therefore, the kind of marriages we will have. It is said, "Politics makes strange bedfellows." That may be true, but marriage is not political maneuverings with an opposing party, but spiritual ministry to a beloved partner. This is because each person is a spiritual being and needs to be appreciated and approached as such. In this regard, Scripture states that we all have eternity in our hearts (Ecclesiastes 3:11)—that is, we have a consciousness that no other creatures have. This is the uniqueness of humanity. God sees us as spiritual beings, and He relates to us in just that way. Perhaps we would better understand ourselves if we related to God before we tried to relate to others of our own gender, let alone those of the other gender. Relating to your spouse as a spiritual being is essential for a marriage to work, for you need to relate to people for who they are, not as you might want them to be. And you are who God says you are—not who your parents, boss, friends, spouse say you are (unless they agree with God!). If neither spouse understands that both spouses are spiritual beings, but relates to the other as a mere physical being with mere physical needs, you will find some spouses understandably see providing for the family's physical welfare as their only real job. Though they might not end in divorce, marriages fail spiritually and break down emotionally because spouses have a wrong perspective of themselves and each other. Since we are spiritual beings with bodies, we must have a spiritual orientation in order to understand marriage.

Your spouse's needs are essentially spiritual. He may think that having three square meals a day and a roof over his head is all there is to meet the needs of his life. This is probably sufficient for his physical life, but it is not enough for his spiritual life. Similarly, she may think that as long as the bills are paid she will be secure. This may be sufficient for her physical welfare, but it is not enough for all that she is in God's sight, that is, for her spiritual life. If we are going to have marriages that work according to Scripture, we need to have a spiritual orientation. This is necessary to understand what makes us tick and what is essential for our lives—who we really are.

The Scriptures have much to say about anthropology (the science of humanity). Often in Scripture, a person might be called a "soul,"[13] and so some may think that's all we are. But to see the full human picture, other Scriptures define humanity more exactly and completely.

"May the God of shalom make you completely holy. May your entire spirit, soul, and body be kept blameless for the coming of our Lord Yeshua the Messiah" (1 Thessalonians 5:23 SN). Humanity is made up of "*spirit, soul, and body*," even though all of these may not be a consideration in our priorities for living. Our spirit, soul, and body are generally quite integrated, and so we understand ourselves as simply a person. But being unaware of who we really are, many people merely respond to the felt needs of their body (hunger, thirst, sexual appetite, etc.), or perhaps of their soul (entertainment in music, visual arts, sports, or vocational challenges, etc.). But our real needs are spiritual. These needs are met by God, for this spiritual connection is the vital and essential key to properly addressing all other felt needs of both soul and body. Personal corruption develops when we attempt to meet our soul and body needs apart from the spiritual connection to God.

Consider the tabernacle that Moses constructed, or the temple that Solomon built. The outer court is where every Israelite goes to bring their offerings to the Levitical priests. This outer court is visible to all and is therefore like our body, where our external activities can be seen. The holy place is where only the priests can serve. There is placed the table of showbread, the seven-branched menorah, and the golden altar of incense. It is there in the holy place that spiritual service is conducted, but that place can be entered only after the priests pass through the brazen, bloody altar, and then the laver for cleansing. This holy place pictures our soul, where we are nourished by the bread of life, gain spiritual insight like the menorah, and formulate our prayers like the golden altar. Then deeper still, past the holy place, the holy of holies is located. Here, only the high priest enters once a year on Yom Kippur to come before the presence of the Living God, Who is enthroned on the mercy seat between the cherubim. It is here that true spiritual communion with God is possible, but only if all that preceded it in the outer

---

13. This is especially the case in the literal KJV, where the Hebrew *nephesh* or the Greek *psuche* for "soul" would in modern translations be "person," as in Genesis 46:18, 22; Acts 7:14, etc.

court and the holy place is properly accomplished.[14] Without genuine spiritual communion with God in the holy of holies, all the other activities in the outer court and the holy place are mere religious activity. In Messianic marriages, without genuine communion with the living Lord, all else we do is mere religiosity, hypocrisy, and uselessness. Our real needs are met in communion with the Lord, which then validates all that properly brings us before Him. It is the couple's true communion with the Lord that gives them genuine and meaningful fellowship with each other.

Since we're created with the express purpose of relating to God and thereby representing His will to creation, these three aspects of who we are can be considered in this regard:

I. Your spirit is intended to embrace the divine will.

As noted, the *"breath of life"* (*nishmat chaim*) is God's spiritual work and spirit in us, to be His spiritual beings in His image—as opposed to the angels, who are spiritual beings but who are not created in His image (thus Hebrews 2:16). Humanity alone is able to represent and relate to Him. The breath of life not only makes us alive, but alive to Adonai! This imparted spirit is how we commune with our Creator.

The uniqueness of the human spirit is maintained throughout the Scriptures: *"Thus says the LORD, Who created the heavens and…the earth…Who gives breath [neshemah] to the people on it and spirit [ruach] to those who walk in it"* (Isaiah 42:5). And so, *"The spirit of man is the lamp of the LORD, searching all the innermost parts of his being"* (Proverbs 20:27). Therefore, God relates to you—not as lost sinners—but as His spirit-born children in Yeshua.[15]

II. Your soul is intended to express the divine will.

Your soul is your personality, but some identify the soul with the spirit. The spirit and soul can be easily confused, since both are invisible, intangible, and immortal, but these can be divided,[16] and they are essentially you. Let's carefully understand the process of creation to appreciate more fully the uniqueness of humanity and your own individuality. By His breathing the breath of life (our spirit) into us, we became a living soul.

All animal life, including humanity, has a *nephesh*, or "soul" (Genesis 1:20, 21, 24, 30; 2:19). Thus, besides a spirit, every human being also has a soul. The other creatures are also called a "living soul" (*nephesh chayah*). But our human soul was

---

14. The awful consequences of the priests not carefully following the biblical protocols are seen in Leviticus 10 and 16. The closer to the holy of holies the priests had to serve, the more circumspectly they had to walk.
15. *"You have forgotten the exhortation which is addressed to you as sons"* (Hebrews 12:5).
16. *"For the word of God is living and active and sharper than any two-edged sword, and piercing as far as the division of soul and spirit"* (Hebrews 4:12).

solely intended to match with the spirit we have from God. This is emphasized by the unusual phrase "***L'nephesh chayah***," where the *L'* means "**for** (this kind of) a living soul." The human soul was created by God to especially express the human spirit from God. How great is God? He is beyond all human comprehension (Isaiah 55:8–9) and certainly more than any merely mortal person could adequately express!

In today's terminology, we normally don't use the word *soul*; instead, we call it *personality*, since it reflects our individuality though our individual differences of personality, which then shows itself in our fashion tastes, entertainment preferences, political inclinations, and other differing interests. Perhaps with your pets you've noticed that two birds or two dogs may have very different personalities from each other. That's true for all creatures, including humans. Even identical twins can have quite different personalities.

So, your individual soul (personality) has the unique combination of mind, feelings, and will to express the one true God. You reflect a slightly different facet of the divine diamond of God's nature from anyone else in the world! That's why each person is always of great value and why there are no throw-away people according to God's perspective. You are of amazing value to God, and so is your spouse. That is why the Redeemer "*has come to seek and to save that which was lost*" (Luke 19:10), "*for God so loved the world*" (John 3:16), which includes you and your spouse.

The differences in our human personalities are accounted for in Scripture by the fact that the soul (or personality) is made up of three different but integrated parts:

- Your intellectual self (thinking)[17]
- Your emotional self (feeling)[18]
- Your volitional self (will)[19]

The intellectual you

The intellect refers to your mind for thinking, as to thoughts, ideas, perception, memory, reason, knowledge, imaginations, and intelligence. Once one is spiritually redeemed one can have a redeemed mind, which the Bible calls a "*sound mind*," disciplined, or sensible.[20] Minds are corrupted by sin; thus, God saw all our thoughts as wicked.[21] However, as a believer, and upon offering our lives as living sacrifices for His service, God enables and encourages each of us to "*not be*

---

17. Genesis 6:5; Deuteronomy 15:9; Proverbs 23:7, Ezekiel 11:5; Matthew 9:4; Romans 2:15, etc.
18. Exodus 34:6; 1 Samuel 23:21; Song of Solomon 5:4; 2 Corinthians 6:12; Philippians 2:1, etc.
19. Genesis 24:5, 8; Exodus 2:21; Psalm 54:6; Hebrews 10:26; 1 Peter 5:2, etc.
20. Mark 5:15; Luke 8:35; Romans 12:3; 2 Corinthians 5:13; 1 Timothy 3:2; 2 Timothy 1:7; Titus 1:8; 2:2, 5, 6; 1 Peter 4:7, etc.
21. Genesis 6:5; Ecclesiastes 9:3; Jeremiah 17:9; Matthew 15:19; Mark 7:21–23; Ephesians 2:3, etc.

conformed to this world, but be transformed by the renewing of your mind" (Romans 12:1–2). In Messiah, we are empowered to tear down the strongholds of arrogant thinking, and to take every thought captive to Messiah's Lordship (2 Corinthians 10:4–5). This is the process to have the renewed mind that seeks to think God's thoughts and honor Him in all our thinking. This is how you spiritually mature in your intellectual self, and why some are said to have godly wisdom.

The emotional you

Your emotions refer to your feelings of anger, fear, contempt, disgust, sadness, happiness, joy, surprise, etc. God also helps us to mature in our emotional selves. Many strange practices that people "enjoy" are the outworking of our corrupted emotional selves. These defiled feelings can become any number of sociopathic, traumatic, and uncontrollable emotions that rack and ruin the individual who does not trust in Messiah. However, once you are saved and redeemed, and as the image of God is being renewed in you, you can obey God and start to transform your emotions to more properly reflect the image of God. Thus, we are Scripturally encouraged to *"rejoice in the Lord always"* (Philippians 4:4) and to compassionately *"mourn with those that mourn"* (Romans 12:15 SN). This is so vital in the Messianic marriage, where our homes have to be safe places and provide the mercy and forgiveness that is unavailable and unknown in the world. As we mature in the Messiah, we can turn the TV or radio channel when visual or auditory messages are emotionally corrupting to us. By repenting of wrong emotional responses and obeying God's Word, we can each emotionally mature, so that our Messianic marriages can live out the truth, *"The joy of the Lord is your strength"* (Nehemiah 8:10)!

The volitional you

Your volition refers to your will and is seen in your convictions, decisiveness, resistance, yieldedness, boldness, and persistence. As a believer, your volition (will) is also being renewed in the Lord. This is your will power (or *won't power* for resisting temptation) that enables you to be yielded and obedient to God and His Word. Scripture often refers to believers as servants, or slaves, of the Lord.[22] The word *slave*, though sometimes translated "servant," refers to someone who has surrendered their own will to only do the will of their master. There is only One who is our Lord and Master and that is the Lord Yeshua. His will be done. And as we mature in the Lord, we thereby volitionally yield our will to Him and become increasingly compliant to the Holy Spirit. At the same time, amazingly, we become increasingly stubborn against sin, which previously got the best of us. In so doing, we are relying upon the Lord and resisting the enemy, and we thereby *"overwhelmingly conquer through Him who loved us"* (Romans 8:37). As God's will becomes our own, the Messianic marriage is the beneficiary, for in

---

22. Greek *doulos* or Hebrew *ebed*; see Numbers 11:11; Luke 12:43; 1 Corinthians 7:22, etc.

that redeemed relationship the marriage bond is strengthened by the faithfulness that resists temptation. The everlasting love of God[23] secures the Messianic home.

As mentioned before, spirit and soul are intangible. The "person" that we are is integrated, and we see ourselves as a whole individual, not divided into spirit and soul. The spirit and soul interface in what may be thought of as a blended area. Yet a division can be seen (Hebrews 4:12), so careful distinctions can also be made. The area of spirit includes our faith, hope, love, light, fruit (of the spirit), and reverence, among others. The area of soul includes character, attitude, integrity, conscience, intuition, guilt, and wisdom, among others. The soul is so impacted by the spirit that it may understandably seem blended, but as we mature in Messiah, each specific area can have its own challenges and opportunities for expression. Our maturity through marriage will need mutual compassion, encouragement, and prayer as we seek to grow together in Yeshua and not grow apart.

III. Your physical body is intended to execute the divine will

Our sovereign Maker intends us to physically execute His will, and our source material reminds us to execute His will in all humility. God formed us from the dust of the ground. The Hebrew word translated "formed" (*yatsar*) means to be "formed according to plan." This informs us that we are formed for His purposes, not ours. We read of *yatsar* in, "*The people whom I formed for Myself will declare My praise*" (Isaiah 43:21). And again, "*Everyone who is called by My name, and whom I have created for My glory, whom I have formed, even whom I have made*" (Isaiah 43:7). Humanity is "formed" for His glorious purpose. Though this purpose was lost by sin, it is now renewed in Yeshua.

Thus, as Messianic individuals and Messianic couples, you are to "*present yourselves to God as those alive from the dead, and your members as instruments of righteousness to God*" (Romans 6:13). Our redeemed bodies have a renewed purpose that is fulfilled as we "*present*" the members of our bodies to now be "*instruments of righteousness to God*" and no longer as instruments of selfish desires and loveless behaviors. But some may think, But we're just made from dust, not gold. What can be expected from creatures made from lowly dust? Our source material reminds us to humbly execute His will. We're molded from the dust, like all the animal life (Genesis 2:19). How very humble are our origins. The Hebrew word *aphar* is used for common, loose dirt—just add water and you have mud or clay! This should remind us that He is literally the Potter, for we are literally the clay! And so what a great Creator! Yes, "*we have this treasure in earthen vessels, so that the surpassing greatness of the power will be of God and not from ourselves*" (2 Corinthians 4:7). We were created to depend on God and thereby to glorify Him, not ourselves or our marriages. Our Messianic marriages are "*earthen vessels*," that the power to live out His image will be of God, and to Him be the glory.

---

23. Jeremiah 31:3.

The redeemed "Three in One"

Being created in God's image, we commune with God through a spiritual connection. That is, since "*God is spirit*" (John 4:24), He relates to us and empowers us through our spirit. In spiritual connection with God, the spiritual life of God is worked out through our soul (*nefesh* in Hebrew or *psuche* in Greek). This spiritually impacted soul impacts the physical body to now do, act, and behave according to what we think, feel, and will. In other words, when you are made alive to God by faith in the Messiah, you can now spiritually renew and transform your soul to reflect His life and values. This will be reflected through your thought life, emotional life, and volitional life, which will then be acted out as good deeds to His glory, pleasing to the Lord. All this is opposed to doing mere activities (even religious activities) without being spiritually motivated; those are called "*dead works*" (Hebrews 6:1; 9:14).

This new life is by the Spirit of God's power. You received the Holy Spirit upon initial faith in Yeshua; He is now maturing you in these areas as you obediently yield them to Yeshua. Through this process, your personality will not change, but it will mature. Becoming an adult, you put away childish things (1 Corinthians 13:11).

This is how your Messianic marriage will mature in fruitfulness, growth, influence, self-control, and ruling your stewardship responsibilities to God's glory. As you and your spouse are experiencing this growth, you need to understand what is happening spiritually to encourage growth, to pray for each other to continue growing, and to appreciate with praise these blessings from the Lord. We are spiritual beings, so we need to have a spiritual orientation in order to understand life, ourselves, and our marriages. Otherwise, we will end up treating each other in a fleshly way that will only result in failure. Scripture states that without this spiritual life, we are but people for whom "*the things of the Spirit of God…are foolishness…because they are spiritually appraised*" (1 Corinthians 2:14). But in Messianic marriages yielded to the Lord, we understand that though only God can meet our spouse's deepest spiritual needs, we are each called and empowered to compassionately minister to our spouse's spiritual needs, and thereby be God's instrument of blessing to our spouses.

The implications of human nature for dating, engagement, and marriage

All vital relationships must be foundationally spiritual to fulfill His purposes. This divine purpose of marital unity will guide your dating, engagement, and married life. Relationships founded upon the Messiah are founded upon Him right from the beginning.

Spirit unity is developed through the *friendship* phase of dating. During this time, couples should be discussing the spiritual values, victories, and challenges in their individual lives. They develop spiritual unity as they realize that they share the same spiritual values and commitments. If the relationship develops no further, these two will have at least developed a long-term friendship and spiritual alliance. Spirit unity is foundational to all other proper unity for the married couple. Without spirit unity, the foundation is destabilized until they repent and have Messiah as their foundation for living and the Holy Spirit helping to reorient and renew them through Messianic discipleship.

Soul unity is built on the foundation of the unity of shared spiritual values and commitments. During the *dating* phase, the couple's discussions revolve around those intellectual, emotional, and volitional matters that reveal their level of maturity as an outgrowth of their spiritual convictions. The principles that articulate one's spiritual faith reveal whether the person's mind is yielded to the Lord. Solomon teaches us, "*For as he thinks within himself, so he is*" (Proverbs 23:7). The New Covenant reiterates this in Romans 12:1–2 and 2 Corinthians 10:4–5. We're not conformed to the world if our minds are transformed to demonstrate that God's will is the "*good and acceptable and perfect*" way to live. So too, what we laugh and cry about reveals whether we are concerned with what concerns the heart of God. Do we weep over Jerusalem (Luke 19:41), and rejoice in the Lord always (Philippians 4:4)? Our willingness to trust and obey the Lord, or willingness to give in to any temptation, reveals whether or not God's will is our will. As soul unity develops, this becomes the courting process that leads to engagement and marriage.

Body unity is experienced and developed after the wedding, since under Torah, virginity is the expectation (Deuteronomy 22:23). Engagement is not the time to have sex. Only after the wedding is the couple to consummate the marriage. In the Torah, casual sex with an unengaged virgin means marriage (Deuteronomy 22:28–29), whether or not they are otherwise compatible. Thus, the New Covenant assumes the propriety and blessing of the marital bed and judgment on all fornication—that is, premarital sex and adultery (sex with anyone but your spouse: Hebrews 13:4; 1 Corinthians 7:1–2; 1 Thessalonians. 4:3, etc.). For married couples, sexual union is to be counted as a delight (Proverbs 5:15–19), as well as a duty (1 Corinthians 7:3–4).

Far too often, couples having an initial attraction to each other, have physical unity (sex prior to marriage), and then try to get to know one another, remaining spiritually dead to God and each other. They didn't have true unity; they merely had sex. They may even get married, hoping that marriage will provide their dysfunctional relationship with the significance and security that they deeply desire. In doing so they are attempting to use a marriage differently than God intended, and their "marriage" becomes a spiritually eccentric relationship. When children are raised in this environment, their genuine needs as well—that is, their spiritual needs—are never understood nor adequately addressed. This family may even try religion, but their immense spiritual problem can never be resolved by mere religious activity. The only hope for this and any marriage is the forgiveness, grace, love, and new life provided in Messiah. This Good News, in accord with God's original design, provides a whole new orientation for their lives, their marriage, and their family.

Our humanity is realized through our commitments. Living for the flesh, in or out of marriage, is failure. By *flesh* we mean the natural inclinations and desires that arise from our sin-corrupted soul. This is *"the lust of the flesh and the lust of the eyes and the boastful pride of life"* (1 John 2:16) that motivates us to covet, fear, be envious, greedy, hateful, and every other defiling impulse in the sinful human soul. On the other hand, our spiritual values, priorities, and commitments as Messianic believers are what reflect God's will and His image in us. Our spiritual commitments in agreement with Scripture make us authentically human in accord with God's original design. Many people search their whole lives to discover who they really are. They do not understand themselves from God's perspective, and so they search within themselves, like peeling away the onion one leaf at a time, thinking that somewhere down there is the real you. But in the end, they find out that they are just a bunch of tightly wound onion leaves. They search within, but they search in vain. *The truth of who we are is defined by our spiritual commitments and not by our fleshly identity.* We may have developed many survival tactics in growing up or getting through our teenage years. Once redeemed in the Lord, all of those matters can now become useful, not where they are depended upon, but rather, yielded to the Lord for His healing and renewal. By His grace, these idiosyncratic behaviors can be transformed, and that transformation is revealed by that person's spiritual commitments, priorities, and values.

When you want to know who you are, look at your commitments. You need to understand yourself and your spouse in this way. According to your spiritual commitments, you will use your time, talent, and treasure in your relationships, either for His glory, or not. Your commitments reveal who you really are, just like looking at your checkbook tells you where your heart really is (Matthew 6:21).

As you then counsel those who are married, your Scriptural commitments will evaluate them from God's perspective. Apart from Scripture, you will not be able to help them follow the Lord in their Messianic marriage. You need to restore the spiritual orientation through Scriptural commitments that a marriage must have in order for it to be spiritually functional and following the Lord.

Most people do not understand what marriage is all about, or what their calling is in it. Some people get married because they want another "mommy" or "daddy" figure. As long as this new "parent" tells them what to do, they will think that this dysfunctional relationship is the right relationship for them. Conversely, others coming out of dysfunctional homes may marry to have someone to dominate. They may merely be reliving their youth, by making sure they have someone to boss around. These dysfunctional marriages merely reinforce corrupted desires that are not of God. Our spiritual commitments must define the image of God in us and in our relationships. Before people get married, they need to make sure that they and their potential spouse are properly discipled in the faith and—by God's grace through faith—ready to make spiritual commitments and encourage, minister to, and spiritually address the many issues they will face in a Messianic marriage.

Messianic discipleship can reorient the believing Messianic couple to have biblical values and make spiritual commitments that both reflect God's image in their lives and glorify God through their marriages. Faith-reliance in Yeshua the Messiah is the start, and faith-obedience to the Lord is the re-orienting, renewing, and redemptive lifestyle for the healthy Messianic marriage.

The Marriage Relationship Is Serving, Not Dominating

> *The LORD God planted a garden toward the east, in Eden; and there He placed the man whom He had formed. Out of the ground the LORD God caused to grow every tree that is pleasing to the sight and good for food; the tree of life also in the midst of the garden, and the tree of the knowledge of good and evil.* (Genesis 2:8–9)

Your work identity as God's servant, not as the owner

The garden of Eden (*gan aiden*) is "*planted*" by God on the third day, in preparation for humanity to be created on the sixth day. It is planted by God as His "lab experiment" to develop and prepare humanity for greater responsibilities. The word *Eden* means "delight," and it was meant to be the garden of delight. Life without sin is a delight; life with sin is a disgrace. Here God "*placed*" (set) and established "*the man*" (the definite article before man—the Hebrew *adam*—indicates a representative human for us all). The purpose for both humanity's creation and placement in the garden is to represent God. God prepares the place for the prepared person. First God makes the person; then God puts him in the right place. With job changes and other issues, marriages can be a "moving" experience. But be assured that God goes ahead of you and prepares His place for His people. Even as God went before Israel through the wilderness to the promised land (Exodus 13:21; Numbers 14:14), so too He goes before you. As a Messianic couple, sincerely be God's people for Him, and you will surely be set into God's place for you. But if you're not His people, then there's no place that will be His place for you.

The garden contains trees that are both beautiful and bountiful (2:9). Two other trees are specifically mentioned: "*The tree of life also in the midst of the garden, and the tree of the knowledge of good and evil.*" Since Adam already has life and has no concern of death, the tree of life provides no temptation for him (nor later for Eve). But "*the tree of the knowledge of good and evil*" has something that Adam doesn't yet have: wisdom, discernment, and the experiential *"knowledge of good and evil."* Since people—even untainted people—only want whatever they don't already have, the imperative from God in 2:16–17 would be much-needed advice.

The garden of Eden is also called "the garden of HaShem," or "of God,"[24] so it was very likely meant to be a "heaven on earth" for humanity. One Greek word for "garden" is *paradeisos*. The paradise of Eden mirrors God's own paradise in heaven. Yeshua promises the thief on the cross that he will be there *"in Paradise"* with Him that very day (Luke 23:43). Paul *"was caught up to the third heaven...into Paradise"* (2 Corinthians 12:2, 4).

The *"third heaven"* above the sky, (which is the first heaven), and above the stars, (the second heaven), equates to *"Paradise."* Messianic overcomers are promised by Messiah *"to eat of the tree of life which is in the Paradise of God"* (Revelation 2:7). In the book of Revelation, the *"tree of life"* is located in the New Jerusalem, in the New Heaven and New Earth (Revelation 22:2, 14, 19); evidently this eternal paradise will be our future garden of Eden. By this we can understand that the garden of Eden was all that pre-sin humanity needed to be satisfied.

The location of the garden is open to much speculation. Evidently, there was the land mass of Pangea, one large supercontinent, prior to two cataclysmic events—the flood and the dispersion of humanity after Babel. Once Pangea became broken up and divided, the location of the areas mentioned can be assumed to have spread globally. The water flowed out of Eden into four great rivers, the names of two of which, the Euphrates and Tigris, remain as rivers today. Adam's sufficiency is not in himself but in the all-sufficient provision from God. These waters point to what God has for Israel and for all other people who trust in Him and Him alone. This is why Yeshua stands at the temple at Sukkot and cries out, *"If anyone is thirsty, let him come to Me and drink"* (John 7:37). To all who will trust in Him, He is still the fountain of living waters for your heart and your home.

The descriptions of the rivers and the precious metals in those lands (Genesis 2:10–14) assures Adam that wherever God sends him, there will be sufficient resources for his life and well-being. Yet, although Adam and Eve have all they need for a perfect life, their marriage fails. And it fails for the same reason every other marriage fails: they don't trust God. They take really bad advice and disobey God, and every other relationship is damaged as well.

Understanding yourself as a servant is intrinsic to every relationship. The marriage relationship is for God's purpose, which is our mutual service to each other, not domination over each other. Before Adam had a wife, he had to learn how to serve, and was settled in the garden for this purpose. How different society would look today if people understood themselves as the servants, not as the owners!

---

24. Genesis 13:10; Isaiah 51:3; Ezekiel 28:13; 31:8–9.

God has put us here to serve in our families. Parents do not own their children—they are merely managers of them. Every husband is called to serve his wife, and every wife to serve her husband. People who go into marriage understanding this are more likely to find success. If people get married in order to be served because they think of themselves as "the boss," or the one having the leverage, they will find themselves in corrupt, dysfunctional relationships. Even Yeshua did not come to be served, but to serve (Matthew 20:28). We are here to serve. As people spiritually mature, they become better servants of each other.

God's garden was created for His fellowship with those created in His image. This is where God would walk with His people (Genesis 3:8). Here it was always to be the Sabbath, a time of fellowship between God and humanity. A healthy relationship is intrinsic to God's being, and therefore relationships are especially and extremely meaningful to Him. God loves relating to others; He loves you! In fact, God is love (1 John 4:8). He created the garden in order to have Shabbat fellowship with His beloved people. So is it in the life of the redeemed Messianic couple: God's fellowship with His people means His people's fellowship with each other. When they lose fellowship with God, they are out of fellowship with one another as well. Is your marriage lacking loving fellowship with one another? Both need to get back to fellowship with God, that your home may be like the garden of Eden, by His grace and love.

> *Then the* LORD *God took the man and put him into the garden of Eden to cultivate it and keep it.* (Genesis 2:15)

"*God took the man and put him into the garden.*" If Adam has free will, why does he allow God to take him and put him wherever He desires? Isn't that demeaning? Of course not! Before sin, Adam simply trusts God! As followers of the Messiah, this trust is what characterizes our lives, "*for we walk by faith, not by sight*" (2 Corinthians 5:7). As He takes the people of Israel from Egypt and puts us into a promised land, so in Messiah He takes us from the bondage of sin and puts us into the place of His eternal promise.[25]

Adam is placed in the garden to "*cultivate it and keep it.*" The word "cultivate" is from the Hebrew word *abad*, which means "to serve." "Keep" (*shamar* in Hebrew) means "to watch or guard." These two words are very special words in the Hebrew Bible because they are also used to describe the duties of the priesthood in the tabernacle (Numbers 18:5, 7). Adam and Eve were to be God's priests in the garden. Humanity was to be a priesthood representing God to creation and creation to God. Then, fallen humanity needed a priesthood. This was the purpose of God's calling of the nation Israel in Exodus 19:5–6. Then, failed Israel needed a priestly tribe to represent them before God. But with the failure of the Levitical

---

25. "*He rescued us from the domain of darkness, and transferred us to the kingdom of His beloved Son*" (Colossians 1:13).

priesthood (Malachi 2:8), we needed the Messiah as the divine High Priest for the tribe of Levi, the nation Israel, and for all humanity.

In the book of Leviticus, we see that God gives the tabernacle to be a renewal of what humanity had in the garden of Eden. As a result of the atoning sacrifices offered by the priests in the tabernacle, sinful people can again have fellowship with a holy God. As the priests who serve in the tabernacle are representatives of God to the people and the people's representatives before God, we also are called in Messiah's high priesthood to be a His holy Messianic priests: *"You yourselves, as living stones, are being built into a spiritual house to be a holy priesthood for God to offer acceptable spiritual sacrifices to Him through Yeshua the Messiah"* (1 Peter 2:5 SN).

This adequacy of the service of the priest is based on the sufficiency of the sacrifice of the priest. Inadequate sacrifices are not only poor service by the priests, but also provide no help to the people. In Malachi, God rebukes the priests for their unworthy offerings and instruction that stumbles the people, leading to divorce, which God hates (Malachi 1:6–2:16). Our service for God as His Messianic priests in the home and congregation is based on the total sufficiency of the sacrifice of Messiah, through whom we *"offer acceptable spiritual sacrifices"* that will change all to whom we minister.

God's design for humanity to be priests representing God to creation and creation to God is now restored in Messiah, our Cohen Gadol (High Priest). Though we do a poor job at it now, when Messiah returns and reigns on the earth, we may be vastly improved, as we're told, *"You have made them to be a kingdom and priests to our God; and they will reign upon the earth"* (Revelation 5:10). So when Messiah's atonement redeemed us from the depravity of sin, it also restored us to the dignity of God's service.

As you trust in Messiah's perfect sacrifice, you grow in His priestly service. That is how your heart and home become *"a temple of the Holy Spirit who is in you, whom you have from God, and that you are not your own…. For you have been bought with a price: therefore glorify God in your body"* (1 Corinthians 6:19–20). This is our spiritual service to one another. Yeshua's recipients of grace through faith become God's instruments of grace by faith to others. All that is needed has been provided for us in Yeshua's atonement. That's why Paul urges us *"by the mercies of God, to present your bodies a living and holy sacrifice, acceptable to God, which is your spiritual service of worship"* (Romans 12:1). Perhaps the reason you're not adequately providing spiritual service to your spouse is you have not yet *"presented your bodies a living and holy sacrifice."*

Yes, the problem with a living sacrifice is that it keeps trying to crawl off the altar! Where you haven't presented yourself as a living and holy sacrifice is where you are not adequately ministering to your spouse. Remember, "the adequacy of the service of the priest was based on the sufficiency of the sacrifice of the priest." Only sacrificial service adequately ministers graciously and effectively to your spouse.

In God's economy, *ruling* in the home means *representing* Him from the heart. God loves His creation, and wants humanity to represent His love by affirming and appreciating all that He has made your spouse to be. We are called to do the cultivating, the tending, the serving, the keeping, and the guarding, just as the priests did in the tabernacle. In a redeemed home, we need to reject the idea that ruling is characterized by domination. Many people do not have a sense of comfort until they have control. We need to mature out of this mindset and begin to trust God and live by His priorities, learning to care for each other rather than try to control one another. But as servants of the Lord, our work identity is as His servant, not as the owner. We raise our kids as His managers and by His Word.

Before the curse (Genesis 3:17), humanity serves the land as priests, but after the curse, we serve the land as slaves. For the most part, we work as we did in the garden, but after the curse it becomes like slave labor rather than willingly serving the living God. This is how most of the world still views work today. However, the redeemed home is to be different from the world. Kids will learn how to be godly adults as they see their parents modeling values that are in contrast to the world's values. God's values must be seen for what they are—the baseline, the standard. Neither laziness[26] nor being a workaholic[27] is acceptable to God.

In the garden, God has a job, and people have a job. In Genesis 2:9, we see that God is the One who causes things in the garden to grow; He gives the increase. It is not Adam and Eve's job to figure out a way to force the plants to grow. No, God gives the increase. We see this principle in 1 Corinthians 3:6–7; we are to plant and to water, but it is God who gives the increase. Likewise, in marriage, husbands are not to try to grow their wives, nor are wives to try to change their husbands! Scripture does not tell us to train up our spouse in the way they should go. No, God grows wives and also grows husbands! They report to Him because they rest in Him.

So, what are we to do? We guard and serve our spouses as they develop, as God meant for them to grow. We encourage, care, affirm, and appreciate, thinking of ways to encourage in what God has called us to do together. Seek opportunities to bless your spouse and help them to grow. If your wife is interested in writing, encourage and help her in this, but leave it to God to give the increase.

We are called to love and appreciate our spouses for who they are. If you are growing apples but want potatoes, don't try to change the apples into potatoes.

---

26. "*If anyone is not willing to work, then he is not to eat, either*" (2 Thessalonians 3:10).
27. "*So there remains a Sabbath rest for the people of God*" (Hebrews 4:9).

Learn to love apples! Learn to adjust to the call of God, and *"run with endurance the race that is set before us"* (Hebrews 12:1). Embrace it! This is the calling of marriage.

God is the one who gifts and enables our spouses and our children. In the Bible, the Greek word *ektrepho* means "to nurture." But it is only used twice in the New Covenant and both times only for men; men are called to be the family nurturers, both to wives and children (Ephesians 5:29 and 6:4). In the Greek translation of the Tanakh, this word *nurture* is used in Genesis 45:7, as Joseph explains that what he did for his family was *"to keep you alive"* (*chayah*). That's what a husband and father does, as he lovingly rules his marriage and family by grace through faith in Messiah. We will look at this principle in greater depth later in our study. However, in Scripture, it is the husband's and dad's responsibility to nurture and develop others; this is the biblical leadership model. The leadership role is to nurture others as they grow in Messiah to all that God has created them to be in living out His image. Husbands serve their family, just as Adam first served the garden of God. If Adam did not do a good job with the garden, he could not be entrusted with the responsibility of a wife. However, if he was able to handle the garden, then perhaps he could be trusted with a wife. People are much more valuable than gardens.

Before we go further, let's take another *selah* here to better absorb what we've learned so far in this chapter. You might wish to spend time pondering on your own or discussing with your spouse what Shabbat means to you. Pause and reflect on God's purposes for humanity as seen in His creative work and rest. Consider the meaning of the word *covenant*, and what place covenant holds in your life. Do you have a clear vision of the spiritual nature of your marriage? Have you discovered the godly joy of serving others? Take a moment to think, and when you're ready, move on to the next section.

The Marriage Relationship Is Obedience, Not Arrogance

The LORD *God commanded the man, saying "From any tree of the garden you may eat freely; but from the tree of the knowledge of good and evil you shall not eat, for in the day that you eat from it you will surely die."* (Genesis 2: 16–17)

The third aspect of relationship is obedience (to God) and not arrogance (toward others). One reading this may be thinking, that's what I want—I want her (or him) to obey me! However, the real issue is your obedience to God, not your partner's obedience to you. Disobedience toward God is self-defeating arrogance.

In this text, the only restriction God places on Adam's freedom in the garden is to NOT eat from the tree of the knowledge of good and evil. Let's remember that, like all other trees that God has made, this tree is also *"good for food"* (2:9).

God's purposes and calling for His people include commanding what is best for them and prohibiting what is wrong for them in light of His calling for them. Thus, it's "*good for food*," but it's not food for you. This initial prohibition is now the foundation of all food laws, and every other prohibition. All wholesome relationships are based on trust and trustworthiness. God is teaching us how to order a home by His Word, by what He says. His gracious restriction reveals that seeking more than His provision is really sinful distrust in Him. The safest place to be is in the will of God; His Word is His will. When you transgress His Scripture, the home is now in grave danger. With that restriction come the awful consequences of disobedience, "*for in the day that you eat from it you will surely die*." The text uses an emphatic form of "die" (*mot tamuth*). "*You will surely die*," that is, absolutely die. Thus, "*The soul who sins will die*" (Ezekiel 18:4). The death that is referred to by "*you will surely die*" is two-fold: one death is by the effects and by the offense of sin. Though this may contradict some popularly held beliefs about death, death is not annihilation (i.e., cessation of existence), but rather, it is separation. As to the spiritual offense of sin, this death is immediate, and it is a spiritual death that separates from spiritual life. Being "*dead in your trespasses and sins*" (Ephesians 2:1) means that when you pray, "*your iniquities have made a separation between you and your God, and your sins have hidden His face from you so that He does not hear*" (Isaiah 59:2). This spiritual separation also takes place in a marriage when we offend one another. Certain aspects of a married couple's relationship (kids, in-laws, finances, etc.) become like a "dead zone" where the couple doesn't relate well. As with the Lord, forgiveness and repentance are needed to bring life back to sin-deadened souls.

The physical effects of sin, as with Adam and Eve, may not take effect for quite a while. Through sin, death entered into the human condition.[28] And so, as with the rest of humanity to follow, God solemnly says, "*For you are dust, and to dust you shall return*" (Genesis 3:19). But, as noted earlier, what happens upon physical death is not annihilation, but another separation. This physical death is a separation from physical life. But this is not the end of the soul of that person who physically died. For the believer in Yeshua, "*to be absent from the body... [is] to be at home with the Lord*" (2 Corinthians 5:8). Paul tells the Messianic community, "*My desire is to depart and be with Messiah, for that is very much better*" (Philippians 1:23 sn). It's not just "*better*," but "*much better*." But it's not just "*much better*," but "*very much better*"! You can see why God doesn't reveal more of the believer's glorious future—we couldn't stand to stay here away from the Lord! But for the non-believer in Messiah, physical death leads to their future judgment. "*It is appointed for men to die once and after this comes judgment*" (Hebrews 9:27). Physical death is not their final judgment, but their physical death leads to the

---

28. "*Therefore, just as through one man sin entered into the world, and death through sin, and so death spread to all men, because all sinned*" (Romans 5:12).

final judgment. And because their sin has already caused a spiritual offense that caused a separation from God, if they physically die in that spiritual separation from God, they will remain eternally separated from Him. "*Behold, now is the 'acceptable time,' behold, now is the day of salvation*" (2 Corinthians 6:2). Oh, "*seek the Lord while He may be found*" (Isaiah 55:6)! The situation for humanity is catastrophic, but not without divine remedy. God, being rich in mercy, promised the Messiah to die in your place! And what God promised, God provided, so that by faith in Him we are delivered out from death. His death paid for the offense of your sins, and His gift regenerates the effect of your sins.

Yeshua declared, "*Truly, truly, I say to you, he who hears My word, and believes Him who sent Me, has eternal life, and does not come into judgment, but has passed out of death into life*" (John 5:24). Now that's Good News for those who will believe.

Though there are quite deadly results of sin, we must not look upon this verse as if God is threatening Adam with murdering him unless he obeys God. No, it's not a threat at all; it is a warning. Love warns, and God is love. Love warns their beloved who is heading for a cliff (though you may be tempted to not say anything to an enemy who may likewise be heading for danger!). God knows that His Word is our wisdom for living, and that our obedience brings a blessed consequence for our lives, but also that disobedience brings certain dire consequences,[29] not merely for offending God, but for doing what is contrary to our own best-interests. God cares about our best interests, and His Word is a lamp unto our feet[30] to attaining what is eternally best for our lives.[31] Apart from God's Word, "*there is a way that seems right to a person, but that way leads to death.*"[32] Walking out of an open window only proves that the law of gravity works every time, whether you believe in gravity or not. So too, the "law of sin" also works consistently, whether you believe in God or not. Heed God's warnings, even if they may not make sense to you at first.

We can deceive ourselves by seeking shortcuts (i.e., like eating from the wrong tree) to try and gain discernment and wisdom from experiencing the knowledge of good and evil. We cannot gain true and godly wisdom from the *knowledge of evil*—that only leads to our spiritual corruption. Rather, true wisdom is only achieved from knowledge *and* obedience to God's Word. We gain wisdom by walking by faith and revering God. Proverbs 1:7 states, "*The fear of the Lord is the beginning of knowledge; fools despise wisdom and instruction.*" Similarly, Psalm 111:10 teaches us, "*the fear of the Lord is the beginning of wisdom; a good*

---

29. See Numbers 32:23, "*Be sure, your sin will find you out,*" and Ezekiel 18:4, "*The soul who sins will die.*"
30. Psalm 119:105.
31. See 2 Timothy 3:15.
32. Proverbs 14:12; see also Jeremiah 6:16; 17:9.

understanding have all those who do His commandments; His praise endures forever." These verses are meant to teach us that first and foremost, a right attitude towards God is necessary for true wisdom. Along with a right attitude towards God, we need consistent application of the Word as well: Strong teaching *"is for the mature, who because of practice have their senses trained to discern good and evil"* (Hebrews 5:14). Having your *"senses trained"* refers to the consistent application of God's Word in your daily married life; this produces godly discernment and wisdom for you and your spouse. God's restrictions are meant to protect us from unnecessary pain and misery! Trusting God and His Word is His way of life for you, your marriage, and for all humanity.

Godly standards

The Word teaches us how to manage our homes by God's standards and within certain parameters. We are free to make decisions within those parameters, but we are not to transgress them. When we disobey, we put our homes and relationships in danger, as we will sadly see in Genesis 3. Our loving homes are meant to reflect His loving standards. And yes, all of His holy standards are His loving help to you and to your family. Yeshua said the greatest commands are to love God and to love others, and that all the other commandments are tied to these.[33] Paul restates this as, *"Love fulfills all Torah"* (Romans 13:10 sn), for without God's love you miss the very heart of God's intention for you and your marriage in His Torah. Perhaps you were not brought up in a believing home, and the standards that your home lived under were contrary to what God teaches in the Scriptures. But you do not have to continue that way. Discipleship helps us to follow the Lord's biblical standards in our lives and in our homes. If you feel guilt because there are areas for you and your spouse that lack biblical standards, remember that God loves you. If the Holy Spirit is surfacing some area in your life and marriage that needs some attention, then thank Him. And rather than feel guilt, go to the Lord in prayer, thanking Him for the forgiveness in Messiah, and asking Him to help you and your spouse to grow a bit more in that area that He revealed.

Guilt is like a hot fire. When a hand gets too close, we immediately draw it away from the heat. So also, when we feel guilt, we tend to draw away from the law that makes us feel guilty. We already have a perfect "guilt offering" in Messiah! We need to simply repent (i.e., recognize and turn away from our bad attitudes and actions), by asking for God's help to outgrow our immaturity and grow into whatever area He has revealed. Through discipleship, we can learn together about His godly standards for the marriage and home, which you can then commit to as a couple. It's not your guilt, but your Scriptural commitments that should define you and your Messianic marriage as a temple of the Holy Spirit. Messiah redeems relationships as well as individuals, but having a Messianic marriage as a redeemed

---

33. Matthew 22:37–40.

relationship only works under the authority and blessing of His Word. Blessing? Yes, Yeshua said, *"If you know these things, you are blessed if you do them"* (John 13:17). The blessing is in the doing, not just the knowing, for Torah was given not only to be learned, but to be lived (Leviticus 18:5)!

This brings us back to the matter of Messianic discipleship, which is assumed in the Bible (Matthew 28:19). As a couple, discuss, memorize, and make a commitment to follow these foundational principles *together* in your home:

- *We will have no other gods before us.* What comes before God in your time, talent, and treasure? (See Matthew 4:8–10.) If not God, then who or what are you trusting for your security and significance as individuals and as a couple?
- *No idolatry.* As individuals and as a couple, what do you really depend on for your significance, satisfaction, and security? Career, appearance, wealth? (See Luke 12:15–21.) Do your possessions possess you?
- *We will honor His Name, and not take His name in vain.* Do our attitudes honor His name? (See 1 Corinthians 12:3.) What circumstances tempt us to dishonor His name with bad attitudes, lack of character, or vain imaginations? (See Psalm 14:1.)
- *Honor the Sabbath.* Is Yeshua, *"Lord even of the Sabbath"* (Mark 2:28), exalted by you as a couple in your worship and walk? As a couple, is there a congregation where you're committed to corporate worship? (See Luke 4:16.)
- *Honor your mother and father.* Are you both respectful of your parents and each other's parents in your hearts and as well as with your speech and activities—despite their parental and personal shortcomings? (See Matthew 15:3–6.)
- *No murder.* Yeshua said that hating others is heart murder. (See Matthew 5:21–22.) Have you forgiven those (even your spouse) who have offended you, based on Messiah's death for those offenses? Or are you waiting for their "proper apology" first? Since Messiah's death is for all sins (against God and against you), your forgiveness of the offender frees you from the *"root of bitterness"* from the offense. Their apology can never heal the past hurt they caused, nor be adequate recompense for your hurt; that's only adequately addressed through Yeshua's sacrifice for those sins. Their apology is their reconciliation with you.
- *No adultery.* Are you both committed to no flirting, to not excusing other people's adulterous affairs (even celebrities), and to not indulging in any pornographic entertainment? (See Matthew 5:27–28.)
- *No stealing.* Are you stealing from God, or are you both committed to tithing? (See Malachi 3:10–11.) Are you shortchanging each other on time

spent together? If you have children, are you spending time with each child, and as a family?

- *No lying.* Are you both committed to truth telling? (See 1 John 2:21.) Do you speak "*the truth in love*" (Ephesians 4:15), or do you use "the truth" as an excuse to hurt others? (Gossipers always use their understanding of the truth to speak about others not in the room.) Or, do you use "love" as an excuse to lie to others? Remember: truth without love isn't truth; love without truth isn't love. Do you believe that a lack of wisdom (not knowing what to say) justifies telling falsehoods? Can you agree as a couple that a lack of wisdom in what to say or not to say is understandable, but it's not justifiable?

- *No coveting* (greediness; desiring something or someone that isn't yours). Are you content, appreciative, and thankful to God for what you have? Or do you desire other things or people? (See Joshua 7:1, 19–22; Philippians 4:11–13; Colossians 3:5; 1 Timothy 6:5–11.) Do you call your dissatisfaction with where you're at and with what you have "ambition" to justify your lusts and greed? Can you, as a couple, trust God to give the increase as you walk with Him in humility and thankfulness?

Although these would be great discussions to have during the first phase of the dating process, in whatever stage you are now, you can discuss these matters to grow together as a Messianic couple. Remember, it is essential to begin practicing God's Word in your home, because God is always going to deal with your home as if you were. He doesn't adjust to your unscriptural standards, but calls each of us to adjust by grace through faith in Yeshua to His standards. Thus, together, we "*press on toward the goal for the prize of the upward call of God in Yeshua the Messiah*" (Philippians 3:14 SN). If you are not walking in the truth, then you are not walking with or following after the Messiah, but in fact you're walking away from Him. The blessing of God is going to be found where His Word is honored. When you trust the Lord, you will trust what He has to say about life, and this will be seen by your application of God's truth in your home.[34]

Once you begin applying the Ten Commandments, you will find there are many other practical applications throughout Scripture for your lives, marriage, and family life. For example, the book of Ephesians chapters 4–5 have much to say about our unity in Messiah. You may have already discovered that marital unity doesn't happen merely from sharing the same last name. And practical application is what the Bible is all about![35] The Bible teaches us that "*all Scripture is*" both "*inspired*" and "*profitable*" (2 Timothy 3:16). It's just as profitable as it is inspired. If you doubt its profitability, you therefore doubt its inspiration. You may ask

---

34. Once again, John 13:17 and James 1:22 seem suitable to consider on this matter, though this is covered a little further along.

35. See Exodus 18:20 on the essential need for application to what the Scripture teaches.

yourself, "Am I expected to follow the entire Bible?" What do you think? *Of course!* As we mature, we implement the Scriptures more and more, because we learn that blessings are found in the doing. This is why Yeshua said in John 13:17, *"If you know these things, you are blessed if you do them."* Think about that. You can't *"do"* these things unless you *"know"* the Scriptures, but knowing the Scriptures is only half of the story—and not the better half. It is the implementation of Scriptural truth that blesses the believing couple, not just knowing about it. Putting the Word into practice is what makes the great difference in anyone's life and family.

Even if you and your spouse are committed to walking in Scriptural truth, any and every marriage can be improved and should be continuing to grow in Messiah. Continue on, and continue to repent of all *"the little foxes that are ruining the vineyards"* (Song of Solomon 2:15)! Repentance is a lifestyle for all of us, since we all are called to *"grow in the grace and knowledge of our Lord"* (2 Peter 3:18). Yeshua *"must increase"* and we *"must decrease"* (John 3:30). We repent of any area of our lives, marriage, and attitudes that does not reveal the image of God. We can all find spiritual improvement as we repent and press on to the mark of our high marital calling living out God's image. If your marriage has only been obedient to the Lord on Shabbat morning, well, that's a start; let's *"not despise the day of small things"*![36] Don't seek short cuts, but now commit together to move on to glorifying the Lord throughout the rest of the week—taking it one day at a time. We want to keep growing this way because this will create a spiritually healthier marriage, which will also make for a healthier home and society.

The Marriage Relationship Is Teamwork, Not Solo Work

Then the Lord God said, "It is not good [lo tov] for the man to be alone; I will make him a helper suitable for him." (Genesis 2:18–22)

What's wrong with this picture? As we noted, up until Genesis 2:18, all is well; everything has been, *"Tov, tov, tov, tov, tov, tov,"* (good) and *"tov me'od"* (very good)! Yes, Adam is busy at work (2:15), and even studying God's Word (2:16–17), and though life is good enough for Adam, it is not good according to God, for in 2:18, God states, *"no good!"* If God had not said it, Adam would not have known it.

Since there is no sin to "foul the waters," why does it suddenly become *"lo tov"* (no good) to God? What went wrong? Nothing! Because relationship is intrinsic to God's nature, He knows that Adam is incomplete without someone suitable to *relate to*. We may be tempted to think "God is enough for me." Because of past traumatic relationships, people may think it's safer not to be involved in a committed relationship. And because of past congregational problems they may not want to be a "joiner," as a member of a local body of believers. It is not uncommon

---

36. Zechariah 4:10.

to hear believers say, "It's just me and the Lord. I've got Him, and I don't need anyone else!" However, such a position is unbiblical!

What does God mean when He says, "*it is not good*"? Since God is good in every way, God knows what is good, and He has already affirmed creation as good seven times in Genesis 1, and that the food is good for eating. So, when it is not good, that means it is not useful, beneficial, or appropriate for His purposes.

In light of God's plan, it's not good for God that man is alone. His purpose for humanity is left unfulfilled if man is alone. It's not good for the world that man is alone. The world was created for humanity to rule, but humanity is to rule as a couple. Man cannot fulfill His calling alone. Everything was planned on there being two of them, not just one:

- His proposal is that *they*, not just *he*, should rule (Genesis 1:26)
- His own nature necessitates that there be two genders, not one (Genesis 1:27)
- His blessing is for *them*, not just *him* (Genesis 1:28)
- His provision of food is for both of them ("*you*" is plural), not just one (Genesis 1:29)
- Even His identity of "*man*" is as a couple, not just as a man (Genesis 5:2)

The creation of woman is for the good of man, God, and the world. But what does it mean to be "*alone*"? "Alone" (*l'vado*) is not merely solitude, but it is to be apart, isolated—and it can lead to an alienated society. This Hebrew phrase is used for an army "*straggler*" (Isaiah 14:31), and a "*lonely*" bird on a housetop (Psalm 102:7). Do you think of yourself as a self-contained person, needing no one else? Perhaps you're more like the prophet's description of the fortified city that is alone, abandoned, and deserted, like the desert (Isaiah 27:10). Have you been cast aside? God understands, for this word is used for the abandonment of the leper by the community (Leviticus 13:46). But remember, Yeshua came to cleanse and restore you. Often, this word is used for God's uniqueness, as in "*who alone works wonders*" (Psalm 72:18). Yes, it is lonely at the top. But then, that's why the perfect and fully self-sustaining God created humanity according to His likeness. The perfect God of love created us for fellowship with Himself.

Therefore, it is no good for people to be alone from others; it is no good for couples to be isolated from the congregation; it is no good for families to be secluded from community; it is no good for communities to be isolated from the larger society; and it is no good for countries to be isolated from the other nations of the world.[37]

---

37. It's true that this Hebrew word is used to describe Israel as "*apart*" from the nations (Numbers 23:9; Micah 7:14), but this is not haughtiness. It is a holy calling and identity to be God's "*special treasure*" (*segullah*, Deuteronomy 14:2). This requires of them that they reach out to the other nations. This word is also used when Israel is "*apart*" from God as a judgment (Lamentations 1:1),

But "alone" in and of itself isn't the real problem. The verb "to be" (*heyot*) is an infinitive construct; that is, "to be" qualifies "alone" as a norm. Solitude for a time is important as well; especially alone time with the Lord. But a person should not remain alone as a lifestyle. Thus, Paul writes that solitude should be "*for a time, so that you may devote yourselves to prayer*" (1 Corinthians 7:5), but the healthy lifestyle for God's people is in community with others.

Marriage is especially important to God, but not as a substitute for, or to the exclusion of, the whole of human society. Instead, it is the foundation of any wholesome community. Appreciation of others is tied to our appreciation of the God who provides others to develop together a healthy community to His glory. This becomes God's priority for all humanity. Our condition remains "no good" until we "love one another."

Ezer kenegdo

God also said, "*I will make him a helper suitable for him*" (Genesis 2:18).[38] The Hebrew word *ezer* is from the common word for "help," or "helper" (i.e., Ezra), found throughout the Scriptures. The Hebrew word *kenegdo* is only used in Genesis 2:18 and 20, referring to what would be indispensable in a life-mate for Adam. *Kenegdo* is made up of the prepositional *ke*, meaning "like," and *negdo*, literally meaning "opposite him" (Joshua 5:13; 6:5, etc.). Together these words mean "like his opposite" or "according to his opposite," indicating woman would have a role beside the man as his "complementary co-worker." English translations such as "suitable for," "matching," and "corresponding to" all capture the idea. While the translation "partner" accurately emphasizes equality between the man and woman, it doesn't reflect the aspect of similarity and suitability in relating well to him. Thus, there is in *kenegdo* an emphasized equality because of the man's assumed leadership initiative later in the text (2:24). Paul states that Adam is in a leadership role because of "seniority," for God made him first (1 Timothy 2:13), but he is only to be a first among equals, possessing neither inferiority nor superiority.

The intrinsic likeness implicit in *kenegdo* has good reason. There are many animals around Adam, so "*it is not good for the man to be alone*" means apart from others of his own species. He needs someone to be a helper to him in his calling to represent God as God's image.[39] Since woman too was created in the image of

---

because they lost their sense of calling and holy identity and tried to be like the other nations.

38. As another reminder of the mystery of God's nature, God doesn't say, "It is not good for you to be alone." He says, "*It is not good for the man to be alone*." He's not talking to Adam but about Adam. But whom is He talking to? This is one of three places in the creation account where God talks about someone, but it's not mentioned to whom He is speaking (1:26; 2:18; 3:22). He is talking to Himself, that is, conferring within Himself—within His own counsel. This is further recognized by the rabbis who translated the text into Greek (the Septuagint). They translate the Hebrew "*I will make* [for] *him*" (*eh'eh'se lo*) with the Greek *poi'aisomen auto* that means, "We will make for him." It's seen that God is conferring with Himself.

39. *Talmud*, Yevamot 62b, "no good.... he is also incomplete…and he even impairs the Divine

Two • The Process for Marriage

God (1:27), she too has "*the breath of life*" (2:7). Humanity is unique among all of God's creation; as man is unique, so too, she is unique. As he was created in God's image to relate to God, and in His likeness to represent God, so too must she properly relate to and represent God. As Adam was created to serve and guard, so must she be able to serve and guard. As he must obey God's Word, so must she obey God's Word. The woman must have "*the image of God*" by "*the breath of life*" to help Adam in this unique calling of representing God by ruling creation on Adonai's behalf—and that must be accomplished through their children (see 1:28 above).[40] That's why the marriage relationship is teamwork and not a solo work, and certainly not a solo work when it comes to procreation and training up godly children![41]

God recognizes that it's time for step two in His program for humanity: woman. But how is God going to bring the man to recognize the woman? Interdependence is a hard concept to grasp, especially if you think you have been doing quite well on your own. There may be some people that have an aversion to intimacy and close relationships because of traumatic events in their past. "Alone" may seem like the better alternative to their past pain. And people may get used to being alone, as well.

But independence can be quite difficult too. God allowed man to briefly experience life without a woman to more fully appreciate the joy of having a helpmeet. He experienced work alone, obedience to Torah alone, and naming the animals alone—there was no one to share in his work, no one to fellowship in the Word, and no one to rule and name the animals with him. He was created to serve God together with her, to study God's Word together, and to rule together.

Drawing from a famous chapter on love (1 Corinthians 13), let's apply its theme to this portion: without love my service is vain, for true service builds up others. Without love, all Torah study is vain, for if I am only wise for myself, my wisdom is vain; I am only truly wise when I help another. If I interact with nature, I appreciate it doubly through another's eyes. Without love, I am nothing.

And so, God through marriage is calling Adam to a new phase of living out the image of God, by loving others as he has been loved by God. God must educate Adam on the unique importance of the woman to properly fulfill his creation calling and his life.

---

likeness" (Soncino, Bereshit, on Genesis 2:18).

40. *Talmud*, Yevamoth 61b, Mishnah., "A man shall not abstain from the performance of the duty of the propagation of the race unless he already has children." Zero population growth is not a biblical or traditional idea.

41. Malachi 2:15: "*Did the One not make her with a remnant of Ruach? Then what is the One seeking? Offspring of God!*" (TLV). For more on this matter of raising godly children, please see the appendix. Though our hearts break for the single parents that need to shoulder both jobs in raising their children in godliness, we're also greatly encouraged by those single parents who find God's grace as sufficient for their vital calling.

What's In a Name?

Because people are unique among God's creation, the marriage relationship is also unique. But humanity was required to personally evaluate and identify the rest of creation to fully comprehend our uniqueness. The divinely created human relationship uniquely fulfills our highest stewardship calling. The Messianic marriage reveals and represents the divine image of God.

> *Out of the ground the* LORD *God formed every beast of the field and every bird of the sky, and brought them to the man to see what he would call them; and whatever the man called a living creature, that was its name.* (Genesis 2:19)

Man can relate to the rest of creation because God created both humanity and animal life "*out of the ground.*" So, though humanity is unique—and though marriages are unique—there is no room for sinful pride, since—in some physical ways—we're no better than any other creature. As Adam interacts with nature, his pre-sin human humility reveals the very One who would humble Himself to interact with and intercede for a fallen humanity.

To fulfill his calling as ruler over the earth, God brings[42] every creature that He had formed[43] to Adam for naming. Being *ha'adam* (literally "the ground," as he was made from the ground) makes Adam perfect for the responsibility of ruling over God's other creatures. Though not having the breath of life and God's spirit, they too are creatures with a soul,[44] so they have certain personality traits that we can relate to, and them to us.

The phrase "*to see what he would call them*" refers to God's desire to see what the man would call the animals, relative to himself.[45] The verb "*to see*" not only means to see visually or observe, but to understand or evaluate (Genesis 8:8; 1 Kings 9:12) or to perceive truth (Deuteronomy 29:4; Matthew 13:17). The naming would show God whether Adam recognizes that he is indeed alone, and by "twos" Adam would understand and appreciate that a pair is not a threat for the individual's fulfillment, but a means to express greater fulfillment in God. In seeing the pair of animals, Adam would also notice the complementary gender identities of

---

42. This phrase "*brought them*" was a work of God that He would also do with Noah (Genesis 6:20; 7:9), and in bringing the woman to Adam (Genesis 2:22).
43. This is done on the fourth (birds) and fifth (land animals) days of creation. So, the Hebrew perfect is to be understood as "*which He had formed.*"
44. The Hebrew word for "soul" is *nephesh*, translated as "creature" (Genesis 1:20–21) or "life" (Genesis 1:30) in most English versions. But the point of the Scriptures is that these creatures have a soul. You may have noticed that two dogs of the same breed and litter have different personalities, which is noticed and appreciated by their owners.
45. "*To see what he would call them*" in Hebrew actually includes the word *lo*, "to himself"—that is, God wants to see what the man would name them "to himself." He would name them relative to himself. His naming would indicate what they are in relationship to himself, just as we call some people friend, father, or mom—all "named" relative to ourselves.

each—that one is made for the other. And too, though each species might have its own distinct soul (or personality), he would also see differences within the species between the male and the female. Even here, Adam would see that they are complementary in God's will.[46]

Adam names the animal in light of it being a *nephesh chayah* (living soul). He names it relative to its *nephesh*, its inner being—not merely as to its outward appearance, but as a fellow creature with a soul. Since this is pre-sin, there are no predators or prey animals. Fear and lust are not a component of their beings, as will happen after the fall of man. They too will be subjected to futility with all creation. So, Adam can truly understand their purpose, value, and worth as fellow creatures.

In marriage, certain names reflect the spouse's consideration and sense of intimacy with their other half, i.e., "Lover," "Honey," "Dear," and "Sweetie." Others do not use these names, precisely because they represent personal and intimate acceptance of one another. Relationships that grow distant may reveal their growing alienation by the formalizing of each other's names, referring to each other using their first names, as their friends do.

As God's representative, Adam has an additional dimensional component—he has what no other mere creature has—the spiritual connection with God via "*the breath of life*" (2:7). Adam will also see that as a human, he is qualitatively different from all animal life. This spiritual connection to God makes humanity fit to represent God to His creation and to rule the world on God's behalf. By naming each animal, he is now demonstrating his authority over that creature.[47] As God calls the names of the larger inanimate creations in the universe as their Lord,[48] so man names the relatively smaller animate creatures on the earth as their ruler. Rulership is demonstrated by naming what is under your divine stewardship, whether it is Fido or Belteshazzar (aka Daniel).[49] Adam will initially call his wife "*Woman*" relative to himself (2:23), but in an act of forgiveness and hope after the fall, he renames her Eve (*Chavah*, "life") "*because she was the mother of all the living*" (Genesis 3:20). In his naming her "*Woman*" and renaming her "*Eve*," he is exercising his leadership authority. Both before and after the fall, Adam is still the head of the home. His failure doesn't nullify his call to leadership in the home, nor does it today for us.[50]

---

46. Indeed, many males are named differently than females in Hebrew: bull (*shor*) and he-goat (*tayish*); cow (*parah*) and she goat (*ez*); Rooster, hen, etc.
47. Psalm 8:4–6: "*What is man that You take thought of him, and the son of man that You care for him? Yet You have made him a little lower than God, and You crown him with glory and majesty! You make him to rule over the works of Your hands; You have put all things under his feet.*"
48. Genesis 1:5, 8, 10: "*God called the light day, and the darkness He called night…. God called the expanse heaven…. God called the dry land earth, and the gathering of the waters He called seas.*"
49. The Babylonians demonstrated their authority over their Judean captives by renaming them with Babylonian names (Daniel 1:6–7).
50. First Peter 3:1–6.

In addition to demonstrating Adam's rulership, he would understand each creature in relationship to his humanity, and thereby see if any might be a suitable helper. It may be that a dog is man's best friend, but not the best choice to fulfill God's purpose for the man. So, too, in regard to marriage—until you recognize your divine purpose, you may not recognize the right spouse for you.[51]

The man gave names to all the cattle, and to the birds of the sky, and to every beast of the field, but for Adam there was not found a helper suitable for him. (Genesis 2:20)

The verb in the phrase "*the man gave names*" is now past tense. The momentous naming process is over. And now the overarching purpose is seen in the poignant result: "*But for Adam there was not found a helper suitable for him.*" By naming the animals, Adam realizes that no other creature is fit to be his *ezer kenegdo*—that is, his proper helper, counterpart, and true co-leader. Before God creates woman, Adam first has to recognize for himself his need for a life partner. Often, God brings in help only when we see the need for such help. Because he now recognizes his need for her, he now can appreciate the gift of her. As aforementioned, our interdependence with one another is based on recognized need for one another. Have you forgotten as a married couple that you actually need each other? If you've forgotten your need for each other, it's because you've first forgotten God's purpose for your life that reveals the need for your spouse.[52] Adam now sees that in light of his calling 1) yes, it's not good for man to be alone, and 2) nothing thus far created can be the partner he needs. He is now ready for God to provide the good partner. God reveals all this to Adam as Adam handles his routine responsibilities by naming the animals. God's great purpose is worked out through our ordinary responsibilities. How can I find Mr. Right or Miss Right? As you serve God through your normal stewardship responsibilities. If it's in God's will, He will show what's there and what's not there. And then, in His purpose for you, He will bring about what you need to fulfill His calling for you.[53]

The Forming of the Woman

*So the L*ORD *[HaShem] God caused a deep sleep to fall upon the man, and he slept; then He took one of his ribs and closed up the flesh at that place. The L*ORD *[HaShem] God fashioned into a woman the rib which He had taken from the man, and brought her to the man.*
(Genesis 2:21–22)

---

51. Ecclesiastes 4:8–12.
52. Sin is seen as utterly sinful when Adam, who initially appreciates the woman as God's gift (Genesis 2:23), blames the woman for his sin, and indirectly blames God as well (Genesis 3:12).
53. "Faithful is He who calls you, and He also will bring it to pass" (1 Thessalonians 5:24). "*I can do all things through Him who strengthens me.... And my God will supply all your needs according to His riches in glory in the Messiah Yeshua*" (Philippians 4:13, 19 SN).

Two • The Process for Marriage

For the tenth and eleventh—and final—time in this chapter, the covenant name of God, HaShem, is used in these two verses.[54] From the creation of the male in 2:7 through the presentation of the female to the male in 2:22, God's covenant faithfulness is emphasized to stress the enduring covenant relationship of the marriage between the male and the female and God. It is this threefold bond that Solomon states gives marriage its lasting strength.[55] If your marriage bond does not include God as the binding agent, then the marriage could be one trial away from dissolution.

"*So the* LORD [HaShem] *God caused a deep sleep to fall upon the man, and he slept; then He took one of his ribs…*" (2:21). Adam unconditionally trusts HaShem, the covenant-making and covenant-keeping God. By faith, he so submits to God that God can cause Adam to fall into a deep sleep[56] Therefore, Adam is unconscious of what God is doing, and he sacrificially gives of himself, trusting that God, being faithful and good, will give back something better than what Adam gave.

Like Job, we may want the whys and the wherefores of all the challenges of life, but we must walk by faith, trusting in God's goodness to have all things "*work together for good.*" In the Messianic marriage, the basic requirement is faith in God—not in each other! God provides the love for your spouse by faith (Romans 5:5). Lack of faith in God undermines your love for each other and makes that "first love" a mere fading memory.

Can we trust God with what we don't understand? Is our lack of understanding the reason we don't trust God? For the woman to thrive, the male has to provide a sacrifice without his comprehension of exactly what is happening. In this regard, our trusting submission to God enables us to "*be subject to one another*" (Ephesians 5:21), so that the wife can trust God in submission to her husband. He can lay down his life for his wife as a living sacrifice, that she may be blessed and benefited in God's purpose for her (Ephesians 5:22–27). No great work of God has ever been accomplished without sacrifice. According to Yeshua, marriage is a work of God, for "*what therefore God has joined together, let no man separate*" (Matthew 19:6). His marriage calling reveals the intrinsic trust in God and unselfishness required for all healthy human relationships. God's work in our life and marriage is generally without our comprehension or even consciousness of what He's doing[57] Faith is not knowing what He is doing, but trusting that He knows what He's doing, and that, because He is good, all things will "*work together for good*" (Romans 8:28).

---

54. Genesis 2:4, 5, 7, 8, 9, 15, 16, 18, 19, 21, 22.
55. Ecclesiastes 4:12.
56. As with Abram in Genesis 15:12. But, although Abram received God's vision in his sleep, Adam didn't receive his vision (of Eve) until he awoke!
57. In our fruitfulness (Mark 4:26–27); in our labors (Ecclesiastes 8:17); in our regeneration (John 3:7–8;) and in our resurrection, 1 Corinthians 15:35–38.

The purpose of our physical possessions is to produce and edify others.[58] In marriage, what you have as a couple is to be used to help one another. To have separate possessions, separate bank accounts, separate vacations, and separate social lives amounts to separate lives, insulating you from your spouse. Whatever Adam possessed, he had it to give for the life and blessing of his wife.

The Hebrew word *tsela*,[59] rendered as "rib" in verses 2:21–22, is translated "side" (or "chamber") in every other usage.[60] God evidently creates Adam with that "extra" rib, not needed for his physical functioning nor hindering him previously, but essential for his calling and for the woman's creation. In other words, God has created the man with elements that will only be meaningful if used for the sake of others. In the same way, though we are complete in Messiah (Colossians 2:10), we have within us elements that do not hinder us, but do not help us until they are used to bless others, and especially and more profoundly are intended to minister to our spouse for our greater fulfillment. Created in God's image, you have His love, which will only fulfill you when you love your spouse.

The phrase "*The Lord [HaShem] God fashioned into a woman the rib which He had taken from the man*" (2:22) informs us that God literally "built" (*banah*),[61] that is, constructed using Adam's rib, for the purpose of making a wife. The Hebrew phrase that is here translated "*into a woman*" (*l'ishah*), is used fifty-three times, and each time it is translated as "for a wife" to some man. The purpose of the *ezer kenegdo* is therefore realized in the wife. Wife is her position; *ezer kenegdo* is the substance of what it means to be a wife—a helper counterpart.

Your purpose is not found in yourself (your gender, desires, etc.). Your purpose is found and fulfilled in a wholesome relationship with others. Though marriage is often disparaged in secular society, it is honored by the Lord. Just as the highest calling for Israel was as the wife of HaShem,[62] and the highest calling of Messianic believers is to be the Bride of Messiah,[63] so also, the highest calling of a woman is to be the godly wife of a godly man, and the highest calling of a man is to be the godly husband of a godly woman.[64]

The fact that God brings woman out from a man's side is significant. As Matthew Henry has noted,

---

58. First John 3:17.
59. The other word for "rib" is *ala* in Daniel 7:5.
60. Exodus 25:12, 14; 26:20, 26–27, 35; 27:7; 30:4; 36:25, 31–32; 37:3, 5, 27; 38:7; 2 Samuel 16:13; 1 Kings 6:5, 8, 15–16, 34; 7:3; Ezekiel 41:5–9, 11, 26.
61. In the phrase "*Unless the Lord [HaShem] builds the house, they labor in vain who build it*" (Psalm 127:1), we see the development of God's construction project, the home. He takes a *ben* ("a son") and a *baht* ("a daughter") and "builds" (*banah*) a *bayit* ("house"). So, unless God builds the home, it is just a vain effort.
62. Isaiah 54:5; Hosea 2:19–20.
63. Second Corinthians 11:2; Ephesians 5:25–27; Revelation 19:7–9; 21:2, 9.
64. Ephesians 5:21–22.

Two • The Process for Marriage

> The woman was made of a rib out of the side of Adam; not made out of his head to rule over him, nor out of his feet to be trampled upon by him, but out of his side to be equal with him, under his arm to be protected, and near his heart to be beloved.[65]

All this takes place between Genesis 1:26 and 1:27. Through the creation of woman, we are to see each other as equals. The Hebrew word used in 2:21 for God "closed it" (*sagar*) is used for shutting or closing a gate or door, expressing a sense of completion. For man, creation takes one verse (2:7); for woman it takes five verses (2:18–22), as the careful completion of a project, lest your labor be in vain. The man is unique in his creation. The woman is also unique because of God's careful process of creating her: His declaration (v. 18), comparison (vv. 19–20), and operation (vv. 21–22). Taken from the unique creature "man" and thus having his human DNA and the breath of life, woman will thereby share his unique identity as made in God's likeness and image. The construction of the wife is the completion of the husband.[66]

Yet, the rib from man is constructed into the woman apart from him. She is built outside the man, made independently from him. She has individuality apart from man. Her life as wife to the man is by her consent. Since we're created in God's image with free will, all godly relationships are by consent, or they're not godly. Her individual purpose is to be his wife, but not apart from her free consent to the marriage. Every aspect of God's purpose for your life is to know the Lord and make Him known, but that purpose is not forced by God on anyone. By the individual's consent of faith we trust and follow the Messiah. The decision to marry is made by faith in the Lord and is therefore a consensual choice between man and woman. Adam gives of himself in order to gain for himself. God too gives of Himself to gain for Himself. How? In providing for Adam a wife, God gives up undivided fellowship with Adam.[67] Ultimately, God gives up His Son of His own volition, and the Messiah gives up His life to gain us.[68]

Verse 2:22 ends, *"And brought her to the man."*[69] As with the animals, which are caused by God to be brought to the man (v. 19), so it is with the woman. The animals are brought to him to see what they will be called in relation to him. The woman is brought to relate to man as a wife. As Adam comes to see that none of the animal kingdom could be a suitable partner for him, so he now gets to see for himself that this gift of God is his perfect match in marriage. Remember

---

65. Matthew Henry, *Matthew Henry's Commentary on the Whole Bible* (First published 1710).
66. The Bible consistently teaches that we are interdependent. Cf. 1 Corinthians 11:11.
67. First Corinthians 7:32–34: *"One who is unmarried is concerned about the things of the Lord, how he may please the Lord; but one who is married is concerned about the things of the world, how he may please his wife, and his interests are divided."*
68. Isaiah 53:10–12; John 3:16; John 10:17–18.
69. From God bringing the woman to the man developed the wedding custom of the father giving away the bride.

that, pre-sin, they simply trusted God's grace without resistance to have a fulfilling relationship with each other. But post-fall, there is personal resistance to God that is seen in troubled marriages. His grace has not changed. We need to trust in the Lord to have His grace for our marriages. Faith is still the victory in Messiah. Woman's fulfillment as a person, like Adam's fulfillment, is that together they will make a family and develop a community for a God-revealing society.

Functional subordination

We can wrongly think that the calling upon the woman to be an *ezer kengedo*, a counterpart helper, is the same as being inferior. Thus, the issue of *functional subordination* continually comes up in the Scriptures. In order for society to work well, there needs to be functional subordination.[70] For example, if a police officer tells you to stop, it is wrong to challenge him on the basis of how much Scripture he knows or how much money he makes. Because he says stop, you stop! Why? Because you are functionally subordinate to the government.

All of society works this way. It does not mean the police officer is better than you. (However, if you have a problem with self-esteem, you may feel threatened by anyone who is in a position of authority over you. This is an issue that would benefit from counseling.) The fact that a wife is asked to be subordinate to her husband is for the proper working of society, not because he is better than she is. Just as with the Father and the Son, Yeshua's functional subordination to the Father does not mean the Father is better than the Son. Yeshua said, "*I and the Father are one*" (John 10:30). Messiah is the supreme example of functional subordination for the proper working of life. Between men and women, men are not better than women. Husbands are not better than wives. The woman was created from Adam's side to demonstrate our intrinsic equality. Biblically, a wife is to make herself functionally subordinate to her husband. Meanwhile, the husband is subordinate to Messiah. Husbands are to use their God-given authority for the welfare and protection of wives. Use of that authority for self-serving purposes is abuse of power. We are partners as we work together in the Lord.

Some questions to help apply these teachings

1. In what ways do you see yourself as a spiritual being?

2. What feeds and develops you spiritually? (See 1 Timothy 4:6; 2 Timothy 3:16–17; 1 Peter 2:2)

---

70. This reality in society also reflects the nature of God. Cf. 1 Corinthians 15:28.

Two • The Process for Marriage

3. How often do you spiritually feed and exercise?

4. What are some ways your wife (and kids) are more mature and secure from your leadership?

5. What are some ways you're developing your family in Messiah?

6. Men, are you setting the biblical standards and non-negotiables in the home? What are they?

7. Have you worked out with your wife the spiritual values of the home? What are they?

8. What spiritual commitments do you share together?

9. Do you realize your spiritual need for your spouse as much now as when you were first married?

10. How often have you told your spouse that you spiritually need her/him?

CHAPTER THREE

Foundational Priorities in Messianic Marriage

Genesis 2:22–25

Let us recap what we have covered so far: Genesis 1 and 2 provide the foundation for Messianic marriage. In chapter 1, we looked at the *principles* for the foundation of Messianic marriage. In chapter 2, we looked at *preparation* for the foundation of Messianic marriage. In this chapter we will now look at the *priorities* in the foundation of Messianic marriage.

We are created in God's image to represent Him, chiefly by relating well to others who are in His image. We represent Him best as we love one another. We are called to minister to others and not to be centered on our own identity. The principles of marriage are the basic principles for all of society and community, and vice versa. Just as God is intrinsically relational in His own nature, man was created in God's image for the purpose of representing Him and relating well to others. Loving others involves risk by making ourselves vulnerable. Adam first has to realize his need for another human being. Once the man understands his need, God creates woman from Adam's side, for God's purposes. The goal of creating two and not one is seen in both marriage and community (2:22). The purpose is to relate to others, and relating well is the fulfillment of that purpose. In Genesis 2:23–25 we will consider the foundational priorities that express that fulfilled purpose.

The Marriage Relationship Is Appreciation, Not Toleration
The Appreciator of Suitability

The Lord God fashioned into a woman the rib which He had taken from the man, and brought her to the man. The man said, "This is now bone of my bones, and flesh of my flesh; She shall be called Woman, because she was taken out of Man." (Genesis 2:22–23)

When Adam first lays eyes on Eve, he exclaims, "This one at last!" In other words, he feels God has done it just right. So, appreciating your spouse tops the priority list. We clearly see this in verse 23, but we cannot overlook what it says in verse 22. Who gave the woman to the man? God did! The truth is your spouse is perfectly suited just for you.

1. Authority: appreciate God's sovereignty over you

First of all, Adam's appreciation of Eve is basically appreciation of God, the Giver of all good gifts. To appreciate your wife, you must first appreciate the Giver of your wife, the Lord God. The man appreciates that God has prepared him as a spiritual being whose life is dependent upon God (2:7). He appreciates that he was created to serve God through his vocation as God's representative on the job (2:15). The man further appreciates that God's Word is his guidance and parameters to live the life God created him to live (2:16–17). He appreciates as well that "*it is not good for the man be alone*" to fulfill God's creation calling for his life (2:18). He appreciates that nothing else in creation can be a suitable partner for him other than the woman that God created (2:19–22). This appreciation of God is foundational to man's appreciation of the woman. If he loses appreciation for the woman, it is because the man first lost his appreciation for the God who created and provided her.

Secondly, for a man to properly appreciate his spouse, he must first understand that the husband is called by God to be the spiritual leader in the home. If he will not accept his role as a spiritual leader in the home, he will thereby be relinquishing that role to his wife, and he will never understand or appreciate her from God's point of view. The Bible comments that this is because the man was created first.[1] Remember, though, as we have already studied, true leadership is not selfish domination, but selfless service. In a redeemed home, the husband's leadership, like God's leadership in the pre-sin world of Genesis 1, is seen as affirmation, encouragement, and appreciation; therefore, the husband can be called the "appreciator of suitability," as exemplified in Genesis 2:23. His appreciation of God orients him to properly appreciate his wife from God's point of view and therefore for God's fulfilling purpose for his life. Once more, if the husband loses his appreciation of God, he'll forget why his marriage is still relevant for him and lose appreciation for his wife.

The basis to marital unity is seeing your spouse as the Lord's key earthly provision for your life. Many think that gaining a spouse is like buying a suit. "It's all right in general, but it needs to be tailored to fit me!" They attempt to alter their partner to be what they think will fit them. "Too much talking here, not smart enough there. Too lazy here, not expressing their love there." This is all wrong. You don't get married to change your spouse, but to appreciate who your spouse is. God has called the couple together to rule. For God's will, he and she are perfect and therefore perfect for each other. Accepting your spouse for who that person is and not for who you want that person to be reflects your faith in the Lord and your appreciation of the God who provides for your life. If a person had a desire to be a pro-basketball player but never grew tall enough to play the game professionally, what do they do, buy stilts? "No," they would wisely say, "I'll

---

1. First Timothy 2:13.

give up basketball, and do what I'm made to do with the height I have." Or with the spouse I have, for Father knows best!

Couples can at times think that they're incompatible. Incompatibility is like one tire out of alignment with the other. When a tire is out of alignment from hitting the curb, what do you do? Do you keep ramming the tire into the curb, attempting to beat the wheel back into alignment? No, that will only ruin it altogether. Do you try ramming the other wheel into the curb to put them both out of alignment, so they'll be in alignment with each other? No! That's Ananias and Sapphira's problem in Acts 5! Though this husband and wife were in alignment with each other in their sinfulness, they were both out of alignment with God's will and therefore under His severest chastening.

What is to be done? Obviously, you need to get each individual tire in alignment with the chassis of the car, and then they will both automatically be in alignment with each other! Though the tire seemed to be out of alignment with other tire, it was in fact out of alignment with the chassis of the car. So, get both spouses in alignment with the Lord, and they are both automatically in alignment with each other. When you think you're incompatible with your spouse, you're in all likelihood incompatible with the Lord; you're not walking closely with your God. Both spouses need to be compatible and in alignment with God (via repentance, cleansing, and acceptance in Messiah) to be compatible and in alignment with one another. Our marriage alignment glorifies God. For, in this way, you can "*accept one another, just as Messiah accepted you to the glory of God*" (Romans 15:7 SN).

2. Similarity: appreciate what we have in common

To appreciate our commonality is to recognize that we have more similarities than differences. When Adam first gazes on Eve, he says (in Hebrew), "*zot ha paam*" (literally, "this, the time"). This is best understood as an exclamation: "Now, this is it!" Or quite simply, "WOW!" For the very first time in Scripture the words of a human being are recorded in direct discourse, and it is a "wow" moment! Adam is thrilled with the woman that God has presented to him. Man immediately appreciates the woman.

Adam then says, "*This is now bone of my bones, and flesh of my flesh*." He immediately recognizes her similarity to him and identifies with her. Their similarity is undeniable, since she is made from his rib, which is his flesh and bone. Neither of them is created ex nihilo (out of nothing). Instead, they are both made from available substances (he from dust, she from his rib), and are both formed and constructed as the handiwork of God.

In Scripture, the Hebrew word for "flesh" (*basar*) is a symbol of weakness, and the Hebrew word for "bone" (*etsem*) means "to make strong." Adam recognizes that she is weak in the flesh, like him, but also that she is strong like him. So it is with men and women today—they both have strengths and weaknesses. Adam's leadership is seen in his recognition of that fact, rather than the false idea that she is weak and he is strong.

That humanity would be created in some way weak may at first seem confusing, since there was no corrupting sin that would have weakened people. But we must remember that humanity was created weak, not because of sin, but because humanity was created to be totally dependent upon God. Prior to sin, dependence upon God is the norm. The introduction of sin makes a humanity resistant to God, with a fleshly desire to be independent from Him—the new normal. Weakness is not humanity's problem—it's how we respond to our weaknesses that gives us problems. If we respond selfishly, disobediently, and inhumanely to our weaknesses, this is spiritual defeat in marriage and elsewhere. But if we respond to our personal weaknesses by depending on God, then we will discover that His *"power is perfected in weakness,"* for His *"grace is sufficient"* for us (2 Corinthians 12:9). This grace-supplied power is the true victory in our Messianic marriages, as well as everywhere else.

For Adam to say that Eve is *"bone of my bones, and flesh of my flesh"* is more than just a literal statement in the Hebrew Bible. It is used to affirm that we are alike, we are much more the same than we are different, and we can fully accept each other on that basis.[2] This same phrase is used elsewhere in Scripture as a pledge of loyalty (2 Samuel 5:1). Taken this way, the man's statement *"bone of my bones, and flesh of my flesh"* becomes a covenantal statement of his lifelong commitment to Eve. Often, Messianic couples simply forget how much they have in common. They may take commonalities for granted and end up majoring in the minors, rather than majoring in the majors. It is vitally important for couples to recognize and identify their primary areas of commonality. If they are unable to do so, there may be problems in the marriage.

These first words of humanity recorded in Scripture, used in the wedding ceremony of Adam and Eve, establish the equality of all humankind while setting humanity apart from the animals. Adam and Eve are now partners and *"fellow heir[s] of the grace of life"* (1 Peter 3:7). What a beautiful picture of Adam's leadership in the marriage! His leadership is not seen as dominating her, for before sin and following Messiah's redemption, husbands are called to "nurture" their wives.[3] By application to the larger paradigm of society, these shared values are the foundation of a strong marriage, community, and society, especially for those that are privileged to lead in service to others.

---

2. Thus Laban says to his nephew Jacob, *"You are my bone and my flesh"* (Genesis 29:14). So too, Abimelech says this to his family in Shechem (Judges 9:1–2). So too do the northern tribes of Israel recognize David as king (2 Samuel 5:1). So too David says to the elders in Israel (2 Samuel 19:11–13).

3. Ephesians 5:28–29: *"So husbands ought also to love their own wives as their own bodies. He who loves his own wife loves himself; for no one ever hated his own flesh, but nourishes and cherishes it."* The word translated "nourish" is the Greek word *ektrepho*, which is to bring to maturity or to nurture (*Thayer's Greek English Lexicon*).

The Bible asks, "*Can two walk together lest they be in agreement?*" (Amos 3:3 SN). The assumed answer is No! You have to know what you have in common, and in what areas you are in agreement. There are primary matters of our lives and secondary matters. The secondary matters are generally external issues that will pass away in time. But the primary matters are what God has stated are of primary importance to our lives and marriages. As has been often stated, "We have unity in the primary matters, liberty in the secondary matters, and charity in all matters."[4] In other words, though your looks may have attracted you to each other, that's secondary and will pass away in time. But if that's what your unity is based upon, then your unity will pass away with your youthful appearances. However, if your unity is based on the foundation of Messiah's Lordship over your lives, marriage, and family, then you have a foundation rock that will withstand the worst of storms that may come your way.[5] The storm reveals the quality of the foundation. The primary matters of faith are what we have in common, and these shared values are vital to a successful marriage! These primary matters are those things that are most important in your life. They need to be constantly revisited to keep the marriage renewed and refreshed in the Lord.

We should also take note that the man initiated and established these values in the home ("*The man said…*" [Genesis 2:23]). Though most men are untaught on the responsibilities of spiritual leadership in the home, still it is their leadership that should initiate that crucial discussion prior to the wedding. For, our shared eternal values provide our unity in the here and now. Even so, we must all be focused on keeping "the main thing the main thing," and Yeshua is always and forever "the main thing"! He is both the Creator and Sustainer of the universe, and as such, is to be the centerpiece of our existence, our marriages, and our congregations. Therefore, the Messianic marriage must "*run the race set before us with endurance, looking unto Yeshua, the author and finisher of our faith*" (Hebrews 12:1–2 SN).

During premarital counseling, I'll normally ask the couple to write down qualities of God that they each consider vital for their lives and upcoming marriage. When we compare lists, we take time together to understand what we consider spiritually important for the marriage. As a married or hope-to-be-married couple, what are five primary values (beliefs, goals, hopes, prayers, etc.) that you have in common? Since values are what determine our behaviors, how are these primary values consistently manifested in your relationship together?

3. Complementarity: appreciate God's diversity between you
Similarity is not all that Adam notices. He states in 1:23 that Eve is "*bone of my bones, and flesh of my flesh,*" but he also recognizes the difference between them. The follow-up statement, "*She shall be called Woman [ishah], because she was*

---

4. Attributed to Augustine of Hippo.
5. See Matthew 7:24–27.

taken out of Man [ish]," demonstrates his awareness of her differences, for she was taken out of him. Adam is saying, "She's the missing piece in my life. Though we're the same, we're also different!" You will recall that humanity being created in the image of God precedes our different human genders. In Genesis 1:27, the Scripture states that *"God created man in His own image, in the image of God He created him; male and female He created them."* Thus, in creating the woman, God completes the man, and creation itself is completed. But God creates them male and female. They are both human—both created in the image of God, both having the spiritual connection to God by the breath of life—but they are nonetheless different as well. God could have, if it had been His will, created them to be identical, but God created them to be different. The differences as well as the similarities complete humanity.

The first man names the first female "*Woman.*" Is she named by Adam to identify with himself or distinguish from himself? Both! She is identified with him in her similarities, yet distinguished from him in her dissimilarities. In his leadership role, Adam not only recognizes their similarities, but also their differences, and appreciates them as such. Adam doesn't merely tolerate her differences but appreciates them. Similarly, a husband is called not only to recognize differences between himself and his wife, but to appreciate them as well. You will recall that she is called his *ezer kenegdo*, the counterpart or corresponding helper, and that this Hebrew word is from the root word *neged*, which can mean "opposite."[6] The meaning may imply a mirror image, but not quite. It's more like saying that opposites attract. Those God-made differences are the reason that opposites attract. Opposites are intended to complement and help one another. We are to differ in our perspectives, but not in our values and the primary matters of faith.

Perspectives are meant to differ because things might not always be the way any one individual person perceives them. Where an insecure leader may feel threatened by another's difference of opinion, a true and mature leader recognizes the value of other perspectives. As can happen, many only recognize their differences when they're irritated by their spouse. As we walk in the Spirit and walk in love, our differences are meant by God to be complementary witnesses to God's truth. This concept of "witness" is similar to the idea of two like-minded witnesses in a court of law, each seeing the same facts but from differing points of view.[7] There must be agreement between the witnesses, otherwise there is no case, but if they agree so much that it is as if they both read the same script, there is the possibility of collusion. Likewise, being yielded to God's Spirit creates agreement between two people that testifies of God's truth. This is why Messiah sends out His *talmidim* (disciples) as His witnesses by twos: you need two for an acceptable witness, but you need two who are different to speak on the same facts. For this

---

6. Joshua 5:13; 1 Chronicles 8:32; 9:38; Nehemiah 3:10; Ezekiel 40:13, etc.
7. Deuteronomy 19:15; 1 Timothy 5:19.

reason also, God wants Jewish believers and Gentile believers to remain as such in the Body of Messiah,[8] for you need two witnesses to confirm the facts as true, but they also need to be two who are different. So in a marriage, vive la différence! The husband and wife are intended to graciously complete each other by their dissimilarities as well as their similarities—that is, if they're walking in the Spirit and walking in love.

However, if they are walking in the flesh (in selfishness, fear, guilt, anger, etc.) and not walking in the Spirit, their differences will create a conflicting witness, which is in opposition to and not complementary of one another.[9] God sees a married couple as one.[10] Therefore, opposition against each other is the same as double-mindedness in God's eyes, and their prayers will go unanswered.[11] Remember, a double-minded person is *"unstable in all his ways"* (James 1:8). A married couple must be in unity in the Spirit of God in order to be an effective witness for Him, as well as having a fulfilling married life together. As we walk in the Spirit, our differences are meant by God to enrich one another's lives, not cause division. However, if we walk in the flesh, we will find ourselves at war with one another over our secondary differences! We must repent of such foolishness and self-centeredness that hinders our walk with the Lord and with each other.

Our unity amidst diversity is key for the healthy Messianic marriage relationship. But remember, appreciation begins with God. Does God appreciate you or merely tolerate you? He loves and appreciates you! He is dissimilar and similar to you. Created in His image, you have similarities to God, and He appreciates that about you always. You also have dissimilarities to God (i.e., your frailty compared to His strength), and He appreciates that about you too! You are loved by God, differences and weaknesses and all. Your spousal appreciation is a result of His appreciation of you.

The Initiator of Unity

For this reason a man shall leave his father and his mother, and be joined to his wife; and they shall become one flesh. (Genesis 2:24)

The appreciator is the initiator!

The two verses Genesis 2:23 and 2:24 are linked by the Hebrew phrase *"al ken,"* translated "For this reason," or "Therefore." It refers to a consequence from the

---

8. Compare Romans 11:1 and 11:11.
9. Galatians 5:17: *"For the flesh sets its desire against the Spirit, and the Spirit against the flesh; for these are in opposition to one another, so that you may not do the things that you please."* Romans 8:5: *"For those who are according to the flesh set their minds on the things of the flesh, but those who are according to the Spirit, the things of the Spirit."*
10. Matthew 19:6.
11. James 1:6, 1 Peter 3:7.

preceding action—i.e., "because of that, therefore this." Because of the appreciation of your spouse in 1:23, there results the one-flesh unity with your spouse of 2:24. Your appreciation of your marriage diversity produces your dedication to your marriage unity. Adam appreciates that Eve is God's will for him. Embracing that will, he obeys God and has unity with his wife, as he leaves, cleaves, and weaves (i.e., becomes one flesh with her). In marriage, a lack of appreciation of your spouse is revealed in a lack of unity with your spouse. If appreciation is lost, it all begins to fall apart. If either party begins to take the other for granted, or is so irritated by the other that either one stops wanting to be with the other, it is a sign of sinfulness that must be repented of.

Men who are the most appreciative of their spouses are also the most dedicated to their marriages. The man who wants to be the leader of the home must first be the appreciator of his wife, thus the initiator of unity in the marriage. The responsibility for the unity in the marriage is with the man. If his marriage dedication is lagging, the challenge is NOT to start by "striving to be more dedicated," for that is a kind of fleshly "works" theology. No, to gain proper appreciation for your spouse, start by rededicating your life to the Lord and renew your appreciation of God. For it is His grace that brought her into your life. Lacking appreciation for your spouse is really a reflection of your lack of appreciation for God! Appreciation for God is key to properly appreciating your spouse.

Note the text states, "*For this reason a man shall leave his father and his mother.*" The man leaves his parents. It's not that the woman won't need to leave her parents' home for this new home with her husband, but he is the marriage leader. Therefore, the Scripture notes, the man is the initiator of unity by the act of leaving (and then by his cleaving). This is his first leadership activity. Remember, our proper attitude (2:23) precedes our proper activities (2:24).

The failure of any marriage may have many perceived causes, but one failure inferred from this biblical text is due to the man's lack of spiritual leadership in initiating the biblical leaving (and cleaving). This first leadership activity constitutes spiritual boundaries for the home. There is in the Bible an assumed need for men to be prepared to properly lead in marriage (and certainly before he can then lead anywhere else[12]). There is also an assumed need for wives to be spiritually ready for when their husbands are "*disobedient to the word*" to win them "*without a word*" (1 Peter 3:1). As his *ezer kenegdo*, designated helper, this is her spiritual calling and commitment to his leadership in the marriage and the home. She will, therefore, need to be careful not to usurp his leadership role simply because he is not prepared to lead, and/or he is unresponsive to God.[13] In any case, the biblical

---

12. First Timothy 3:5. And perhaps too, in order to have his marriage in proper order, a newly married man wasn't sent out to war during his first year of marriage, according to Deuteronomy 24:5.
13. Often, the wife may not fully realize her husband's spiritual immaturity or carnality until

principle is that the man is called to lead by leaving the past and cleaving to his wife, to build their future.

Leave: *"A man shall leave his father and his mother."*
What does it look like when a man appreciates his intended wife? The Scripture states that a man would *"leave his father and his mother"* for her! Because of his appreciation that she is God's needed provision for his life, the marriage supersedes all other human relationships, including that with his own parents—and, yes, even with his own children. The word for "leave" in Hebrew is *azab*; it's a strong word meaning "to forsake." He does the leaving to initiate this new life with his wife, not just to leave home.

The first relationship he must forsake is the one he has with his own parents. This can be difficult, as some parents have trouble cutting the apron strings. However, it is vital for the man to shift his priorities to his wife. Still, forsaking father and mother is to be understood in a relative sense, not an absolute sense. Otherwise, the married couple could not fulfill their proper biblical obligations to honor their parents and help them in their time of need, even as the Messiah assumes they will.[14] Honoring father and mother is one of the highest human obligations next to honoring God. His parents will still be honored, but his marriage is now his primary earthly relationship. So, the husband is to see to it that both he and his wife maintain the appropriate distance from their respective parents. During premarital counseling, we discuss these matters, and the couple makes decisions before the wedding about which set of parents they will visit at Thanksgiving, whom they will visit at Hanukkah, etc. As the head of his home, the husband is to see to it that his wife also complies with the mandate to "leave" that he himself is under. All this should be discussed during premarital counseling, before tensions develop regarding the expectations of the in-laws.

When a man gets married, his (and her) priorities must change. Whatever each of you previously cleaved to in your unmarried life, you must now leave! Your loyalty, affection, zeal, priority, and primary commitments have changed for the rest of your lives together! Each must let go of the emotional, psychological, and even spiritual attachments of your premarital life. You can no longer be "married to" your job, your computer, or your favorite sports team! In principle, everything else—jobs, friends, hobbies, etc.—are now to be evaluated based on whether they help or hinder, develop or damage, the marriage relationship. Bill and Joy were blissfully wed. Afterwards, during one of the monthly checkups that I have with newlyweds during their first year of marriage, Bill said that his longtime friend Pete still expected to have a lot of "hang-out" time with him. We discussed it together,

---

after the wedding. In premarital counseling, she needs as much preparation for her role in his leadership responsibilities as he does.
14. Matthew 15:3–6.

and Bill realized he needed to talk to Pete about his new primary relationship with Joy, and how that impacts their friendship. These are not easy matters to handle, but they are necessary nonetheless. He should have that talk with his friends and family, and she, of course, will have that talk with her friends and family. To the degree he can leave, to that degree he can cleave and have godly leadership in his own home. Never give cause to your spouse to suspect that there is anything on earth more important to you than them. Let's take a lesson from our people Israel. Israel's problem was that though they left Egypt, Egypt hadn't left them. They had returned to Egypt in their hearts.[15] They lusted for the past, though it was bondage. They had to forget *"what lies behind"* in order to press on *"to what lies ahead"* (Philippians 3:13). Though this New Covenant portion refers to our ministry of living wholeheartedly for Messiah, remember that once you're married, your marriage is your primary ministry for the Lord.

Have you left the past? Repent and turn away from any other relationship that competes with your marriage, and consecrate your life to your spouse for Messiah's sake. As an exercise, write down five areas you need to leave. Write down whatever areas that you think your spouse needs to leave. Discuss and pray about these areas together.

Cleave: *"...and cleave to his wife."*

"Leaving" leads to "cleaving." When we think about cleaving we need to understand it from the point of view of Scripture. You leave in order to cleave. The implication is that the biblical marriage is monogamous—that is, one man and one woman—since he (singular) cleaves to his wife (singular).[16] This is counterintuitive because of sin and the way the world has led us to believe. However, remember who in the text does the cleaving. The man! We normally think of the woman as the "clinging vine." It is actually the man who is responsible for holding the marriage together. In our society this role has been reversed. Because of sin, men are not stepping up into the leadership role in caring for the family unit—making certain that needs are being addressed, making sure the family is being prayed for, etc. In many marriages, the wife and mother has been forced into a role of spiritual leadership that she has never been called to by God or enabled by God to perform. This role reversal becomes extremely stressful on the marriage. Since people are made up of body, soul, and spirit,[17] full unity must include cleaving in each of these three areas in the Messianic marriage.

---

15. Acts 7:39: *"Our fathers were unwilling to be obedient to him, but repudiated him and in their hearts turned back to Egypt."*
16. Of the 1,231 societies listed in the 1980 Ethnographic Atlas, 186 were found to be monogamous; 1,041 had occasional or frequent polygyny (one husband and plural wives); and four had polyandry (one wife and plural husbands). *Ethnographic Atlas Codebook* derived from George Peter Murdock, *Ethnographic Atlas* (Pittsburgh, PA: University of Pittsburgh Press, 1967).
17. First Thessalonians 5:23.

1. Cleaving assumes spiritual unity

The Hebrew word for cleaving is *deveq*. This word *deveq* is found in Daniel 2:43, where it is translated "adhere." "*They will not adhere...as iron does not combine with pottery.*" The iron and clay are different substances that cannot cleave or adhere to each other. Substantial differences in a marriage will keep the cleaving process from occurring. Mature Messianic believers have faith, Scriptural values, and spiritual purity and are not to be unequally yoked together with non-believers.[18] "*How can two walk together unless they are in agreement?*" (Amos 3:3 sn). Without spiritual unity between spouses, there can't be true harmony and unity in the marriage. And this is because there can't be unity with the Lord if you're not in agreement with Him as to the truth of His Word. The couple that is of one mind in purpose and practice because of single-minded faith, values, and priorities is growing in togetherness. If you do not grow together, you will grow apart. Are there some unbiblical ideas, beliefs, and values that you have not forsaken? Then these will be the areas where you will be uncommitted to God and to each other (unless, like Ananias and Sapphira in Acts 5, you're in agreement with each other in your rebellion to God!) Do you both agree with God on the truth? Is Yeshua Lord of your marriage? Or are you substantially different? Repent of any areas where either or both of you are uncommitted to God's Word and truth, so that you can adhere to your spouse and have unity in your marriage.

2. Cleaving indicates soul unity

The word *davaq* is translated "sticks closer" in the verse "*There is a friend who sticks closer than a brother*" (Proverbs 18:24). To leave one's father and mother and cleave to one's spouse means to sever one loyalty and begin another—a loyalty that is closer than any other family or sibling commitment. The Hebrew word *ahev* in Proverbs 18:24 that is translated "friend" is literally "one who loves." Of course, our greatest friend is the One who loves our souls, that is, Messiah. Messiah calls us to love our spouses as He has loved us (John 13:34–35). This love of God has been poured out into the hearts of all those that trust in Yeshua (Romans 5:5), and this love is what provides the same loyalty to our spouse that Yeshua has for us. This is why our marriages are His ordained witness of His love for His people (Ephesians 5:31–32). The verb "cling" (*davaq*) often designates the maintenance of the covenant relationship (Deuteronomy 4:4; 10:20; 11:22; 13:4; 30:20). Are there areas of disloyalty, falseness, or deception in your marriage relationship? These are the areas in the spouse's soul that are not yielded, or cleaving, to Yeshua. It's only by being fully dependent on the Head that we are fully interdependent on each other (Ephesians 4:15–16).

---

18. Second Corinthians 6:15 (sn): "*What harmony can there be between the Messiah and Satan? What does a believer have in common with an unbeliever?*"

3. Cleaving means physical unity

The story of Ruth and Naomi is a beautiful picture of cleaving in physical unity. Ruth refuses to leave or forsake Naomi, but cleaves to her, even after Naomi begs her to leave.[19] Ruth's cleaving is not sexual, of course, but a God-honoring commitment to stay with Naomi regardless, whether it be in a different location or even in death. Understanding this application of faithfully cleaving for Adam and all other husbands, the Messianic man is never, never, never to forsake his wife under any circumstances. Even if for physical or psychological reasons there is a lack of sexual unity, the husband is never to abandon his wife. For, our marriage testimony is that we have a God who *"will never leave us nor forsake us."*[20] As we trust and abide in Him, we too will be empowered to cleave to our spouse and demonstrate His faithfulness through our marriage. This marriage commitment to cleave is vital for the children to understand also, so they will feel secure in the home. The unity of the parents provides the security for the children.

Weave: *"And the two shall become one flesh."*

The appreciation that leads to the leaving and the cleaving results in the "weaving," that is, the two becoming one flesh.[21] We may wonder why it says "*one flesh*" rather than "one soul." Let's remember that first we are to be of one spirit by having our primary matters in unity. Then we are to be of one soul by having liberty in secondary matters. Finally, the result of these first two matters, spirit and soul, is one flesh in marriage.

This unity is a process in development, and that's why the text states that the two "*shall become*" one flesh. This future sense of the verb[22] indicates that relationships take time to mature into a growing unity. Sex is easy; unity takes time. But this last part of the verse has to do with intimacy and fidelity in marriage. To be married and then to even consider an intimate relationship with someone who is not your spouse is evil! Yeshua says that in so doing, you are committing adultery in your heart.[23]

Even Yeshua's teaching reminds us that we need to depend on the Lord for the love, grace, and power in our Messianic marriages. He reminds us that apart from Him we can do nothing (John 15:5). True and lasting oneness necessitates

---

19. Ruth 1:14–17.
20. Joshua 1:9; Hebrews 13:5.
21. Though it seems absurd to have to say it, this is actually the seedling of teaching against bestiality. This unity is only with a woman, since she has to be "flesh of your flesh," to be "*one flesh*" with you. All animals are of another flesh and prohibited from such degrading intimacy with humans. First Corinthians 15:39: "*All flesh is not the same flesh, but there is one flesh of men, and another flesh of beasts, and another flesh of birds, and another of fish.*" See Leviticus 18:23; 20:15; Deuteronomy 27:21, etc.
22. The Hebrew *hayah* is in a "vav consecutive" verb form, which, with the initial verse imperfect, gives the next two imperfects a future intention.
23. Matthew 5:28.

the Messianic couple to trust daily in Yeshua. He provides the unity in the marriage, even as the couple clings to Him. Like a braid of hair, the marriage appears to contain only two strands, but it is impossible to create a braid with only two strands—if the two could be put together at all, they would quickly unravel. Herein lies the mystery: what looks like two strands requires a third. The third strand, though not immediately evident, keeps the braid tightly woven. Messiah's presence in a biblical marriage is the needed third strand, holding the wife and husband together (though to all casual observers it only appears like two!) And so the Scriptures assure us, "*A cord of three strands is not quickly torn apart*" (Ecclesiastes 4:12).

The phrase "*the two shall become one flesh*" is stated several times in Scripture. Each reference gives us a greater insight on the Messianic unity in our marriage relationship:

This marriage unity is permanent in Messiah (Matthew 19:5)

Messiah's use of the phrase reestablishes that the marriage relationship is a permanent unity. In Matthew 19:3–6, when challenged by the religious leadership on matters of divorce, Yeshua gives the Pharisees a divine commentary of marriage based on Genesis 2:23–24 and adds this further observation in Matthew 19:6: "*So they are no longer two, but one flesh. What therefore God has joined together, let no man separate.*" Marriage permanence is God's original design that He restored in Messiah's redemption. In the first century, as now, because of the hardness of people's hearts, divorce was widespread and often for trivial reasons. Moses had permitted a writ of divorce to protect the woman in this painful matter (Deuteronomy 24:1–4). But the divorce loophole of the "hardness of heart" (i.e., sin) is removed in Messiah's redemption, for in Yeshua we get a "new heart," as prophesied.[24] The redeemed marriage is the only marriage that can have the spiritual unity of one flesh. Messiah's teaching that the married couple is "*no longer two*" interprets the idea of one flesh to make the marriage relationship into a new entity based on having a new heart in Yeshua. This new marriage entity is not caused by a man's actions in leaving and cleaving. Instead, marital unity is the work of God that is lived out by cleaving in faith. For the marriage is now an entity that "*God has joined together*" and should be treated as humanly inseparable. Have you and your spouse recommitted your lives together as an inseparable union by God's divine work? This recommitment can revitalize your marriage when it's based on His redemptive work in Messiah, for "*nothing can separate us from the love of God in Messiah Yeshua our Lord*" (Romans 8:39 SN).

---

24. Ezekiel 36:26–27.

This marriage unity is participatory with Messiah (1 Corinthians 6:16)

As we have stated earlier, it's evil to consider sex—let alone *have* sex—with anyone other than your spouse. But there is also a spiritual dimension about sexuality, and that is why each spouse is to be absolutely faithful to the other, for marital adultery pictures spiritual adultery.[25] First Corinthians 6:16–18 states, *"Or do you not know that the one who joins himself to a prostitute is one body with her? For He says, 'The two shall become one flesh.' But the one who joins himself to the Lord is one spirit with Him. Flee immorality."* Note the text commands us to *"flee immorality."* You're first unfaithful to your God, and next you're unfaithful to your spouse.[26] Your immorality breaks your spiritual union with the Lord, as well as your marriage vows. But in a Messiah-centered marriage, your spiritual union with the Lord is strengthened by your faithfulness to your spouse, for *"sex within marriage is pure"* (Hebrews 13:4 CJB).

This marriage unity pictures the Body of Messiah (Ephesians 5:31)

Finally, in Ephesians 5:30–31 (SN) the marriage unity pictures the Body of Yeshua. It states, *"We are members of the same body, husband and wife, and for this reason a man shall leave his father and mother and be joined together and the two shall become one flesh."* Marriage as seen from the eyes of God teaches us the meaning of marriage for our lives. God chose marriage above every other relationship to represent His relationship to His people of faith. Thus, we are to relate to our spouses as God relates to us. Marriage pictures the unity between Messiah and the congregation. It pictures a greater unity in the Lord. How will the world know of God's love for us if they do not see it pictured in our marriages? They are our testimony of His faithfulness and our witness of His all-sufficient grace that makes us one. This oneness—this unity we have in marriage—is a testimony of God's love for his people. The intimacy in marriage is the closest of all human relationships, for it reflects our divine relationship. Of all human relationships, this is the one relationship that most reflects God's love for His people and, therefore, the marriage relationship pictures our life in Messiah. May your children see the picture and thereby desire His love to be shared with the spouse God has for them.

Since we are told that the one flesh is a mystery referring to Messiah and the congregation, it cannot refer to mere sexual union. This full acceptance, unity, or oneness transcends the physical for the spiritual, and is an expression of God's full acceptance of us as the Body of Messiah. We're one with Messiah. How are we made one? By faith in His atonement, the sin that separated us from God separates us no longer! Yeshua's atonement paid for the sins *to* us as well as *by* us. Thus, our unity as a Messianic couple is based on trusting in His atonement for our offenses, and for all offenses against us as well. Our simple repentance to

---

25. Jeremiah 3:7–10; 5:7; Ezekiel 16:32, 38; 23:37; Hosea 3:1; Matthew 12:39, etc.
26. See Appendix Six for God's purposes for sex in the Bible.

God by faith in Yeshua reconciles us to God! So too, our simple apology to one another by faith in Yeshua reconciles us to one another. Yeshua is the key to why the Messianic marriage matters, and how we can be one in Him.

So, from all these references to *"the two shall become one flesh"* we understand the larger biblical perspective of the importance of trusting in a faithful God, that we might live out His faithfulness in our Messianic marriages.

The Communicator in Honesty:
The Priority of Communication with Your Spouse

And the man and his wife were both naked and were not ashamed.
(Genesis 2:25)

We have looked at the man's leadership as the *appreciator*, then the *initiator*, and now in Genesis 2:25 as the *communicator*. The fact that they were *"naked"* and *"not ashamed"* indicates an open communication between the husband and his wife. They had nothing to hide or to be embarrassed about. They had a trust between them that made them both an "open book" to read and appreciate.

Healthy marriages have great communication, even when they have to use words. Created in God's image, we'd expect great communication, for communication preceded creation. The Word says: "Then God SAID, let US make man" (emphasis added). Good communication brings about creativity in the marriage, in the home, and throughout our lives.

Their openness and honesty in their communication are emphasized and tied to the preceding principle in several ways. The phrase referring to *both* the man and his wife (*sh'neihem*) is the subject of the verse, and so they *"both"* as a unity experience the same result of his appreciation of her, which is honesty in communication.

There are therefore three principles of the first couple's communication that become a pattern for our marital relationships as well.

1. They are connected. Communication is a result of appreciation

Not only the principle of unity and dedication in 2:24, but the principle of appreciation of 2:23 is linked by the word *and* (the Hebrew letter vav) to the honesty in communication realized in 2:25. As is common in Scriptural narrative,[27] the verse is connected by the *"and"* (vav) to the preceding. The account moves along and stays connected by the *"and"* at the beginnings of the verses. The verb tense in 2:25

---

27. Genesis 2:5, 6, 7, 8, 9, 10, 12, 13, 14, 15, 16, 17, 18, 19, 20, 21, 22, 23. Genesis 2:4–7 contains the creation account of the male. Genesis 2:8–25 covers humanity's development account as both male and female. Genesis 2:24 is a parenthetical explanation of the unifying results of the male's appreciation of the female.

changes back to the narrative of 2:23: it is again past tense.[28] This indicates that 2:25 is a direct result of the male's appreciation of the woman as God's gift to him.

The Scripture says that they "*were BOTH naked*" (emphasis added). As noted above, the subject is "both" (*sh'neihem*)—that is, they were both naked, not just one. They experienced this result of appreciation as a "both"—that is, as a couple. His appreciation of her had a positive impact on them both. Appreciating his wife—and thereby dedicated to their unity—resulted in a healthier relationship for him and her. If you ever wonder what you can do in the best interest of both your wife and yourself, appreciate her! If a man selfishly worries that by appreciating his wife he will be short-changed, then I'd advise him to believe God. He assures us that what you sow, you will reap!

Since 2:25 is a result of 2:23 (and 2:24), a lack of communication in marriage is an indicator of his lack of appreciation (and his lack of dedication to their unity). That lack of unity indicates a lack of appreciation of the spouse and also of God. This is then seen in a lack of open communication. So too, our appreciation of God will be seen in our open communication with Him in prayer. If we understand that God is our provider and our sufficiency, then we will appreciate our spouse, and be dedicated to marital unity, and thereby communicate honestly with our spouse in every way. There are no shortcuts; if there is no appreciation (2:23), there's no dedication (2:24), and there will be no open and loving communication (2:25).

You can ascertain your appreciative unity by your open communication. Real unity is seen in full acceptance, sincerity, openness, and honesty. Fake unity (or spiritual disunity) is seen in insincerity, miscommunication, and dishonesty. The congregation is no more than the homes that make it up; the congregation can be no stronger than the homes therein. If the marital insincerity is then applied to the congregation, the result is that the congregation is characterized by hypocrisy. Better to leave your gift at the altar and be reconciled to one another (Matthew 5:23) than to "fake it" and play religious games. There is no room for dishonesty in the home or in the congregation. You must repent to the Lord and apologize to each other for all dishonesty. The Messianic marriage is called and empowered to make the home a "speak-the-truth-in-love" place for each other and the children. To truly love and care for one another requires repentance, forgiveness, mercy, and compassion. All of these we have received and continue to receive from the Lord. By faith in Yeshua, the Holy Spirit joins us to His own Body (1 Corinthians 12:13), and nothing can ever separate us from the love of Messiah (Romans 8:39). As hard as it is to understand, the grace we need from God to be right with Him is the same grace we need to be right with our spouse, and even to accept ourselves. Adam and Eve are joined by HaShem and to HaShem, and the pre-sin result is total honesty with each other. So also with us, our faith in Yeshua is the key to oneness in marriage and openness with each other.

---

28. As a vav consecutive imperfect, it becomes an absolute past.

2. They are candid. Communication is a realization of acceptance

The Hebrew word for "naked" (*arom*) not only means to be without clothing, but it also means to be revealed or exposed.[29] It has more to do with the exposure of the soul than just physical nakedness. In the home, your spouse's soul is exposed and therefore vulnerable to you. Because of this, you must accept each other "as is." Adam and Eve are transparent with one another, open to each other; transparency and open communication are the norm. There are no masks, no games, strategies, or figuring out how to get their needs met, as we too often find in our struggling marriages. God sees everything you do, so stop living like He isn't there! Honestly accept your spouse! "No masks" means accepting each other by the same grace by which God accepts you both in Messiah. Honesty is the openness of unity. In the movie *The Godfather*, Michael Corleone tells his wife, "Don't ask me about my work!" Secrecy is a sad symptom of the sinful life. Are there areas of life that you don't share with your spouse? Do you share them with the Lord, or are you trying to keep secrets from Him, too? You can be honest with God. And then ask Him to help you be open and honest with your spouse.

In 2:25, their nakedness means there is also nothing to conceal; they have nothing to hide from each other. There is no hiding from each other or God until sin enters the human equation. Amazingly, we find a direct parallel with this verse: "*Then the eyes of both of them were opened, and they knew that they were naked*" (Genesis 3:7). They both again experience nakedness, but now, because of sin, the experience is as a self-conscious feeling of vulnerability. And so, they then sew fig leaves together to hide their fear of openness from one another, which before sin they experienced as acceptance in communication. In marriage, there will be times of frustration and feelings of inadequacy. But instead of feeling guilty, take those cares to the Lord and ask for His grace! As areas of weakness surface, ask the Lord to help and strengthen you both, then discuss it with your spouse. Share everything together for your mutual edification.

As Adam knows the animals' souls and is therefore able to name them according to their nature (see 2:19), so, in their openness, the couple knows each other's souls. Pre-sin, they know each other and accept one another "as is." This openness reveals a wholesome and loving relationship. This is what happens when we stop hiding our lives from each other in marriage. The fear is that if we are that open about our frailties, then people—even our spouses—will think we are losers! Actually the opposite is true; unless they are sociopaths, they will love and appreciate you for trusting them with your concerns! Just as sin had Adam and Eve (and us) hiding from each other, Messiah relates us back to God and each other. This is realized more and more as we mature in the Lord. As areas of weakness surface, we must trust the Lord and our spouses, asking the Lord to help us in these areas.

---

29. Job 26:6; Hebrews 4:13, as also the Greek word for "naked" (*gumnos*) is likewise used.

The text says, "*the man and his wife,*" and so "*his wife*" is as much a part of him now as was his rib in 2:21. This phrase "*his wife*" demonstrates his profound appreciation and unity with her. In the Messianic marriage, our profound appreciation that we are one is the opportunity for communication to flourish in the marriage, home, and congregation. Once more, being created in the image of God—who communicated within the inseparable unity of Himself for our creation (1:26)—now manifests in our fully accepted unity through our unguarded communication.

Also, since the woman is seen in relationship to the man as "*his wife,*" the man's leadership role is being reemphasized. As you are called by God to be the *appreciator* (2:23), and it is revealed that you are the *initiator* (2:24), so emerges your calling to be the *communicator* (2:25)! You are called to appreciate and initiate this type of communication in the home as part of your leadership role. This leadership role is pre-sin. A sinful reversal in marital roles is indicated when the Scripture says regarding the forbidden fruit, "*She took from its fruit and ate; and she gave also to her husband with her, and he ate*" (Genesis 3:6). She now wrongly asserts leadership initiative, and gives to "*her husband,*" and Adam now passively accepts from her the very fruit that was forbidden by God.

And because of this sin-originated role reversal, the calling to initiate communication may seem unusual and uncomfortable to many men. Male initiative in communication may even appear contrary to contemporary stereotypes about men in general, and husbands in particular. One old Jewish joke illustrates this: a boy comes home from school and tells his mom that he got the part of the husband in the school play. Mom immediately tells her son to go back to school and insist on a speaking role!

Since some men feel quite unprepared for the communication responsibility, let me give a few words of encouragement. First, pray and ask the Lord to help you love your wife and speak to her with love, affirmation, and kindness, and show her how meaningful she is to you. Then, believe that God answers your prayers, and reach out to your wife. Encourage her as the wonderful gift from God she is. Pray for and with her; join your hearts together in the Lord daily. Take the time to walk and talk with her; go to a coffee house, just to spend your time with her. Read Scripture together, and talk about how the Scriptures apply to your lives and marriage. Just reading a daily devotional together can be unifying for a couple. Buy her flowers, or some token of your love. Help her. Even though she is called to be your helper, show your servant leadership by assisting her when she has a lot to do. And just reach out and hug her, and hold her hand as you walk together. Yeshua told us that we're to love one another as He loved us. Leaders love. Mature leaders love more consistently. Ask the Lord to help you grow in these leadership responsibilities.

This is the goal we have for our homes; to be a growing testimony of the love and grace of God: *"But we all, with unveiled face, beholding as in a mirror the glory of the Lord, are being transformed into the same image from glory to glory, just as from the Lord, the Spirit"* (2 Corinthians 3:18). Admittedly, growth is slow, but let us keep pressing toward the mark of our high calling in our Messianic marriages.

3. They are confident. Communication is a recognition of approval

Genesis 2:25 tells us in closing that Adam and Eve *"were not ashamed."* The word "ashamed" is from the Hebrew word *bosh*. The force of the Hebrew phrase contrasts with the "primary meaning of the English 'to be ashamed,' in that the English stresses the inner attitude, the state of mind, while the Hebrew means 'to come to shame' and stresses the sense of public disgrace, a physical state."[30] What that means for us is that, whereas we get self-conscious and internally feel judged, this Hebrew phrase indicates that they do not cause each other to feel judged, ashamed, or unworthy. They approve of each other in their acceptance of one another. This is quite important for our Messianic marriages. Too often, we can accept one another but do not approve of each other. Thus, we can accept our spouse and ourselves as losers, brutes, dummies, etc. But the biblical text indicates that they accept and approve of each other. Is she perfect? Well, he knows she is perfect for him!

Their communication is undivided in their unity, unguarded in their honesty, and now, unashamed in their security. For many of us, the results of sin have been so devastating that our only sense of security is in our vain hope of not being found out. Often dishonest communication is depended upon, with the hope that a lie will protect or promote the liar. Yeshua taught that *"the truth will make you free."* This may be helpful for some, but for liars, the truth is far too threatening to be trusted. Lying can become a way of life, and we do need to be extremely careful of our lying developing into a marital lifestyle, and what might regrettably become characteristic of your home and testimony. In dysfunctional homes, loyalty is much more highly valued than truth. "Just tell your teacher that you fell down the stairs again." In such a home, the children are corrupted to live by a lie. We need to repent and seek God's help to be truth-tellers with our spouses, that our homes may be safe places for the family.

Pre-sin Adam and Eve are confident in each other's presence, and they do not feel humiliated or anxious. This has three dimensions. First, they are unashamed in their own sight (self-confidence). They feel fully accepted by God. They have no need to judge themselves. There are no personal feelings of guilt and shame in the pre-sin condition—sin produces those feelings. But it's the truth about you as well. Your shameful guilt is a response of your flesh to your feelings of failure, weakness, and inadequacy. But you need not live in guilt, because Yeshua is already

---

30. *Theological Wordbook of the Old Testament*, s.v. *bosh*.

your perfect guilt offering.[31] Thus, since you have a perfect guilt offering, your feelings of guilt are an indication that you're not trusting in Yeshua. Those guilty feelings are a poor and miserable substitute for what Messiah has for you—forgiveness and a cleansed conscience before God.[32] When we put our hand too close to a fire, our immediate reaction is to pull our hand away. So also with guilt. The fiery pain of guilt on our conscience has us draw away, and we substitute evasion and shame for the simple prescription of Scripture: "*If we confess our sins* [to God], *He is faithful and righteous to forgive us our sins and to cleanse us from all unrighteousness*" (1 John 1:9). We're to draw closer to God and not draw away, hiding from Him in guilt and shame. Rather, cast "*all your anxiety on Him, because He cares for you*" (1 Peter 5:7).

Second, they are unashamed in each other's sight (social confidence). Both know they are accepted by their spouse, so neither feels judged, embarrassed, or ashamed by the other. So too, by God's grace, we are to "*accept one another, just as Messiah also accepted us to the glory of God*" (Romans 15:7 SN). Trust in Messiah's grace to accept yourself and your spouse, just as you are accepted by God in Messiah. Yeshua did more than enough for you to be fully acceptable to God. Yes, by the very same grace by which God accepts us in Messiah, we also graciously accept ourselves and others. Those times that you're not accepting yourself by grace, you will find yourself unable to accept others by grace. If this is the case, talk to the Lord about this matter, and review the Scriptures that are meant to assure us of our gracious and full acceptance in the Beloved (Ephesians 1:6).

Third, they are unashamed in God's sight (spiritual confidence). We are complete in Messiah (Colossians 2:10). God is not ashamed of them, and so it is with Messianic believers today. Because of simple yet sincere faith in Messiah, God no longer treats or speaks to you again as "sinners," but as His beloved children.[33] "*And such we are*" (1 John 3:1)! We never need to feel incomplete or falling short before God, for in Messiah "*you have been made complete*" (Colossians 2:10). Therefore, Messiah is not ashamed to call us His brethren (Hebrews 2: 11)! Yeshua died for your sins and took all your sinful shame upon Himself! Isn't that wonderful? Such knowledge gives us confidence (not conceit) in every sphere of life as we grow together in the Lord, for He is with us always. The first couple loves without fear, for they are joined at the heart by Adonai, and His "*perfect love casts out fear*" (1 John 4:18). (If you're concerned about what to do if you faithfully live this way but your spouse is disobedient to God or is a non-believer in Messiah, this will be covered fully when we study 1 Peter 3:1–7 later in the book.)

---

31. See Isaiah 53:10, where the Messiah is prophesied to be our *asham*, or "guilt offering."
32. Hebrews 9:13–14.
33. See Hebrews 12:5–6. As His child, God may chasten you, but He will never condemn you (see Romans 8:1, 31–39).

Three • Foundational Priorities in Messianic Marriage

In summary, this is the way strong marriages and communities are linked together: *suitability for appreciation*, therefore *unity by dedication*, and *honesty in communication*. So, how is that working for you? Have you identified areas that you and your spouse need to bring before the Lord? Some might think that the results of sin leave us with glaring inadequacies. Perhaps, but it's His grace that is to prove sufficient for our marriages. There's an old story about a great dramatic actress from the nineteenth century, Sarah Bernhardt. One night in London, she was playing *Fedora* to a crowded house. As usual, the poison scene drew tempestuous applause, but hardly had the clapping of hands and the stamping of feet died away, when loud laughter was heard in the upper gallery. The serious-minded turned reproachful looks at the "boisterous boors," as they called them. However, their frowns turned to smiles and then to open laughter, when they noticed the cause of the merriment. Yes, right in the front row of the gallery sat two one-armed men. Without realizing that many were watching them, these two fellows were prolonging the applause by clapping their remaining hands together. Can you think of both you and your spouse as two imperfect but redeemed people using your combined resources to appreciate life and glorify God? As a redeemed community made up of redeemed Messianic marriages and families, God has brought the Body together with individual parts meant to depend upon each other and, by that grace, to enjoy peace, testimony, and thankfulness.

What God is doing in Yeshua is restoring us to the original design that is laid out in Genesis 1:26–2:25. In Yeshua the Messiah, we are *fully restored* by grace through faith to an eternal relationship with Adonai that *fully empowers* us to have restored relationships in marriage, family, and community, so that in our hearts and homes Yeshua may be exalted forever!

Some questions to help apply these teachings

1. Have you recognized God's authority in bringing you together with your spouse? (This and all the following questions can be applied to your relationship to community or congregation as well.)

2. What values do you have in common? What goals, beliefs, hopes, prayers, etc. are in common? Write five things you have in common with your spouse.

3. Write five areas that are different but you appreciate about your spouse. Write two areas you have left behind and two that you still need to leave behind. Write out five areas of commitments you have toward your spouse.

4. What five areas express your unity, or need work to express your unity?

5. What areas do you each have to work on in taking initiative in your relationship?

6. What areas with regards to permanence (leaving), purity (temptation), or picturing (witness) are matters of prayer for you and your spouse?

7. How often do you set aside time to talk, discuss, and pray together in a week?

8. What areas are difficult to share with your spouse? Can you pray with your spouse about these matters?

CHAPTER FOUR

Foundational Precautions for Marriage

Genesis 3:1–24

As we have learned, Genesis provides the foundational principles for all relationships in Scripture, especially marriage. God's nature is relational, so He created us in His image (to represent Him), and after His likeness (to relate to Him). Humanity is similar to all other creatures (we're all made from the dust), and yet humanity is also qualitatively different from every other creature (humanity alone was given the breath of life).

In Genesis 2:8 and following, God prepares humanity for marriage. In 2:8–21, God prepares the man for relationship with the woman. In 2:22–25, we see the priorities for the man as the leader in the home, by ministering his appreciation, dedication, and communication in the marriage. Adam and Eve function in sinless conditions before sin enters the human picture, after which appear our present dysfunctional marriages, homes, and society. And as the man is God's appointed leader in the home, he is the one God holds responsible for the marriage failure and the fall of humanity.[1] Remember, in Messiah's redemption, the Messianic marriage is returned to the pre-sin principles to once again enjoy a spiritually functional and God-honoring home.[2] His grace is sufficient for your marriage!

Now in Genesis 3, Scripture reveals the impact on marriage after sin corrupts the first couple. Scripture instructs us how to avoid Adam and Eve's disobedient mistakes. In Genesis we study the marital failure in three sections:

1. The disobedient and deceptive cause of marital failure, 3:1–13
2. The disciplined and corrective consequences of marital failure, 3:14–19
3. The dedicated and redemptive cure for marital failure, 3:20–24

---

[1]. Hosea 6:7: "*But like Adam they have transgressed the covenant.*" Romans 5:12, 14: "*Therefore, just as through one man sin entered into the world, and death through sin, and so death spread to all men…even over those who had not sinned in the likeness of the offense of Adam.*"

[2]. This is the shocking instruction that Yeshua the Messiah teaches His disciples when He is confronted by the religious leaders of His day regarding the divorce and remarriage issues in Matthew 19:1–12. In light of His upcoming redemption, He brings our perspective back to the original design for marriage in Genesis 2:24.

The Disobedient and Deceptive Cause of Marital Failure (Genesis 3:1–13)

First, the spiritual cause of our marital (and social) collapse

> *Now the serpent was more crafty than any beast of the field which the LORD God had made. And he said to the woman, "Indeed, has God said, 'You shall not eat from any tree of the garden'?" The woman said to the serpent, "From the fruit of the trees of the garden we may eat; but from the fruit of the tree which is in the middle of the garden, God has said, 'You shall not eat from it or touch it, or you will die.'" The serpent said to the woman, "You surely will not die! For God knows that in the day you eat from it your eyes will be opened, and you will be like God, knowing good and evil." When the woman saw that the tree was good for food, and that it was a delight to the eyes, and that the tree was desirable to make one wise, she took from its fruit and ate; and she gave also to her husband with her, and he ate.* (Genesis 3:1–6)

This portion of Scripture relates a tragic process that ends with humanity's sinful separation from God and the moral collapse of a marriage. In this portion of Scripture, we see the enemy, Satan, on the attack, and this attack results in the couple's disastrous disobedience to God. Even so, the Scripture also reveals that God is able to redeem the marriage. In this portion, God reveals our human frailty in such obvious terms, but not because He wants us to feel bad—rather, to reveal a problem that needs to be dealt with. God is able to turn disaster into redemption!

I. We're confronted in our dedication to the Word (3:1): Marital relationships are defined by Scriptural commitment.

The primary lesson to be learned from this section of Scripture is that disobedience to God brings about disaster. The father of lies is the enemy of the Truth, and seeks to destroy all who relate according to the Word. He attacks relationships at the point of our commitment to the Word. Since God's Word is God's will, and the safest place for marriage is in God's will, then if you remove the Word of God, your marriage is in grave danger. God designed marriage to be protected, but when we disobey Him, we leave His protection. As a train is only stable if it stays on the rails, so a marriage is derailed by disobedience to God's Word. The problems leading to the marriage failure and the fall of humanity are revealed in this section: fellowship (v. 1), provision (v. 1b), accuracy (v. 2–3), protection (v. 4), identification (v. 5), evaluation (v. 6), and dedication (v. 7).

Our dedication to the Word regarding our fellowship

> *Now the serpent was more crafty than any beast of the field which the LORD God had made. And he said to the woman, "Indeed, has God said, 'You shall not eat from any tree of the garden'?"* (Genesis 3:1)

The first problem revealed in verse 1 is improper fellowship. Relationships are defined by their Scriptural commitment. Homer Simpson's simple evaluation, "You shouldn't go talking with snakes" certainly proves true in this instance! The serpent is an instrumental pawn of Satan, as Jewish tradition[3] and Scripture later identify.[4] Sin did not begin on earth; it began in heaven with Satan's rebellion against God. Sin did not originate with humanity, but in the heart of Lucifer.[5] Sin was imported to earth and has flourished here ever since. God did not permit sin, since permission is consent, and a holy God can never consent to sin. No, He created us with free will, and that freedom gave us opportunity to sin, contrary to His will. Because of our misused free will, our choices bring consequences—either for good or ill, for what you sow, you will reap (Galatians 6:7). We're created fragile—corruptible, though not corrupted. Our need to depend on God is, in a sense, our weakness. A flower's delicateness is its beauty but also its vulnerability, for it is thereby easily crushed. Purity doesn't protect you; rather, you must protect your purity!

Dishonesty puts relationships at risk. Satan is subtle by nature, and the enemy's evil motives are hidden by his friendly manner. The serpent was always wise—he was created wise—but sinful pride (i.e., "I'm the smartest guy in the room") corrupted his wisdom such that he became shrewd, tricky, and crafty. Godly wisdom honors God and godly relationships; ungodly wisdom dishonors God and destroys godly relationships. A couple was having severe marital difficulties. He sought godly counsel, which encouraged him to pray, forgive, apologize, and love. Her counsel came from her hairdresser, who encouraged her to "dump the dude." She followed her hairdresser's advice, ended her marriage, and stopped following the Lord. Since marriage is God's wisdom for humanity, only godly wisdom can help a marriage. Thus ungodly wisdom can only hurt a marriage. Be careful from whom you acquire counsel.

We may wonder why Satan approaches Eve and not Adam. Up to now, the Scripture indicates the main personal interaction is between God and the man. As a predator goes after the weakest in the herd, Satan pursues the person with the least personal experience with the Lord and with His Word. Spiritual maturity is biblically defined as consistent application of the Word of God, which trains our senses *"to discern good and evil."*[6] In his interactions with the woman, the

---

3. Zohar, Vol. 1, p.35b, AND THE SERPENT. R. Isaac said: "This is the evil tempter." R. Judah said that it means literally a serpent. They consulted R. Simeon, and he said to them: "Both are correct. It was Samael, and he appeared on a serpent, for the ideal form of the serpent is the Satan. We have learnt that at that moment Samael came down from heaven riding on this serpent, and all creatures saw his form and fled before him. They then entered into conversation with the woman, and the two brought death into the world. This serpent is the evil tempter and the angel of death. It is because the serpent is the angel of death that it brought death to the world." Sforno: "The serpent represents the Satan" (Bereishis, Vol. 1, Mesorah, pp. 112–113).
4. Second Corinthians 11:3; 1 John 3:8; Revelation 12:9; 20:2.
5. See Isaiah 14:14; Ezekiel 28:13–17.
6. Hebrews 5:13–14.

serpent does not use the expression "HaShem God," because "HaShem" refers to God's covenantal relationship with His people. There is no covenant relationship between God and the serpent. He only speaks of "God," for he doesn't want to remind Eve of HaShem's command given in the context of a covenantal relationship between God and humanity. By Eve merely saying "God," she brings herself down to Satan's creature level, and removes the vital covenantal context for the command. God's Word always expresses His covenantal love for us, even in His warnings. We must never view His Word otherwise, lest we live in mere religion and not the vital relationship with the living God.[7] In the process, the serpent draws the woman into his style of speech, along with his value system, so that she too only speaks of "God." Getting on the same page with someone is fine when you seek to encourage them to consider the truth of God that they may not be considering on their present page. But beware of getting on someone's page that will have you compromise what you know about the Lord.

In speaking to the woman, Satan uses the masculine plural verbs: you both shall not eat (v. 1); you both shall not die (v. 4); you both eat from it (v. 5); you will both have your eyes opened (v. 5); you both will be as God (v. 5); and you both will know good and evil (v. 5). Satan is not merely seeking to get the woman to sin, but to bring them both into sin. He is attempting to make her think that God is trying to keep them both down. He wants them to see eating from the tree as enlightening them both. His subtle suggestion is, "This will be good for your marriage!"

Satan is trying:
- to deceive them by having them trust his lie and not God's Word. So, be discipled and know the Word.
- to undermine God's leadership arrangement, and to thereby divide them by having the woman as the one who will decide about the fruit. So, be submitted and stay humble.
- to morally defile them both by their disobedience to God. So, be obedient and stay cleansed.
- to defeat them, since he knows they are God's representatives and stewards of the world. So, be spiritually aware and strong in the Lord.
- to destroy them, as he knows that sin kills. The Word is godly life; outside of the Word is godless death.

---

7. Some may wonder if we should use "HaShem" in our marital discussions at home. Remember, the covenant tetragrammaton translated HaShem ("the Name") is brought over into the New Covenant Greek writings as Kurios ("Lord"). We are explicitly told that "*whoever will call on the name of the Lord* [Kurios] *will be saved*" (Romans 10:13), and that the name of the Lord is Yeshua, for "*if you confess with your mouth Yeshua as Lord* [Kurios], *and believe in your heart that God raised Him from the dead, you shall be saved*" (Romans 10:9 SN). Thus, for the Messianic marriage and home, the name "Yeshua" is the Name above all other names.

To cast doubt, the enemy challenges Eve's knowledge of God's Word (v. 1): *"Has God said, 'You shall not eat from any tree of the garden'?"* He uses a question to entice a response. He uses the word *said* rather than *commanded*, to change God's authoritative injunction to appear like mere advice, which could be more easily misinterpreted.[8] Do you interpret God's commands to be mere advice? Beware, this is the edge of the precipice that leads to destruction. God puts His priorities for us in the imperative so that the clarity of the Word will be our security in the world. Every command from God is a point of commitment for the believer. But the point of commitment is also the point of attack.

The first sign that the marriage is in trouble can be found by observing with whom Eve is talking. The problem of association can hinder the marriage. The Scripture instructs us to avoid certain people.[9] The principle of leaving and cleaving, alluded to earlier in our study, should certainly be applied here. Any extra-marital relationship must be evaluated relative to your marriage: does it help or hinder the marital bonds? Anyone or anything that could possibly harm the marriage must be left behind, including friends, career choices, or whatever it may be—but especially those individuals who doubt the goodness of God and the veracity of His Word.

As can be seen in verse 3:1, the lack of unity in the marriage begins by associating with someone of differing values. We must ask ourselves with whom we are associating and from whom we seek counsel. When parents try to safeguard their children from associating with the wrong sort of people, their kids might complain, "But we were just talking!" Tell that to Eve! She may not have understood that she was in spiritual danger. Many today are unaware that what they watch, listen to, or ingest can be spiritually damaging and deadly. Even your extended family can be a bad choice if they do not live by biblical values. I've had to counsel with parents that have their children corrupted by misguided grandparents! We must be very careful in our associations! If you look to see how close to the tree you can get, the enemy will help you go the rest of the way! We are to resist the enemy;[10] not try to relate to him!

Our dedication to the Word regarding our provision

The second thing to notice in verse 1 is the issue of provision. The first question the serpent asks is meant to bring doubt into Eve's mind regarding God's provision. Look closely at the verse: *"Indeed, has God said, 'You shall not eat from any tree of the garden'?"* The very question assumes that God is keeping Adam and Eve from

---

8. How does the serpent know of the command to Adam? Since his disobedience means the subjection of all creation to futility (Romans 8:20), when man as God's leader over creation is prohibited from eating from the tree, it thereby prohibits all other creatures subordinate to man from eating from the tree as well.
9. Psalm 1:1; Proverbs 4:14–15; Romans 16:17; 2 Timothy 2:16–18; 3:2–5; Titus 3:9, etc.
10. Jacob (James) 4:7; Ephesians 6:10–13; 1 Peter 5:7–9!

what they need to properly live. What the serpent is really asking is, "Can God be trusted? Is God holding out on you? Can He really meet your needs? Are you being short-changed?"

The enemy of our soul will always try to cast doubt in our minds as to whether or not we can trust God to provide for us. Will we give in to fear or covetousness, wanting more and more to hedge our bets against the future? We must be in prayer together about these things, so we can be prepared against the attacks of the enemy. We must be consciously thankful to God for His provision, asking Him to meet our needs by giving us *"this day our daily bread."*[11]

II. We're compromised in our deficiency in the Word (3:2–5):
Marital relationships are damaged by biblical confusion.

Our deficiency may be understood as a limited knowledge of the Word, or especially an inaccurate knowledge of the Word.

Our Deficiency in the Accuracy of the Word

The woman said to the serpent, "From the fruit of the trees of the garden we may eat; but from the fruit of the tree which is in the middle of the garden, God has said, 'You shall not eat from it or touch it, or you will die.'" (Genesis 3:2–3)

The third spiritual problem is that Eve misquotes Scripture—twice! Inaccuracy concerning the knowledge of God's Word leaves gaps that the enemy wants to fill with lies. A careful examination of verse 1 will reveal that the serpent is not only raising doubt in Eve's mind as to whether she can really trust God, but he is also probing the extent of her knowledge of God's Word! The enemy will constantly test you on your knowledge of God's Word. What keeps you in God's protection zone, so to speak, is your ability to be *"accurately handling the word of truth."*[12] We may think that proficiently *"handling"* the Word is only for professionals, but that too is a lie of the enemy. God's Word is for you, even as His protection in the Word is for you.

Eve's answer is inaccurate on three points:

1. *Her inaccuracy in the Word*: She is confused about the precept. God did not say anything about touching; it was eating that was the problem. Adam and Eve may have thought that the tree was poisonous and physically dangerous (rather than spiritually dangerous) and that even touching may be lethal. The snake was probably touching the tree or the fruit, thereby proving that touching did not bring any judgment, and setting her up to think that therefore eating it would not bring judgment either.

---

11. Matthew 6:11.
12. Second Timothy 2:15.

2. *Her uncertainty about the Word*: She is confused about the penalty. She uses a Hebrew form for "*or you will die*" (*pen-t'mutun*) that lacks the emphatic quality of HaShem's original warning, which was, "*you will surely die*" (*mot tamut*). Not only does she add to God's Word ("*or touch it*"), she also takes away from the power of it, implying she is unclear about the actual consequences. What she says softens the warning from God, implying that she considers the consequence of death a possibility rather than the certain result.[13] Her inaccuracy in the Word leads to her uncertainty about the Word. At that moment, the enemy knows he has her.

3. *Her impoverishment of the Word*: She is confused about the Person. Though it is HaShem who gave the command, she calls him by the generic "God" ("*God has said*"). The name translated "Lord God" in most English translations is in Hebrew the tetragrammaton—yud-hey-vav-hey—the sacred four-letter Name of God, which is His covenantal name (we translate it as HaShem, "the Name").[14] The command HaShem gave was part of a covenant relationship with humanity. By using the name "God" instead, Eve impoverishes the meaningfulness of the Word for her life, for she is unwittingly removing the covenant relationship from His instruction. This reduces the Word to mere rules and regulations, instead of the loving warning from a God who cares for His people. Only in relationship with our covenant-keeping God do we understand His intention in His instruction. Remove relationship and you're left with religion. Marriages reflect this as well. The true value of your marriage is in the loving relationship, which gives meaning to all your communication with each other. Take out the loving covenant relationship from your interactions and marriage becomes mere toleration of one another. Marriage takes constant renewing of your covenant love in the Lord for each other.

We may ask where she got this misconception. After all, God gave the command to Adam, not her. Therefore, she either added to what Adam told her, or he added to the command himself, hoping it would keep her further away from the tree and the danger. In rabbinical Judaism, fences are established around the Torah. The premise is to help protect the people from the possibility of breaking the Torah by keeping them further away from it. This is like the fences that parents provide for their children, warning them to "stay ten feet away from the curb." Eve added a fence to the Word, but it was no protection; it was a deception. By adding to God's Word, we transgress His Word. "*Do not add to His words*" (Proverbs 30:6). Being deceived by evil begins with our lack of personal accuracy in the Word.

---

13. Though she says that the forbidden tree is "*in the middle of the garden*," it is in fact "*the tree of life*" that is in the middle of the garden (2:9). That text also mentions the tree of the knowledge of good and evil, but its location is not pinpointed. She may have been totally confused on what tree was where.

14. In the New Covenant, His covenant name is Yeshua. See Acts 4:12; 10:42–43; Romans 10:9; etc.

In recognizing Eve's inaccuracies, we are not calling her a sinner—at least not yet, for even with her inaccuracies, she has not yet eaten of the forbidden fruit. Sadly, by changing God's Word, when she speaks to Adam, she becomes a false teacher to her husband. That act of disobedience is the corrupting and condemnable transgression. Her misunderstanding of Scripture is not in and of itself a sin. But her inaccuracies make her vulnerable to the enemy's deception and temptation. Remember, Satan cannot force you to disobey God; he can only suggest you do so. The disobedience is your fault for acting on his temptation.

The lesson is quite clear: a lack of accuracy in knowing the Word becomes the very area in which you are exposing yourself to the enemy. If you are a new believer, then God will help you in this area, as long as you don't arrogantly assume that it doesn't matter. God will help you by having a discipled community of believers that can give you feedback and guidance when you're not sure of God's will for your life. Obviously, it would have been good if Eve spoke with Adam before eating of the fruit. Similarly, it is best for couples to talk together about all decisions that will impact them both before acting on an impulse.

Many of us may also have the general sense of what Scripture teaches, but we do not know it exactly. Think of all the wrong thinking that is in direct contradiction to Scripture but is often accepted as wisdom: "Internet porn is a victimless crime." "A small lie is necessary at times." "I'm not making enough money to tithe." "My body is my business!" "My vocation is my validation." When believers are unaware of the biblical Word, they may easily fall for worldly wisdom.

This can be disastrous for any married couple today, as it was for our first parents in the garden. As a married couple, commit to the Word to lead and guide you both. We must beware of the "ignorance (of Scripture) is bliss" attitude.

Let us diligently apply ourselves to learning the Scriptures and applying them to our lives. A mature believer not only knows what the Scripture says but faithfully follows it as well. Maturity is consistency.

Our Deficiency in Our Protection by the Word

*The serpent said to the woman,
"You surely will not die!"* (Genesis 3:4)

1. The enemy's sinful denial

Eve's inaccurate perception of God's Word is the basis of the enemy's next attack, a lie in which he directly contradicts God's command to Adam in 2:17. Recall that God told Adam that in the day he eats from the fruit he *"will surely die."* The enemy tells the woman they *"surely will NOT die"*! The woman chooses to believe the lie, and the consequences are devastating. As can be seen in Genesis 2:16–17, God's Word is stated in such a way that we can clearly understand it and follow it.

As the father of lies (John 8:44), Satan tells a big lie, taking advantage of Eve's great uncertainty. This is a common ploy of the enemy's pawns. Liars confidently deny the truth, knowing that a believer's uncertainty about the truth will then cause them to think that the liar's apparent certainty means that the liar is right. "Yeshua is not Lord," the deceiver says, and your lack of biblical certainty, combined with their certainty, undermines your faith. And that's how people go astray in marriage, and go apostate from the Lord. If a believing couple is unaware of what the Bible says about marriage, they can become unsettled and led astray by false assertions. Have you ever heard, "Marriage is a fifty-fifty proposition!" That's a lie. The Bible teaches that marriage is a 100 percent-100 percent proposition, because both spouses have to fully sacrifice themselves in order to love as they're called to love.[15] But if you don't know what the Bible teaches, you may believe that marriage is about fairness, and therefore a fifty-fifty deal. And since you may feel that you have already given your 50 percent, you can resent your spouse for not doing his or her fair share. By believing a lie, you have resentment, anger, guilt, and fear. Believing a lie removes God's protection in the truth.

We can learn from Adam and Eve's tragedy that our own protection and marital security is found ONLY in following God's will, as clearly stated in His Word. Your home is not secure if you are not in His Word and not following His will. To live otherwise is to believe and follow the enemy's lie. The lie is that your sin has no consequences. The marital lie is that you can deceive one another, be unkind to each other, choose not to pray together or pray for each other, etc., and that those sins won't really matter or have any long-term impact on your lives and home. Sins? Yes, we are called and commanded to love and minister to one another, not merely tolerate one another. To do otherwise is to invite disaster. Because the first couple chooses to believe the enemy's lie, they give up the only protection they have, and the consequences are tragic. The enemy seeks to do the same to you. Scripture states that *"your adversary, the devil, prowls around like a roaring lion, seeking someone to devour"* (1 Peter 5:8). Satan will constantly test your knowledge of the Word, and will attack any area of weakness that he perceives in your life and marriage. But, just as he could not make Eve eat what was forbidden, so he cannot make you do what is wrong. He can only suggest, tempt, and lie. Therefore, we're repeatedly taught to resist him.[16] We battle the enemy as we resist him, so as not to be sidetracked from the righteousness that God would have for us. We are sidetracked by either yielding to the enemy's evil temptation or by merely focusing all our attention on fighting him.

---

15. Yeshua taught that we're to *"love one another, even as I have loved you"* (John 13:34). Wives are to *"be subject to your own husbands, as to the Lord"* (that is, completely), and husbands are to love their wives, *"just as Messiah loved us and laid down His life for us"* (Ephesians 5:22, 25 SN). Love is measured by Yeshua's sacrifice.
16. Ecclesiastes 4:12; Ephesians 6:13; James 4:7; Hebrews 12:4; 1 Peter 5:9.

However, it bears repeating, the lesson to learn in this biblical account is to accurately know the will of God in God's Word and follow it, for therein lies our only protection! The Scripture is something that is meant to be protection for us, not to restrict us. God's Word is not a fence keeping us from happiness, but guardrails keeping us from a shameful disaster.[17]

2. The enemy's substitute delusion

"For God knows that in the day you eat from it your eyes will be opened, and you will be like God, knowing good and evil."
(Genesis 3:5)

In verse 5, the enemy ramps up his attack by aiming at the trustworthiness of God. He realizes that her inaccurate knowledge of God's Word means she also has an inaccurate knowledge of God, for God's Word is His true self-revelation of His nature, character, and purpose. The enemy therefore proposes that God said they would die just to frighten them, in order to keep them from the fulfillment that comes from eating from the forbidden tree. By stating, "*For God knows,*" Satan implies that God is intentionally tricking them. As with Adam and Eve, the enemy will try to make you feel or think that you are being cheated and shortchanged in marriage—the same marriage that you confessed at one time was God's blessing for you! And, he suggests, your real happiness is to be found outside your marriage. He will try to convince you that God is intentionally withholding the good life from you.

Or the enemy might take a different tack, lying that your life purpose is to be happy, and that whatever God has said must be interpreted to satisfy your fleshly desires and vain curiosities. Since many people live merely for their own sense of happiness, comfort, and pleasure, they can be duped to think that God merely wants them to be happy, and interpret the Scripture accordingly. Televangelist Jim Bakker thought that way for a while. He cheated on his wife and cheated his donors out of their money by foolishly twisting the Scriptures to fit his own perverted view of God and life. The enemy can play you from both directions: either God is keeping you from the joy that disobedience brings, or God really wants you to be happy, so everything should be interpreted toward that end.

In the enemy's audacity in his first ploy, he states that God knowingly prohibited Adam and Eve to keep them from eating fruit that would give them the fulfillment of their creation. Satan assures Eve that "*in the day you* [both] *eat from it,*" God knows there will be results. God actually knows that in the day you eat from it you will have three important changes that He doesn't want you to have:

---

17. Second Timothy 2:15 states, "*Present yourself approved to God as a workman who does not need to be ashamed, accurately handling the word of truth.*" The Scripture assures us that our confidence in living life comes from accurately handling the Word of God.

comprehension, deification, and discernment! God will have competition with humanity as His equals.

Admittedly, the results of eating the forbidden fruit, *"your eyes will be opened, and you will be like God, knowing good and evil,"* could be understood in a harmless way by God's direction. Opening eyes is something God does for His servants, and for believers in general (Genesis 21:19; 2 Kings 6:17; Acts 26:18). Making us like God is what God has already done for all humanity, since He created us according to His likeness (Genesis 1:26). In fact, it is said that under very special circumstances, *"the house of David will be like God"* (Zechariah 12:8). Additionally, knowing good and evil is not necessarily wrong, since this is what King Solomon prayed for (1 Kings 3:9), and this is what God provides all mature believers in Yeshua (Hebrews 5:14). The problem is in the process for receiving those results. Eating of the fruit is disobedience to God, and the result of all acts of disobedience is corruption. The end does not justify the means.

So, Satan's assurance that their eyes will be opened, meaning that they will have insight and comprehension on spiritual reality as it really is, is true. So they eat and their eyes are opened (3:7), but what do they see? They see themselves as sinners, with overwhelming guilt and fear, feeling vulnerable, ashamed, and condemned!

Their act of disobedience opens their eyes and they become spiritually blind! This is the condition of all the nations, despite the philosophers, wise men, and wizards! *"The Gentiles also walk, in the futility of their mind, being darkened in their understanding, excluded from the life of God because of the ignorance that is in them, because of the hardness of their heart"* (Ephesians 4:17–18). In marriage, disobedience to God makes you spiritually blind, darkening your understanding so that both spouses can misconstrue and misunderstand each other, producing marital alienation and a divided home. Yeshua explains this problem: *"The eye is the lamp of the body; so then if your eye is clear, your whole body will be full of light. But if your eye is bad, your whole body will be full of darkness. If then the light that is in you is darkness, how great is the darkness!"* (Matthew 6:22–23). A "clear eye" is a spiritually clarified and cleansed eye that brings info in that will edify and enlighten the person. But a "bad eye" brings in the same info as moral darkness, and that soul's corruption is profound. The insight gained through disobedience is spiritually counterfeit. There may be vague similarities to the truth, but it's false fruit from a rotten root. In my forty years of providing marriage counseling, I've found that misperceptions account for the greatest number of marital problems. Often, talking through these misunderstandings can resolve the believing couple's problems. But not always, since sin can cause great suspicion and guilt that can cripple a couple's trust of each other. So there needs to be a spiritual eye salve, and not anything the world provides. As Yeshua says to the lukewarm congregation at Laodicea, *"Because you say, 'I am rich, and have become wealthy, and have need of nothing,' and you do not know that you are wretched and miserable and poor and blind and naked, I advise you to buy from Me gold refined by fire so that you may become rich, and white garments so that you may clothe yourself, and that the shame of your nakedness will not be revealed; and eye salve to anoint your eyes so that you may see*" (Revelation 3:17–18).

The city of Laodicea had a famous medical school and exported a powder (called a "Phrygian powder") that was widely used as an eye salve. Though famous worldwide, their own salve won't help them. They need to come to the Messiah, so that, by applying His spiritual eye salve of grace repentance in His cleansing atonement, they may see what is eternally true and be spiritually fervent instead of lukewarm. This eye salve is the Good News of Messiah, which Paul was entrusted to proclaim, which is meant "*to open their eyes so that they may turn from darkness to light and from the dominion of Satan to God, that they may receive forgiveness of sins and an inheritance among those who have been sanctified by faith in Me*" (Acts 26:18). If your marital perspectives of each other are starting to dim, then be renewed together in Yeshua's forgiveness and blessing.

"*You will be like God.*" The phrase doesn't promise that Adam and Eve will be God, but that they will be "*like God*" (*k'Elohim*)—that is, similar to God. As noted earlier, this is not intrinsically a problem, for since we need to relate to Him as our Creator and represent Him to creation, in many ways God created us to be like Him, for God said, "*Let Us make man in Our image, according to Our likeness*" (1:26). However, in the absolute sense, no one can be like God, since God is God by nature, and we are His creatures, created according to God's will for us. We are like God in some ways, and yet we are quite different from Him in many other ways. Once again, the process of being like God is satanically defiled by disobedience. And then any such defiled likeness to God is a mere counterfeit and wholly ungodly in its application. And so, unredeemed marital love is reduced by sin to mere lust, which can only bring dissatisfaction in its application. The wickedly subtle enemy attempts to develop in humanity an unholy dissatisfaction with who we are, by saying we can be like God. Are you also dissatisfied with who you are? In your "opened eyes," are you too short? Too tall? Too smart? Too stupid? Too old? Too young? This is the result of the lie of the enemy that we have accepted and that makes us dissatisfied with ourselves and with others. Who you are in Messiah is all you need! Upon coming to faith in Messiah, we are taught that we are complete in Him (Colossians 2:10). That means that in Messiah you have all you need to be fully accepted by God and completely empowered to do everything God called you to do.

To run the whole race set before us in Messiah, there are many aspects that assume our spiritual maturity to fulfill our whole calling. Marriage is a calling from God, and Messianic couples need to spiritually mature in Yeshua to fulfill their marital calling. There will be many times when much more prayer will be needed, and times when much more forgiveness will be required. This maturing process is not to be dismissed, but rather embraced. And so, with Satan's temptation to be like God, we need to understand the ambition we need to have and the ambition we need to avoid. Simply put, all of Satan's ambitious designs necessitate disobedience to God. All of God's goals for us require faith-obedience to realize. Are believers to be ambitious? Of course! Paul writes, "*Therefore we also have as our ambition, whether at home or absent, to be pleasing to Him*" (2 Corinthians 5:9). God calls His people to be holy, as He Himself is holy (Leviticus 19:2; 1 Peter 1:15–16), and Yeshua reiterates this as, "*Therefore you are to be perfect, as your heavenly Father is perfect*" (Matthew 5:48), and "*Love one another, even as I have loved you*" (John 13:34–35). As we embrace our high calling by faith in Messiah, we will spiritually mature and thereby love others with God's love, and separate ourselves from that which displeases the Lord. But Satan's ploy offers an apparent shortcut through disobedience. There are no godly shortcuts. By faith in Messiah's atonement we are sanctified forever (Hebrews 10:10, 12, 14). Yet, though your spiritual position as His child is perfect in Yeshua, you still need to spiritually mature in practice into who you are called to be—a full-grown man or woman of God. This means abiding in Yeshua, running the race looking to Yeshua, faith-obedience in our daily lives, etc. And this is where marriage comes in as God's divine instrument for our growth and growing testimony. With most people, you can tolerate being around them before you go back to your personal agenda. Not with marriage. Marriage is 24/7/365. It is this marriage commitment that matures the believer in love, grace, mercy, forgiveness, and patience. As the Messianic man cleaves to his wife, he is nurturing and edifying her in the Word and prayer. This mortifies the flesh and builds up the family. As the Messianic wife submits to and respects her husband, she mortifies her own flesh and edifies her husband. This Messianic marriage now is maturely able to impact their congregation and community. This is how your circumstances, working together for good, conform the couple "*to the image of His Son*" (Romans 8:28–29). Husband and wife become more and more like God (that is, godly) in their character, attitudes, and lifestyle. Satan attacks this first marriage because the Messianic marriage is the means of God's love and grace, representing God and permeating society.

But sadly, by eating the forbidden fruit, Eve accepts Satan's shortcut. Like Satan's own evil and prideful desire, this temptation to be like God through disobedience corrupts people so thoroughly that the best of a ruined humanity cried out, "*Wretched man that I am! Who will set me free from the body of this death?*" (Romans 7:24). Satan ruins himself by desiring to be like the Most High, therefore he seeks to infect our first parents with the same desire, that he might ruin them too and have them join in his futile rebellion. All of us are made in the image and likeness of God, for the glory of God.[18] But if we leave God out of our married lives, or put Him in second place by living selfishly, we have become our own god,

---

18. Genesis 1:27; Romans 3:23; Isaiah 42:8; 1 Corinthians 10:31.

trusting in ourselves for our own sufficiency, security, and satisfaction. Perhaps not consciously or even intentionally, we have yielded to the temptation of Eve.

"*Knowing good and evil*" is the result of having their eyes opened and being like God. Once more, the mere knowledge of good and evil isn't wrong in and of itself—in fact God planned for us to have this knowledge—but in the right way, without shortcuts. God's way of obtaining wisdom is through consistent faith-obedience to His Word, as stated in Hebrews 5:14: "*But solid food is for the mature, who because of practice have their senses trained to discern good and evil.*" The word *practice* emphasizes the need for implementing the Word as part of our lifestyle. But when knowledge of good and evil is obtained by disobedience, it becomes wholly corrupted knowledge that will only fully corrupt humanity. This is why the prophet declares, "*And all our righteous deeds are like a filthy garment*" (Isaiah 64:6). Your righteous deeds are not so good when they are the fruit of a poisonous root.

Like money, authority, and other resources, knowledge is not something that in and of itself provides a positive benefit. Like all resources, it depends on what you do with it. And what you do with it will reveal the state of your soul. If you're selfish, any resource you have will merely reveal your selfishness, and the more of that resource you have, the more of your selfishness is revealed. Knowledge as a resource reveals your inner reality, whether it is corruption or purity. And the more you have, the more your inner self is revealed. You can't educate away unbelief. There are many people who go for religious training only to find themselves not only unchanged, but worse off than before. Ananias and Sapphira were a couple who heard the apostles' teaching like the others, but rather than helping them, knowledge only made their sinfulness more culpable (Acts 5:1–11). Some hear of the grace of God and are grateful to God and thereby gracious to others; but some hear of that same grace and think they can thereby sin with impunity. The unrepentant heart is not helped by knowledge, but is merely hardened in its waywardness. I live in North Carolina, and it gets quite warm in the summer. The same hot Carolina sun accomplishes two very different effects: it melts the wax, and it hardens the clay. So, too, the knowledge of Messiah is "*death unto death*" and "*life unto life*" (2 Corinthians 2:15–16 SN). "*This commandment, which was to result in life,*" Paul says, "*proved to result in death*" (Romans 7:10). It's not that the Torah is in any way sinful. Absolutely not! But sin, showing itself to be utterly sinful, made the Torah, which is good, to become an instrument of my condemnation because of my wretched sinful state. Why is something good or evil? God alone is good (Luke 18:19). Something is good or evil relative to God; He defines whatever is good as good. Anything that reflects His character is good; anything contrary to His character is evil. So, the knowledge of good and evil obtained by disobedience reveals sinful transgression, worthy of death, for now they will see that God is good, but that they are evil. "*Knowing good and evil*" through a disobedient action makes all the knowing a revelation of Adam and Eve's condemnation. Their condemnation is experienced as the guilt of sin and the dread of God, as they hide from Him in the garden (Genesis 3:7–8). Adam and Eve were always naked, but it was morally irrelevant in their pre-sin condition. With sin, they now know they are naked, and sin makes them self-conscious and guilty for their awareness. Therefore, they try to hide their nakedness with fig leaves (Genesis 3:7). The end doesn't justify the means. The married couple's knowledge of one another will only edify their souls if they are walking in the Spirit with a deep love for one another. A Messianic married couple must first in humble repentance commit to honor God with their lives and with all the resources at their disposal, rather than seek their own fulfillment and honor. This must occur before the Word, or any other resource, can bring the life and blessing to their relationship that God intends it to bring. The Messianic marriage requires the humble attitude of repentance to receive God's Word in God's way for the life it can bring. Arrogance will merely bring greater condemnation by that same Word. God's way of obtaining wisdom is through following His Word. Though Satan seeks to tempt you with disobedient shortcuts, God will bless your obedience to God's Word, as you use your resources of time, talent, and treasure all for His glory.

The couple's self-serving desires blind them to God's standard of obtaining knowledge and discernment His way, and are in direct opposition to His stated command. Learning to obey God's will takes training, time, and practice, but this is the Lord's way of teaching us true knowledge and discernment. Taking shortcuts to obtain wisdom is never a good idea.

In Genesis 3:1, we learned that (I.) we're confronted in our dedication to the Word. Marital relationships are defined by Scriptural commitment. In Genesis 3:2–5, we learned that (II.) we're compromised in our deficiency in the Word. Marital relationships are damaged by biblical confusion. Now we will learn that:

III. We're conquered in our disregard for the Word (3:6):
Marital relationships are destroyed by spiritual corruption.

> *When the woman saw that the tree was good for food,*
> *and that it was a delight to the eyes, and that the tree was desirable*
> *to make one wise, she took from its fruit and ate; and she gave also*
> *to her husband with her, and he ate.* (Genesis 3:6)

Principle: Our distrust of the Word will deceive us. Up to now, it was the serpent's denial of God's Word that deceived her; now it's her own distrust that will be her deception. Please note Eve's points of failure:

1. *Autonomous ego* ("*The woman saw*"): "I'll determine what is right for me." Self-deception is the worst form of deception. People will often say, "Well, I sincerely considered it for myself." True, but Scripture warns us of being

self-deceived by our own sincerity. "*Cursed is the man who trusts in mankind,*" for "*the heart is more deceitful than all else and is desperately sick; Who can understand it?*" (Jeremiah 17:5, 9). The world interprets Jeremiah by stating, "The road to hell is paved with good intentions!" King Solomon warned, "*There is a way which seems right to a man, but its end is the way of death*" (Proverbs 14:12). By disobeying God's Word, the married couple abandons themselves to their own godless destruction.

2. *Autonomous evaluation*: This refers to self-centered measurement. Genesis 3:6 is both descriptive and definitive on the corrupting process of sinful decision-making. Eve is merely a human representative of each of us. There are three aspects of her self-centered evaluation that cause her to disobey God: "*When the woman saw that the tree was good for food, and that it was a delight to the eyes, and that the tree was desirable to make one wise.*"

Because Eve foolishly gives ear to the tempter (even though her husband is standing with her!), she finds that his temptations arouse thoughts and feelings within her that she evaluates as personal requirements in order to be personally gratified, regardless of God's Word. The enemy attempts to have Eve identify herself with a wrong standard for her life: that is, to have her goals for her life measured by her perceived, or felt, needs. Her assessment that "*the tree was good for food*" is an attempt to address her fleshly lust. Is it wrong to eat? Of course not. The question is whether your appetite justifies eating whatever you want to appease your hunger. As we see in Genesis 2:16–17, God, as our Creator, is authorized to tell us what is appropriate food for humanity. To make a ludicrous illustration, cannibalism is wrong, not because people are inedible, but because God forbids us from eating other people. Even though in desperate situations some have done so, the necessity of a desperate situation emphasizes the prohibition, for the exception proves the rule. All the trees that God made are "*good for food*" to someone, except that God prohibited that one forbidden tree. That the forbidden fruit is good for food is not in question. But whether it is good for food for you in God's sight is another question. Sometimes an individual's appetite will misguide him to eat what is not right to eat. And for some, when it's wrong, an additional layer of sweetness is added to the eating. Solomon says, "*Stolen water is sweet; and bread eaten in secret is pleasant*" (Proverbs 9:17). Sin, like tasty poison, might at first taste good to you, but that doesn't mean it's good for you.

The biblical food laws (kashrut), as God's divine guidance for people, is disputed by some, but the dispute only highlights the question: What authority will you give God's Word for your lives and marriage? If you think your decisions are determined simply by what you see as "*good for food*" for you, then you will probably agree with Eve. Remember that in agreeing with Eve, you're disagreeing with God. How you evaluate life around you will define what you actually value and demonstrate by what values you truly live. Those who are God's redeemed people are called to follow God's redemptive Word in how they live and in their marriages. Admittedly, in the world, this is a minority opinion, but beware of following the world's values, for "*friendship with the world is hostility toward God*" (James 4:4).

Eve then realizes that the tree is "*a delight to the eyes,*" that is, the tree is visually desirable (*ta'avah*) to her. The root *avah* is "desire" or "want" in the positive sense, and "covet" or "lust" in the negative sense. Often, the thing you desire will reveal whether you have a godly desire (2 Samuel 3:21) or a wicked lust (Proverbs 21:10). What God provides, we should desire; but what God prohibits, we should never seek. When God made the garden of Eden, He "*caused to grow every tree that is pleasing to the sight and good for food*" (Genesis 2:9). So, all the trees in the garden were "*pleasing to the sight,*" including the forbidden tree. The word for "pleasing" (*chamad*) in the positive means "to be precious" (Proverbs 21:20), "delight" (Songs 2:3), or "desirable" (Psalm 19:10). In the negative, it means "to covet what's not yours" (Exodus 20:17). When you desire what God has prohibited, then that is the sin of covetousness. A neighbor's spouse may be good looking, but desire to have what is someone else's is coveting and condemned by God. The eye gate is here the instrument of sin, but it only reveals a heart that is already rebelling against God's command. This lust of the eye gate is the problem of many heroes of Scripture: Lot (Genesis 13:10), Samson (Judges 15:1–3), and David (2 Samuel 11:2). God warns us not to look upon the uncovered nakedness of anyone other than one's own spouse (Leviticus 18:6–18; 20:17–21). Thus, married couples need to beware of the wandering eye and dressing provocatively to get the attention of the opposite sex. Messiah warns us about the lust of the eyes: "*If your eye causes you to stumble, throw it out; it is better for you to enter the kingdom of God with one eye, than, having two eyes, to be cast into hell*" (Mark 9:47). But remember, it's not merely the eye—it's the rebellious, covetous heart that requires a deeper repentance and dedication to the Lord. We're reminded of this each week when we recite the V'ahavtah, "*These words, which I am commanding you today, shall be on your heart.... You shall bind them as a sign on your hand and they shall be as frontals on your forehead*" (Deuteronomy 6:5, 8). For the couple, it begins by committing the marriage to the Lord and accepting the maturing disciplines that help us to grow into that commitment.

One of the disciplines I placed on myself as a younger married man was to put a sign on the TV set that read, "*I will set no worthless thing before my eyes*" (Psalm 101:3). It helped somewhat, but I still needed to grow much stronger in my thought life. So, another verse I committed to memory and drew upon often was, "*We demolish arguments and every arrogance raised up against the knowledge of God, and we are taking every thought captive to the obedience of Messiah*" (2 Corinthians 10:5 SN). I attempted thereby to head off the covetousness of the eye gate by "*taking every thought captive to the obedience of Messiah.*" This is a lifelong discipline for every Messianic disciple. Those that say, "There's no harm in just looking" may be agreeing with Eve, but the looking is a covetous desire when God has forbidden it, and is just a step towards the disobedience and condemnation of sin. You may ask, "Can God forgive me?" Well, of course He can and does forgive you in Messiah's atonement. But do not commit the sin of presumption, committing sin while planning on His forgiveness. This will bring God's severe chastening, for it's a sin of presumption that is the mark of the lost hypocrite.[19]

There's a difference between your felt needs and your real needs. Your felt needs are what your flesh desires; your real needs are defined by God's Word for you. A small child may desire to eat candy for lunch, but the wise parent knows what's best for their small child. Not all felt needs are wrong. In some cases they're only wrong because of how you attempt to address them. We are all created to relate to others, and you may feel lonely. It is wrong to seek the company of evil-minded people, but right to seek the fellowship of God's people. Young adults who feel hormones exploding are wrong to address that felt need with premarital sex, but are right to seek a Messianic marriage relationship to address those genuine felt needs (1 Corinthians 7:9). Our felt needs wrongly addressed are demonstrated by Eve and biblically characterized as *"the lust of the flesh and the lust of the eyes and the boastful pride of life"* (1 John 2:16).

For us, there always seems to be an attitude of "what's in it for me," and the enemy will constantly try to exploit this attitude as a felt need, not your real need. Felt emotion, such as fear, insecurity, and feeling disrespected, are all a result of sin. Feeling fearful is common, but God's Word teaches that He has not given you a spirit of fear, but of love, power, and a sound mind (2 Timothy 1:7). Which are you going to believe? Human need is so profound we don't even know what our real need is. That is why your spouse will never be able to *fulfill* your real needs, but will only be able to *address* your real needs. Your real needs can only be met in Messiah, so do not look to your spouse for answers they cannot provide. This will only cause frustration and resentment for both people. That's how Sarah felt when Abraham was told that the promised child would come from his loins. Now she felt pressure to produce a child when that was the one thing she could not naturally do. So, her solution was Hagar (Genesis 16:1–5), despite the fact that Genesis 2:24 taught that God's plan was one husband and one wife. When stressed to produce what only God can produce, we're all likely to give in to a "Plan B" mentality: B immoral, B selfish, B disobedient. All of which only brings about unwanted long-term consequences, as in Ishmael. Only the Lord can meet our real needs; we can only address those needs in love and kindness.

As we can see, the lies of the enemy contain a strong but deceitful allure. First, Eve *identifies* with her own felt needs and her desire to be like God. Then she *evaluates* the situation by what seems right in her own eyes, and this proves to be her undoing.

---

19. Read Luke 12:45–48.

And so it goes with all of us! The apostle John saw Genesis 3:6 as the basis of all sin. He authoritatively interpreted that Scripture this way: *"For all that is in the world, the lust of the flesh* [good for food] *and the lust of the eyes* [a delight to the eyes] *and the boastful pride of life* [the tree was desirable to make one wise], *is not from the Father, but is from the world"* (1 John 2:16). Yes, *"the lust of the flesh and the lust of the eyes and the boastful pride of life"* describes the fundamental corruption of every human soul.

As humans, because sin has corrupted our understanding,[20] we tend to judge things inaccurately. However, it is said of Messiah in Isaiah 11:3–4, *"And He will delight in the fear of the* LORD, *and He will not judge by what His eyes see, nor make a decision by what His ears hear; but with righteousness He will judge the poor, and decide with fairness for the afflicted of the earth."* However, we frequently evaluate things with unrighteous judgment, in that we judge merely by what we perceive with our eyes and hearing, not as things actually are. Therefore, it is important in marriage not to assume "facts" that are not in evidence. For example, there is a big difference between asking your spouse why they sound upset, and assuming they are mad at you and going on the defensive.

Why do we act unrighteously? First, because of sin, our flesh rebels against the Word of God (Romans 8:5–8). Second, because we do not have the Word of God as foundational in our soul, we decide by our own self-centered reasoning. Once more, *"There is a way which seems right to a man, but its end is the way of death"* (Proverbs 14:12). Hebrews 5:11–14 teaches that we can *"become dull of hearing"* and can even remain in infancy, spiritually speaking. We may need to learn very basic things all over again and then learn to act upon them. Believers who are not reading, studying, and applying the Word to their life will find themselves in all kinds of immaturity-based trouble. They are not accustomed to *"the word of righteousness,"* so that, regardless of time and service, they are really spiritual infants. And this problem is double-trouble in any marriage where the Word of God is neither foundational nor followed. Couples can be religiously deceived if they're wedded in the Name of Messiah, but they're not also living to the glory of that Name by obeying His Word.

Hebrews 5:14 tells us that *"solid food is for the mature, who because of practice have their senses trained to discern good and evil."* How do you discern good and evil? It only comes by the Word of God. If we look at Eve, we need to understand why she was wrong. Her error had its beginnings in her inaccurate knowledge of the Word of God, followed by her disobedience to it. She did not see the value of the Word's protection, so she evaluated the situation based on her felt need, which was the lust of the flesh, the lust of the eyes, and the pride of life. She lacked spiritual discernment. Do you?

---

20. Ephesians 4:17–19.

"She took from its fruit and ate; and she gave also to her husband with her, and he ate." This leads us to the matter of dedication—what do we mean by dedication? What happens next has a certain kind of logic. Rather than seeking her husband for counsel on the matter, she decides for herself. She is now sinfully smarter than he is, because she is first to eat from the forbidden fruit of the knowledge of good and evil. Initially, she has a knowledge he does not have, and therefore, she is able to get him to eat from it also. She assumes the leadership in the home, and he submits to her authority. What we have now is role reversal, and instead of submission of the wife to the loving authority of her husband, it now becomes a game of one-upmanship ever after. Even today, the home is frequently a battleground between a woman's sense of insecurity and her husband's sense of inadequacy.

Eve's failure is seen in her lack of dedication to her husband's leadership. Adam's failure is seen in his lack of dedication to God. He decides that unity with his wife is more important than God's command. The text states that after she eats, *"she gave also to her husband with her, and he ate."* Though Adam is there with her, he keeps silent while his wife is being manipulated by the enemy.[21] His lack of dedication to God is seen in his abdication of leadership responsibility in the marriage. Does he not know how to protect his wife and family from wrong spiritual influences? Or does he foolishly think that she can make her own decisions? Whatever the case may be, it is essential for a husband to be properly discipled on his spiritual leadership responsibilities in the home. *"And he ate."* Her problem was deception. His problem was defiance, for he had heard from God and knew what God expected from him. So, they ended up with a unity that is likened to Ananias and Sapphira in Acts 5—they had unity in sin, not unity in righteousness. Ananias and Sapphira agree together to say one thing and do another. They promise to give all their funds to the Lord, but hold back a portion for themselves. It's not uncommon for individuals or couples to want to appear more dedicated than they are. Their hypocrisy is declared to be lying to the Holy Spirit (Acts 5:3).[22] Hypocrisy and lies are the same thing. Marital unity only provides value if it is in the righteousness that comes from *"speaking the truth in love"* (Ephesians 4:15)!

Sadly, these three corruptions totally corrupted all people. We learn in Scripture that we are each made up of three aspects: body, soul, and spirit.[23] Our body has been corrupted by *"the lust of the flesh."* Our soul has been corrupted by *"the lust of the eyes."* Our spirit has been corrupted by *"the pride of life."* Paul would therefore declare, *"there is no good thing in my flesh!"* (Romans 7:18 SN). Our spirit

---

21. See another instance of the disastrous effects of the leader of a family (Jacob!) keeping silent, in Genesis 34:5. Where proper authority underreacts, improper authority will overreact. See too the husband's responsibility to say something when a wife makes a vow (Numbers 30).
22. First John 2:21: *"Because no lie is of the truth."* Indeed, those who lie to themselves and others are following Satan, *"the father of lies"* (John 8:44), and are in spiritual conflict with the Holy Spirit.
23. As detailed in 1 Thessalonians 5:23.

is where we fellowship with God; but that's corrupted. Our soul includes our intellectual self (our thoughts), emotional self (our feelings), and volitional self (our will), all corrupted and useless for God's purposes. The same sad state of affairs is true for your spouse and for yourself. But there is Good News! When Messiah came, Yeshua defeated Satan in the same three areas that Eve failed: body, soul, and spirit. Though He had a human body like yours, and could therefore be tested in each area like you can be tested, Yeshua gained the victory by total dependence upon God and obedient reliance upon the Word.[24] In your marriage and home you can have the same victory in Yeshua's grace and power. But only by abiding in Yeshua as a Messianic married couple will you both experience what it means to be more than conquerors through Him who loved you.[25] Otherwise, as with Adam and Eve, whose disobedience brought sin, death, and judgment into the world,[26] our disobedience to Adonai will bring sin, death, and judgment into the home. Sin means corrupted and corrupting lives; death means separation from each other; judgment means the Lord will chasten the disobedient home unless there is repentance and faith-obedience by the married couple. Repent quickly in Messiah!

We need to understand from this tragic passage that God did not create marriage to fulfill our lives; rather, as we learned earlier in our study, marriage is a calling to represent Him faithfully to all of creation. You can never find true fulfillment in your spouse! Your real needs can only be met in the Messiah. You can then minister grace to your spouse, and your marriage testifies to that saving grace. Adam and Eve learn this the hard way. It is vital for us to understand all the steps that lead to their demise: taking counsel from the wrong source, doubt of God's goodness, not obeying God's Word but instead leaning to their own understanding. These are all contributing factors to their debacle. Now, as we look at the consequences, let us always bear in mind God's ultimate plan is to redeem the failing marriage. Yes, a marriage can indeed learn from disaster!

The Condition of Marital Collapse

Then the eyes of both of them were opened, and they knew that they were naked; and they sewed fig leaves together and made themselves loin coverings. They heard the sound of the LORD God walking in the garden in the cool of the day, and the man and his wife hid themselves from the presence of the LORD God among the trees of the garden. Then the LORD God called to the man, and said to him, "Where are you?" He said, "I heard the sound of You in the garden, and I was afraid because I was naked; so I hid myself." And He said, "Who told you that

---

24. See Matthew 4:1–11.
25. Romans 8:37.
26. Romans 5:12–14.

you were naked? Have you eaten from the tree of which I commanded you not to eat?" The man said, "The woman whom You gave to be with me, she gave me from the tree, and I ate." Then the LORD *God said to the woman, "What is this you have done?" And the woman said, "The serpent deceived me, and I ate."* (Genesis 3:7–13)

This passage shows the dead condition of the disobedient marriage.

Our dead condition observed

    I.   The death of our open communication (3:7–9): Humanity needs redemptive leadership.

    II. The death of our obedient supervision (3:10–11a): Humanity needs righteous discipleship.

    III. The death of our original appreciation (3:11b–13): Humanity needs responsible fellowship.

At the end of Chapter 2, we saw that there was perfect communication between Adam and Eve. However, this was the first thing to go after *"the eyes of both of them were opened."*

Sin has us concealing from our spouse, 3:7

The first casualty of the couple's sin is the loss of communication between them, and from that further distrust develops. Their eyes are opened, but this is not always a good thing in Scripture, particularly when they are opened too late, as will be the case for those that die in unbelief and only realize too late the horror of their future existence.[27] Chapter 3 verse 7 states: *"Then the eyes of both of them were opened, and they knew that they were naked; and they sewed fig leaves together and made themselves loin coverings."* Suddenly they know they are naked, revealing their feelings of guilt and exposure. They have been naked all along, but now sin produces a self-consciousness about their bodies, and they now see being naked as being vulnerable. So, they hide from one another by covering themselves with fig leaves. Being naked is not a sin, but now they have feelings of guilt that they act upon. At the end of Genesis Chapter 2 (and before sin entered their lives), the Bible says that they were *"naked and were not ashamed,"* but now open communication is lost, and with it, the openness and acceptance of each other is lost as well. They have knowledge of what is natural, but now they become neurotic by the corruption of sin. This neurosis stems from living in the guilt and trauma of their past sin and applying it to the present situation. They evaluate their nakedness that is morally neutral as morally wrong. They become judgmental of themselves and threatened by others, even their own spouse.

---

27. Luke 16:23: *"In Hades he lifted up his eyes, being in torment, and saw Abraham far away and Lazarus in his bosom."*

Sin makes natural nakedness both a threat and a shame. Sin now produces impure motives and covetousness. We're not to be ashamed of the body unless it is a tool of sin and not of righteousness (Romans 6:13). Nakedness is now a danger because of unbridled lust. Being unashamed of one's own body doesn't mean that nakedness is to be permitted, because of the lust of others. Thus, nakedness before anyone but your spouse can be a point of condemnation in Torah, prohibited as well in the New Covenant.[28]

The fig-leaf cover-up is ironic on two grounds: leaves in Scripture are symbolic of testimony,[29] but here the testimony is one of fear and unbelief. Furthermore, in sewing fig leaves, we see the first human industry—making loincloths from fig leaves—prefiguring all the other industries that will attempt to avoid responsibility, cover-up offenses, and escape reality (e.g., false religion, drug culture). The great difference between the righteous and the unrighteous is not in how good a life they live (for all have sinned), but whether they cover up or confess their sins to the Lord.[30] The answer to restoration of their marriage, or any sin-broken relationship, is never covering up—it is confession, acceptance, and forgiveness. Both spouses need to confess their guilt to God and to each other, accept His grace, and forgive each other. Instead, Adam and Eve become distrustful of one another. The principle is just as true today as it was then. To the degree that you lack openness with your spouse, distrust will develop. When a marriage relationship fails, it is from a lack of total openness and appreciation of each other.

As counterintuitive as it may seem, drawing near to God in our weaknesses is where we find grace for ourselves, and where we also find unity in the marriage! Unity in marriage is never found in hiding, denying, and judging one another. It is found by acknowledging our sin to one another and to God, and by forgiving one another. In order to have good communication, there has to be restoration by admission—in other words, we must confess our sins to God and to each other. Good communication occurs with repentance of our sin and openness to God. In the Greek, "to confess" (*homologeo*) your sin means to agree with God that it's wrong, and as wrong as He says it is.

Do you have a fig-leaf marriage—that is, a marriage that is secretive, suspicious, and distant? The remedy for restoration is confession, acceptance, and forgiveness. Because of the human condition and the residual effects of sin, these problems can occur at any time. But the remedy in our Redeemer is available and to be applied whenever we're tempted to use fig leaves to protect ourselves from our spouse.

---

28. Leviticus 20:11–21; 1 Thessalonians 4:3–7.
29. Psalm 1:3; Proverbs 11:28; Jeremiah 17:8. However, when there is leaf and no fruit, it's condemned as a false testimony, Mark 11:13.
30. Job 31:33: *"Have I covered my transgressions like Adam, by hiding my iniquity in my bosom?"*

Sin has us hiding from our God, 3:8–10

As we shall see, Adam and Eve's lack of openness with each other reveals their lack of openness with God. Later in this section, HaShem has to drag the confession out of their throats before marital restoration can begin.

The next Scriptural expression of their sin is to hide from God. "*They heard the sound of the LORD God walking in the garden in the cool of the day, and the man and his wife hid themselves from the presence of the LORD God among the trees of the garden*" (Genesis 3:8). Not only are Adam and Eve trying to hide from each other, they are also attempting to hide from God! The absurdity of attempting to hide from the omniscient God is an apt illustration of sin. Sin is stupid, absurd, and foolish and only makes sense from within the mindset of anxiety and fear. Rightly has the psalmist asked, "*Where can I go from Your Spirit? Or where can I flee from Your presence?*" (Psalm 139:7). And the prophet reiterates the matter: "'*Can a man hide himself in hiding places so I do not see him?' declares the LORD. 'Do I not fill the heavens and the earth?' declares the LORD*" (Jeremiah 23:24). Because of our fear of people, we learn to wear masks (if not fig leaves). With God, this is not only absurd but unnecessary because of His love and concern for His sin-damaged children.

Why is God walking in the garden? Recall that this is now Shabbat, and it is never supposed to end. There was no evening and morning on the seventh day as found in the other six days of creation. What's implied is that we were created for endless relationship and fellowship with God. God is seeking fellowship with humanity.[31] Shabbat orients us around our developing relationship with our Creator and Redeemer. Even for God, relationships with people take time to develop. But fellowship with God assumes a holy people,[32] for sin separates us from Him.[33] For humanity, our Shabbat rest ended that day, but not for God. It is this rest that He freely offers in Messiah, who declared, "*Come to Me, all who are weary and heavy-laden, and I will give you rest!*" (Matthew 11:28).

Verse 9 tells us, "*Then the LORD God called to the man, and said to him, 'Where are you?'*" He called to the man, since Adam is the leader. But has not Eve assumed the leadership role? Yes, but despite what humanity asserts, God still holds the man responsible for the family. Even in your homes, you may allow your wife to lead, but God still holds the husband responsible. Verse 9 is the first question from God in the Bible.[34]

---

31. Leviticus 26:12: "*I will also walk among you and be your God, and you shall be My people.*"
32. Deuteronomy 23:14: "*Since the LORD your God walks in the midst of your camp to deliver you and to defeat your enemies before you, therefore your camp must be holy; and He must not see anything indecent among you or He will turn away from you.*"
33. Isaiah 59:1–2.
34. Genesis 3:11; 4:9; 16:8; 18:9; Exodus 4:2, Isaiah 6:8, etc.

There's much to love about the Lord in how He manages this disaster.

1. *I love His timing*: God comes to them after they are covered in their fig leaves, so they will not be further humiliated by their weakened conscience.
2. *I love His "sound"*: He allows His sound to announce His approach, so in their weakened state they will not be overwhelmed by His presence.
3. *I love His style of questions*: Though rhetorical—since the all-knowing God knows their whereabouts—He asks open-ended questions 1) to encourage dialogue within the parameters of a relationship, and 2) so that they will understand that if He wanted to harm or condemn them He would not ask a question, but 3) this gives them a chance to admit their failure (repentance), and 4) for their healing to take place they must again relate to God, even as they interact with Him.

They sinned and are now spiritually dead to God! Yet God seeks to raise the dead, for He has planned His sacrificial provision for sin in order to redeem the sinner. By that same grace, your marriage can be revived. As a spouse, ask inviting questions rather than making accusatory statements. Remember that the believer's role is always to be restorative. This is summarized in Galatians 6:1 (SN): *"Brothers and sisters, if a person is discovered in some sin, you who are spiritual restore such a person in a spirit of gentleness. Pay close attention to yourselves, so that you are not tempted too."*

When your spouse does anything contrary to God's Word, always seek to restore with a gentle attitude, being especially careful not to be tempted to think yourself better than your spouse. Godliness is being like God. So, open-ended questions will develop healthier discussions, and bring about redemptive interaction that provides healing for the marriage.

"Where are you?" Do you think God does not know where Adam is? God knows everything. So, if God knows everything, why does He raise the question? He asks for Adam's sake, because by hiding, Adam is not where he is supposed to be. A question necessitates a response from Adam: "I'm here and I'm hiding." The same question rings forth from God today: Where are you? Where is your marriage? Is it hiding from God? God is seeking you and your marriage to cleanse and forgive. Will you respond? Messiah taught us that this was His purpose, *"For the Son of Man has come to seek and to save that which was lost!"* (Luke 19:10).

Adam's answer in verse 10 is evasive and revealing at the same time: *"He [Adam] said, 'I heard the sound of You in the garden, and I was afraid because I was naked; so I hid myself.'"* You can see from this verse a phobia developing as a result of sin. We can be sure the issue is not Adam's nakedness—it is rather his feeling of vulnerability and the fear of judgment. Adam's response contains the first-person pronoun "I" four times. This may be thought of as a simple response to God's question, but without any *we* included, the answer shows that marital unity is gone. Every man for himself! Sin makes one self-centered, which is a change of values—and thus his self-justifying evaluation.

There are three sinful values that are revealed in Adam's response.

1. *The dread of self-concern*: "*I was afraid.*" Adam doesn't say, "I was concerned for Eve." He does not answer the rhetorical question of *where* he is hiding, but the unasked question of *why* he is hiding. Adam now attempts to justify himself. Sin lives in dread of God, for it fears punishment (1 John 4:18). After all, God did warn him that the day he ate of it he would die (Genesis 2:16–17). We find the first emotion from sin: guilt-producing fear. Sin interprets God's warnings of love as threats. Adam and Eve hide from each other with fig leaves, but they hide from God with a forest! They hide because of fear. His fear-induced fight-or-flight reaction is an immediate result of sin. Fear of what? Fear of death entered the human psyche. The knowledge of good and evil gained from sin causes not the means to victory and success, but the realization of defeat, and fear of punishment. In marriage, fear is not uncommon—fear of displeasing your spouse, fear of losing your spouse, etc. Though it's not uncommon, it is also not of God. Scripture explicitly states, "*For God has not given us a spirit of fear, but of power, love and a sound mind*" (2 Timothy 1:7 SN). When fear rears its ugly head, go immediately to God for the assurance of His love that He desires you to have, for His "*perfect love casts out fear*" (1 John 4:18).[35] God's love will refocus their fear into reverence for God, which is "*the fear of the LORD*" that "*is the beginning of wisdom*" (Psalm 111:10). God's love is the restarting place for any relationship.

2. *The deception of self-consciousness*: "*I was naked.*" Though some may call this modesty,[36] his fear reveals that Adam is feeling his utter vulnerability. But what is Adam confessing as to why they are hiding? "I was afraid at your sound because I am naked." This is a desperate and absurd confession. After all, what command does Adam think he has broken—as if God is going to punish them because he broke the "no shoes, no shirt, no service" law? He confesses fear of punishment rather than shame of sin. Though Adam's fig leaves cover him somewhat, they still leave him feeling naked before God. What may have eased his fears before Eve is no help whatsoever when facing the living God. He feels naked, since his sin is exposed and cannot be covered up with mere fig leaves. Though a

---

35. The danger of fear is addressed quite often in Scripture, which should be a constant reminder never to allow it to rule our hearts or homes. Romans 8:15: "*For you have not received a spirit of slavery leading to fear again, but you have received a spirit of adoption as sons by which we cry out, 'Abba! Father!'*" Hebrews 2:15: "*...and might free those who through fear of death were subject to slavery all their lives.*" First John 4:18: "*There is no fear in love; but perfect love casts out fear, because fear involves punishment, and the one who fears is not perfected in love.*"
36. Abarbanel, Bereshis, Vol. 1a, p.124, Mesorah, Artscoll Tanach Series.

spouse may attempt to cover vulnerable areas (with lies, anger, evasion, drugs, etc.), sin is as exposed to God as a neon-flashing billboard.[37] We have no secrets before God.

3. *The decision for self-protection*: "*I hid.*" Notice Adam's thinking process to justify hiding from God. Adam says, "I hid because I was afraid, and I was afraid because I was naked." With sin now corrupting his thinking, Adam thinks that his real problem that justifies hiding from God is his nakedness, as if his fear of vulnerability would be addressed by hiding from God. Sin has already so completely corrupted his thinking with fear that he just gives lame excuses. Before eating from the forbidden tree, Adam was naked and felt no fear or vulnerability. He says all this nonsense rather than admit the real problem: sinful disobedience to God. The painful truth is that his flesh is now in charge of his thinking. He is trying to rationalize sinful behavior by what sounds reasonable only to the fleshly mind. What could Adam understand now about why God gave the command? Did Adam think that God didn't want him to eat from the tree because it would make him *feel* naked, or that it would *reveal* him as naked? All sin-acquired knowledge made him stupid, not wise. All sin-acquired wealth makes you poor, not rich.[38] Sin-acquired fame makes you lonelier, not popular. Sin diminishes your potential and does not enrich your life. Who Adam is has not changed, but his perspective is skewered. He now sees his nakedness as a deficiency, a negative, an inadequacy, and a threatening vulnerability. Fig leaves seem better than nothing, like a drowning man grasping at straws. Sin so perverts his mind that his life now seems desperate, and his God now seems a threat to him. Similarly, David sought to use Goliath's sword,[39] feigned madness,[40] lusted after a woman and killed her husband,[41] and was a terrible, guilt-ridden father.[42] So also, Jacob lied to his father and brother[43] and kept silent when he should have spoken up.[44] Peter desperately boasted that he would never forsake Yeshua[45] and then even more desperately denied his Lord[46] and played the hypocrite before Paul.[47] These examples emphasize the sin-motivated desperation

---

37. Hebrews 4:13: "*And there is no creature hidden from His sight, but all things are open and laid bare to the eyes of Him with whom we have to do.*"
38. Read Haggai 1:2–6 and Revelation 3:15–18.
39. First Samuel 21:9.
40. First Samuel 21:13; Psalm 34: title.
41. Second Samuel 11.
42. Second Samuel 13–18.
43. Genesis 27; 33:12–17.
44. Genesis 34:5.
45. Matthew 26:35.
46. Matthew 26:70–75.
47. Galatians 2:11–14.

that brings both the married and single to hide behind lies, swords, and lust. Are you hiding from God, or in God? Is sin, or God, your hiding place? God so wants to be![48]

For Adam, there is a confusion of values: between hating the facts of sin and hating the results of sin. Humanity sees sin as a problem because of its results, as if the fear, shame, exposure, guilt, and judgment are the real problems of sin. In which case, hiding is some sort of inept remedy to avoid the sin's consequences. We are not guilty for feeling pain, shame, and fear; these are the resulting conditions and the mere symptoms of the sin that should indicate to us that we need to repent. What humanity wants healing for or an escape from are these resulting conditions (fear, shame, etc.). A woman may ask, "I'm depressed that my boyfriend left after he said he loved me and made a baby with me. What do I do for my depression?" My response: "Repent of being emotionally entangled with someone who is not a man of God and of having sex outside marriage. Accept His forgiveness for you in Messiah's atonement. Then raise the child by the grace of God to the glory of God. The problem for you to resolve is not the depression, but the sins that separated you from God. The depression is a symptom that should warn you to return to the Lord."

God then asks two more questions of Adam in verse 11. The first is, "*Who told you that you were naked?*" A very interesting question! This is not intrinsic knowledge, for Adam was naked before without fear or shame, and now the same naked condition causes fear and shame. His perspective, and not his circumstances, have changed. Those who are Spirit-led and those who are sin-led are easily distinguished by seeing whose counsel they follow. Who has been informing you? Who informed you that you're naked and that "naked" is your real problem? Who's your teacher? Who told you that you are stupid, ugly, lazy, etc.? Was it your dad, mom, friends, first traumatizing boss? You are who God says you are, not what others say you are. In other words, where are you getting your information from? That's who you trust to protect you with their counsel. Some trust that their fears are better protection than their faith. Sin will always be seen in what we act on, whether it be anger, fear, frustration, or whatever. The answer to God's question to Adam is, of course, sin! It was sin that told Adam he is now vulnerable and needs the protection of fig leaves. Adam only compounds his sin by trying to deflect God's question with his nakedness rather than deal with the real issue of his disobedience.

When it comes to making judgment calls, you can only judge what is within your stewardship responsibilities, and that judgment should be objective and not

---

48. Psalm 32:7: "*You are my hiding place; You preserve me from trouble; You surround me with songs of deliverance.*" Psalm 119:114: "*You are my hiding place and my shield; I wait for Your word.*" Colossians 3:3–4 (SN): "*For you have died, and your life is hidden with the Messiah in God. When the Messiah, who is our life, appears, then you too will appear with Him in glory!*"

subjective.[49] For example, you can judge whether your child has washed their hands. On the other hand, why tell someone they're inadequate just because they disappoint you?[50] This first question from God reveals God's understanding that Adam's awareness of his nakedness is a result of sinful disobedience, which God's next question will then pinpoint.

God's next question to Adam

God's next question in verse 11 is, "*Have you eaten from the tree of which I commanded you not to eat?*" You would think a simple yes-or-no answer would suffice. Simple remedy: Confess quickly, and draw near in Messiah! But sin does not act this way, as we shall see. What is God doing with this question? He wants Adam to recognize the source of his fears: disobedience. God is love. God lovingly seeks to surface your sin so it can be remedied, just as a doctor's x-ray reveals a medical condition that needs to be cured. There is no way for you to feel guilt, fear, and shame other than by disobedience. If you had not eaten you would not feel ashamed, afraid, and guilty. He is seeking what from Adam? He seeks simple recognition of wrong-doing on Adam's part, so that repentance and apology can follow. Repentance brings about restoration of relationship. Sin and disobedience are not a marriage's real problem, for God has a remedy for sin, which is Messiah's atonement. The real problem is not acknowledging your sins as sins. What does God want from you? He wants your straightforward repentance, and He wants you to seek His mercy. Because all have sinned and fallen short of God's glory (Romans 3:23), we all need the same atonement, forgiveness, and mercy. None of us is in an exalted position to look down our noses at our spouse's failures. Every Messianic marriage between two mere mortals assumes there will be the need for much forgiveness for the marriage to become healthy and continue forward. With Adam and Eve's marriage, it would take a bit more divine ministry to bring them both to accept His simple remedy.

The Blame Game, 3:12–13: the evident loss of appreciation

> *"The woman whom You gave to be with me,*
> *she gave me from the tree, and I ate."* (Genesis 3:12)

The foundations of marriage in Genesis 2:23–25 are based upon three elements: *appreciation* (2:23), *unity* (2:24), and *communication* (2:25). Sin has effectively destroyed all three elements. The fully open communication between them is lost once they use fig leaves to hide from each other (v. 7). Adam's self-justification

---

49. Paul gives great advice about judgment calls in 1 Corinthians 4:3–5. In short, your judgment of me tells me more about you than it tells me about me. That is, your judgment tells me about your values by how you evaluate and thereby validate or don't validate. This info about what you value helps me to better understand you, without it meaning much, if anything, about me.

50. Judgment on another's character shifts the focus away from your own feelings of inadequacy and unworthiness.

demonstrates the loss of his initiative to maintain unity in the marriage (v. 10). Now we see why the other two foundations are lost, for Adam's appreciation of his wife is lost by their sin (v. 12). What he once appreciated as God's blessing for his life he now blames as the cause of the failure of his life. Once our appreciation is lost, there seems to be very little reason to maintain unity, expressed through open communication.

When God asks Adam if he ate of the tree, the entire scene deteriorates. Again, a simple yes or no is all that is required, but Adam's response is to promptly blame Eve *and* God at the same time! "*The woman whom YOU gave to be with me, she gave me from the tree and I ate.*" She is now "*the woman*" and no longer "my wife" (2:24–25).

Adam blames Eve, and worse, he blames God for making a poor personnel decision! Adam's response in this section is a complete reversal of his original reaction to Eve in Genesis 2:23 ("Wow, she's perfect for me!"). But sin has now corrupted their relationship into a blame game.

Now there's a not-too-subtle accusation against God as Adam blames his wife, with the words, "*The woman whom You gave to be with me.*" Lack of appreciation of God is what causes a lack of appreciation of God's gift. Adam's lack of appreciation of God leads to a separation from God that will bear sinful fruit in his other close relationships, especially with his wife. Just as our total dependence upon Messiah produces total interdependence on each other,[51] so sin against God divides us from Him and then leads to sin against each other, which divides our marriages. We must first restore our relationship with the Lord by His grace through our faith. That enables us to restore our relationships with our spouses. For, apart from Him we "*can do nothing*" (John 15:5).

Throwing our spouse "under the bus," as Adam did, is another symptom of sinful guilt that should bring us to quickly repent. Acting on our feelings of guilt and blaming others is sin's self-justifying disguise. Adam is deceived by sin into believing that Eve is guiltier than himself. As head of the home, God holds him responsible, and this disaster will be forever known as "*the offense of Adam*" (see Romans 5:12–21). Sin makes you defensive, and you switch from flight to fight. Rats run until they're cornered.

Because of Adam and Eve's sin, a sin-caused glitch in the human condition now works in their souls and will be passed on to all humanity. It will remain until the Lord either calls us home or returns. Along with physical DNA, God created us with a spiritual DNA that reveals that we're created in God's image as we represent Him to His creation. But with the impact of sin, our spiritual DNA is corrupted, and we now misrepresent Him, even in our marriages.

---

51. As Paul demonstrates in Ephesians 4:15–16.

From this time forward, the glitch in the human condition will be played out in the courtroom of the mind, the heart, and the soul. Paul speaks of this condition in Romans 2:15: "*They show the work of the Law [Torah] written in their hearts, their conscience bearing witness and their thoughts alternately accusing or else defending them.*"

What does that mean? In Adam and Eve's case, that mitzvah—that one command they received—now shines a light on where they fell short! When people say they want to "follow Torah" they are unwittingly asking for trouble. For whether it's one mitzvah or a whole Torah full of mitzvot, we require total reliance on the Lord to fulfill any of them. The more you try to follow Torah apart from the Lord, the more sin you will see in yourself.[52] The Torah was not given to declare you righteous; it cannot do that because it is the holy standard of God. It was meant to show us our inability to meet God's standard, and our need for humility, so that we will come to Him for grace and mercy and be led to hope in Messiah.[53] Slowly but surely we learn to love one another and mind whom we talk to, and what we are to properly do with our lives.

So now we have this courtroom always going on in our minds, and we must beware of thinking that knowing more Torah somehow makes us more righteous; it will only make us guiltier! And God holds us accountable for what we know. "*From everyone who has been given much, much will be required*" (Luke 12:48). We should always desire to know more of God's Word—not so we can feel better about ourselves, but to better understand His mercy and grace and thereby grow into the things we learn. For we all need His grace to grow into His knowledge, which is why Peter writes, "*But grow in the grace and knowledge of our Lord*" (2 Peter 3:18). We can understand our spouses only by God's grace. Let us not abide apart from Him, for our acceptance of ourselves and of our spouses is found only in Him.[54]

As we have noted previously, God made us all different from each other, and not only as male and female. Because of sin, those differences have now become wrong and threatening in our sinful eyes. When God made male and female, He gave us basic similarities ("*bone of my bones, and flesh of my flesh*"), but He also engineered differences ("*because she was taken out of Man*"). Similarity and dissimilarity—that's all there is, and opposites attract. Whoever you marry will bring out aspects of yourself opposite to him or her. Along with this, we are gifted with an amazing ability to adapt. Paul speaks of Adam as the one from whom all the endless varieties and ethnic groups sprang. Differences and diversity are a joy to the Lord, since true unity is based upon our dependence on Him, and not our gender or ethnicity.

---

52. Romans 7:7–24.
53. As Paul taught in Galatians 3:19–24.
54. Ephesians 1:6; Romans 15:7.

Couples often blame their differences for the problems in their marriages (i.e., incompatibility). But this is only the case if you are walking in the flesh. Our flesh makes us contrary and competitive. But as God designed marriage, walking in the Spirit makes us compatible and complementary to each other. That is how God intended it to be. If you are walking in the Spirit, your spouse's differences are intended to enrich your life, even as you see life through your beloved's eyes. Otherwise, the differences will irritate you and then alienate you if there is no repentance. As we love one another, the Holy Spirit brings about unity, not uniformity. We all see life differently. Love allows you the freedom of seeing the world through someone else's eyes without feeling threatened.

Through this section of Scripture we see that the very differences Adam appreciated about Eve in chapter 2, he now blames her for in chapter 3. He not only blames her, he blames God. When you find yourself blaming your spouse, you need to realize you are really blaming God, for He brought you together. When you appreciate the gift, you also appreciate the Giver. When you despise the gift, you despise the Giver. A shaky marriage is a consequence of being out of fellowship with God, so you need to examine your own walk with the Lord before you go blaming your spouse.

The sin of ingratitude is now fully displayed: "*You gave…she gave…I ate.*" It's as if Adam is saying, "It's really God's fault for giving me a 'gift' that is defective. Besides, once she ate, she had a wisdom I didn't have, and was thereby able to get me to eat. It's not my fault; don't blame me." With this same mentality we can always say to God, "It's Your fault for giving me the ability to go on the Internet and watch porn." Sin either accuses or excuses, but it is always resistance to God.

God does not rebuke Adam for his disrespect and implied blame of God. God accepts responsibility for His universe. When Moses complains that God made him with an inability to accomplish the work that God called him to do, rather than rebuke Moses for such a complaint, God admits that He makes men "*mute or deaf, or seeing or blind*" (Exodus 4:10–11). God assumes His grace alone is our sufficiency.

Though it is wrong to judge your Creator, still He takes responsibility for your frailty, since He created you not to be all powerful in yourself but to depend on His grace as your sufficiency. His "*power is perfected in weakness*" (2 Corinthians 12:9)! Perhaps you ask God, "Why did You make the universe this way?" It is created for His plan to show His grace as sufficient—not for your agenda, nor to allow you not to need God! His grace alone is sufficient for your marriage as well, and your spouse's weaknesses are intended to prove that every day. So, look to God to fulfill your life, not your spouse. When you look to the Lord, even your spouse can be God's instrument of grace and blessing for your life and home.

Adam concludes with, "*And I ate.*" God accepts this as an admission of guilt, since He no longer asks anything of Adam. But is this sufficient for repentance? Wouldn't the rationalizations by Adam disqualify this as his confession? No, Adam's weakness because of sin made it almost impossible for him to say anything that would be a pure confession of unqualified repentance. For, he may not have been aware of sin's awful impact and the depth of his own depravity. But God accepts "*and I ate*" as an admission in repentance, as weak as it might be. God does not ask us to jump through hoops to walk with Him. He knows how dreadfully weak we truly are, and He accepts the simplest admission as sufficient repentance, because the basis of His forgiveness is in Messiah's perfect sacrifice, not in your (even the most perfect imaginable) repentance. Like Adam, we're all unaware of the awful depravity of our soul. Only in heaven will we know as we "*have been fully known*" (1 Corinthians 13:12). How easily do you accept your spouse's apology? Do you make them show some high degree of absolute remorse? No one's apology or repentance will ever be equal to the pain the offense has caused. God accepts your simplest confession and admission of fault as perfect repentance because of Messiah's death in your place. His death alone can fully pay for, cleanse, and heal the awful impact of our offenses against God, others, and even ourselves. How dare any of us expect more from fellow sinners, and especially from our beloved spouses! His great desire to reconcile with us compels Him to accept any admission by us and to fully pardon us in light of Messiah's perfect salvation. As we mature spiritually, our repentance will become much deeper, as Yeshua must increase and we must decrease (John 3:30).

Before responding to Adam, "*the LORD God*" turns His attention to Eve, and says to the woman, "*What is this you have done?*" The woman responds, "*The serpent deceived me, and I ate*" (v. 13).

Though she impersonally speaks of Him as "God" in verse 3, He speaks to her relative to His covenant relationship to her, as HaShem. Your lack of love for God does not reflect upon God; He still loves you with an everlasting love,[55] and His proof of His eternal love for you is Yeshua.[56]

These are the first recorded words of God directed to the woman. That God speaks to women as well as men should not be ignored. In marriage, our relationship to each other is contingent on each of us first having a personal and intimate relationship with God. He addresses her as responsible for her own deeds. Though God created them equal to each other, she is functionally subordinate to her husband as his helpmeet from God (which is her calling in life). But she is counted by God as an equal in her responsibilities, for what she does as Adam's helpmeet she does as God's provision for Adam's life. She is called on the carpet for her own actions, for which she is responsible before God, not Adam.

---

55. Jeremiah 31:3.
56. John 3:16; Romans 5:5–11.

God's question to Eve is really quite simple. He's asking for her to say what she did, not why she did it. "I was deceived." Why you did wrong doesn't justify the wrong that you did. Besides, God already knows the whole story before anyone says anything. Then why ask? He is seeking her simple repentance for reconciliation with Himself. But as with Adam, her sinful guilt desperately tries to justify itself by shifting blame for her misdeeds. As popular as this silly excuse has become, here we see the first time it is used: "The devil made me do it!" We must remember that Satan cannot make us do anything. He merely suggests and tempts but cannot force you to disobey God and sin. That is on you. The devil did not make you do it, nor the alcohol, nor the drug habit—you are guilty for your own actions. You're wrong for accepting bad counsel, taking drugs, and getting drunk, as well as acting from those influences. You can't blame the counsel you received from another for the disobedience you committed. So you will be blessed if you do not follow counsel contrary to God's Word. *"How blessed is the man who does not walk in the counsel of the wicked, nor stand in the path of sinners, nor sit in the seat of scoffers!"* (Psalm 1:1). Do not walk in their counsel, stand in their paths, or enjoy fellowship with those that disobey God. Marriage is built upon His Word, but it is destroyed by disobeying it. Don't blame the counselor for your disobedience—husband or wife, take responsibility for your actions.

In proving that the priesthood of Melchizedek is superior to the Levitical priest through Aaron, the Scriptures reveal a profound truth: as Levi was in Abraham when he gave tithes to Melchizedek (Hebrews 7:4–10), so Levi and his priesthood is subordinate to Melchizedek and his priesthood in Messiah. In the same way, though still in Adam when God gave him the command (as *"bone of my bones"*), Eve was subordinate to the command and responsible as well as Adam for her obedience to the command. She was therefore in Adam in receiving the command and culpable for her disobedience. In the same way, we were all in Adam and culpable for the sin of disobedience to God's Word, a sin which has played out in our lives in a variety of ways: *"Therefore, just as through one man sin entered into the world, and death through sin, and so death spread to all men, because all sinned...even over those who had not sinned in the likeness of the offense of Adam"* (Romans 5:12, 14). Sin impacted us all in its corruption and in our culpability. The Messianic marriage is where we find solace and healing, as the couple trusts in the Redeemer of marriage, *"so that, as sin reigned in death, even so grace would reign through righteousness to eternal life through Yeshua the Messiah our Lord"* (Romans 5:21 SN).

Eve is held responsible more for being deceived than for eating the fruit. First Timothy 2:14: *"And it was not Adam who was deceived, but the woman being deceived, fell into transgression."* Second Corinthians 11:3 (SN): *"But I am afraid that, as the serpent deceived Eve by his craftiness, your minds will be led astray from the simplicity and purity to Messiah."*

The consequences of eating the fruit are shared (their eyes are opened), but Eve's greater sin is being deceived. It's as if God is saying, "He deceived you, but you believed him, and you actually believed I was keeping you from blessing!" She is deceived, not merely in eating the fruit, but in distrusting God. Though she uses being deceived to mitigate the sin of eating and giving the fruit to Adam, she is responsible for her actions and her naiveté.

God doesn't see the enemy's deception of Eve as any excuse for her at all. Her deception is a self-deception, for she herself evaluated the fruit and deemed it good for food. As the prophet states to other self-deceivers, "*The arrogance of your heart has deceived you*" (Obadiah 1:3). Scripture encourages us all to become discerning, not by sinful shortcuts and disobedient substitutes like eating the forbidden fruit, but by studying and following God's Word: "*Strong teaching is for the mature, who by reason of use have their senses trained to discern good and evil*" (Hebrews 5:14 SN). So, let us as couples "*desire the pure milk of the Word that we may grow in respect to our salvation*" (1 Peter 2:2 SN).

"*And I ate.*" Eve finally admits eating the forbidden fruit. As with Adam, this is accepted by God as her confession and therefore a form of repentance. Her admission means her repentance of her iniquity. But there is a vital point to keep in mind: her confession means her repudiation of the enemy. She's no longer his ally but now is back to walking with God.

Neither Adam nor Eve shows regret or remorse for their sins. This sometimes comes later, as it did with me. Three months after trusting Yeshua as my Messiah, I heard a sermon that the Holy Spirit used to bring me under overwhelming conviction for my sins—sins for which I had already been forgiven. Only then did I realize just how offensive they were to God. As I mature, I'm still learning the depth of that lesson. Adam and Eve will have more remorse, regret, and deeper realization of their sinfulness as they live through the consequences of their disobedience. So too, accepting a weak apology from your spouse may not be the final stop of that train as your spouse further matures and realizes the pain that their actions and attitudes caused others. Messiah already paid the full penalty for that offense so fully that we can fully forgive others as we have been fully forgiven by our offended God. Indeed, in the New Covenant promise, God states that He will forgive our iniquity, and our sin He "*will remember no more*" (Jeremiah 31:34). As we mature in our New Covenant relationship in our Messianic marriage, we too can graciously forgive and forget.

Adam blames Eve, and she in turn blames the snake. But the poor snake has no one else to blame! So, let's not continue the blame game; rather, let's repent of it. Development and appreciation in the marriage comes from taking responsibility for your actions, repenting, apologizing, and then accepting God's forgiveness. In shifting blame, you are sidestepping God's healing process in Messiah.

This is a good spot to take a *selah*, as we are faced with the ugly reality of human sin. We are about to examine the consequences of moral failure, and we look forward to God's provision of a remedy. Yet, the Good News found in Yeshua cannot be fully appreciated without seeing just how bad the bad news is. Let's take a pause from reading now and reflect on the sad condition of our first father and mother, and how their choices have affected all humanity through history since they fell. We are their children and have inherited their fallen nature.

The Disciplined and Corrective Consequences of Marital Failure (Genesis 3:14–19)

I. The discipline upon the divisive serpent, 3:14–15: its complete doom

II. The discipline upon the dissident woman, 3:16: her compliant duty

III. The discipline upon the disobedient man, 3:17–19: his cursed domain

The blame game in Genesis 3 shows us that no one wants to take responsibility for their own actions and awful mistakes. Adam and Eve expect the consequences that they desire, but only end up with what God's Word says they will gain from sin: death.[57] But it's far worse than that. Disobedience to God not only breaks relationship with God and with each other, but also the awful consequence of any sin is the curse: condemnation to eternal death.

We have learned from this chapter about taking responsibility, admitting what you have done, and not making excuses. We can now learn how to heal from all these disasters in a marriage. This is vital for every marriage to grasp, because Adam and Eve's disaster has impacted your marriage and every other marriage. In other words, your marriage is a disaster waiting to happen except for the grace of God that is applied to your marriage by faith in Yeshua.

The priority for restoration of marriage relationships is to live under God's divine discipline for the marriage. The grace-filled Messianic marriage lives under the Lord's divine discipline. His discipline when followed makes us His faithful disciples through our marriage relationship. In 3:14–19 we see God apply discipline to the snake and the wife and the husband. As His disciples, discipline is normative throughout the Bible. The rest of the Bible, when it teaches about relationships—especially marriage—assumes this discipline.

Good News: your marriage is going to be functional but only by the grace of God. Without the grace of God, your marriage is spiritually dysfunctional, as it resists His disciplines. Every marriage relationship is made up of two sinners who may specialize in the blame game, resentment, domination, manipulation, or any number of devices to vainly attempt to have their needs—if not met, at least adequately addressed. Though we will be dealing with these issues more fully, for now a few quick pointers:

---

57. *"There is a way which seems right to a man, but its end is the way of death"* (Proverbs 14:12).

1. Agree on the divine priorities for marriage, 2:23–25: review and agree.
2. Pray about the destroyed priorities for marriage, 3:1–13: review and pray.
3. Commit to disciplined priorities for marriage, 3:14–19: review and commit.

> *The LORD God said to the serpent, "Because you have done this, cursed are you more than all cattle, and more than every beast of the field; on your belly you will go, and dust you will eat all the days of your life; and I will put enmity between you and the woman, and between your seed and her seed; He shall bruise you on the head, and you shall bruise him on the heel." (Genesis 3:14–15)*

The Discipline upon the Divisive Serpent, 3:14–15: Its Complete Doom

As we consider 3:14–15, we find a three-fold identification of Satan and therefore a three-fold curse upon him. The three-fold identification: The "*serpent*" is a pawn of Satan. Its "*seed*" is the progeny of Satan.[58] The "*head*" is the person of Satan.[59] The three-fold curse: A. The serpent's sinful existence is degraded as sin. B. The serpent's sinful seed is detested by the saints. C. The serpent's sinful supremacy is destroyed by the Savior.

A. External sign: The serpent's sinful existence is degraded as sin, 3:14

1. Diminished in honor: the obligation upon sin

Regarding the serpent, we see the discipline on the serpent is very severe.[60] Only the serpent is not called to confess. It is condemned. Biblical confession is for spiritual reconciliation. The serpent is summarily condemned and cursed. God asks you to confess your sins and accept His promised and provided bloody covering (3:21), that you might not be condemned. The supernatural Satan used the natural serpent as his perhaps unwitting tool. You may ask, "Why is the animal responsible, since it was duped and used by Satan?" As Eve was responsible for being duped by the enemy, so too was the snake. Transgressors are culpable for sins of ignorance.[61] You or your spouse may be unaware that your attitude or behaviors are wrong in God's sight, but the Scripture says that you too are under a curse.[62] All who sin are cursed and subject to the wrath of God. If we love what God has

---

58. *"By this the children of God and the children of the devil are obvious: anyone who does not practice righteousness is not of God, nor the one who does not love his brother"* (1 John 3:10).
59. *"The great dragon...the serpent of old who is called the devil and Satan"* (Revelation 12:9 and 20:2). Satan is called *"dragon"* and *"serpent"*—thus, the serpent in the garden is Satan.
60. For those that study snakes, it's evident they once had legs. See Delaney Ross, "Why Snakes Don't Have Legs (For Now)," October 23, 2016, *National Geographic*, news.nationalgeographic.com.
61. Leviticus 5:3; Luke 12:47–48.
62. Deuteronomy 27:26: *"'Cursed is he who does not confirm the words of this law by doing them.' And all the people shall say, 'Amen'."*

cursed—sin—it does not disprove God's curse. It demonstrates our depravity, rebellion, and waywardness.

2. Debased in humiliation: the designation for sin

Cursing the serpent turns this into a symbolic designation for defeat, a constant reminder of the degradation of Satan, and a strong warning regarding rebellion against God. *Nachash* ("serpent") is also used as a word for practicing divination that is condemned and forbidden (Deuteronomy 18:10). "*On your belly you will go.*" Every slithering snake is a sign and a symbol of the disgrace, dishonor, and humiliation of Satan.[63] In the wilderness, when the people complain about the manna,[64] God punishes them with deadly, fiery serpents. Upon their confession of sins, God tells Moses to place a fiery brass (*nechoshet*) serpent on a pole. A bitten person who looks to the brass serpent will live.[65] In the tabernacle, brass speaks of divine judgment through the brazen altar and self-judgment through the laver of brass. The brass serpent that Moses lifts pictures God's cure for the deadly, sin-caused condition of the people. The serpent is a symbol of sin that is judged. The Messiah was made sin for us,[66] and all who look to Him will not perish! So, the New Covenant states, "*As Moses lifted up the serpent in the wilderness, even so must the Son of Man be lifted up; so that whoever believes will in Him have eternal life*" (John 3:14–15). The serpent, a symbol of judgment, reminds us of One who took our judgment. Looking to Him brings our healing and eternal life. The redeemed Messianic marriage is therefore a symbol as well, of the Messiah and the assembly who are free of judgment.[67] But the defeated, unredeemed marriage is also a symbol, of lives built on the lies of the enemy rather than the truth of God, and of those that will not look unto Him "*whom they have pierced*" (Zechariah 12:10).

3. Dissatisfied in hunger: the desolation of sin

Just as the serpent entices Eve to eat what is defiling, so is he cursed to eat what is demeaning. Snakes have no taste buds. They eat from hunger, but derive no pleasure from eating food. All food is like dust to the snake. This is its age-long curse (Isaiah 65:25). But its further humiliation is this: "*And dust you will eat.*" This is a sign of defeat. When an enemy "licked the dust," it meant they fell in battle to the ground. In Psalm 72:9, we read: "*Let…his enemies lick the dust*" (also Isaiah 49:23, Micah 7:17). Licking dust is a symbol of being vanquished—totally defeated and brought low, down to the lowest level. So too, marriages that deny

---

63. Leviticus 11:42: "*Whatever crawls on its belly…you shall not eat them, for they are detestable.*"
64. As a symbol of Messiah, the despised manna is a symbolic rejection of the Living Bread from Heaven, indeed the Lord of Glory Himself. First Corinthians 10:9 (SN): "*And let us not put the Messiah to the test, as some of them did, and were destroyed by snakes.*"
65. Numbers 21:4–9.
66. Second Corinthians 5:21: "*He made Him who knew no sin to be sin on our behalf, so that we might become the righteousness of God in Him.*"
67. Ephesians 5:32.

the truth, resist the Lord, and follow the father of lies lose the very joy of what they hoped for in their marriage.

In God's sight, marriage is sacred. Let your mind dwell on that for a moment. For us, marriage may be convenient, it may be legally necessary for some situations, or it may be enjoyable or merely tolerable. In God's sight, it is sacred. From this the Lord says, "*Let no man separate.*" Dividing a relationship is what the serpent does in order to conquer and destroy humanity. As Yeshua taught, a "*house divided against itself will not stand.*"[68] If you are going to destroy your house, your family, and your marriage relationship, then dividing the spouses is how it is effectively done. The warning here to dividers is that they all will be punished. As the serpent (Satan) is most subtle of the creatures, he is most judged. Again, to whom much is given, much will be required. The more you have, the more you are held responsible. All dividers will be judged. Think about this and jot down some notes for your own relationship. Are there people with whom you associate who are not edifying and building up your relationship? In other words, does their interaction with you encourage you to live less interdependently with your spouse? That extra-curricular relationship is a threat to your marriage, since God does not want you to be independent from your spouse. Rather, as you both spiritually grow into full dependence upon Yeshua, you will grow into full interdependence with each other. That is God's will for your marriage. Any relationship that hinders your marital interdependence is not from God and should be viewed by both spouses as a threat to your home.

Explaining this further in Matthew 19:6 (SN), Yeshua says, "*Where God has declared one, they are no longer two but one.*" Even though you may feel that you are two different people, God treats you as one. It is a sacred relationship. God looks at it this way, though we may not. Who do you think has to change perspective, us or God? Obviously, we are the ones that have to do the adjusting. God is expecting both spouses to mature into His perspective on the Messianic marriage relationship, as well as other relationships. Part of our maturity in Messiah is evaluating our relationship as sacred in His eyes, recognizing our sacred unity as His seal of approval on the Messianic marriage.

B. Internal sense: Satan's sinful seed is detested by the saints

*"I will put enmity between you and the woman,
and between your seed and her seed."* (Genesis 3:15a)

God established enmity, hatred, and hostility to protect His people from identifying with Satan's evil seed. God is love and hates sin, because sin destroys His people, whom He loves. You would hate whatever would harm your children as well. God hates sin, but loves sinners. God has called and enabled us to love, but

---

68. Matthew 12:25.

not love everything. Created in His image, we're to hate sin too.[69] This antagonism is part of the will of God to maintain the distinctiveness of His godly ones so that they are not attracted to and absorbed by what is contrary to God in this rebellious world. *"You adulteresses, do you not know that friendship with the world is hostility toward God? Therefore, whoever wishes to be a friend of the world makes himself an enemy of God"* (Jacob [James] 4:4). Avoid the failure of Eve by keeping enmity between you and the evil of this world: *"Do not love the world nor the things in the world. If anyone loves the world, the love of the Father is not in him. For all that is in the world, the lust of the flesh and the lust of the eyes and the boastful pride of life, is not from the Father, but is from the world"* (1 John 2:15–16). As good doctors love health and therefore hate disease, so God has called us to love righteousness and hate evil. Those without a knowledge of the Scriptures may think that good and evil, right and wrong, etc., are not very clearly discerned. But they are: *"By this the children of God and the children of the devil are obvious: anyone who does not practice righteousness is not of God, nor the one who does not love his brother"* (1 John 3:10).[70] In marriage, there are obvious and very clear lines drawn that should never be crossed. A couple prayerfully commits to not have entangling and intimate relationships with those outside their marriage. Those who do not live to honor God and who despise the Lord are seed of the enemy. Be committed as a couple to what is right in God's sight and you both will hate what is wrong, evil, and destructive to your marriage and home.

Those who follow the truth in Messiah are of His spiritual seed.[71] Those who live by a lie are followers of *"the father of lies."*[72] Evaluate your own life and marriage. Whom do you both follow—the truth of Messiah or the lies of the world? For all of us, there is hope: *"In which you formerly walked according to the course of this world, according to the prince of the power of the air, of the spirit that is now working in the sons of disobedience"* (Ephesians 2:2). Did you see the word *formerly*? It can be formerly for you and your spouse, too. Even now, take your spouse's hand and together trust in Yeshua. He will pour His love into your heart, and you will love what He loves and hate what He hates.

C. Eternal success: Satan's sinful supremacy is destroyed by the Savior

*"Her seed; He shall bruise you on the head,
and you shall bruise Him on the heel."* (Genesis 3:15b)

---

69. Psalm 97:10 (SN): *"Hate evil, you who love HaShem."* Romans 12:9: *"Abhor what is evil; cling to what is good."*
70. Also, 2 John 1:7 (SN): *"For many deceivers have gone out into the world, those who do not acknowledge Yeshua the Messiah as coming in the flesh. This is the deceiver and the anti-Messiah."*
71. *"He shall see His seed"* Isaiah 53:10 (SN).
72. John 8:44.

I. Satan's defeat provides the restored honor for the woman

"*Her seed*" is our hope. Amazingly, in the midst of this curse is a redemptive promise and a Messianic prophecy—the first promise of redemption and the first prophecy of the Messiah in all the Scriptures! This promise of the seed of the woman is recognized as referring to the coming of the Messiah in non-Messianic as well as Messianic faith.[73] In the midst of the curse, there's a promise! You may have lost hope and think that your marriage is cursed, but in the midst of your marriage there is a promise. Messiah is the true redemption of your marriage!

The "*seed*" of the woman? Do women have seed? Though *seed* in English is limited to males, in Hebrew it is used for the offspring that the woman produces as well.[74] But why does the Scripture bother to refer to "*HER seed*" at all? For, the Lord God's redemption for the marriage—His redemption of all humanity—brings restored honor for the woman. The redemptive grace for all women is given in Messiah. The essential honor for all women is restored in Messiah's birth. Though the enemy deceived her, her validation as God's creation is found in her Seed, the Messiah. The Bible's mention of her failure is not meant to demean females any more than its many references to Adam's sin is intended to demean males. For, the woman's self-worth (that the enemy attempted to destroy along with her marriage) is restored and validated in her Seed! By their personal faith in Messiah, her seed become God's children. By their personal unbelief in Yeshua, the enemy's seed become God's enemies. She is now and forever the matriarch of the godly seed, as distinguished from the enemy's seed. But remember, the woman's self-worth is not found in herself, but in her Seed, Messiah. Only in her Seed is honor is to be found. And whoever honors her Seed is honored by God.

In marriage, the woman's self-worth and validation does not come from her husband but from the Messiah, regardless of the husband's appreciation or disapproval of her.[75] Apart from her husband's approval, the wife is empowered by Messiah's redemption to minister God's love and fulfill her divine calling to represent the Lord—once more, regardless of her husband's disposition.

II. Satan's defeat produces the death sentence upon the enemy

"*He shall bruise you on the head*." Being bruised "*on the head*" refers to a death blow; Satan's defeat is his utter destruction. Then why does Satan still prowl "*like a roaring lion, seeking someone to devour*" (1 Peter 5:8)? This is part of the three-phased program of the enemy's destruction by the Messiah, which directly applies to Messianic marriages. Since his deception ruined marriage, his destruction restores marriage through the Messiah.

---

73. "[She hinted at] that seed which would arise from another source,... viz. the king Messiah." (Midrash Rabbah Bereshit 23:5, *Soncino Classics Collection* [Brooklyn, NY: Judaica Press, 1973; Soncino Press Ltd., 1990]). As to the victory over Satan, see New Covenant: Romans 16:20; Hebrews 2:14; 1 John 3:9–10, etc.
74. Genesis 4:25; 16:10; 19:32, 34, etc.
75. See 1 Peter 3:1–6.

Phase 1. All believers in Yeshua are delivered from Satan's control through Messiah's redemptive work on the cross. In providing our redemption, Messiah came to destroy the works of the devil.[76] Yeshua's death started Satan's destruction by delivering all believers in Yeshua from Satan's deception. Messiah came to deliver the slaves of the devil.[77] This slavery is a slavish fear of death that manifests in all manner of fears for self-protection—protecting one's ego included. All other phobias stems from this fear of death, and the fear of death results from the fear of condemnation upon sin.[78] Messiah's death delivers all believers from Satan's dominion.[79] Fears, lies, and abuse are part of Satan's spiritual realm. But Yeshua delivers us from Satan's bondage, so by His grace through faith, we can now live and love reflecting Messiah's realm that is our eternal home. Because the devil is still at liberty and actively seeks "*to devour*" (destroy our lives and witness through his ungodly temptations), Messianic believers need to resist him by actively submitting to God (James 4:7). The marriage that is not actively submitting to and obeying God is not resisting the enemy. These are the homes where the enemy is wreaking havoc through wrong attitudes and sinful behavior among family members. Both spouses are called to "*fight the good fight of faith*" (1 Timothy 6:12) and put on the full armor of God (see Ephesians 6:10–18).

Phase 2. Now the enemy is at liberty, but at Messiah's return Satan will be bound for one thousand years (Revelation 20:1–3). This is Satan's millennial captivity and detention in the bottomless pit. The point of Satan being bound and not being destroyed at Messiah's return is to demonstrate the undeniable need for God's grace. For, even with Messiah sitting on His glorious millennial throne in Jerusalem, and even though Satan is bound for those one thousand years, still people will not trust in God and humble themselves. Rather, they will be hypocritical. This is evidenced at Satan's release, as he is quickly able to bring the nations into the final rebellion against the Lord (Revelation 20:7–9). This period will reinforce what all history is intended to prove: that God's grace alone in Messiah is the only hope for humanity. This is especially important in the Messianic marriage: His grace through faith in Messiah is the only hope for the family, now and forever.

Phase 3. This refers to the destruction of Satan in the lake of fire at Messiah's final battle (Revelation 20:10). Messiah came to doom the very existence of the devil. At the end of Yeshua's one-thousand-year reign, Messiah finally quells the last devilishly inspired rebellion and throws Satan into the lake of fire forever! This is followed by the second resurrection of all non-believers to appear before

---

76. "*The Son of God appeared for this purpose, to destroy the works of the devil*" (1 John 3:8).
77. "*That by Yeshua's death He might render the devil powerless...and might free those who through fear of death were subject to slavery all their lives*" (Hebrews 2:14–15 SN).
78. "*There is no fear in love; but perfect love casts out fear, because fear involves punishment, and the one who fears is not perfected in love*" (1 John 4:18).
79. "*For He rescued us from the domain of darkness, and transferred us to the kingdom of His beloved Son*" (Colossians 1:13).

the great white throne judgment and receive their degree of eternal punishment (Revelation 20:11–15).[80]

This threefold destruction of Satan is not only the destiny for all non-believers in Yeshua, but is the pattern for all non-Messianic marriages. In phase one, couples are divided over lack of mutual love and support. In phase two, a bondage of fear, pride, and resentment keeps them from being able to care for each other. In the last phase, there is the death-like state of either stalemated indifference or a marriage-destroying divorce, both of which picture the destiny of those who follow the father of lies into the lake of fire. But by faith in Yeshua it can be turned around and the marriage can be redeemed. By trusting in Yeshua, you're submitting to God and resisting the devil. By His grace we are fully accepted in Messiah and can thereby accept one another. By Yeshua's forgiveness of all our sins we can forgive our spouses for their sins as well. Do not wait until your heart is so hardened that you can no longer turn your hopes to Yeshua. In spiritual warfare, go for the head, for we battle not against flesh and blood, but against spiritual forces in high places (Ephesians 6:12). Your spouse is not your enemy, but at worst is only a mere unwitting pawn of the enemy. Pray for one another.[81] Speak truth in love.[82] Be gentle toward those in opposition to the truth.[83] By faith in Messiah we all can enjoy the victory together over those who would divide the marriage.

III. Satan's defeat requires the redemptive suffering of the Messiah

"*And you shall bruise Him on the heel.*" Messiah's death for our sins is first referred to as the enemy's wounding of His heel. This is the first biblical picture of Yeshua coming into this world to suffer in our place. Out of this small seed of promise come all the sacrifices and types, and hundreds of prophecies, including the well-known prophecies of the Suffering Servant, such as: "*He was pierced through for our transgressions, He was crushed for our iniquities*" (Isaiah 53:5). Then, in the fullness of time, the fulfillment of these types and prophecies comes in the person of Yeshua the Messiah, born to die for us. In His once-and-for-all death, Yeshua both destroys the enemy and redeems humanity. In doing so, He also restores marriage to its original design. He takes the curse of our destruction to give us hope in His resurrection! He takes the curse of our humiliation to give us the gift of His glorification. He takes the shame of our depravity to give us His grace for our dignity. He takes the curse of our enmity so we can have His love for our unity. He takes the full measure of God's wrath to give us His peace beyond human measure.

---

80. See *The Messianic Answer Book* for more on the subject of the various degrees of penalty in judgment.
81. James 5:16 (SN): "*Confess your trespasses to one another, and pray for one another, that you may be healed. The effective, fervent prayer of a righteous* [spouse] *avails much.*"
82. Ephesians 4:15.
83. Read 2 Timothy 2:23–26.

Yeshua's sacrifice enables us to see how sacrifice is foundational to the marriage. Built upon His work, we live out His sacrificial love toward our spouse. As noted, marriage is not a fifty-fifty proposition, but it is a lifestyle of 100 percent-100 percent grace giving for the sake of the other. Those Messianic marriages that depend on His great sacrifice are thereby empowered to live out His love as a thanksgiving offering to His glory. Whereas our selfishness reveals a lack of reliance upon Yeshua, our faithful service for the Lord is revealed in our sacrificial service to our spouse.

A popular slogan used by believers regarding the death of Messiah is, "It's Friday now, but Sunday's coming!" The point is that on Friday, Yeshua was dead and buried and considered by most people to be a failed attempt at redemption, having been defeated by the Roman government, a pawn of our enemy the devil. But "Friday" was not the last word on the redemption matter, for on the first day of the week, He arose in resurrection power. And one day the victorious truth that is believed by many will be clearly seen by all: "Yeshua defeated the enemy!" Right now, since *"we see in a mirror dimly,"* you may be wondering if the message of your home is sadly, "Our Messianic marriage defeated." It may be "Friday" for your marriage, but there is resurrection power available for you both right now! By faith in Yeshua, you will one day see the whole truth—we will know as we've been known—and Yeshua's victory in your lives will be declared: "In Yeshua, our Messianic marriage defeated the enemy!"

The Discipline upon the Dissident Woman, 3:16: Her Compliant Duty

Adam and Eve picture our lives: our great potential, our grievous failures, and our gracious redemption. When they both eventually and weakly confess, *"and I ate"* (3:12–13), relationships are finally restored. But, as in our lives, there are some painful consequences. The discipline placed by God upon the repentant Adam and Eve reflects much of our lives in general: pain and toil. For the serpent, and all the unrepentant, the consequences of sin are certain doom and condemnation. But for people who repent before God and accept Messiah's death in our place, even the most severe chastening is always redemptive and always for our ultimate good.[84] Because Messiah's work will "reverse the curse" for all who repent, we can learn how Adonai intends even bad consequences for good for any who trust in Yeshua.[85]

The hurting discipleship of bearing children

> *To the woman He said, "I will greatly multiply your pain in childbirth, in pain you will bring forth children; yet your desire will be for your husband, and he will rule over you."* (Genesis 3:16)

---

84. The "good" is clearly revealed in Romans 8:28–30. Also, *"Before I was afflicted I went astray, but now I keep Your word"* (Psalm 119:67).
85. *"You meant evil against me, but God meant it for good"* (Genesis 50:20).

Four • *Foundational Precautions for Marriage*

Eve accepts the sorrow in her discipleship calling: in both birthing children and in raising them. As far as the marriage discipline upon the woman, God first informs her that there will be pain in childbirth. *"I will greatly multiply your pain in childbirth, in pain you will bring forth children."* If bearing children is painful—which it is—then raising those little sinners can seem like torture. It can be a painful situation from start to finish. The sufferings of labor pain typify the sufferings that all endure because of judgment and the pain of living.[86] The very means of redemption through the seed of the woman would also cause her pain and sorrow before He could redeem. Thus, women prefigure the sufferings of Messiah in their labor pains.[87]

This discipline upon the woman is that she must endure the pains of motherhood while living holy unto God. The call of discipleship is not enduring the pain, but living holy unto God and representing His love to others while enduring the pain of life. For this, the grace of God is required. This was always the case, but before the fall, grace living was just plain living. After the fall, we now need intentional faith to depend on His grace for our sufficiency. This demonstrates what He alone can do through us, for His *"power is perfected in weakness"* (2 Corinthians 12:9). In this way, we more closely identify with God. We can more fully appreciate the grief that God endured with His first children, Adam and Eve, and endures with all the rest of us that grieve the very One who loves us.[88] Restoration unites you forever with the Lord! What breaks His heart will break yours! What grieves the Spirit will grieve you too! Your discipleship as a parent is to love even those children who disobey and disrespect you. As God disciplines us,[89] we know how to discipline our children and develop them to become His faithful Messianic disciples.

Childbirth is a reminder not just of the painful consequences of our sin, but more importantly of the Messiah who will destroy Satan, the serpent. For, every childbirth reflects the cry of creation awaiting in pain His removal of the curse and of His redemption of the world.[90]

The woman must never blame her children for her pain. She recognizes the pain of being a mother as a discipline from God. As you love your children and

---

86. Isaiah 13:8; 21:3; 26:17; Jeremiah 30:6; Hosea 13:13; Micah 4:9; Matthew 24:8; John 16:21–22; 1 Thessalonians 5:3.
87. Genesis 4:2; Psalm 22:10; Isaiah 7:14; Jeremiah 31:22; Micah 5:3; Luke 2:7; Galatians 4:4–5.
88. *"The Lord was sorry that he had made man on the earth, and He was grieved in His heart"* (Genesis 6:6). *"Do not grieve the Holy Spirit of God, by whom you were sealed for the day of redemption"* (Ephesians 4:30).
89. Proverbs 3:11–12; Hebrews 12:5–6.
90. Romans 8:19–22: *"For the anxious longing of the creation waits eagerly for the revealing of the sons of God. For the creation was subjected to futility, not willingly, but because of Him who subjected it, in hope that the creation itself also will be set free from its slavery to corruption into the freedom of the glory of the children of God. For we know that the whole creation groans and suffers the pains of childbirth together until now."*

love your God, amidst your pain you are actually in a redemptive role. Pain is never an excuse for rebellion and resentment, for the Lord gave you this discipline as a redemptive testimony of His grace as sufficient for you. All women getting married need to understand that to have kids there will be tears to shed in the best of marriages.

**The humble relationship with your husband:
She accepts him as her God-appointed leader**

"Yet your desire will be for your husband, and he will rule over you."

Because it regards her renewal as wife and partner, this is the wife's Torah,[91] not the husband's. That is, it is not for him to force her to obey this discipline. Her response to God will determine her obedience to His discipline for her. It is God's discipline for her, not her husband's discipline upon her. Husbands that try to dominate or manipulate their wives with the use of Scripture show themselves too insecure to properly lead their families. They should seek discipleship or counseling to develop them for the proper leadership role in the marriage and home.

Humble submission to proper authority is the testimony of all the redeemed, as we all are submitting ourselves to God's appointed authority.[92] If we're restored to the Lord and submit to our calling as His people, submission to proper authority is seen in all our relationships—in our marriages, families, and community as well. Those who don't submit to God's appointed authority are not submitting to God.[93] Unfortunately, the only behavioral models that some people have had are dysfunctional parents who have manipulated one another attempting to get their needs met. They grew up that way, and all their wiring is connected in such a way that it is the only way they know to relate to others. They did not understand what it is to properly submit to one another[94] without feeling demeaned. However, the redeemed condition is revealed when the wife is submitted to her husband and her self-worth is, therefore, found and secured in the Lord.

Her discipline is highlighted by the word *desire*.[95] This same word *desire* is used in Genesis 4:7 regarding Cain, which states, *"If you do well, will not your countenance be lifted up? And if you do not do well, sin is crouching at the door; and its desire is for you, but you must master [mashal] it."* There is often a one-upmanship

---

91. *"Wives be subject to your own husbands as unto the Lord, for the husband is the head of the wife, as Messiah also is the head of the Congregation, He Himself being the Savior of the body"* (Ephesians 5:22–23 SN).
92. See Appendix Seven: The Five Biblical Levels of Delegated Authority from God.
93. There are some famous exceptions to this, when human authority blatantly conflicts with God's revealed Word: Acts 5:29, *"We must obey God rather than men."* But in these exceptional situations, believers must also be ready to accept the painful consequences for their faith decisions.
94. In Ephesians 5:21–24, the wife's instruction to submit to her husband follows the instruction for mutual submission.
95. Hebrew: *teshuqah*.

that comes about in the marriage relationship, where the undisciplined and undisciplined couple attempts to gain a sense of their self-worth from each other. Thus, just as sin will have its "*desire*" to rule Cain, so she will have her desire to rule her husband. But, like Cain must master sin's desire to control him,[96] so the woman must master her desire to control her husband, for he is to rule (*mashal*) her. All people have needs. In general, women and men have needs for security and significance, respectively. These needs are addressed and met in Messiah. But if we resist God's discipline and seek to meet our needs through our spouse, the wife will expect her husband to meet her need to feel like a worthwhile and secure person. This is not good, for this will lead her to manipulate or control him so she will feel secure. Her felt need for security is genuine. But this need is met only by the Lord and not by the husband. For she too is created in God's image and her genuine needs are only properly met in Messiah, as she relates to God by faith. However, if she is not depending on the Lord, her fleshly desire for that security will be directed toward her husband. This is totally futile for her, because her husband is just as desperately needy! If he's not walking with the Lord, he will seek significance from his wife, which is total futility for him as well. Both her desire for security and his desire for significance are only fulfilled in the Lord, not in each other. Fulfillment can only come from the Messiah because only in Him are you complete.[97] She must by faith yield to the Lord, and thereby discipline herself not to allow her desire to control her husband, to control her.

The statement "*He will rule over you*" (and the "*He*" is emphatic) is a return to the original divine order, but is a discipline because of her fallen human condition. The word for "rule" in Hebrew is *mashal*, meaning to have managerial oversight. At the first usage of *mashal*, the sun and moon are said "*to govern* [*mashal*] *the day and the night*" (Genesis 1:18). As the most prominent luminaries over day and night, their rulership is intended to maintain the order and stability that the Lord God has ordained. As Eliezer rules all of Abraham's possessions (Genesis 24:2), we see that *mashal* is a managerial role, not an ownership in any way. Eliezer is to handle matters according to Abraham the owner's instructions. Husbands are to manage and provide orderliness to the home as the Lord God has instructed, but the husband is not to act like the owner. Rule is therefore to have oversight, and to manage well.

The husband rules over his wife not by battling or dominating her, but by *leaving* all else for her, *cleaving* only to her, and *weaving* with her in unity (as God commanded in 2:24). But Adam failed to rule, though he was standing right there when his wife was deceived by the serpent. Sin is subtle, and its appearance to Adam didn't seem harmful to him, though it was. Rather, it appeared to him—as to her—as a way to find fulfillment. That is sin's (and Satan's) great deception.

---

96. See Psalm 19:13 and Proverbs 16:32.
97. Colossians 2:10.

Internet porn appears to satisfy your urges, yet it is a subtle trap to addict you to immorality and utter corruption. So the woman's conscious motive in her desire for the man was not to harm Adam, but to "help" and feed him. But her ways were contrary to God's ways. Men have to resist their wives' offers of the forbidden fruit to maintain their proper leadership in the marriage. They must righteously rule (manage) to have marital unity according to God's design. Eve was self-deceived by sin, for her fulfillment could only come as a helpmeet and when he righteously ruled in the marriage. Her attempts to stabilize, secure, and satisfy their lives by her own initiative were in themselves rebellious to God's order. They could only lead to the husband's disobedience by abdicating his leadership responsibility and not properly leading by insisting, "We will not eat what God has forbidden us to eat." So, to Eve it is said, *"He will rule."* This was her only hope and God's sage advice to get her back on track for a fulfilling married life according to God's Word.

In Scripture and in Messiah there is total equality of male and female, with only functional subordination for the wife as to her divine calling as his helpmeet. The male's leadership calling is as a servant of all in his family.[98] For him to either oppress his wife or abdicate his leadership is to rebel against God's calling. Likewise, for her to resist the man's leadership or to usurp his leadership is to rebel against God's calling for her.

This discipline creates functional subordination for the sake of orderliness and stability.[99] Scripture does not teach that males are superior to females, or that husbands are superior to their wives. That would be a misunderstanding of proper governance in the home and society. So, when the cop—male or female—says stop, I stop. I do not check out his prayer life before submitting to his position and obeying his order. And I do not for a moment think that his authority to order me to stop makes that police officer superior to me. But rather, I respect his position in the government, so I stop. I am subordinate to his authority, but not inferior to his person. My obeying the law and submitting to his authority maintains a functional society.

Since the husband will rule and oversee in the marriage relationship, in pre-marital counseling I tell couples, especially the woman, "Do not marry a man who is not ready to be a spiritual leader. It is going to be grievous to you. For, in that case you will be led by someone who does not know how to be a loving and caring leader." With one couple that I have counseled, the woman understood his responsibility to lead in the home and committed herself to wait until her boyfriend had a prayer life before she took him seriously as husband material. It was a wise commitment on her part. Though some foolish women think they will improve their husbands by strongly influencing them, they usually end up

---

98. Matthew 20:26–27.
99. "Functional subordination" is covered more fully later in this book when considering 1 Corinthians 11:3.

greatly disappointed, a mere nag, and quite unhappy. Getting married is always an "as is" proposition. Look before you leap.

The wife needs to understand that in order for this to be a redemptive marriage, the woman's discipline from the Lord requires both her willing mothering of her children and her willing submission to her husband, for the Lord's sake. Otherwise, she is rebellious against the Lord's discipline in the marriage, and things go from bad to worse. In her proper submission, we find that for her part, the Messianic marriage is wholesome, faithful, and blessed in the Lord.

Women, reconsider getting married if you cannot accept the discipline of the Lord in raising children or in submitting to your husband. Marriage may not be God's calling for you. Men, be careful to discuss with any woman you would consider marrying if she fully understands these disciplines as part of the ministry of marriage. If she balks at these matters, then that may not be the right wife for you.

The Discipline upon the Disobedient Man, 3:17–19: His Cursed Domain

Then to Adam He said, "Because you have listened to the voice of your wife, and have eaten from the tree about which I commanded you, saying, 'You shall not eat from it'; cursed is the ground because of you; in toil you will eat of it all the days of your life. Both thorns and thistles it shall grow for you; and you will eat the plants of the field; By the sweat of your face you will eat bread, till you return to the ground, because from it you were taken; for you are dust, and to dust you shall return." (Genesis 3:17–19)

To Adam God says, *"Because you have listened to the voice of your wife."* God is saying to Adam, "You listened to the voice of your wife instead of to Me!" God tells Adam not to eat, and Eve then gives him to eat. Adam tries to blame Eve for giving him the forbidden fruit, but God says that he's responsible for the wrong counsel he follows. But Scripture is not teaching husbands to ignore their wives. As your helpmeet, she is responsible to give you counsel from her perspective, and because she is your opposite, her counsel may be quite different from your point of view. That is her calling in her husband's life. But any counsel—whether from your wife or anyone else—that is contrary to the Word of God is false. If followed, it can be a curse and not a blessing. This is also Abram's problem in Genesis 16, when his wife Sarah, feeling the stress of having to provide a baby that she is not naturally able to conceive, gives Hagar to her husband as another wife. Sarah's counsel conflicts with Genesis 2:24, God's one-husband-one-wife rule. The Ishmaelite consequences trouble Israel to this day. Because Adam substitutes the voice of his wife for the Word of God, Adam and all men since have God's discipline placed upon them. When you try to break God's Word, you're the one that gets broken! Though God's Word may seem difficult, we should see this not as His punishment upon men, but as His discipline for our ultimate spiritual benefit.[100]

The disciplines upon the man bring a dual reversal of fortune for him: a land reversal and a life reversal. His disobedience is the root cause for the cursed ground and for death as humanity's new normal.

The land reversal: "*Because you have listened to the voice of your wife, and have eaten from the tree about which I commanded you, saying, 'you shall not eat from it'; cursed is the ground because of you.*" You disobeyed by eating, so you are disciplined through eating. What you sow, you reap. God's discipline is just. By definition, Adonai's disciple is under Adonai's discipline. Work is godly, even when it is grievous.

Adam was the Lord's disciple before the fall, but because Adam abuses the blessings he was given, those blessings are hereafter to be gained much more strenuously. In the garden, the vegetation grows by the work of God. The garden is planted by God for man, not planted by man for God: "*Out of the ground the Lord God caused to grow every tree that is pleasing to the sight and good for food.... Now a river flowed out of Eden to water the garden*" (2:9–10). But that will no longer be true. Adam will now slave for his food, for "*plants of the field*" refers to what God does not provide. If you insist on living apart from God in disobedience, you also lose His blessing and provision that come only by faith and obedience. You want a happy marriage, but you live in disobedience to the simplest of His commands, simply because they're not convenient for you. Really? And you wonder why He withholds His blessing?

The discipline of the Lord is the opportunity for our growth in service for Him.[101] The discipline delivers the disciple from his self-centered and disobedient approach to living and focuses him on God's obedient way of life.[102] Our discipline is His faithfulness to His promise to mature His disciples in His grace and mercy.[103] By delighting in God's Word through our discipline, we are spiritually nourished[104] and also "*conformed to the image of His Son.*"[105]

This too is God's way of disciplining His disobedient people Israel: "*But they will become his slaves so that they may learn the difference between My service and the service of the kingdoms of the countries*" (2 Chronicles 12:8). This is the same discipline the Lord applies to all His Messianic disciples today: "*All discipline*

---

100. "*All discipline for the moment seems not to be joyful, but sorrowful; yet to those who have been trained by it, afterwards it yields the peaceful fruit of righteousness*" (Hebrews 12:11).
101. "*Before I was afflicted I went astray, but now I keep Your word*" (Psalm 119:67).
102. "*It is good for me that I was afflicted, that I may learn Your statutes*" (Psalm 119:71).
103. "*I know, O Lord, that Your judgments are righteous, and that in faithfulness You have afflicted me*" (Psalm 119:75).
104. "*If Your law had not been my delight, then I would have perished in my affliction*" (Psalm 119:92).
105. Romans 8:28–30.

for the moment seems not to be joyful, but sorrowful; yet to those who have been trained by it, afterwards it yields the peaceful fruit of righteousness" (Hebrews 12:11). Our faith-acceptance of His discipline as for our good helps us to live out His redemptive grace to others. As those who *"bless the L<small>ORD</small> at all times,"*[106] we are His witnesses of merciful grace. This is also how we are sure to never fall prey to Satan: *"Submit therefore to God. Resist the devil and he will flee from you"* (James 4:7). Our obedient submission to God as His disciples is our victorious resistance against the devil.

God's grace-through-faith program enables His disciples not only to endure His disciplines, but to reveal His redemptive call for all. When Corrie ten Boom and her sister Betsy were challenged by a fellow inmate as to why God would send His children to Ravensbruck Concentration Camp, Betsy simply responded, "To obey Him."[107] Because we share this fallen world with the rest of humanity, in the midst of our mutual toil we get to shine as lights in the darkness to declare our blessed hope in Messiah. From Genesis 3:17–19, Paul teaches this same reversal of fortune in Romans 8:17–25.[108] Paul says that our relationship to the Lord calls us to suffer with Messiah so that we may also be glorified with Him. But then, Paul, a man who suffered much in his service for Yeshua, states that whatever our suffering may be, it cannot be compared with the glory to come! The suffering is not limited to humanity, but all creation *"was subjected to futility,"* because God cursed the ground due to our human failure. The earth was given to us as a stewardship, and our disobedience cursed the ground.

But Paul teaches that both the truth of our suffering and the promise of glory to come move us to eagerly live for our blessed hope and not to seek fulfillment in our labor, making it into idolatry. For the disciple of Messiah, the hope of the glory to come is the only true hope of the Messianic marriage. Both the painful parenting and the toil by the sweat of our brow provide the Messianic marriage with the opportunity to testify that our hope is in the Lord. For those who think it is just too difficult, you're right—the discipline teaches us the foolishness of disobedience. Will humanity learn and live for God? No. Next comes the flood,

---

106. Psalm 34:1
107. Mark and Phyllis Kirchberg, *The Profound Mystery: Marriage—The First Church* (New York: Vantage Press, 2008), 116.
108. *"And if children, heirs also, heirs of God and fellow heirs with [Messiah], if indeed we suffer with Him so that we may also be glorified with Him. For I consider that the sufferings of this present time are not worthy to be compared with the glory that is to be revealed to us. For the anxious longing of the creation waits eagerly for the revealing of the sons of God. For the creation was subjected to futility, not willingly, but because of Him who subjected it, in hope that the creation itself also will be set free from its slavery to corruption into the freedom of the glory of the children of God. For we know that the whole creation groans and suffers the pains of childbirth together until now. And not only this, but also we ourselves, having the first fruits of the Spirit, even we ourselves groan within ourselves, waiting eagerly for our adoption as sons, the redemption of our body. For in hope we have been saved, but hope that is seen is not hope; for who hopes for what he already sees? But if we hope for what we do not see, with perseverance we wait eagerly for it."*

when the already-cursed earth is then destroyed in water. Will we learn then to be faithful in the midst of it and work hard? Apparently not. We live in a world where many think they are entitled to whatever benefits they can grab, while trying to avoid the hard work of godliness. Godliness? Yes. We were created to labor. Labor as toil is a consequence of sin; before sin, God rested from His labors on Shabbat. Thus, labor is godly. It's the cursed ground that makes labor now a toil and a frustrating thorns-and-thistles experience. When we live by faith, this hard-work discipline reveals our humble spirit, acknowledging that we are but dust. There is no reason for human pride, other than as continued rebellion against the Lord, which is even further foolishness that brings further painful consequences.

Though there are thorns and thistles (the weedy frustrations of life), and even though death will come to us all, God's disciples don't shy away from hard work, but rather accept as His discipline this calling to work "*by the sweat of your face.*" And with all our labor-saving devices, there is even more stress, anxiety, and fear—not from the hard work, but because humanity attempts to work apart from the grace of God. They do not work as His disciples under His discipline, and this causes tensions regardless of the job you have. Unless in prayer you cast your anxieties on the Lord,[109] you must bear all your anxieties upon yourself.

If we could only grasp that our creation calling is to relate to God (according to His likeness) in order to represent God (in His image), we would accept His discipline as our sacrificial service to live Him out in all our ways. Our sacrificial service pictures the One who took our eternal judgment with a crown of thorns and reversed the curse so that by faith we might live with Him forever.

In marriage, men are to work hard; laziness is sin. Women, beware of marrying a lazy man. The Lord cannot bless laziness. Men, set an industrious example for your family so that your children will understand that the Lord's disciple thrives under the Lord's discipline. This is a lesson to be learned by those who are in a subordinate role to others. You, like the ground, can be impacted by your leader's misdeeds. Therefore, be careful whom you marry, whom you work for, and in what country you live.

The life reversal: Before their first sin, death was not a concern for our first parents, but it became humanity's "natural" condition from then on. Death is actually unnatural for humanity. Enoch and Elijah were not meant to die; they were meant to live. Like Enoch and Elijah, Adam was not meant to experience death. Though the human body is made fragile and weak and can therefore potentially die, God's grace through the tree of life was His ongoing provision for an ongoing, deathless life. But God warned Adam about the forbidden tree, "*The day that you eat from it you will surely die.*" The most immediate death took place spiritually, as sin caused a spiritual separation between God and humanity. Biblically, death

---

109. First Peter 5:7.

is separation, not non-existence. Physical death is separation from physical life with people. Spiritual death is separation from spiritual life with God.[110] Upon physical death, the body is buried or "sleeps" in the ground, but the soul goes either to eternal judgment apart from Adonai,[111] or, for believers in Messiah, to the eternal presence of Adonai,[112] for neither *"death, nor life…will be able to separate us from the Love of God in Messiah Yeshua our Lord."*[113] In either case, the Scriptures instruct us that following physical death, the soul is conscious.[114] So, although one day Adam and Eve will physically die, the spiritual death they now experience is that they have lost their most intimate communion with the Lord. For each of us as well, even in our present Messianic redemption, *"we walk by faith, not by sight."*[115] Following our physical deaths, believers in Messiah will be immediately transported to His heavenly presence and we *"will know fully just as [we] also have been fully known."*[116] As His disciples under His discipline, we work hard, and then to dust our physical bodies will return.

Eve learned in her discipline as a mother that sin produces pain. For Adam, his discipline reveals that sin produces death. And so the prophet declares, *"The soul who sins will die"* (Ezekiel 18:4). *"Till you return to the ground, because from it you were taken; for you are dust, and to dust you shall return."* In your self-deception, you forgot who you were, mere dust. You believed Satan's lies that you could be gods. But you are who God says you are, and that's more than enough. Accept yourself by the grace by which He accepts you; by your simple faith and humility in Messiah, gain His glory as His free gift. The result of your sin is your physical death, and then, without repentance and faith in Yeshua, your eternal death, that is, your eternal separation from God. But the result of Yeshua's grace for you is His everlasting life and His eternal glory.

The Dedicated and Redemptive Cure for Marital Failure: Marriage Lasts unto Death (Genesis 3:20–24)

Now the man called his wife's name Eve, because she was the mother of all the living. The Lord *God made garments of skin for Adam and his wife, and clothed them. Then the* Lord *God said, "Behold, the man has become like one of Us, knowing good and evil; and now, he might stretch out his hand, and take also from the tree of life, and eat, and live forever"—therefore the* Lord *God sent him out from the garden of Eden, to cultivate the ground from which he was taken. So He drove*

---

110. Isaiah 59:1–2; Ephesians 2:1.
111. Hebrews 9:27.
112. Philippians 1:21–23; 2 Corinthians 5:6–8.
113. Romans 8:38–39 (SN).
114. First Samuel 28:12–15; Luke 16:23–26; 20:37–38.
115. Second Corinthians 5:7.
116. First Corinthians 13:12.

the man out; and at the east of the garden of Eden He stationed the cherubim and the flaming sword which turned every direction to guard the way to the tree of life. (Genesis 3:20–24)

People often wonder, "Is there life after death?" Though the Bible guarantees that fact, the real question is, "Is there life *before* death?" Biblically, life is not mere animation or existence, but being in relationship with the living God. Separation from Adonai is death, even if you still exist. In Genesis 3:20–24, we learn from Adam and Eve what it means for a fallen, corrupted, yet repentant couple to genuinely possess life before death.

I. Their ministry roles for life before death, 3:20: The saving faith of the repentant

II. Their Messianic redemption for life before death, 3:21: The sovereign grace to the redeemed

III. Their merciful restriction of life before death, 3:22–24: The severe mercy for the removed

I. Their ministry roles for life before death: The saving faith of the repentant

Now the man called his wife's name Eve, because she was the mother of all the living. (Genesis 3:20)

Not only do we live under discipline and learn from disasters, but marriage in the sight of God lasts "until death do us part." In verse 20, Adam names his wife Eve. In Hebrew, "Eve" is *Chavah*, meaning "life." He sees the discipline of God upon her—that is, motherhood—to be her renewed calling as *"the mother of all the living."* Created in God's image, Adam now realizes that humanity is loved by God, even at our worst, even while "dead in our sins."[117] This divine love becomes a chief theme in Scripture: "*God demonstrates His own love toward us, in that while we were yet sinners, Messiah died for us*" (Romans 5:8 SN). Adam believes the promise of Messiah the Redeemer—the Seed of the woman who destroys Satan, the one who deceived them out of life. Adam and Eve will live before and after their physical death! This the hope of the Redeemer, even as another ancient declares: "*As for me, I know that my Redeemer lives, and at the last He will take His stand on the earth. Even after my skin is destroyed, yet from my flesh I shall see God; whom I myself shall behold, and whom my eyes will see…. My heart faints within me!*" (Job 19:25–27). And so too, the prophets promise: "*He will swallow up death for all time, and the Lord* GOD *will wipe tears away from all faces*" (Isaiah 25:8). The Talmudic writers recognized this Redeemer as the hope of Israel: "The world was created only for Messiah" (Sanhedrin 98b). "All the prophets prophesied only for

---

117. Ephesians 2:1.

the days of the Messiah" (Berachot 34b). When the Redeemer came, Yeshua said, "*Truly, truly, I say to you, he who hears My word, and believes Him who sent Me, has eternal life, and does not come into judgment, but has passed out of death into life*" (John 5:24). By faith in the promised Redeemer, Adam and Eve have a living hope.

Adam has just blamed his wife for his own failures. Yet, instead of blame-naming her (I will name you "Fruit Loops" or "Dodo" or "Oops!" or "It's my entire fault"), he now shows a repentant spirit by caring tenderly for his wife and honoring her with a name to reflect her life-giving calling—that she will give birth to children, giving life to humanity. Despite their past failure, there is a future of hope in the Seed of the woman. This displays a restored leadership role on Adam's part. In Genesis 2:19–20, Adam demonstrated his leadership role that represented God to His creation by naming the creatures. Naming demonstrates leadership. Daniel and his friends were forced as slaves in Babylon to accept new Babylonian names, thereby submitting to the Babylonians as their masters. Parents name their children, thereby taking responsibility for raising them, whereas surrogates do not name or raise the infant. Adam's repentant heart is seen as he reasserts his leadership authority in naming his wife as a testimony of life and hope in God. You are a growing leader in your home when you are forgiving, tender, uplifting, edifying, and honoring to your wife, despite her mistakes and errors in judgment. Adam renews his wife's calling of life, not death. So we minister life to our spouses. Eve accepts her divine discipline by accepting the name he graciously gives her as her renewed leader in the home. The wife's support of her husband's godly leadership reveals her as Messiah's disciple.

II. Their Messianic redemption for life before death: The sovereign grace to the redeemed

> *The LORD God made garments of skin for Adam and his wife, and clothed them.* (Genesis 3:21)

The couple is redeemed through death. They choose fig leaves, but that is not suitable covering for them. The covering from God has to do with His redemption. The animal skins represent the first physical deaths in the Bible. These animals are not killed for food—they are killed for sacrifice. This is the first actual clothing, the first physical death, the first sacrifice for humanity—the innocent victim for the repentant sinner. This foreshadows the bloody sacrifices that will develop later and is the first type of Messiah as our sacrifice, for Scripture states: "*He made Him who knew no sin to be sin on our behalf, so that we might become the righteousness of God in Him*" (2 Corinthians 5:21). The first biblical clothing foreshadows our eternal garments as well: "*As many of you as were immersed into the Messiah have clothed yourselves with the Messiah*" (Galatians 3:27 SN). This is how God the Father restores every prodigal yet repentant child, as pictured in the father's words about his repentant prodigal son: *"The father said to his slaves, 'Quickly bring out the best robe and put it on him,... for this son of mine was dead and has come to life again; he was lost and has been found'"* (Luke 15:22, 24). God the Father's grief over our awful sins now becomes rejoicing over the repentance of every one of His returning children. He wants only to clothe you in Messiah, His robe of righteousness for you.

The couple is redeemed by Adonai's sacrificial provision, which is the only way that God works to redeem a struggling couple. The enmity that was revealed in their blame game is now removed in the promise of the Redeemer, for Messiah came to make the two into one: *"For He Himself is our peace, who made both groups into one and broke down the barrier of the dividing wall, by abolishing in His flesh the enmity...so that in Himself He might make the two into one new man, thus establishing peace, and might reconcile them both in one body to God through the cross, by it having put to death the enmity"* (Ephesians 2:14–16). God covers them in redemption, not excuses! The redeemed and renewed leadership in the home does not hide behind the fig leaves of hypocrisy, but trusts in the blood of Messiah's redemption.

III. Their merciful restriction of life before death: The severe mercy for the removed

> *Then the* LORD *God said, "Behold, the man has become like one of Us,*[118] *knowing good and evil; and now, he might stretch out his hand, and take also from the tree of life, and eat, and live forever"—therefore the* LORD *God sent him out from the garden of Eden, to cultivate the ground from which he was taken. So He drove the man out; and at the east of the garden of Eden He stationed the cherubim and the flaming sword which turned every direction to guard the way to the tree of life.*
> (Genesis 3:22–24)

Removal priority is for man's penalty, 3:22: **The merciful reason for this restriction**

> *Then the* LORD *God said, "Behold, the man has become like one of Us, knowing good and evil; and now, he might stretch out his hand, and take also from the tree of life, and eat, and live forever"*

The Lord discerned our ungodly wisdom

Adam was not prohibited up to this point from eating from the tree of life. Though he was created as a physical being, it is assumed that he would be enabled to live forever by eating from that life-giving tree. The problem now is that he is a

---

118. God said *"Us"* to whom? To angels? No, for it states, *"has become like one of Us."* The angels are not identified as being like God. To Himself? This "Us" is also in Isaiah 6:8, etc., where the triune God is speaking.

corrupted being, and living forever would be awful for him. God is rich in mercy (Ephesians 2:4–5); every restriction by God is an expression of His mercy to us, whether we're aware of it or not. Knowing good and evil through corruption has only produced fear, resentment, and blame. Why is something good or evil? It is good or evil relative to God. Anything that reflects His character is good, and anything that contradicts His character is evil.

If *knowing* merely means that humanity understands right and wrong, it would not necessitate the measures enacted. But if *knowing* (as in Genesis 24:22) means to determine—to evaluate for oneself—then humanity will now determine what is good and what is evil. They will decide sinfully and selfishly, on the basis of whether or not it is "good for me." Their conclusions are fig leaves and hiding fearfully from God. They will get *knowing* sinfully wrong every time, since it is selfishly evaluated. Our corruption reverses good and evil, even as the prophet declares: "*Woe to those who call evil good, and good evil*" (Isaiah 5:20).

Gaining the knowledge of good and evil through disobedience is now part of the corruption of our mind and conscience, like a hair-trigger gun in the hands of a rebellious child. In mercy, God removes us from further temptation. What is meant for good, sins perverts into an instrument of wickedness. Similarly, sin made the Torah, which is holy and good, into an instrument of death, as Paul exclaims![119] So too with our marriages. They were meant to be good, but sin perverts them into hurtful relationships. With repentance and God's mercy in Messiah, like the Torah, redeemed marriages can now reflect His saving grace in Yeshua.

The Lord dreaded our unending wickedness

The believer in the Lord, as hard as it is for some of us to grasp, accepts death to be a mercy. Death is in fact a very gracious mercy. That's why Paul could say, "*For me, to live is Messiah, to die is gain*" (Philippians 1:21 SN). Gain? Yes, and that's why both the removal from the garden and our death (the removal from physical life) are a gracious part of our divine discipline. We are not permitted in our present physical bodies to live forever. Praise the Lord! It would be hell on earth for such wickedness to continue without the blessing of physical death. Adonai's everlasting love for us not only provides physical death, but removes Adam and Eve from the proximity of the tree of life.

However, there is a promise to us of a resurrection body that will be imperishable and incorruptible. The resurrection body will be impervious to sin and its resulting death. "*Now I say this, brethren, that flesh and blood cannot inherit the kingdom of God; nor does the perishable inherit the imperishable. Behold, I tell you a mystery; we will not all sleep, but we will all be changed, in a moment, in the twinkling of an eye, at the last trumpet; for the trumpet will sound, and the dead will be raised imperishable, and we will be changed. For this perishable must put on*

---

119. See Romans 7:9–14.

the imperishable, and this mortal must put on immortality. But when this perishable will have put on the imperishable, and this mortal will have put on immortality, then will come about the saying that is written, 'DEATH IS SWALLOWED UP in victory'" (1 Corinthians 15:50–54).

God's merciful restrictions now, if faithfully followed, are to keep us secure to enjoy His greatest blessings forever. As parents restrict their kids from driving a car until it's safe for them, so we too as Messianic marriages need to accept the discipline of restrictions that His redemption mercifully provides, so that we might have the eternal hope in what His Word promises for every Messianic believer.

Removal purpose is for man's progress, 3:23: **The merciful relocation in this restriction**

> *Therefore the LORD God sent him out from the garden of Eden,*
> *to cultivate the ground from which he was taken.*

Is God relocating you way outside of your comfort zone? That's certainly what it must have felt like to Adam and Eve. He sends them out to protect them from further hurt. In being removed from the garden of Eden, Adam and Eve are being given an opportunity to serve the Lord—that is, to live out His life calling and impact the world, even through a farming career. The faithfulness of God compels Him to remove us from harmful places so we can fulfill our creation call. He is faithful in His desire to redeem the world. When He blesses Adam and Eve (Genesis 1:28) to impact the world, it is always and only the blessing of grace that fulfills our lives and calling. Now, following their sinful failure, grace is more evident as they trust the Lord outside the garden. Our locations change; our calling continues! The purpose of restriction and relocation is to be serving elsewhere. God closes the door for Paul in Asia to open the door for Paul in Europe![120]

Do you and your spouse accept your divine Messianic calling? Yeshua said, *"Go…make disciples of all the nations…and lo, I am with you always"* (Matthew 28:19–20). Though Galilean Peter may never have wanted to leave his familiar surroundings, his creation call is fulfilled in Messiah's mandate to reach out. Is your family's security in their present location or in the Lord Himself? Your true security will be revealed as you yield yourselves to His calling.

Jonah the prophet had to be expelled from a great fish to reach out to the non-Jewish world. Is your Messianic marriage concerned about reaching out, or obsessed over "internal affairs" that only make you carnally ingrown and not spiritually mature? The unhealthy marriage is ingrown, but the spiritually healthy Messianic couple seeks to reach out with Good News together to their neighbors and friends.

---

120. Acts 16:6–10.

Removal permanence is for man's protection, 3:24: The prevention of reentry

So He drove the man out; and at the east of the garden of Eden He stationed the cherubim and the flaming sword which turned every direction to guard the way to the tree of life.

God kicks them out. If it were up to our first parents, they would have never left. But often God has to take matters into His own hands to get us where we need to be. When the people would not reach the world, but rather, resisted their outward call and built a tower of Babel upward, God had to disperse them.[121] When Yeshua called His disciples to reach the world, but they preferred to stay together in Jerusalem, God had to permit a persecution and disperse them to fulfill their calling.[122] What will it take to move us to fulfill our calling? A job change?[123] Health issues?[124] God is faithful to help us fulfill our creation and redemption calling, while He may not be too concerned about maintaining our creature comforts, luxuries, and conveniences. Are you as a couple more committed to your comforts, or to your calling? Your wrong commitments for each other develop wrong relationships with each other.

God keeps them out. The angels guard the tree, but why? Why not destroy it and be rid of the problem? God wants us to partake, but not in a corrupted state. As they guard the tree, so also they guard the holy of holies and the mercy seat. Why? Only through the blood sacrifice can you approach the Lord. The angel's fiery sword reminds us that only with the fire offering can we approach fellowship with the Holy One of Israel. We fight fire with fire. So also, only through the blood offering of Messiah can we eat of the tree of life, having life eternal in the Son. So too in your home, the blood of the Lamb is required for the presence of the living God in your marriage.

All that you see in the previous chapters regarding the formation of rivers and the locations is pre-flood. That shifts and changes after the great flood. In the New Covenant we see the conclusion of all these matters once God's program of redemption is completed. Revelation 22:1–3 talks about the new heaven, the new earth, the new Jerusalem, etc. "*Then he showed me a river of the water of life, clear as crystal, coming from the throne of God and of the Lamb, in the middle of its street. On either side of the river was the tree of life, bearing twelve kinds of fruit, yielding its fruit every month; and the leaves of the tree were for the healing of the nations. There will no longer be any curse; and the throne of God and of the Lamb will be in it, and His bond-servants will serve Him.*" Verse 14 goes on to say, "*Blessed are those who wash their robes, so that they may have the right to the tree of life.*" Those

---

121. Genesis 11:1–9.
122. Acts 8:1.
123. Acts 18:2–3.
124. Galatians 4:13.

who have not washed their robes in Messiah's atonement are eternally excluded from the tree of life. The tree of life is for the redeemed alone.

We need to appreciate the graciousness of God in His discipline. Marriage lasts until death, "Till death do us part," as we are taught in Scripture, and usually in most marriage ceremonies. We are expected to be faithful until death.

Some questions to help apply these teachings

1. With whom do you associate that may be considered a hindrance to proper relationships?

2. In what areas do you have trouble trusting the Lord in regards to your provision and calling?

3. What decisions are you making by God's Word? And which ones do you fudge by your own reasoning?

4. What activities do you engage in that are not according to His will? What restrictions of God do you accept or not accept readily?

5. What areas can you discern as right or wrong by God's Word? What areas are most unclear to you? What matters do you evaluate as good and right and wrong and bad for you?

6. What areas do you discuss together? What areas do you not discuss together? Are they both by agreement? What areas are you ashamed about and tend to disguise, lie, or disengage over?

7. In what areas are you fearful of God?

8. From what instructors besides the Word are you getting your teaching on right and wrong, good and evil?

9. In what matters are you blaming others? Do you have any responsibility in those matters? Are you blaming or resenting God?

10. What spiritual battles are you facing? Who are your allies in the battle? In what areas do you resist proper submission?

11. Are there areas of service that you murmur about or resent? What areas of unforgiveness reside in your soul?

CHAPTER FIVE

The Tanakh's Take on Marriage

Illustrations, Divorce, Prophets, and Proverbs

Following the marriage disaster of Genesis 3, the Tanakh both illustrates and regulates the hardness-of-heart condition in marriage that results from the sinful corruption of humanity. Our illustrations are from both well-known and lesser-known marriage problems in the Scriptures. They indicate a diversity and similarity of difficulties in broad-spectrum marriage matters, all of which are intended by God as preparatory lessons, like a tutor leading us to the redemption in Yeshua the Messiah.[1]

Tanakh Marriage illustrations

Abraham and Sarah: **their Hagar strategy**[2]

The call upon Abraham and Sarah is tough on them, especially on Sarah. Though Abram attempts to provide himself an heir through Lot[3] and through his servant Eliezer,[4] God tells Abraham that the promised child will be from his own loins (Genesis 15:4–5). Sarah is not only incapable of having children, but at age seventy-five she is beyond natural childbearing years. The promise of an heir evidently causes her great stress, with its pressure to produce what she is incapable of providing. She goes to "plan B," attempting to fulfill the will of God by circumventing it.

In an earlier marriage fiasco, Abraham leaves the promised land during a drought and goes to Egypt. There he asks Sarah to lie about being his wife and to say she is his sister, since he fears for his life. To get Abram to leave Egypt quickly, Pharaoh gives him some Egyptian handmaids, one of whom serves Sarah. Her name is Hagar. Under the stress to produce, Sarah gives Abram her handmaid Hagar to have a child in her place. Though local custom permitted a barren woman to use her maid in this manner, it goes against Genesis 2:24 and God's one-man-one-wife marriage program. The impatience (and lust) of Abram and the self-induced stress of Sarah bring about the Ishmaelites, who have had a long-term troublesome relationship with the Jewish people ever since.

---

1. Galatians 3:23–36.
2. This illustration proves that the end never justifies the means.
3. Genesis 12:5.
4. Genesis 15:2.

Lesson: God's promises are fulfilled by His power, not ours. Our "shortcuts" only produce unintended and negative consequences for the relationship and the future family. God's promise takes twenty-five years to be properly fulfilled by Sarah producing Isaac. Don't give in to fear, impatience, stress, or lust. Cheating on taxes, watching immoral movies, or using illicit activities to gain immediate relief or gratification can only do much more harm than good. Trust the Lord completely, patiently, and obediently for His perfect provision for your Messianic marriage. And repent quickly when you don't!

Isaac and Rebekah: **marriage choice between truth and loyalty**

We noted that Abraham lies about his wife Sarah being his sister, but he actually lies twice![5] Following this lying behavioral model will negatively impact your children, for we then find Isaac making exactly the same moral mistake and saying his wife Rebekah is his sister, and for the same reason—in fear for his own life.[6] This fear is not from God, *"for God has not given us a spirit of fear, but of power, love, and a sound mind."*[7] Homes that opt for loyalty over truth bring grievous corruption to their children.

Having your child lie to protect Dad's drinking problem can only undermine the child's trust in the parents and all future authority. This is especially true when there is abuse in the home, and you tell your child to say that he fell down the steps again. This is not family loyalty; it is damnable corruption. When Isaac lies about Rebekah as his sister, she herself uses lying and has Jacob lie to get the Abrahamic blessing from Isaac.[8] Lying to one another or for one another is lying to God, as with Ananias and Sapphira in Acts 5. Our faith is in the God who is the truth and *"cannot lie."*[9] When a marriage depends on lies for their supposed security, significance, and/or satisfaction, the couple is deceived to think that God would bless such an ungodly arrangement, for *"no lie is of the truth."*[10] Rather, God's chastening hand will be upon such a marriage until there is repentance, forgiveness, and obedience to the truth. For only *"the truth will make you free"*[11] from the bondage of lies.

Jacob and Leah and Rachel: **favorite wife problem**

As noted, Jacob has a problem with truth-telling. Jacob's infamous lies[12] will unfortunately characterize him to many Bible students. But what he sows, he will

---

5. Genesis 12:12–13 and 20:2.
6. Genesis 26:7.
7. Second Timothy 1:7 (SN).
8. Genesis 27.
9. Titus 1:2.
10. First John 2:21.
11. John 8:32.
12. Genesis 27; 33:14–17.

also reap. Laban, his relative, deceives him into marrying his older daughter Leah and then tricks him again to work longer than agreed to for his other daughter, Rachel, whom Jacob loves. The Torah of Moses will later prohibit a man from marrying two sisters,[13] and forbid playing favorites among the children of your wives.[14] But part of Isaac and Rebekah's lifestyle is having favorites among their two sons: Isaac loves Esau, and Rebekah chooses Jacob. Though his first wife is Leah, Jacob loves Rachel above her, and therefore is inclined to love her son Joseph above his brethren. This causes havoc in his marriage relationship, as his wives compete for his attention (Genesis 29:30–30:25) and great treachery arises among ten of his children, who sell Joseph, his favorite, into slavery and then lie to their father about the matter. There's so much wrong with this picture, where do we start? Equal weights and measures—that is, evenhandedness—is required by God.[15] No favorites, let alone playing one off against the other. God loves us all the same, both Jew and Gentile are equal in His sight, and He is *"no respecter of persons."*[16] If His love constrains our hearts,[17] then we should love as He loves all members of our family the same.

Joseph and Asenath: forced to marry outside the faith

Though Joseph is not rebuked by God for any fault, when it comes to marriage, he accepts a wife given to him by Pharaoh, *"Asenath, the daughter of Potiphera priest of On."*[18] Marrying a false worshipper from a family of such probably was the acceptable thing to do in Egypt. In any case, you cannot say no to Pharaoh, who just released you from prison. That said, marrying a non-believer is later forbidden under the Torah of Moses[19] and in the New Covenant.[20] Yet at that time there was no commandment on the matter.[21] Even so, both Josephs' sons, Ephraim and Manasseh, were leaders of two tribes of Israel. Despite his wife's religion—or perhaps she became a believer in HaShem—Joseph raises his sons to be followers of the one true God of Israel, even while in Egypt. There are countless stories of Jewish-Gentile Messianic marriages, where the non-Jewish believing spouse

---

13. Leviticus 18:18.
14. Deuteronomy 21:15–17
15. Leviticus 19:36.
16. Romans 3:29–30; Acts 10:34.
17. Second Corinthians 5:14.
18. Genesis 41:45.
19. Deuteronomy 7:3.
20. Second Corinthians 6:14.
21. One could gain insight from Abraham's refusal to have his son Isaac marry a Canaanite woman (Genesis 24:3), and from how grievous it is for Isaac and Rebekah to have their son Esau marry pagans, and their refusal to have Jacob marry a Canaanite woman (Genesis 27:46; 28:6–9). In the story of Judah's marriage (Genesis 38), Judah marrying the Canaanite woman Tamar is a biblical indication that the people of God are becoming Canaanites, and thus Joseph's divinely inspired plan (Genesis 41–44; 45:7–8) to remove his brothers and father from Canaan to maintain them as the people Israel.

commits to raising their children as Messianic Jews. They do this because they realize that the calling in the New Covenant on all Jewish believers is to maintain their testimony as present-tense Jewish people to demonstrate the present-tense faithfulness of God, that He is not forsaking the Jewish people. Though you may have a Jewish-Gentile Messianic marriage, raise the children for who they truly are: Jews. And raise them as Jews who love their Messiah and their people Israel.[22]

Moses and Zipporah: **his first wife**

Scripture records that Moses had two wives, a Midianite woman and an Ethiopian woman.[23] His first wife Zipporah is a Midianite, one of the daughters of Jethro, whom Moses rescues along with her sisters from some shepherds[24] after he escapes from Egypt.

When he is called to serve God and help deliver his people the Israelites from their Egyptian bondage,[25] it turns out that he is not prepared. He has not circumcised his son. This foot dragging is offensive to God, and God is prepared to take the life of Moses.[26] Moses's wife is forced to remove her son's foreskin, and she calls Moses a bloody husband because of the B'rit Milah (the covenant of circumcision) she has to perform. Though Moses is prepared to take her and their sons to Egypt,[27] we no longer hear of her (or his sons) until after the deliverance from Egypt.[28] What happened?

Some marriages are unprepared for the calling of God. Admittedly, this calling is a surprise to Moses as well. But for Zipporah, it is a bloody matter, and he apparently decides she isn't ready for such a calling and sends her back[29] to her father. Moses and Zipporah have a marriage separation because they are spiritually unprepared for the calling of God.

We're not sure what happens to Zipporah after that Exodus 18 reunion. She may have gone back to Midian, for neither she nor Moses's sons are heard from again. Despite the fact that God miraculously calls Moses and powerfully enables Moses to lead Israel out of bondage, and despite the presence of the living God in the camp, she doesn't want this unusual and bloody calling from God. Circumcision? Yes, if there is at least one Jewish parent, as with Timothy,[30] then B'rit Milah is Scripturally expected. But there may be other matters we are unprepared for in a Messianic marriage. Are you and your spouse prepared for God to throw

---

22. Our book, *Messianic Wisdom*, can help in this regard.
23. Exodus 2:16, 21; Numbers 12:1.
24. Exodus 2:17.
25. Exodus 3:10–4:10.
26. Exodus 4:24.
27. Exodus 4:20.
28. Exodus 18:1–6.
29. Exodus 18:2.
30. Acts 16:3.

Five • *The Tanakh's Take on Marriage*

you both a curveball? The curveball can be an unexpected change of finances, an unexpected medical condition, or the loss of a loved one. This will test your genuine trust in Yeshua. Couples need to be praying for God's will to be done, and expect that He will do just that through them. Often our faith is seen in our ability to flex with the Lord when matters take a sudden and unanticipated shift.

Shlomo[31] was anxious to plant a Messianic congregation, but his wife Lisa thought it a strange idea. In counsel with him, I held him back for three years before starting the ministry until his wife was sure this was a calling from God for them both. Ministry takes couple-power and marital unity to model a wholesome family life in the Lord. In marriage, God made the two one in His sight, and any calling on one is a calling on the other as well. Be prayerfully prepared together.

David and Bathsheba: a marriage to kill for

David is the archetypical king of Israel, who had great faith in God against Goliath as a teen and went on to become a successful leader. But though he was "*a man after* [*God's*] *own heart*" (1 Samuel 13:14), he wasn't perfect. Though God's ideal is one-man-one-wife (Genesis 2:24), and even though Torah warns against "*multiplying wives*" (Deuteronomy 17:17), still David is attractive and attracted to the ladies—far too attracted. Instead of going to work (2 Samuel 11:1), he stays home and sees a woman bathing from his kingly perch. As the most powerful man in Israel, he uses his position to have an adulterous relationship with Bathsheba, and then has her husband killed to cover up the affair! This not only brings shame to his reputation, but it desecrates God's name, and the terrible results include rape, murder, and insurrection in David's family and the kingdom of Israel. The "*lust of the flesh and lust of the eyes and the boastful pride of life*" (1 John 2:16) are lived out through that awful period of David's life. And he is someone who loves God!

Take warning for your marriage from David. Beware the wandering eye, immoral sexual desires, and the vanity to think you can cover it up—God sees it all. Live daily in yieldedness to God. Fred and Lola planted a congregation, but his eyes wandered, and his flesh seduced him to leave Lola for another woman. His life became one long disaster, and he eventually came to his senses and repented. He's now following the Lord, but is not able to serve Yeshua in the same ministry capacity. Beware of the lust of the flesh. It will destroy your home and testimony for Adonai. For this reason, I never meet with any woman alone other than my wife, not merely to avoid temptation, but to keep any allegation from being made that could taint either of our reputations. Be filled with the Holy Spirit to be empowered to follow the Lord through all the distractions of life. Repent immediately of any sexual desire in your heart for anyone but your spouse. This is spiritual adultery in God's sight.[32] Renew your commitment and vows to each

---

31. All names throughout the book have been changed to protect the privacy of the individuals.
32. See Matthew 5:27–28.

other personally and publicly. And "*put no worthless thing*" before your eyes,[33] but run the race set before you with endurance, looking unto Yeshua.[34]

Solomon and his wives: compromised marriages

King Solomon was a complicated man. In 1 Kings 3 he demonstrates great and humble faith in the Lord, asking for wisdom to handle his kingly responsibilities. God also blesses him with great wealth and honor. But for all his great wisdom, and despite building a temple to HaShem, Solomon still disobeys God's Word and marries pagan women.[35] And as the Scriptures warn,[36] these pagan wives turn Solomon's heart from fully following the Lord.

Like his father David, Solomon also multiplies wives in disregard of the Scriptures (Deuteronomy 17:17), but Solomon multiplies wives way beyond his predecessor, for he has seven hundred wives and three hundred concubines. Wives are like gods; if the right one is not enough, one thousand wrong ones can't possibly help. Whether he multiplies them out of lust, pride, or for political alliances, he abuses his leadership role and cannot be a moral role model for Israel. In fact, God says that his kingdom will be torn away from his son (1 Kings 11:11–13). God also raises up adversaries against Solomon, all because his marriage failures turn his heart from the Lord. And so, his son Rehoboam loses the greatness of the kingdom, for as wise as his dad was, he himself follows foolish counsel.[37] Disobedience to the Lord means disaffection from the Lord. Either marriage will build up your faith or tear down your faith. Both spouses need to follow the Lord with a whole heart to have unity in the home, for the unity of the parents provides the security for the children.

In a more common marriage situation, but one that in principle has the same problem of being unequally yoked, Diane contacted me with a difficulty. She had married an unsaved Jewish man during a backslidden period in her life. Later, when she came back to the Lord and realized her disobedience by marrying an unbeliever, she wanted to know what God's will for her would be in this situation. Paul teaches us to remain in such a marriage if the unbeliever is willing to stay married to the believer.[38] My counsel was: "First, repent of your previous sinful disobedience in marrying an unbeliever, and thank God for His forgiveness, for Yeshua's atonement covers all our sins. Then, live faithfully now for the Lord in your unequally yoked marriage, praying that God will open your unsaved husband's eyes to the truth of Messiah. It may be hard, but that is now your calling." If you're in a marriage with an unbeliever, you have to repent if you were a believer when you wed, and now you have a divine calling to win your spouse to Messiah.

---

33. Psalm 101:3.
34. Hebrews 12:1–2.
35. See 1 Kings 11:1–12.
36. Exodus 34:12–16.
37. First Kings 12:8–11.
38. First Corinthians 7:10–15.

Ahab and Jezebel: the audacity of idolatry

As we've already stated, it's not true that "Power tends to corrupt and absolute power corrupts absolutely." Remember that Yeshua had all authority, but He was never corrupted by His absolute authority. But power will reveal what is there. King Ahab (874–853 BC) of the northern kingdom, Israel, was certainly corrupt, and becoming king not only revealed his corruption, but gave this wicked man even more opportunity to do evil.[39] To complete his wickedness, he marries Jezebel, the Sidonian pagan princess. Her counsel to her husband is only wicked, for her heart is not only sinful (for all have sinned) but has been thoroughly corrupted by her pagan worship. The Scriptures state: *"Surely there was no one like Ahab who sold himself to do evil in the sight of* [HaShem], *because Jezebel his wife incited him"* (1 Kings 21:25). This is a murderous marriage made in hell. And though they have Elijah the great prophet speaking to them, repentance never enters their minds. When HaShem endeavors to woo Ahab back to the true faith by providing Ahab a victory over the Syrians, he only despises the Word of the Lord even more. Why? This ninth-century BC "power couple" only reinforce each other's evil attitudes and behaviors. Their future holds only condemning judgment from the Lord. Beware of marrying an unbeliever! This sort of marriage only reveals your own unbelieving heart through such an act of disobedience to the Lord. If you are considering such a union, beware and repent before you destroy your life and others.

Hosea and Gomer: marrying the immoral

Being a prophet is not all it's cracked up to be—take it from Hosea (760–720 BC). God calls him to marry a harlot as God's testimony against Israel, because Israel is involved in spiritual harlotry, or idolatry (Hosea 1:2). While the Bible does not teach that it's fine to marry a corrupt person, it happens. How do we respond when we realize we have committed such foolishness? Hosea has to live faithfully with an unfaithful spouse to testify of God's faithfulness to unfaithful Israel. It is hard, but that is the calling.

A dear friend, Susan, shared her story with Miriam and me. Susan was young and naive when she married Bill. She was a sincere believer, but didn't know enough to ask some follow-up questions when Bill said he was a believer in the Lord. Poor dear! He soon showed his true colors as both a drunk and a womanizer—even bringing other women home with him. Susan prayed and prayed for Bill. For twenty-six years of miserable marriage she prayed. But she would not break her marriage vows, and would not divorce Bill. Finally, he told Susan that he was divorcing her in order to "marry a woman who would be more fun." After the divorce, she continued to pray for Bill.

One day, two years later, she received a phone call from her ex. "Susan, thanks for praying, for now I'm born again! But what do I do now, since I'm now married

---

39. Ahab's whole awful reign is recorded in 1 Kings 16:28–22:51.

to a drunken wife who cheats on me?" Susan could only say what she knew was true, "Pray, Bill, pray. It may take a while, but God does answer prayers." Not all unequally yoked marriages are as evidently awful as Susan's marriage, but in God's sight, one married to an unbeliever is actually a missionary to that unbeliever. Certainly, you should repent of any naiveté or wrong-headedness that led you into such a marriage, and be strong in the Lord to love the unsaved and thereby win the lost.[40]

Tanakh on Marriage, Divorce, and Remarriage Regulations

As noted in the Scriptures, the Tanakh[41] was meant as regulatory[42] until Messiah would come and establish the New Covenant based on His redemption and salvation from our hardness-of-heart condition.[43] This condition is what the Torah reveals and what its regulations were meant to restrain.

In the Torah

In the Torah, the marriage discussion is of course regulatory, especially in those sections that deal with slaves (especially female slaves as wives in Exodus 21 and Deuteronomy 21), and those sections that deal with second wives (even the fair treatment of second wives who are slaves, Exodus 21:10–11). In our present day, this whole matter of slavery reeks of social injustice that we proudly consider expunged long ago from civilized society. Understood.[44] But we must remember the Torah was not intended to bring about humanity's redemption from sin, but to bring about Israel's regulation of their sinful behavior. Slavery in the pagan countries of the world was often without any regulation or help for the slaves; they were treated and disposed of as property. The Torah of Moses brought regulation so that Israel would treat slaves humanely as real people, though with very limited civil rights. But to reinforce a more humane treatment, God, through Mosaic Torah, repeatedly reminds His people that *"you were a slave in Egypt."*[45] As for the second wife, though Genesis 2:24 one-man-one-woman marriage is what God designed, with human corruption multiple wives (and in some countries, multiple husbands) became socially acceptable and needed regulation as well. In this regard the basic provisions for a second wife stated, *"If he takes to himself another woman, he may not reduce her food, her clothing, or her conjugal rights"* (Exodus 21:10). Though we may live in states or countries where all properties and possessions are equally

---

40. More of this will be covered under our study and application of 1 Peter 3:1–7.
41. Tanakh: the Torah (Law), N'vi'im (the Prophets), and Ketuvim (the Writings)
42. Hebrews 9:10: "...*regulations for the body imposed until a time of reformation.*"
43. Matthew 19:8.
44. For a further discussion on slavery then and now, listen to the author's 15-part teaching series on the letter to Philemon.
45. Exodus 13:3, 14; 20:2; Leviticus 26:45; Deuteronomy 5:6, 15; 6:12, 21; 7:8; 8:14; 13:5, 10; 15:15; 16:12; 24:18, 22.

divided in a divorce, we must remember that humankind once lived according to a might-makes-right mentality. Women were often abused and discarded by evil men. This precept was meant to regulate for the women's sake a fair treatment when the flame of love (or lust) had long since been extinguished.[46]

There is also Torah on the moral matters regarding marriage, such as uncovering a woman (Leviticus 18), adultery (Leviticus 20; Numbers 5), and married women keeping their vows (Numbers 30). The Torah also wrestles with the issue of inheritance for females in a patriarchal society, regulating on the side of the woman (Number 27 and 36), and with the general fair treatment of a wife (Deuteronomy 22:13–30), and the levirate marriage (Deuteronomy 25:5–11) that allows the brother's name to live on in Israel.[47]

But the matters that may be best known from a New Covenant perspective have to do with the divorce regulations that Yeshua discusses in Matthew 19:2–9.

Divorce Matters: The Conditions that Prohibit Remarriage to a Former Spouse

Deuteronomy 24:1–4[48]

Of the many ceremonial limitations upon the Levitical priesthood (Leviticus 21), is the prohibition of a priest against marrying a divorced woman (or a widow, etc.). This portion helps to explain the ceremonial defilement involved with marrying a divorced woman.

> *When a man takes a wife and marries her, and it happens that she finds no favor in his eyes because he has found some indecency in her, and he writes her a certificate of divorce and puts it in her hand and sends her out from his house, and she leaves his house and goes and becomes another man's wife, and if the latter husband turns against her and writes her a certificate of divorce and puts it in her hand and sends her out of his house, or if the latter husband dies who took her to be his wife, then her former husband who sent her away is not allowed to take her again to be his wife, since she has been defiled; for that is an abomination before the* LORD, *and you shall not bring sin on the land which the* LORD *your God gives you as an inheritance.*
> (Deuteronomy 24:1–4)

---

46. Paul seems to have this instruction in mind when he writes 1 Corinthians 7:1–6.
47. For a discussion on the spiritual values in the levirate marriage, read the author's commentary on the book of Ruth, pp. 176–187.
48. The portion's structure: Deuteronomy 24:1 belongs to a longer list of *ki + yiqtol* [imperfect] clauses (see 23:10, 22, 25; 24:5, 7, 10, 19, 20, 21; 25:1, 5, etc.) These are circumstantial situational clauses. A reader would check the other clauses of this type in the context to see how they are put together. As far as making vv. 1–4 one long sentence, the "*v'haya im*" ("and if" v. 1) phrase introduces the *prodosis*. The *veqatals* (vav + perfect) follow ("and he shall write," "and he shall give," "and he shall send," etc.). The apodosis doesn't come until verse 4 ("then"). Thus, syntactically, vv. 1–4 belong together (If X = vv. 1–3, then Y = v. 4).

This portion is evaluated by Yeshua the Messiah as caused by "*hardness of heart*," which necessitates Moses to permit divorce under certain conditions. But this portion was primarily meant to keep marriages sacred before God in the context of Israel's calling as His holy people.

The purposes of this portion:

First purpose: to keep the land *tahor* ("clean")

Second purpose: to regulate divorce—for the wife to have a certificate of divorce so she may remarry

Third purpose: to hinder a fickle husband from too easily divorcing his wife

Fourth purpose: to prohibit remarriage to a former spouse after her second marriage to another man

The requirements of Scriptural divorce (24:1–2)

> *When a man takes a wife and marries her,*
> *and it happens that she finds no favor in his eyes because he has found*
> *some indecency in her, and he writes her a certificate of divorce and*
> *puts it in her hand and sends her out from his house, and she leaves his*
> *house and goes…*

Seven steps are required for an approved divorce, including two initial conditions:

1. *The man initiates a Scriptural marriage to the woman* (according to Genesis 2:24) by choosing a woman to marry, and then properly marrying her. This portion does not apply to forced marriages ("shotgun weddings," as in Deuteronomy 22:28–29), arranged marriages, common-law marriages, etc. This application is to first-time marriages of a virginal groom and virginal bride via Scripturally approved conditions. God is attempting to keep the first marriage pure for the people to remain pure, that His land may remain pure.

2. *The man finds some indecency in her* (*ervat davar*, "a shameful thing"). The calling of a holy people necessitated public modesty, for "*the Lord your God walks in the midst of your camp*," so the camp must be holy.[49] This shame of public nakedness was not a matter for divorce, but a capital offense requiring the death penalty.[50]

In Scripture,[51] it was always another who "*uncovered the nakedness*" of the wife—never the husband—for he should uncover her nakedness as part of healthy marriage. If his wife's nakedness is uncovered by another man, there is presumed adultery, and they both die even as if it were incest.[52] If she publicly exposes her

---

49. Deuteronomy 23:14.
50. Leviticus 18:6–19; 20:11–21.
51. Leviticus 18:6–19; 20:11–21.
52. Leviticus 20:10–11, 17.

own nakedness, this is lewdness and also worthy of death, not divorce.[53] The point is that though some couples may have been indiscreet about their moral failures, Torah did not teach divorce for such behavior, but only death. This section would not be contradicting those other sections of Torah by teaching divorce for such an offense, so there is something else being taught here by Moses.

The shameful matter (*ervat davar*) of the wife is the nakedness of the husband. This is some weakness and vulnerability about her that shames him in his own eyes. He seeks to remove her to protect his own self-esteem. But there is no actual occasion in which the husband "finds" an *ervah*, that is, a shameful matter. For if he did, he would cover it to protect his own honor. It is only when there is a public shame (i.e., adultery, idolatry, lewdness, etc.) that the husband is expected to take public action (i.e., divorce or even death) according to Torah. Thus the premise of this whole discussion (i.e., that he privately finds something shameful about her) is to bring him to realize his own selfishness or his easily offended orientation. In Scripture, a wife's nakedness to the husband's shame is "uncovered," not by the husband, but by a son, nephew, etc. For "*the man and his wife were both naked and were not ashamed.*"[54] If the indecency was adultery, she would be condemned under Torah, not divorced.[55] If she was proven not to have been a virgin upon marriage, that too was condemned,[56] but that was not a matter of divorce under Torah.

So, in Deuteronomy 24:1, the indecency (shame) is in the eye of the beholder, that is, the shame is in the husband's own self-esteem, not in the objective indecent behavior of his wife. This indecency could be that they're incompatible (in his opinion), or that he doesn't feel respected by her, or her lack of companionship, etc. But it has nothing to do with her having a condemnable behavior. Rather, it has everything to do with his perception of his self-esteem. Because of sin, he now perceives her weakness as his vulnerability. Is there not shame? Yes, shame on him for his insecure self-centeredness! Yet, because of the sinfulness of humanity, the Torah could only regulate, and in so doing, hopefully bring people to look deeper into their selfish hearts, repent, and remain married.[57]

---

53. Ezekiel 23:18. In the New Covenant, when Joseph suspects Miriam of adultery, he plans to "*send her away secretly*," or divorce her (Matthew 1:19). But she could have publicly faced the death penalty under Torah.
54. Genesis 2:25.
55. Leviticus 20:10.
56. Deuteronomy 22:21.
57. This word *ervah* refers to weakness (undefended areas), shameful nakedness, something dishonorable, or humiliation. Genesis 9:22–23: "*nakedness [ervah] of their father.*" Noah was a shame that brought a curse to Canaan. The *ervah* was also the "*undefended*" part of a country (Genesis 42:9, 12). Modesty, as opposed to shamefulness or immodesty, was required among priests (Exodus 20:26; 28:42). Saul saw Jonathan's support of David as a "*shame*" upon his father, and called it "*the shame of your mother's nakedness*," in that it dishonored him as the dad (1 Samuel 20:30). Notice that although his mother is not in the story, the phrase is used in reference to the dishonor of the father.

3. *She finds no favor in his eyes*. The husband has to first find some indecency in her, for then she will not have "*favor in his eyes.*" It can't be that he doesn't care for her and then goes looking for some excuse, which is not a just cause for him to seek to divorce her. It must be that he first finds some indecency, and then she loses favor in his eyes. Mind, this does not at all justify his seeking to divorce, but rather, forces him not to merely lose interest in her and then go looking for excuses of indecency about her.[58]

Three matters are thus far required: 1) He has chosen to marry her, 2) he has found some indecency in her, and 3) she then finds no favor in his eyes. Have you asked enough questions of the person you choose to marry? Will there be something that comes up later on that will be off-putting or "indecent" for you? Is there something about her or him to make you feel like you've made a bad choice? Then don't get married in the first place!

Now, for this to be a legit divorce that will give opportunity for the prohibition against remarriage to be in effect, there are several other steps the husband must personally take.

4. *He writes her a certificate of divorce*. No lawyer is mentioned. By having to do it himself, he is forced to deal with his own peculiar rationale and self-interest

---

Thus, the word *ervah* became a synonym for "shame" (Isaiah 20:4; 47:3 [as a reproach]; Lamentations 1:8 [to despise]; Ezekiel 16:8 [this *ervah* was only for the husband to see and cover as his own]; 16:36–37 [as lewdness]; 23:18 [as harlotries]). Idolatrous and immoral living is characterized as "*they have uncovered their fathers' nakedness*" (Ezekiel 22:10). For invaders to have "*uncovered her nakedness*" (Ezekiel 23:10) meant to have their way with Israel, even taking her children at will, and property (Ezekiel 23:39). Israel uses the blessings of the Lord for idolatry, etc., as an act of *ervah*. The Lord removes those blessings to cover "*her nakedness,*" thus stopping the shame to the Father and Husband of Israel.

In Ezra 4:14, for the king to be tricked in the loss of revenues is considered "*to see the king's dishonor*" (*ar'vat mal'kah*). Deuteronomy 24:1 in the Greek translation of the Tanakh (LXX, or Septuagint) uses the word *aschemon* for "unattractive," "indecent," "unpresentable"—referring to the parts of the body that should be kept private and covered. Also it is used for "disgraceful," as in the rape of Dinah (Genesis 34:7). So too, in the New Covenant: "*And those members of the body which we deem less honorable, on these we bestow more abundant honor, and our less presentable [aschemon] members become much more presentable*" (1 Corinthians 12:23).

Aschemon appears elsewhere in the Septuagint (Leviticus 18, 20, etc.). And it is used in Greek writings in Jewish culture: "The necessities of life are water, bread, and clothing, and also a house to assure privacy [*aschemon*]" (Sirach 29:21). Paul alludes to this in 1 Timothy 6:8, when he speaks of food and covering. Paul uses it of homosexuals "*committing indecent acts [aschemon],*" in that they are dishonoring the Creator, not merely themselves. Revelation 16:15 states that blessed is the one who "*keeps his clothes*" so as not to be naked, and none would "*see his shame [aschemon].*" As previously noted, Joseph, as a righteous man, wanted to quietly divorce Miriam for her pregnancy until it was revealed to him as God's divine work (Matthew 1:19–22). But the idea of divorce recognized her pregnancy, not merely finding "*some indecency in her,*" for with her death would also come the death of the child she was carrying.

58. On this matter, the traditional rabbinical community has taken a position that is voiced by the French rabbi of the eleventh century, Rashi: "It is his duty to divorce because she should not find favor in his eyes." So, advancing beyond with what Yeshua had to contend, the rabbinical opinion of His day had so devolved that divorce was what must take place where she has no favor in his eyes, a position directly contrary to Moses's intention.

in the matter. By outsourcing all this to a lawyer, the pain of having to write down all your self-serving reasons for this divorce would certainly be removed. But no lawyer is permitted; it must be written down by the husband for this to be a legitimate divorce.

5. *He puts it in her hand*. We see no mention of a messenger to deliver the papers. By putting it into her hand himself, he has to look at her, and live the reality that he is causing her pain by his actions, for it is solely his initiative that is causing this divorce, not hers.

6. *He sends her out from his house*. We see no mention of a sheriff or a judge sending her away. By sending her away himself, he has to again live with the pain of his heartless rejection of his wife. All this is meant to bring him to his senses.

7. *She leaves his house*. She may not actually leave, for there may be other extenuating circumstances which require her to stay. It may not be his house, but someone else's. If the house belongs to another, he has no biblical right to ask her to leave. It may be her house as part of her father's gift, in which case she may also rightly refuse to leave. If she doesn't leave, the divorce is in question, though if he leaves, it now may be seen as his abandonment of the marriage and not the biblical divorce that Moses requires.

If all these seven steps have been carefully followed, then there is a divorce under Moses's regulations. This "writ of divorce" placed into her hand now proves that she was not at fault, for he had to write down why he disliked something about her, and why she did not have favor in his eyes any longer. This writ actually guarantees her innocence as a victim in the divorce. All this is for her protection. It's only further hardness of heart that misinterpreted the teaching of Moses as a problem for any woman.

The prohibitions to remarry his first wife (24:2b–3)

> [She] *becomes another man's wife, and if the latter husband turns against her and writes her a certificate of divorce and puts it in her hand and sends her out of his house, or if the latter husband dies who took her to be his wife...*

1. *The condition that prohibits his remarriage to his first wife* (24:2b). The wife may choose not to remarry, choosing rather to go back to her father's home, etc., and await possible reconciliation. For she may see this as his temporarily foolish hardness of heart and that he's a double-minded man who may come to his senses and come back to her. In any case, this divorce may only be seen afterwards as a separation, since the prohibition is not in effect if she chooses to remain unmarried. Paul refers to this in 1 Corinthians 7:10–11, in that a divorced person must remain unmarried, or if they wish to remarry, go back to their spouse.[59] But it's her remarriage that makes the divorce final.

So, she marries another man (*l'ish acher*).[60] This is simply some man other than her first husband.[61] By remarrying under these conditions,[62] though she is now defiled to her first husband, the first husband is culpable,[63] and the second husband is now also guilty of adultery as well. But this is not viewed as the sort of adultery with capital punishment attached, but as a ceremonial state of defilement because the divorce was forced upon her.

2. *The further conditions that prohibit remarriage to the first husband* (24:3). There are several further measures that her new husband must take for the prohibition to be in effect. There is one general condition with four facets in her second divorce. The phrase "*the latter husband turns against her [s'neah]*" seems parallel to the first husband finding "*some indecency in her.*" This is Moses's way of redefining the first husband's real problem, that is, that the first husband initially turned against her as well. The phrase expresses an emotional attitude toward persons and things that are opposed, detested, despised, and with which one wishes to have no contact or relationship.[64] This matter of turning against her, or hating her, is also seen in marriage in Deuteronomy 22:13–19, where the husband who hates his wife is not permitted to make false accusations of immorality against her, for then he can never divorce her. If the accusations of immorality are found to be true, there's no divorce either, since she is executed for her proven wickedness (22:20–21), hatred or not.[65] That said, without genuine cause (adultery, etc.), the

---

59. In the prophets, there is quite a bit of discussion of God sending away adulterous Israel and Judah (Isaiah 50:1; Jeremiah 3:1–8). But it is always with the idea that Israel will not "remarry" by permanently accepting false gods. In due time, Israel will return and be accepted by Adonai (Isaiah 54:6–7; Jeremiah 3:12; Hosea 3:5; 6:1–3). But her spiritual harlotries will require a New Covenant for His ancient people (Jeremiah 31:31–34).

60. The phrase "*another man,*" as in Genesis 29:19 and Leviticus 27:20, is also found in Jeremiah 3:1 where God complains about Israel as "*a harlot with many lovers.*" This phrase is also used for a transformation in Saul by the Spirit (1 Samuel 10:6), when Saul becomes for the moment someone other than himself. The harsh view by Rashi is: "He has turned the wicked woman out of his house whilst he has taken her into his house."

61. In fact, she is ideally not to remarry another man, for she is actually still married to the same man before God. But if forced to stay with him, it may have been even worse for her, as in a parallel Muslim culture today you can see that jealous husbands have been known to pour acid on their wives' faces with impunity. So, the "get" was a more benevolent option because of the hardness of heart in humanity. But what choice does she have—starve to death? In that society, to be unmarried was to be a prostitute or a gleaner, in which case you were literally up for grabs. Even so, Paul instructs younger widows to marry (1 Timothy 5:14).

62. Of course, she could not marry a priest (Leviticus 21:7; Ezekiel 44:22).

63. Yeshua rightly understood this whole matter (Matthew 5:31–32).

64. Rashi: "These words mean, the other man will hate her and divorce her, and if not she will bury him (be the cause of his death)." But I think Rashi's comments tell us more about him than about Moses.

65. A home with hatred is a hard place to live in for sure (Proverbs 15:17; Genesis 37:4–8), and left unresolved, it may lead to division.

actual motive for a divorce is just hardness of heart. In fact, hating a fellow Israelite in your heart is forbidden to the people of Israel (Leviticus 19:17).

Hatred, as selfish as it is, is often a cause for sending someone away (Genesis 26:27). The husband who hates his wife without cause places the wife in a place of blessing before the Lord (Genesis 29:31–33). Hatred of a wife is no reason to hinder her firstborn son to you to be removed from his proper status.[66] This senseless hatred that rejects a spouse was the motive that rejected Messiah as well.[67] Messiah came to give us new hearts because we had all become afflicted with hardness of heart, which is especially seen in the plague of divorce both then and now. Though God hates divorce (Malachi 2:16), people are hard hearted toward God and therefore to their spouses as well.

For her second divorce, her second husband also must write her a certificate of divorce and, as with the first writ, it is his opportunity to see that this is all based on the fact that he turned against her, which on its face seems quite self-serving.

Her second husband must also put it "*in her hand,*" which, as noted, must make him face the person that he is hurting because he has turned against her, not that she has turned against him. This further hardness of heart should (by the work of the Holy Spirit) also reflect to the second husband that he is quite unlike God, who is ever faithful to Israel according to His promises.

Her second husband must also send her "*out of his house,*" at which point his heartlessness contains all the difficulties noted above: he has to send her, she has to leave, it must be his house, etc. In other words, this is a replay of her first divorce with all its hindrances to accomplish the divorce, and further hindering the prohibition of remarriage to the first husband from coming into effect.

The second condition in her second marriage that may prohibit remarriage to the first husband is the second husband's death. If they're happily married and she becomes a widow, she can remarry without concern, but not to her first husband. What if he remains ill but doesn't die? She remains faithfully married to him.

The prohibitions in light of these conditions (24:4)

> *Then her former husband who sent her away is not allowed to take her again to be his wife, since she has been defiled; for that is an abomination before the* Lord, *and you shall not bring sin on the land which the* Lord *your God gives you as an inheritance.*

Considering the limiting conditions noted above, there are four final prohibitions that are meant to nail shut any consideration of a remarriage to his first wife, so

---

66. Deuteronomy 21:15–17. It should be noted that hatred as a Hebraism can also mean "to love less than someone else." For example, Jacob hating Leah is usually translated as "loved less" (Genesis 29:31), and therefore this Hebraism is also used in the New Covenant (Luke 14:26, etc.).
67. Psalm 69:4; John 15:25.

that the aforementioned husbands will hopefully realize the offensiveness in God's sight of a self-serving divorce.

1. *It is legally prohibited*. This is a sin against Torah, for it states: "*Then her former husband who sent her away is not allowed to take her again to be his wife.*"

Remarriage to your former wife under these precise conditions is prohibited. The phrase translated "*not allowed*" is simply "cannot" (*lo-yukhal*). It's not saying that he is not physically able, but that in God's eyes it is morally or legitimately impermissible.[68] This is the basis of God's complaint against Israel: "*God says, 'If a husband divorces his wife and she goes from him and belongs to another man, will he still return to her? Will not that land be completely polluted? But you are a harlot with many lovers; yet you turn to Me,' declares* [HaShem]" (Jeremiah 3:1). God was faithful, but Israel was unfaithful. Can He legally take her back again? What the Torah can't do because of the weakness of our flesh, God did in Messiah.[69] That is, through Messiah, a regeneration and a renewal and New (marriage) Covenant are provided.

Remarriage to a first wife who remarried is prohibited, among other reasons, for Torah forbids it.

Notice the first husband is defined as 1) the former, *harishon*, the first; he is the first, he cannot also be the third, since he is the first; 2) as the one "*who sent her away.*" Though the second did likewise, he is the one who sent her away from his house. "To return" is masculine, thus he wants to return to her, but he cannot. He gave his word that she is indecent and he cannot take it back. You can't call her indecent, send her away, and think you can just have her when you're so inclined. As Israel wanted to return to the land and could not, for they had not returned to the Lord, so you too are not able to return to the woman you defamed in Israel.[70]

"*To take her*" is to claim her as your wife,[71] but that claim has been taken by another. You cannot take what you have previously taken and then forsaken, after she was taken by another. "*To take her again*" is literally "to become to him," as God delivered us from Egypt and chose us "to become to Him" for a people.[72] Foreigners are "to become to Him" as His servants.[73] This becoming between the wife and first husband, as such, has already happened, and so it cannot happen again. It's like going apostate and wanting to come back as if it's a new salvation; you can't re-crucify Messiah to be saved again.[74]

---

68. As Benjamin leaving Jacob to go to Egypt would have been improper (Genesis 44:22).
69. Romans 8:3.
70. Jeremiah 22:27: "*But as for the land to which they desire to return, they will not return to it.*" Hosea 11:5: "*They will not return to the land of Egypt; But Assyria—he will be their king because they refused to return to Me.*"
71. As in 1 Samuel 25:39.
72. Deuteronomy 7:6; 14:2; 26:18.
73. Isaiah 56:6.
74. Hebrews 6:6.

The phrase "to be his wife" (*l'ishah*) is first used in Genesis 2:22 and speaks of the original purpose. It is therefore used as a purpose statement.[75] But you cancelled that purpose for her when you declared her indecent and sent her away. Now, a widow can be taken by another for a wife.[76] But in this situation, he cannot return to take her to become to him a wife after she has been defiled. (She is not defiled by being remarried to another. Read on.)

2. *It is humanely prohibited*. This is a sin against her, since she has been defiled by him. She has become defiled (*tame*, meaning "unclean"). How? By marrying another. Why would that make her unclean? There are at least two possibilities: 1) She is defiled in general; 2) She is defiled by him. Regarding the first possibility, is she defiled in general by her immoral behavior? This can't be, for then she would be killed and certainly not permitted to remarry again. So, is she defiled by him? How? She was caused[77] by him to become defiled. She has not made herself defiled; he caused her to be defiled to him. How? By his heartless treatment of her for the supposed shame that he found in her, which he now chooses to carnally overlook. How can you bring her before the altar in remarriage after you ungraciously hated her and found indecency in her? All of that should disqualify her, right? But now you want to call clean what you have declared unclean. She is not intrinsically defiled, but no longer fit for you as a wife because of your writ of divorce that caused her to marry another and be ceremonially unclean—and all this is because of you!

She has been made defiled by another man. But you are the guilty one. *Defiled* can be considered ceremonially,[78] or morally.[79] Yeshua states that unbiblical divorce makes her commit adultery, and anyone who marries her also commits adultery.[80] Is she an adulterer? No, she was forced into divorce and remarriage and is considered guiltless. But to you she is now an adulterer, for she has been defiled as your wife, and you have now made her unacceptable to become your wife again. And the second husband? He too commits adultery by marrying her, for she is still married in God's sight, though she has been spurned by her first husband. Yeshua is not asking for the death penalty for an improperly divorced woman—a woman divorced by her husband's hardness of heart—but is saying that her husband forced her into a ceremonially defiled position relative to her second married state as pertaining to her first husband.

---

75. Genesis 12:19; 16:3; Deuteronomy 21:11, 13; 25:5, etc.
76. As with the Moabite widow taken by Boaz (Ruth 4:10, 13). There too, God's infinite grace is revealed. See further in the author's commentary on the book of Ruth.
77. The passive causal Hebrew grammatical form (*hothpaal*) is applied to "defiled" (*tameh*). The "defiling" was done to her; she did not defile herself.
78. John 18:28.
79. Titus 1:15.
80. Again Matthew 5:32.

To take her for a wife again would be to further dishonor her, since you have declared her indecent. To the second husband, this is like participating in harlotry, which is always forbidden. As Dinah would not be given to her rapist for further abuse,[81] so the wife is not to be further defamed in Israel.

3. *It is divinely prohibited*. This is a sin against God, "*for that is an abomination before* [HaShem]." "Abomination" (*toevah*) is a gross impropriety before the Lord.[82] So the practice of any abomination means rejection from the New Jerusalem.[83] Yes, this is prohibited because it demeans God, who hates divorce. You have despised Him in divorcing her and then taking her back again after her remarriage ended. "*For that is an abomination before* [HaShem]." What is "*that*" that is an abomination?[84] It refers not to the woman as the abomination before God, but to the man for his remarrying this woman, whom he sent out, causing her to be ceremonially defiled by her remarriage.

4. *It is redemptively prohibited*. This is a sin against the land: "*And you shall not bring sin on the land which* [HaShem] *your God gives you as an inheritance*." This remarriage to your first wife is causing[85] sin on the land. This very action pollutes the land,[86] and is the cause of exile from the land.[87] All this for remarrying your ex-wife after her remarriage to another? This is a holy land that permits no unholiness. There can be no causing of sin in the land by the corrupting action described here by Moses, for the Lord your God gave the land to you as an inheritance for a possession.[88] It was not given to be corrupted by remarrying a woman you defiled by sending her out to marry another. But you are to be a faithful people to God by being faithful in marriage, as God is faithful to you in the land. The land is symbolic of the redemptive promises to the Fathers—that is, the promise of Messiah, who, as the true Seed of Abraham,[89] would be the Savior of the world, for He would be the blessing for the nations. All of this is tied within the very covenant that divinely promises the land to Israel.[90] To so abominably defile the

---

81. Read of this awful account in Genesis 34.
82. It is like homosexuality (Leviticus 18:22), idolatry (Deuteronomy 7:25–26), apostasy (Deuteronomy 13:13), transgenderism (Deuteronomy 22:5), giving immoral gain as an offering (Deuteronomy 23:18), etc.
83. Revelation 21:27.
84. Is "*that*" referring to the woman as an abomination before the Lord? Or is remarrying her an abomination? "*That*" refers to the antecedent abomination, but the subject of the sentence (and especially this verse) is not her being defiled but his remarrying her.
85. This is an active Hebrew causative verb (*hiphil*).
86. Jeremiah 16:18.
87. Leviticus 18:25, 28: "*For the land has become defiled, therefore I have brought its punishment upon it, so the land has spewed out its inhabitants…so that the land will not spew you out, should you defile it, as it has spewed out the nation which has been before you.*" Numbers 35:34: "*You shall not defile the land in which you live, in the midst of which I dwell; for I the* LORD *am dwelling in the midst of the sons of Israel.*"
88. As the Hebrew for "inheritance," *nachalah*, would mean.
89. Galatians 3:16.
90. See Genesis 12:1–3 for the three-fold promise to Abraham that is an irreducible complexity,

Five • *The Tanakh's Take on Marriage*

land through one's self-serving actions is to personally abandon the redemptive hope for Israel and the nations.

In summary: the husband cannot remarry his wife that he sent out, since she has been defiled to him by her marriage to another. The process for such a prohibition is to make it almost impossible to be carried out, to make divorce for hardness of heart extremely difficult and biblically rare. But the hardness-of-heart tradition attempts to evade the problem, and divorce plagues the land. Remember why God made it so hard for divorce regulations: marriage pictures HaShem's relationship to His people,[91] so God hates divorce.[92] All of this leads us to better understand marriage and divorce in the prophets.

Marriage and Divorce in the Prophets and Proverbs

Though mentioned briefly throughout in the prophets,[93] the matters of marriage and divorce are extensively referred to in the last writing prophet Malachi. The prophet has rebuked the merely ritualistic worship in the temple (1:6–14) and superficial teaching from the priesthood (2:1–9). He now demonstrates the negative impact of that externalist religiosity on society, especially the marriage and family. False teaching, undermining HaShem's faithfulness to His people, undermines faithful marriages. As we studied in Genesis 3, Satan corrupts humanity by attacking the marriage relationship with bad teaching about God. Since marriage best pictures HaShem's love for His covenant people, it is the marriage relationship that is most attacked. Messiah's restoration of a lost humanity to God is best revealed in the restored lives of healthy marriages. But the priests' false teaching in Malachi's day further corrupted the weakened moral fiber of society. If you want to destroy society, start with the family, and if you want to develop society, start with the family. The foundation of a community is the family; the foundation of the family is faith in God. Marriages are the bricks of a wall that provide the protection of a community. Weak family bricks make an insecure community.

> *"Do we not all have one father? Has not one God created us? Why do we deal treacherously each against his brother so as to profane the covenant of our fathers? Judah has dealt treacherously, and an abomination has been committed in Israel and in Jerusalem; for Judah has desecrated the sanctuary of HaShem which He loves and has married the daughter of a foreign god. As for the man who does this, may HaShem cut off from the tents of Jacob everyone who awakes and answers, or who presents an offering to HaShem of hosts. This is another thing you*

---

which Paul calls God's Good News to Abraham (Galatians 3:8).
91. Ephesians 5:31–32; *"For your husband is your Maker, whose name is* [HaShem] *of hosts"* (Isaiah 54:5).
92. Malachi 2:16.
93. Isaiah 54:1, 5; 62:4–5; Jeremiah 2:2; 3:1; Ezekiel 44:22; Amos 4:1, etc.

> *do: you cover the altar of HaShem with tears, with weeping and with groaning, because He no longer regards the offering or accepts it with favor from your hand. Yet you say, 'For what reason?' Because HaShem has been a witness between you and the wife of your youth, against whom you have dealt treacherously, though she is your companion and your wife by covenant. But not one has done so who has a remnant of the Spirit. And what did that one do while he was seeking a godly offspring? Take heed then to your spirit, and let no one deal treacherously against the wife of your youth. For I hate divorce," says HaShem, the God of Israel, "and him who covers his garment with violence," says HaShem of hosts. "So, take heed to your spirit, that you do not deal treacherously."* (Malachi 2:10–16 SN)

Two repeated words in this section identify the theme: the word "treacherous" (*bagad*) is mentioned five times. This portion deals with treachery within the community, family, and marriage, and how to avoid it. Treachery is an act of deliberate betrayal of a trust. This Hebrew word is also translated "deceitfully" and "faithless," in other words, the treacherous are the untrustworthy.[94]

The other repeated word is "HaShem," representing the covenant name of God in the Tanakh. This name represents His faithfulness to His covenant and covenant people. HaShem is mentioned seven times in six verses! Remembering again that marriage pictures HaShem's relationship to His people,[95] Malachi's theme for this portion is that God sees our unfaithfulness to the marriage covenant as misrepresenting His covenant faithfulness to His people, and He hates it.

Trustworthy families have integrity. Integrity is undivided completeness. It's having moral soundness. While treachery will destroy our society, families with integrity produce a morally sound and spiritually healthy community. From Malachi's rebuke of His community's spousal failures, we can learn how to have socially wholesome communities by developing spiritually healthier marriages.

To understand the positive application of Malachi 2:10–16 for our marriages, we learn that marriages with integrity are consecrated to oneness. Thus, to avoid treachery to your faith community (2:10), if you marry, marry a faithful believer (2:11–12). If you're already married, be faithful to your spouse (2:13–16). The following outline of Malachi 2:10–16 can help us follow Malachi's train of thought as to why marriages with integrity are consecrated to oneness:

I. One Father expects integrity in marriage, 2:10

II. One faith encourages integrity in marriage, 2:11–12

III. One family exhibits integrity in marriage, 2:13–16

---

94. The word is translated as "unfairness" (Exodus 21:8); "deceitfully" (Job 6:15); "betrayed" (Psalm 73:15); "faithless" (Proverbs 23:28), etc.
95. Ephesians 5:31-32; Isaiah 54:5.

I. One Father Expects Integrity in Marriage (2:10)

*"Do we not all have one father? Has not one God created us?
Why do we deal treacherously each against his brother
so as to profane the covenant of our fathers?"*

In this verse, there are two reasons for God's expectation of integrity, and it's all based on the unique oneness of God as our Father:

We're responsible to our Father's community: "*...one Father? Has not one God created us?*" Because there's only one God, there's only one overarching community purpose as detailed in the covenant stipulations.[96]

This God who creates doesn't merely create in general, but He specifically creates a covenant people with His wholesome purposes for them.[97] All others in that covenant relationship share with me the same covenantal purpose for our community. If we revere the Head, we respect the hands. The oneness of God and its unique impact on the marriage and family are addressed in the often-quoted Shema and V'ahavtah of Deuteronomy 6:4–9:

> *Hear, O Israel! The Lord is our God, the Lord is one! You shall love the Lord your God with all your heart and with all your soul and with all your might. These words, which I am commanding you today, shall be on your heart. You shall teach them diligently to your sons and shall talk of them when you sit in your house and when you walk by the way and when you lie down and when you rise up. You shall bind them as a sign on your hand and they shall be as frontals on your forehead. You shall write them on the doorposts of your house and on your gates.*
> (Deuteronomy 6:4–9)

Since there is only one God (v. 4), we as a people, as a community, and as a couple are to love Him only (v. 5), and completely, with all our spirit (heart), soul, and body (might). If this is so, then His words will be on our hearts (v. 6) to spiritually nourish our being, influencing our soul in what we think, feel, choose, and therefore do with our physical being. Thus, as a couple, we can teach them to our children (v. 7). Since God's Word applies to every area of life, we diligently take every opportunity at home or away, early in the day or late, to teach his Word to our homemade *talmidim* (disciples)—our children. God's own words (v. 8) will direct our actions (as a sign on our hands) and our attitudes (on our foreheads). This then becomes the witness (v. 9) for our family (doorposts of our houses) and for our community (on our gates), for all the world to see. But it all begins with

---

96. In Scripture, the covenant stipulations are found in the Torah and the mitzvot. Each covenant has its own Torah and mitzvot. For more on this matter, read the author's book *Messianic Foundations*, pp. 157–167.
97. Isaiah 43:1 (SN): "*Thus says HaShem that created you, O Jacob.*"

the oneness of God and His one covenant purpose for His people, both in the home and in the community.

We're responsible to our Fathers' covenant

> *"Why do we deal treacherously each against his brother*
> *so as to profane the covenant of our fathers?"*

In the amazing prophecy regarding our people's repentance for our national rejection of the Messiah, Isaiah 53:6 reveals our desperate need for Messiah in the phrase, *"each of us has turned to his own way."* We have each turned to our own way, not only from HaShem, but from each other. In the marriage relationship, sin separates us from each other when we're separated from God. As I have previously taught on this verse in Malachi, "I am my brother's keeper when I keep our Fathers' covenant."[98] But the same can be said for being our spouse's keeper. If you hurt one, you hurt us all; we're family, community knit together in the bonds of love. And so too, "We treat the covenant as holy when we treat our brothers as worthy." For our spouses, this is even more so, since Yeshua said we are regarded as one by God.[99] A brother's keeper is a covenant keeper; a spouse's keeper (think caregiver) is a marital covenant keeper as well. The very covenant that united us with God also unites us with each other. To despise the covenant with our spouse is to despise the covenant with the Father. As the united Messianic family is a community cornerstone, so the oneness of God brings unity to a redeemed society.

II. One Faith Encourages Integrity in Marriage (2:11–12)

Marriages united in faith honor His Lordship (2:11)

> *"Judah has dealt treacherously, and an abomination*
> *has been committed in Israel and in Jerusalem;*
> *for Judah has desecrated the sanctuary of HaShem which He loves*
> *and has married the daughter of a foreign god."*

"Judah" is the remaining national Israeli territory that the Jews returning from Babylon reestablished. By speaking of Judah, Malachi is speaking of a national problem: intermarriage between Jewish people and pagan women (*"the daughter of a foreign god"*). This is not speaking about the marriage of a Jewish believer in Adonai and a Gentile believer in Adonai (who at this point in history would be called a *proselyte*), but a believer marrying a non-believer or a believer in a different faith, as here. This is consistently condemned in Scripture.[100]

---

98. From my sermon delivered to Hope of Israel Congregation on July 9, 2011, "Marriages that Honor HaShem," from Malachi 2:10–16.
99. Matthew 19:5–6.
100. Exodus 34:16; Deuteronomy 7:2–3; Ezra 9:1–2, 11–12; 10:19; Psalm 106:35; 1 Corinthians

Unbelievers have no relationship with HaShem.[101] Intermarriage is characterized as "an abomination" and "desecrated." It's easy to see that God is deeply offended. Such a marriage could never expect God's blessing, but should expect His severe rebuke and condemnation. This Jewish believer spoken of in this portion may be quite nominal in his faith. It appears that this man was perhaps initially dedicated in the sanctuary—which God "loves"—and so the sanctuary is now desecrated in God's eyes. Being married in a house of worship these days may be seen as giving some validating approval to the couple, but it is a desecration unless the wedding and the marriage give glory to Adonai. God's love is expressed in holiness, as seen in married lives set apart to Him. His love despised is treachery, as with so-called believers whose lives are lived apart from Him.[102] God's love is holy, and through Messiah that love is given in holiness and ministered in holiness in a marriage. A Messianic marriage should never despise and defile His love. But if this happens there needs to be repentance and forgiveness in Yeshua, and sincere recommitment to follow Messiah in the marriage. Where the sin of intermarriage is committed, the believer needs to confess their intermarriage as sin before God, and then follow 1 Corinthians 7:12–15 under their congregation leader's guidance.

Marriages united in faith have His fellowship (2:12)

> *"As for the man who does this, may HaShem cut off from the tents of*
> *Jacob everyone who awakes and answers,*
> *or who presents an offering to HaShem of hosts."*

The Hebrew phrase *"tents of Jacob"* is used to speak of the nation of Israel. The sinful believer who intermarried, who now *"presents an offering"*—that is, who attempts to "draw near" (*nagash*) with offerings to placate God—is removed, or *"cut off"* from fellowship in the believing community. Loss of fellowship reflects removal from intimacy with God. To marry outside the faith is to leave the fellowship of the faith. This may seem harsh, but a congregation and the families that make up that community are a holy people before the Lord and must see themselves this way. And though the intermarried may attempt to look more righteous than they are by giving offerings, God is not fooled. Such gifts are seen by God as attempted bribes from a corrupt person.[103] Often, those who have committed the sin of intermarriage may attempt to compensate with more religiosity, thinking that this will offset or make up for their disobedience and prove they are righteous. How often has a believing spouse of a non-believer done everything possible—dragging the poor non-believer from one meeting to another—to

---

7:39; 2 Corinthians 6:14–16.
101. See Ephesians 2:11–12.
102. First Corinthians 5:1–13.
103. In this regard, the most appropriate verse is *"Behold, to obey is better than sacrifice!"* (1 Samuel 15:22).

have their spouse saved in a vain attempt to validate their sin of intermarriage? Often, their sin of intermarriage undermines their testimony to their unbelieving spouse, as their faith is made to appear like a sham. Faith that doesn't impact our life decisions can't testify to His life-changing grace, for the life has not been changed. Once more, repentance and confession of sin are required. The congregation leader should provide guidance for the repentant through 1 Corinthians 7:12–15, even while the person is under some form of congregational discipline. If they were warned by the congregation leadership beforehand not to marry the non-believer and they did anyway, removal from membership may be required to bring such a person to terms, not merely with the sin of intermarriage, but with their sinful rebellion against the congregation leadership! In any case, beware of the sin of intermarriage.

III. One Family Exhibits Integrity in Marriage (2:13–16)

In this next section of Malachi, a different marriage problem is explored: unfaithfulness. If we remember that the marriage reflects Adonai's relationship with His covenant people, we can start to understand how our unfaithfulness in marriage is so offensive to the Lord. But remember, despite an unfaithful spouse, HaShem will remain faithful! The marriage's integrity is reviewed in its worship of Adonai, by warning from Adonai, and through its witness for Adonai.

Integrity in a family's worship of HaShem (2:13–14)

In these two verses, the married couple's worship, especially the husband's, is a mere vanity and substitute for actual worship, which must begin with repentance.

HaShem stops delivering His blessings (2:13)

> *"This is another thing you do: you cover the altar of HaShem with tears, with weeping and with groaning, because He no longer regards the offering or accepts it with favor from your hand."*

Tears don't count without genuine repentance, which must include a change of attitude about the offense and a change of the activity that caused the offense. Many religious people think that tears are a reasonable substitute for repentance and obedience. That is, people can deceive themselves by thinking that their sincere heartache reveals that they are actually good people, since they are so very pained by their own offenses. This is self-deception. A sincere heart is still a sinful heart.[104]

Offerings don't cleanse without repentance. *"No longer"*—that is, something has changed. The hard-hearted nominal believer not living in obedience to the Word of God may realize that God's blessing is removed from his life. His worship

---

104. Jeremiah 17:9: *"The heart is more deceitful than all else and is desperately sick; Who can understand it?"*

experience seems shallow, superficial, and irrelevant, regardless of how much he gives to the temple. God requires sincere repentance and obedience, not insincere offerings. The only sincere offering that is acceptable to God is Yeshua, when your faith in Him is expressed in your accompanying repentance from sin. One must recognize that desiring divorce, seeking divorce, and attaining divorce is all a sin against God. The only provision for sin is Messiah's offering of His life for your sins. All other offerings in the Tanakh are only good-faith "promissory notes" that Yeshua made good and paid off in His once-and-for-all sacrifice for sins. All other sacrifices offered after His death are only memorials to His final sacrifice for sin. His sacrifice alone is effective for the forgiveness of sin.

When you start despising His blessing (2:14)

> *"Yet you say, 'For what reason?' Because HaShem has been a witness between you and the wife of your youth, against whom you have dealt treacherously, though she is your companion and your wife by covenant."*

"For what reason?"[105] Since sin confuses our minds, the nominal so-called believer may be in a real quandary over his unblessed faith: "Let's see, did I forget to water the plants, have I missed vital TV news or not responded to my emails, is it because I divorced my wife, or am I reading too many spy novels? Hmmm, what can it be that has God miffed at me? I don't know—it's all such a mystery."

God is witness between you and your wife! Remember that your wedding that was conducted in His name made God a chief witness to your union.

The husband has an experiential responsibility to his spouse. She is *"the wife of your youth."* You owe her heartfelt appreciation for her faithful life she gave to you as your wife. She may be older and perhaps not as appealing to your particular fleshly lusts. Grow up! Repent and stop living for your flesh. She deserves and has earned your loyalty and devotion.

The husband has a spiritual responsibility to his spouse. The wife *"is your companion"* in faithfulness. The word for "companion" in Hebrew (*chaveret*) has a root that means "to be joined," as in "to have joined forces" and to be an ally.[106] She is your ally in your spiritual battle and warfare. You have joined forces to *"fight the good fight of faith"*[107] together. To desert your ally in battle is treachery, and this is why you experience defeat before the enemy.

---

105. Israel's questioning doubts about God's concerns over their spiritual failures is a theme in the book of Malachi: 1:2, 6; 2:14, 17; 3:8, 13.
106. Genesis 14:3; 2 Chronicles 20:35.
107. First Timothy 6:12.

Your betrayal of your wife is a betrayal of your Commander in Chief who brought you together as one flesh.[108]

The husband has a legal responsibility to his spouse. The words "*your wife by covenant*" reflect the vows made before God. The vows are the specific stipulations that define the particular covenant.[109] As a covenanter with you before God, your spouse deserves your obedience to your vows. To break your marital vows is a treacherous act that no one should overlook. If you will break your word to God by forsaking your spouse, why should anyone ever believe you will keep your word to them? You are a covenant breaker. This treachery is despised, and only repentance and going back to your spouse will bring acceptance by others. Remarrying (as is often done) may be socially acceptable, but for a healthy Messianic community, remarriage after a treacherous divorce should be looked upon as adding sin to sin. Indeed, marriage is not to be lightly entered into without serious premarital counseling, and then regular follow-up during the first year of marriage.

Integrity in a family's warning from HaShem (2:15–16)

"But not one has done so who has a remnant of the Spirit.
And what did that one do while he was seeking a godly offspring?
Take heed then to your spirit, and let no one deal
treacherously against the wife of your youth."

The first phrase,[110] "*But not one has done so who has a remnant of the Spirit,*" declares that the initiator of a divorce does not walk in the Spirit. The Holy Spirit's power enables one to bear all things and forgive all manner of offenses. One who lives by the flesh will seek ungodliness as a means to deal with their problems.

The second phrase, "*And what did that one do while he was seeking a godly offspring?*" is considered by commentators[111] as a reference to Abraham seeking a seed by having sex with Hagar because of his wife Sarah's inability to have children. Going outside the marriage union is wrong even for Abraham and only proves problematic, as we noted above. The end never justifies the means, but rather the means reveals the end. If you live like hell, that's a warning sign to where you're heading. Divorce does not testify of someone who believes that God will be faithful to save them by grace in Messiah regardless of what sins they've committed, since they can't forgive their own spouse for lesser offenses.

---

108. Matthew 19:6.
109. In premarital counseling, I suggest strong vows that reflect a strong marriage commitment to each other.
110. The Hebrew is literally: "*And not one has done, and a remnant of the Spirit to him.*"
111. The Hebrew phrase is literally: "*And how is the one seeking a seed of God.*" The NET Bible comments, "This is an oblique reference to Abraham who sought to obtain God's blessing by circumventing God's own plan for him by taking Hagar as wife (Genesis 16:1–6)." Net Bible, Malachi 2:15, classic.net.bible.org/verse.php?book=Mal&chapter=2&verse=15#.

Five • The Tanakh's Take on Marriage

His sovereignty makes two into one as a testimony of His sovereign grace to create unity. He blesses a couple as a couple.[112] God could have given Adam six wives by the Spirit, but He only gave him one wife. This one-man-one-woman marriage is what Yeshua reiterated (Matthew 19:6). His Spirit works in two that are one. The Spirit doesn't work in disunity, and disunity hinders the couple's prayers.[113] Divorce resists God's Spirit. The life we're created, redeemed, and called to live is rejected through the initiator of the divorce. A godly seed results from two that are one. It takes two that are one to make one godly seed. As Solomon proved, the more wives you have, the less stable and godly your life. A couple's oneness produces godliness. God's purpose is to have godly children, not just children. Divorce hinders godliness in the child. Children need to see unity and love in their parents to envision unity and love for themselves. Children of such homes far too often have deep emotional wounds, and lack behavioral models for their future marriage and home. Dysfunctional homes produce future dysfunctional homes. Once more, the unity of the parents produces the security for the child.

The third phrase of 2:15 reads, "*Take heed then to your spirit, and let no one deal treacherously against the wife of your youth.*" Since the two are to be one for the Sovereign's purpose, beware of treachery. By your commitment to family oneness, you instill godliness, for faithfulness honors God. Please note that the warning is to take heed to your spirit. The problem in the marriage is essentially spiritual. Your rebellion against God begins in your spirit, and that is then reflected in your soul—that is, in your thought life, feelings, and volition. Divorce is rebellion against God. How do we take heed, or guard, our spirit? Here are some questions to consider on the matter: Have you actually trusted Yeshua for your salvation? As a believer, have you yielded your life to Him as your Lord, with the commensurate repentance and obedience to Him? Have you been discipled in the faith so that you have a Scriptural assurance of your salvation, consistent prayer life, daily devotions in God's Word, an unashamed testimony of faith in Yeshua before others, and a commitment to a local Yeshua-loving, Bible-teaching congregation? Assurance of salvation, prayer, Word, sharing our faith, and a commitment to a faith community are the areas that help us to guard our spirit. The unguarded spirit is already compromised in the corrupted soul, unsubmitted to God, and not resisting the enemy of our faith, as he actively seeks to destroy every marriage that would honor the Lord.

A prenup is treacherous! It prepares the couple for divorce, and its existence undermines the couple's commitment to prayerfully, graciously, and faithfully work through the difficulties that arise in any and every marriage. Divorce is such a plague that the idea of marriage has become comical to many. When it comes to marriage, the world fears the danger of unreasonable expectations more than

---

112. See Genesis 1:28.
113. See 1 Peter 3:7.

it fears rejecting God's marriage warning to guard your spirit. How will you and your spouse respond to God's warning? Remember, a warning is not a threat, but rather it's a sign of love and concern.

The integrity of a family's witness to HaShem (2:16)

"For I hate divorce," says HaShem, the God of Israel,
"and him who covers his garment with violence," says HaShem of hosts.
"So, take heed to your spirit, that you do not deal treacherously."

HaShem's reason for the warning is frankly stated: *"For I hate divorce."* The word "hate" in Hebrew is *sanah*, which is a word for an enemy. Divorce is the enemy of God. Are you considering divorce? Consider carefully that you will become God's enemy. We should be very careful as well not to water down God's hatred of divorce just because it is so prevalent in our world today. Scripture states that God is at war against sin and has fierce anger toward all those who live in sin.[114] Messiah is His peace for humanity,[115] and the New Covenant is His peace treaty. But don't accept the New Covenant peace treaty and then act treacherously—this will prove that you are His enemy, for you fraudulently accepted what you now betray. God hates divorce now as much as He did in the day of Malachi. Do you agree with God and hate divorce as well? Or will you attempt to think that the matter is in doubt, so you will not have to accept the truth of this Scripture—so you can do what you carnally wish to do anyway? You must understand it is not a gray area or a doubtful issue for God. He hates divorce, and He will act toward you in accordance with His Word regardless of your indifference on the matter. Do what He loves and hate what He hates.

The phrase *"his garment"*[116] is a symbol of the husband's protection over his wife. But rather than protect her as a garment, he brings violence. God has the husband as the protector of the wife, but he is deeply offended when a husband brings harm and thereby corrupts the holy calling that was intended as God's witness to His loving care. How do your actions reflect upon God? How does your marriage relationship reflect upon His covenant love for His people? It seems simple: Don't harm those you're called to protect! But sin corrupts our souls when we do not take heed to our spirit! By taking heed to our spirit, we are prevented from acting treacherously in the marriage.

Do what God would do. A testimony of marriage is a testimony of God's faithfulness. For this witness, we must abide in Yeshua to bear fruit of faithfulness

---

114. Romans 1:18–19: *"For the wrath of God is revealed from heaven against all ungodliness and unrighteousness of men who suppress the truth in unrighteousness, because that which is known about God is evident within them; for God made it evident to them."*
115. Isaiah 9:6; Romans 5:1; Ephesians 2:14; Philippians 4:7.
116. As in Ruth 3:9.

and kindness. So, singles might prayerfully say: "I pledge unto God that I will not marry anyone not dedicated to Messiah." For the married, prayerfully say together: "We pledge unto God that we will not divorce, and we will not neglect the spiritual priority for our family." Let us all pledge unto God that we will each glorify Yeshua in all our relationships. Can we do any less?

A tree depends on its root system. Roots have two purposes: they anchor the tree, providing stability, and they gather water, providing nourishment. So also, the root of our relationships is our relationship with the one true God. Let us work on the foundation—the roots—that we might have His blessing in our Messianic marriages.

The Proverbial Marriage

Marital counsel from the book of Proverbs

The book of Proverbs provides divinely authorized advice and counsel for godly living. The portions referring to marriage address various real-world matters. In general, the idea of having a home that is either blessed or cursed is laid out rather simply: "*The curse of the Lord is on the house of the wicked, but He blesses the dwelling of the righteous*" (Proverbs 3:33). "*Righteous*"? Believers are called the righteous because they are imputed righteousness from God by faith in Messiah, either faith that anticipated God's provision in His coming, or faith that appropriates that provision in the One who came to die for us. This imputed righteousness is then lived out by that same saving faith by which Yeshua's righteousness was received. This faith-obedience reveals Messianic believers as "*the righteous*" in Messiah. Since we obediently live by faith, the righteousness we received and live out is from the Messiah and to His glory. The wicked live otherwise. Thus, this righteous and blessed home would be committed to a lifestyle that honors Adonai in all that they do and say, with the commensurate repentance and recommitment as needed.

Proverbs has extensive portions on the folly of immorality and the destruction that follows by those who follow the wisdom of the world in their marriages and not the wisdom of the Word (Proverbs 2:16–19; 5:1–14; 6:23–35; 7:6–23; 9:13–18). This verse is a constant reminder for me: "*Stolen water is sweet; and bread eaten in secret is pleasant*" (9:17). Though the water is the same for anyone, our sinful flesh finds greater pleasure from illicitly obtained goods than from the goods properly obtained. Spouses may try to spice up their relationship with illicit sex, porn, and other corrupting influences. This is futility, folly, and destruction for the soul, with no long-term enhancement for the marriage.

Solomon's proverbs on marriage include observations on spouses who are foolish, those who are wise, and comparisons of the two.

Foolish spouses

Proverbs 27:8: *"Like a bird that wanders from her nest, so is a man who wanders from his home."* Though a bird is prone to wander from her nest, it is unsafe and unwise. A man with sinful inclinations may be prone to wander from his home, but this is always unsafe and unwise. The commitment to the Lord is a commitment to your own home, which equates to coming to your own home for dinner every night. Commitment creates consistency.

Proverbs 17:1: *"Better is a dry morsel and quietness with it than a house full of feasting with strife."* "Strife" (*riv*) is always to be avoided, and quietness is always to be the goal. The simplicity of life ("*a dry morsel*") may seem boring, but only by those who do not have a quiet spirit before the Lord (1 Peter 3:4). Strife is divisive (Genesis 13:7–8), and demonstrates rebelliousness to God (Numbers 27:14). Despite a lavish lifestyle, the family is spiritually impoverished when there is strife in the home. There is a need for Messianic discipleship to teach biblical values rather than worldly standards for what makes a happy marriage and home.

Proverbs 21:9: *"It is better to live in a corner of a roof than in a house shared with a contentious woman."* This is considered so important that it's recorded twice (Proverbs 25:24). The "*corner of a roof*" is small, outside, and lonely, but it is still better than sharing a house "*with a contentious woman*"! Elsewhere, rather than fleeing to the roof, the husband flees to a desert island to avoid a quarrelsome wife (Proverbs 21:19). "Contention" (*madon*) is similar to strife, but its spiritual root is perversity (Proverbs 6:14), that is, a heart with deceptive ulterior motives. The spreading of strife is the result of a perverted heart.

Contentiousness is not limited to the wife, for the husband can be a shock emitter instead of being a shock absorber (Proverbs 26:21). In a marriage, this strife builds such distrust that the contention produces "*bars of a citadel*" (Proverbs 18:19). That is, the spouse just closes down to any kind of communication. A contentious woman is also like "*a constant dripping*" (Proverbs 19:13), that is, a prickly nagging that erodes a loving relationship and makes the overwhelmed husband take to the roof to avoid this Chinese water torture of constant bickering. Into such a relationship, a third party who can objectively speak the truth in love is needed to bring the contentious person to realize that their heart is embittered at God, though they may not realize it at first. Scripture assures us, since we all fall short of the glory of God, we must be exceedingly careful "*that no one comes short of the grace of God,*" for then a bitter root will defile all those around (Hebrews 12:15). The grace of God in Messiah[117] is the cure for the contentious soul: be fully accepted by His grace in Messiah, accept yourself by that same grace, and then accept others graciously too.

---

117. Ephesians 1:6; 2:5-8; Romans 15:7.

Proverbs 30:21, 23: "*Under three things the earth quakes, and under four, it cannot bear up:...under an unloved woman when she gets a husband...*" The unloved, or "hated" (*s'nuah*) woman, when she is married, now is prideful. So it is for Leah, who has to have Jacob deceived to gain a husband. Her children are matters for her self-validation (Genesis 29:31–34), leaving little wonder as to why they turn out the way they do. As Rachel's children become Jacob's favorites, so with an unloved wife it is natural to discount her children. Yet the Torah forbids such favoritism (Deuteronomy 21:15–17). To look to any but the Lord for your self-worth is a dog chasing its tail—futile and self-destructive. Your husband can't understand his own needs, let alone meet your needs. All that can be done in the redemptive home is to allow the acceptance of the Lord to be your foundation for relationship, so that you can then minister to your spouse and not manipulate in the vain attempt to have your needs met—the fulfillment of which needs is beyond your understanding, let alone your futile strategies.

Wise spouses

Two proverbs teach that a godly wife is God's gift to the husband and home. Proverbs 18:22: "*He who finds a wife finds a good thing and obtains favor from [HaShem].*" Proverbs 19:14: "*House and wealth are an inheritance from fathers, but a prudent wife is from [HaShem].*" The book of Proverbs hearkens back to Genesis, where God informs the man that it is not good for him to be alone (Genesis 2:18). It is good to find a wife, which reminds us that this is God's favor to the husband, even as it was initially for Adam. This wife is godly since she expresses God's favor (*ratson*, meaning "good pleasure") in the marriage. HaShem blesses such a home, for it keeps covenant with God and each other. Part of this godly wife's tool kit is "prudence" (*sakal*), a godly quality of practical, get-it-done wisdom. The godly wife is the practical woman that reveals the wisdom of God in a home that honors HaShem. In Proverbs, this particular wisdom shops when it is best to gather (10:5), knows when to keep silent (10:19), and is living for the upward call of God (15:24), for she obeys "*the Word*" (16:20).

Comparisons of the foolish and wise spouses

Proverbs 12:4: "*An excellent wife is the crown of her husband, but she who shames him is like rottenness in his bones.*" Whereas the excellent wife enhances her husband's life like a crown, the shaming wife enervates his beleaguered soul like having rotten bones. The "*crown*" refers to the wife's acceptance and support of the husband's God-given position of leadership in the home, as stated in Genesis 3:16. Far too often, wives that do not accept the husband's rightful role of spiritual leader in the home find ways to cut him down, emphasize his inadequacies, and shame him. For this husband, going home is going back to dreaded salt mines of a failing relationship. To shame your spouse is self-destructive in God's sight, since He says the married couple is one flesh (Genesis 2:24; Matthew 19:5–6). Messianic discipleship regarding the ministry of marriage is desperately needed if the marriage is ever to fulfill its purposes in God's plan for the wife as well as the husband.

Proverbs 14:1: *"The wise woman builds her house, but the foolish tears it down with her own hands."* Wisdom is a result of having reverence for God (Psalm 111:10) and is the application of biblical knowledge. The fool may have biblical knowledge but not the application to her heart and life. By her life, her heart is saying, *"There is no God"* (Psalm 14:1). To "build your house" means to edify your family by God's love and Word. To "tear down your house" is to tear down the family in your home. Once more, a third party to objectively speak the truth in love is needed while there is still any home left to rescue. But the wise woman should not be overlooked or taken for granted. She should be deeply and often appreciated for her yieldedness and obedience to the Lord.

Portrait of the Godly Wife

Solomon concludes his proverbs by giving a full-orbed view of the godly wife par excellence from Proverbs 31. She is *"an excellent wife"* who is invaluable to her family (v. 10). Her husband implicitly trusts her, for she diligently and consistently cares for his life and home (vv. 11–14). Her family is her primary calling, but in fulfilling her vocation, she has a creative home-business that she works at when her family is asleep (vv. 14–19), and in all seasons (vv. 24–25). In her godliness, she can also care for the poor (v. 20) as well as her household (vv. 21–22). Her lifestyle has so enhanced her husband that he becomes a community leader (v. 23), and there he blesses her (vv. 28–29). And this victorious spiritual and marital life is because she *"fears the L*ORD*"* and is praised by all who know her (vv. 30–31).

And so, the Tanakh's take on marriage closes on the ministry of marriage with strong encouragement, regulation, and counsel for a healthy, godly marriage.

Some questions to help apply these teachings

1. Since we grow slowly into our restored original design, what areas in your lives and marriage have you regulated to keep from stumbling into sin (e.g., covenant eyes, accountability groups, expecting your spouse to tell you when you're doing wrong, etc.)? Is your spouse aware of these matters to pray for you as you spiritually grow?

2. As with Abraham, what improper shortcuts have you used to fulfill the "burdensome" responsibilities in your marriage, such as entertainment as a substitute for conversation, immoral stimulants instead of foreplay, lies to avoid awkward social moments, using authority other than the Bible to

have your way, or abusing the Bible to get your way?

3. As with Joseph, if your marriage is made up of a Jewish believer and Gentile believer, what areas demonstrate commitment to have a Messianic home, and what areas have you compromised for the wishes of the non-Jewish spouse?

4. As with Moses, what areas in your Messianic marriage hinder your calling? These areas can include godly discipline in the home (i.e., being both loving and restraining), lack of hospitality, lack of commitment to community, not praying for and sharing your faith with friends and family, lack of devotion to prayer and the Word, etc.

5. As with David, in what areas are you using your authority, private time, business trips, office friendships, etc. to indulge your fantasies and gratify your desires, boredom, and feelings of insecurity? Pray with your spouse about any of these areas.

6. As with Solomon, have you married an unbeliever? If so, have you repented for that act of disobedience? Have you accepted your calling to model God's love, grace, and forgiveness before your spouse? Remember, we cannot model perfection to our children, but only repentance in living for the Lord.

7. As in Deuteronomy 24:1–4, what qualities in your spouse cause you to be turned off, to despise, or to suffer embarrassment? Go to the Lord quickly, for this is where you stopped appreciating the gift, for you have already stopped appreciating the Giver of the gift!

8. As in Malachi 2, what areas of "treachery" have existed in the marriage because of a lack of covenant commitment to God but have been swept under the carpet? Have you fully repented of any consideration of divorce?

9. As in Proverbs, what areas in the marriage trigger contention (e.g., nagging, irritations, bristling, outbursts, etc.)? Have you consistently apologized, forgiven, and prayed together? Have you each handled contention by going to a "corner of the roof" (e.g., another room, leaving to see friends, staying late at work, etc.)? Pray together about this.

10. How has your wife moved toward achieving the Proverbs 31:10–31 ideal for the wife? How has your husband moved toward achieving the Psalm 1:1–3 ideal for the husband? What words of encouragement can you offer to one another?

PART II

The Restoration of Marriage

CHAPTER SIX

The Spirit-Filled Life

Ephesians 5

1 Corinthians 11

Before studying the New Covenant's teachings regarding divorce and remarriage, we must first understand the redeemed marriage in Messiah. The Messianic marriage has redemptive resources that are intended to make divorces very rare, but this can only be the case if those resources utilized. Torah was given to be lived, not just learned.[1] Yeshua taught, *"If you know these things, you are blessed if you do them"* (John 13:17). The blessing is not in the learning, but in the implementation of what we learn as we abide in Messiah.

The Spirit-Filled Marriage (Ephesians 5:18–32)

The operation of the Spirit-filled walk: "Be filled with the Spirit"

> *And do not get drunk with wine, for that is dissipation, but be filled with the Spirit,*
> *speaking to one another in psalms and hymns and spiritual songs,*
> *singing and making melody with your heart to the Lord;*
> *always giving thanks for all things in the name of*
> *our Lord Yeshua the Messiah to God, even the Father; and be subject*
> *to one another in the fear of Messiah.* (Ephesians 5:18–21 SN)

In 5:18–21, the background of the Spirit-filled marriage is seen in the larger context of a Spirit-filled community and home, by our mutually edifying interactions. Each believer has a spiritual responsibility and Spirit-filled ability to the congregation to edify one another by *"speaking to one another in psalms and hymns and spiritual songs; singing and making melody with your heart to the Lord; always giving thanks,"* and lastly, being *"subject to one another in the fear of Messiah."*

This means being in submission to one another. Elders are submitted to the congregation to serve the congregants. Likewise, all members are to be submitted to the elders and to one another. So too in the family—the parents are submitted to the children to serve the children, and the

---

1. Leviticus 18:5.

children are submitted to their parents and each other. This can only be accomplished through the working of the Holy Spirit within the congregation, home, and each member. Everything that the marriage and congregation require from those involved is dependent on the power of the Holy Spirit.

Being filled with the Holy Spirit is often quite misunderstood, as are all the works of *Ruach HaKodesh* (the Holy Spirit). Here is a brief overview on His various works in your life. There are four works of the Holy Spirit,[2] and these works are essential in your walk with the Lord. The first three works of the Holy Spirit are: 1) His regeneration, 2) His indwelling, and 3) His immersion. All three occur at the point of salvation when you trust Yeshua as Messiah, Lord, and Savior. The fourth work of the Holy Spirit is the filling of the Holy Spirit, and this ongoing work is essential to living out the life of Yeshua as we fulfill our creation calling to represent God's image to His creation.

What does it mean to be filled with the Spirit? Have you ever experienced being filled with rage,[3] or awe,[4] sorrow,[5] or jealousy?[6] To be filled[7] with something (or someone[8]) is to be under the influence of that something (or someone). Likewise, to be filled with the Holy Spirit is to be under His influence in order to accomplish His specific work for you.[9]

In the New Covenant, we see the apostles being filled with the Spirit repeatedly,[10] such that they had to constantly yield themselves to be in compliance to His will in order to honor the Lord Yeshua in various circumstances. Being filled with the Holy Spirit is an ongoing activity of the Holy Spirit, because there are many different activities the Holy Spirit wants us to do. We are all commanded in Scripture to be filled with the Holy Spirit.[11] Here is how His filling of us works: in obedience to Yeshua and His Word and in compliance to *Ruach HaKodesh*, we obey three specific commands regarding the Holy Spirit:

1. Do not grieve the Spirit

Ephesians 4:30 tells us, "*Do not grieve the Holy Spirit.*" When we come to faith in Messiah, the Holy Spirit takes up residence within us.[12] When we do things

---

2. The person and works of the Holy Spirit are further developed in the author's book *Messianic Discipleship*, pp. 75–92.
3. Luke 4:28; 6:11.
4. Luke 5:26.
5. John 16:6.
6. Acts 5:17.
7. Greek, *pleroʻo*.
8. Besides the Holy Spirit, one can be under the influence of an unholy spirit: Acts 5:3.
9. Luke 1:15, 41, 67; Acts 2:4; 13:9, etc.
10. Acts 2:4; 4:8, 31; 9:17; 13:9.
11. In Ephesians 5:18, "*be filled*" is a present imperative meaning "be filled and stay filled."
12. As Yeshua prophesies in John 14:17, the Holy Spirit, which prior to Shavuot (the Day of Pentecost) abided with or came upon believers, will thereafter indwell believers in Yeshua. Also see

contrary to the will (i.e., the Word) of God, the Holy Spirit is grieved, meaning He is offended. He remains offended until we repent. If we refuse to repent, then the Spirit remains grieved, and we are therefore unable to be filled with Him! For example, wanting to have marriage on your terms is enough to grieve the Holy Spirit, for God created marriage to be lived out on His terms, not yours. If you stubbornly persist in that desire, you will not be influenced by the Holy Spirit—in fact, you will be resisting Him! This can bring God's discipline on your life, and you may wonder why things are going so badly.[13] However, when we commit by faith to live God's way, we will also find the Holy Spirit's empowerment to do His will. Your resistance doesn't have to be the last word on your life—repent! Recognize your sinfulness, your non-compliance, your rebellious spirit, or whatever it may be, and repent! Then follow through on that repentance with obedience.

2. Do not quench the Spirit

The second command is found in 1 Thessalonians 5:19: "*Do not quench the Spirit*." What does that mean? The Spirit is quenched, or stifled, when His promptings to yield, respond, and obey God's Word go unheeded. For instance, you may go to the Lord and say, "Lord, I am sorry I did not trust you with my finances and have not tithed. Forgive me in Messiah's atonement for my disobedience." You are forgiven because you repented and trusted in Yeshua's cleansing. You are now under the Spirit's influence and He directs you to start tithing. If you resist His prompting by thinking it's much more cost effective to repent than pay your tithes, you have just quenched the Holy Spirit and grieved Him all over again! This will bring the Lord's chastening on you, probably on your finances. In another example, you may ask the Lord to forgive you for harboring unforgiveness in your heart toward your spouse. Once more, if you do not change your attitude and apologize to your spouse, you are quenching the Holy Spirit, and by doing so you grieve Him. If you resist Him, you are not only grieving the Holy Spirit, but you are quenching the fire of His influence as well. God not only desires our repentance, He also wants us to act upon our repentance with obedience to whatever Scripture we repented for disobeying.[14] Again, if you quench the Spirit's influence by not following through on your repentance with obedience, you cannot be filled with Him. If you are not filled with the Spirit and empowered by Him, you will be unable to do the Holy Spirit's work, and your marriage and life will suffer as a result.

3. Walk in the Spirit

In Galatians 5:16 we read, "*But I say, walk by the Spirit, and you will not carry out the desire of the flesh.*" The third command regarding our yieldedness to

---

Romans 8:9–11; 1 Corinthians 3:16; 2 Timothy 1:14; Galatians 4:6; 1 John 4:4.
13. Study Psalm 32:1–8, which covers this matter as well.
14. Matthew 3:8: "*Therefore bear fruit in keeping with repentance.*"

the Holy Spirit is to "*walk by the Spirit.*" In the original language, "to walk"[15] is another way of referring to how you live your life. To walk by the Spirit is to live out your life by depending upon and obeying the Holy Spirit. In obedience to Galatians 6:1, "*Brethren, even if anyone is caught in any trespass, you who are spiritual, restore such a one in a spirit of gentleness; each one looking to yourself, so that you too will not be tempted.*" If you see your spouse in a trespass—that is, in clear contradiction to God's Word—you have a spiritual responsibility to restore him or her "*in a spirit of gentleness*" (not in a rebuke!), careful of being self-righteous or seeing yourself in any way better than the other. You may feel uncomfortable approaching your spouse, but if you will pray for your spouse and prayerfully yield to the Holy Spirit to be His instrument of restoration, God will empower you to do His will through the work of the Holy Spirit. He will enable you to have a spirit of gentleness, through which you can minister to one another in love. If your spouse is fearful or anxious to do what the Lord requires (e.g., discipline the children, report a crime, etc.), pray for your spouse and ask the Lord to fill you to encourage your spouse in their walk with God.[16] Walking by the Spirit refers to the loving and obedient lifestyle that represents the image of God in our marriages and to the world.

If you attend to these three commands, you will be a Spirit-filled person, and therefore a Spirit-filled husband or a Spirit-filled wife. Just loving each other is not enough, for your flesh is stronger than you are and will inevitably rebel and fail.[17] Be filled with the Holy Spirit, that you may love one another and have a marriage that represents God's love for His people.

The Spirit-Filled Community (Ephesians 5:18–21)

As noted, Paul begins his teaching on the Spirit-filled life by starting with the Spirit-filled community. That is because Spirit-filled communities are made up of Spirit-filled families. The congregation can be no more spiritual than the families that make it up, and the homes can be no more spiritual than the members of the family (and yes, we should disciple our children in the Spirit-filled life as part of our parenting ministry).

The Spirit-filled community is described in Ephesians 5:19–21. We minister to one another and worship the Lord with spiritual songs, etc., first in the family and then the community. Let's briefly consider these verses.

---

15. The Greek word for "walk," *peripateo*, is literally "to go about," or "to walk around."
16. Isaiah 35:3: "*Encourage the exhausted, and strengthen the feeble.*" First Thessalonians 5:11, 14: "*Therefore encourage one another and build up one another, just as you also are doing.... We urge you, brethren, admonish the unruly, encourage the fainthearted, help the weak, be patient with everyone.*"
17. "*For the flesh sets its desire against the Spirit, and the Spirit against the flesh; for these are in opposition to one another, so that you may not do the things that you please*" (Galatians 5:17).

*Speaking to one another in psalms and hymns and spiritual songs,
singing and making melody with your heart to the Lord;
always giving thanks for all things in the name of our
Lord Yeshua the Messiah to God, even the Father;
and be subject to one another in the fear of Messiah.*

The outworking of being filled with the Spirit in 5:18 is seen in the verbs in 5:19–21: speaking, singing, making melody, giving thanks, and being subject. All these verbs except for the last one are participle present active—that is, they are the spiritual activities that we keep doing on an ongoing basis. As often as we are filled with the Spirit, we are expressing the Spirit's presence in these ways. The last verb, "*be subject*," is a present participle passive, which means we are being submitted to one another by our profound reverence[18] of the Messiah. This, too, expresses being filled with the Spirit.

It is also important to note that our speaking, singing praises, etc. is not only among ourselves, but within ourselves: "*with your heart*." Before we can edify others with His praises, we must edify ourselves! This is the same principle in the V'ahavta in Deuteronomy 6:5–7. Since we love God with all our heart, His words will be upon our hearts first, so that we can then teach them diligently to our children. This idea of always praising and thanking Yeshua in our hearts, and then in edification to others in the home, may seem a bit unusual—if not idealistic—but it seems that way to us only if we lack the good habits that Messianic discipleship should produce in us and through us. Taking every thought captive to Messiah (2 Corinthians 10:5) is a discipline and good habit that needs to be developed in every believer so that we are not "*conformed to this world*," but transformed by the renewing of our minds to demonstrate what is the good, acceptable, and perfect will of God (Romans 12:2). These godly habits produce wholesome homes and a godly congregation. Paul concludes in 5:21 that if we are Spirit filled as a community and a family, we will be in submission one to another.

Understanding Headship in 1 Corinthians 11:3

Before moving on to the Spirit-filled marital relationship, we will briefly consider the matter of submission through the foundational verse on headship in the marriage, 1 Corinthians 11:3 (SN): "*But I want you to understand that Messiah is the head of every man, and the man is the head of a woman, and God is the head of Messiah.*"

This verse shows us that functional subordination is built into the very nature and Person of God. That is, the Son of God is submitted to God the Father. Why? Because everything is done properly and in order[19] in heaven, in the congregation, and in the home as well. This verse is *not* saying the Father is better than

---

18. "Fear" in Greek: *phobos*.
19. First Corinthians 14:40.

the Son, for they are equal in divine nature.[20] Nor is the husband better than his wife—they are equal in quality and human nature. But there is a functional subordination between the Father and the Son as to specific responsibility,[21] and this should likewise be reflected in the home between the husband and wife.[22] When Messiah came in the flesh, He taught of His equality and yet also His subordination to the Father.[23] As a servant, Messiah's functional subordination to the Father in no way demeans His Person. So too, the wife is in no way demeaned by her subordination to her husband's leadership role in the home.[24] This does not mean that a spiritually immature woman won't misconstrue the matter to feel demeaned where there is no biblical reason to feel that way. Nor does it mean that a spiritually immature husband will not misconstrue the matter and foolishly think that he is superior to his wife. These matters of spiritual immaturity should be addressed through proper discipleship, premarital counseling, and ongoing biblical instruction before the wedding.

In the Spirit-filled marriage, functional subordination reveals the love of God for His people, even as *"the Father loves the Son."*[25] Headship in the Spirit-filled marriage reveals His Lordship in our home through His discipleship in our hearts.

Keeping this ministry of headship in mind, we move on from the Spirit-filled community to the Spirit-filled family (Ephesians 5:22–6:4). In this present section (5:22–33), we consider the Spirit-filled couple and their roles as Spirit-filled wife and Spirit-filled husband.

The Spirit-Filled Family (Ephesians 5:22–6:4)

The Spirit-filled couple (5:22–32)

The Spirit-filled wife: **Functional subordination**

> *Wives, be subject to your own husbands, as to the Lord.*
> *For the husband is the head of the wife, as Messiah also is the head of*
> *the Assembly, He Himself being the Savior of the body.*
> *But as the Assembly is subject to Messiah, so also the wives*
> *ought to be to their husbands in everything.* (Ephesians 5:22–24 SN)

---

20. Philippians 2:7; Colossians 2:9; etc. This matter of the Messiah's divine nature is further studied in the author's book *Messianic Discipleship*, pp. 54–62.
21. See *Messianic Discipleship*, pp. 72–73, 75.
22. This was discussed previously in Genesis 2:18 in the matter of the wife being the husband's *ezer kenegdo*, his partner and helper, as well as in the renewal of his family leadership role in Genesis 3:16.
23. John 5:17–27.
24. To see how functional subordination works throughout society, see Appendix Seven.
25. John 5:20.

This describes the functional subordination on the part of the Spirit-filled wife for the sake of orderliness in the home. There are four helpful principles in Ephesians 5:22–23 to apply in her role as wife.

1. *Her subordinate role to her husband is consensual*. The wife is directed to willingly "*be subject*." Remember that verse 22 is written in the immediate context of verse 21, which states the community is to be subject to one another in the reverence of Messiah. In 5:22 the text states, "*Wives, be subject to your own husbands*." In better English translations, the words "*be subject*" are italicized. When Bible translators italicize words, it's not for emphasis, but to indicate that these particular words are not in the original text, but were added later by the translators to enhance the reader's understanding. These italicized words in Ephesians 5:22 were added to carry forward the main verb from 5:21, for there is no verb in 5:22. Read literally, verses 21–22 say, "*And be subject to one another in the fear of Messiah. Wives, to your own husbands, as to the Lord*." The wife is called to be subject, that is, functionally subordinate, to her own husband, in the same way that community members are subject to one another.

Every wholesome relationship in the Bible is consensual, and marriage is no exception. When she says "I do," she is consenting to her husband's leadership in the marriage. When he says "I do," he is consenting to love her sacrificially as her husband. They are each consenting to submit to their respective roles in the marriage. The members of the community are submitted to each other, beginning with the wife. When this is properly lived out, the home and community become a gracious and loving testimony to the rest of the world. Even though submission is commanded, it is still by her consent. The woman voluntarily consents to be subject to her own husband. Thus, nowhere in Scripture does it say, "Husbands, get your wives to submit to you." Any husband that forces, manipulates, or bullies his wife to be submitted to his leadership is in disobedience to God, corrupts his soul, and negates his spiritual ministry in the marriage. No, her role is by her willing consent. Remember, God formed the woman, not to be her husband's slave, but to be his partner and counterpart in the marriage.[26] When couples say "I do," it should be clearly understood that the wife is consenting to submit to her husband, and the husband is consenting to love His wife as Messiah loved the Assembly (the Body of Messianic believers).[27]

We may naturally be concerned that we might be taken advantage of when we mutually submit to one another. For this reason we need proper discipleship before the wedding so both spouses understand these matters very well and are prepared for the spiritual ministry to their counterpart. This also assumes not merely being

---

26. Review Genesis 2:18–22 on this matter.
27. "Assembly" is used for the Greek word *ekklesia*, since in the Septuagint, this Greek word is used for *qahal*, the Hebrew word for "assembly" in the Tanakh (Deuteronomy 4:10; 9:10; 18:16; 1 Chronicles 28:8, etc.).

a well-taught couple, but a Spirit-filled couple, for the Holy Spirit will empower you to both properly submit and sacrificially love in Yeshua the Messiah. Be very careful of substituting being well taught for being filled with the Holy Spirit, for His power makes His Word practical and applicable to our lives. Also, be just as careful not to substitute being Spirit filled with being well taught, for His power is only to fulfill what the Word of God teaches. Ignorance of His Word will lead to misinterpreting His power for our own selfish desires. Both being well taught in the Word and being filled with the Spirit are essential for the growing, godly marriage that continues to reveal the image of God to His glory.

1. *Her subordinate role to her husband is vocational*. "*Wives, be subject to your own husbands, as to the Lord*" (5:22). The wife is called by God to minister to her own husband. Note the limitation is to her own husband, not to anyone else's husband or any other man. Her stewardship is limited to her own husband. She is responsible to learn his language, which means learning his sensitivities and what may upset him. Many men can too easily feel disrespected and are therefore fragile. She must be responsive and respectful of this accordingly. There is a relationship between the community and the home. Those who do not submit in the home will have a hard time submitting in the community, and then marriage issues become congregational issues. So, the Bible does not teach that women are to be subject to men, but that the wife is to be functionally subordinate to *her own* husband, and therefore to no one else's husband, let alone to another man. This limits the matter to her marriage relationship, and may not be applicable to any other situation. Though she is subordinate to her husband in the marriage, she may be her husband's supervisor at work, where he would be subordinate to her, without the work situation confusing their home life together.

2. *Her subordinate role to her husband is tactical*. Two aspects are brought out here: "*For the husband is the head of the wife, as Messiah also is the head of the Assembly, He Himself being the Savior of the body*" (5:23 SN). First, the "*Assembly*" is an organization, while the "*body*" is an organism. *Organization* refers to the systems and orderliness for the sustained functionality of the Assembly.[28] This is true as well for the home. The family is to have an orderly structure (we eat dinner at 6 p.m. as a family, we worship as a family at the Messianic synagogue on Shabbat morning, we do family laundry on Sundays, etc.). The wife is to submit to her husband as the leader of the organization in the home. Her role becomes tactical as she implements his direction. Second, the husband is the protector ("*Savior*") of the organism. As a result of her husband's headship, she enjoys both the organization's direction and protection. Since her husband is responsible for everything, she is responsive to him. Yeshua is the Savior of the body, as He died

---

28. For more on the functional and healthy structure of the congregation (and home), see the author's book *Developing Healthy Messianic Congregations*, pp. 103–114.

for the sins that were offensive to Him. Just so, the husband should not judge his wife. As her protector, he should be willing to die for her sins, just as Messiah did.

3. Her subordinate role to her husband is developmental. "*But as the Assembly is subject to Messiah, so also the wives ought to be to their husbands in everything*" (5:24 SN). Why is it developmental? "*In everything*" informs us that there may be circumstances up ahead that we are not yet prepared for or mature enough to handle. Not yet, at least. The text clearly states that the husband is responsible before God for everything in the home, and all that goes on in the home. He is also responsible for the spiritual welfare of the entire family. There are situations that come about in a marriage that neither the wife nor the husband is prepared to handle, like a "woops" baby, physical disability, or unexpected financial problems. These can test the spiritual maturity of any Messianic couple. When the Scripture says "*in everything*," we are reminded that we will be growing in the Lord together through trials that we're being prepared for even as we live faithfully for Yeshua through matters we are dealing with today.

Unfortunately, during serious trials, the undisciped spouse can bail on their responsibility, and the other spouse is left doing double duty. This is a difficult situation—but not uncommon—that many marriages have endured. If the wife finds herself in this situation, studying the life of Abigail, who lived during King David's time (1 Samuel 25:1–38), can be an encouragement. Abigail is married to a man named Nabal, whose name appropriately means "fool." She is a godly woman who has to constantly clean up after her husband's follies. If you find yourself in that situation, God will give you, like Abigail, the grace and power through the Holy Spirit to get through it victoriously. For husbands in this situation, review the life of Joseph, whose pagan wife could not possibly prepare her children for the spiritual leadership in Israel required of them.[29] Joseph evidently had to assume the spiritual instruction of his two sons, which is the calling upon every father.[30]

Husbands and wives both grow into their roles as they mature in the Lord. In my experience, most men are not prepared for the ministry of marriage. Often, younger men are highly motivated by the urge for regular and legitimate sex, but may not understand at all the leadership responsibility they are accepting. Even so, the husband is called by God to be a prayer warrior and to minister the Word to his family, since he is responsible before God for everything in the home. His wife should therefore be responsive to him and support him as the spiritual head of the home.

Eve ate the fruit first and thought thereby she could lead the home, because she was one bite smarter than her husband. By contrast, the Spirit-filled wife trusts the Lord as she supports her husband's leadership in everything. That is the abiding testimony of the Spirit-filled Messianic home.

---

29. Genesis 48:8–20.
30. Ephesians 6:4.

***The Spirit-filled husband:* Known by his faithful love for his wife**

In this section, Paul lays out three aspects of the husband's love for his wife:

1. His faithfulness in the ministry of love, 5:25–27
2. His oneness in the maturity of love, 5:28–31
3. His witness in the testimony of love, 5:32–33

> *Husbands, love your wives, just as Messiah also loved the Assembly*
> *and gave Himself up for her, so that He might sanctify her,*
> *having cleansed her by the washing of water with the word, that He*
> *might present to Himself the Assembly in all her glory,*
> *having no spot or wrinkle or any such thing; but that she*
> *would be holy and blameless.* (Ephesians 5:25–27 SN)

His faithfulness in the ministry of love (5:25–27)

The Spirit-filled husband faithfully ministers in his sacrificial love to protect his wife (v. 25), his sanctifying love to purify his wife (v. 26), and his Scriptural love to present his wife (v. 27).

This portion of Scripture answers the question, "How shall a husband love his wife?" The answer is that the husband is to mirror Messiah's sacrificial love. In Ephesians 5:25, we find that husbands are to love their wives just as Messiah loved the Assembly and gave Himself up for her. Loving the wife sacrificially is the dynamic equivalent of the wife being submitted to him, as we saw in 5:21, for just as the community is to love one another and be submitted to one another, so is the husband to be submitted in the home by loving his wife sacrificially. The leader is the servant of all.[31] Therefore, the husband is to sacrificially love his wife and be in submission to her, which he does by dying for her in every area where he has responsibility in the home—which, as we learned in 5:24, is everything! This is his ministry of love in the home.

First, the Spirit-filled husband's ministry is to protect his wife, as we read in Ephesians 5:23. From what should he protect her? From her own faults! Just as we bring judgment upon ourselves for our own sins, and Messiah took our sins upon Himself to take our judgment on Himself (and yet, He was the offended party!), so husbands are to take the hit for their wives. Instead of saying, "She brought that on herself," the husband, in sacrificial love, is to "fall on the grenade," so to speak. The calling of husbands is not to point the finger, but to extend grace with mercy and forgiveness. They are to take responsibility for the home and thereby protect her. At this point, men may ask if there is alternative job. Yes, it's called being single.

---

31. Matthew 20:26–27.

Six • *The Spirit-Filled Life*

The husband's second ministry of faithful love is to sanctify his wife. Verse 26 states that Messiah gave Himself up for the Assembly "*so that He might sanctify her.*" What does 5:25 mean by suggesting that, like Messiah, husbands are to die for their wives? And how is a wife sanctified, set apart, and treated as special? These are achieved when the husband takes the hit so that judgment doesn't fall on the wife. This principle is seen in Numbers 30 regarding vows. When a wife makes a commitment (a vow), the husband must approve it upon first hearing. If he says nothing, the vow stands. Let's say the wife spends money on something and then tells her husband about it. If he says nothing, the vow stands and the bill must be paid. If he disapproves, it is his job to say so upon first hearing. (I would counsel that the husband should not make commitments [vows] without conferring with his wife as well, since she is his partner in the marital ministry, and she may have a different and helpful perspective on the matter.) Remember, the husband is responsible for everything in the home; therefore he is to take responsibility. This frees her from anxieties that are not her responsibility, and this freedom sets her apart as special. By taking the leadership responsibility in the home, the husband makes decisions that treat the wife as special. If you owned a precious Ming vase, you would not put your garbage in it—no, you would treat it as special. Likewise, a husband makes decisions in his wife's best interest, and treats her as precious in his sight.

Treating your wife as special is also a purifying kind of love. The husband is never to tarnish, defile, or corrupt his wife, nor is he to do anything that would defile the home or marriage. That means no Internet porn, lying, bullying, or bailing, and no screaming battlegrounds. The husband is to make sure that he is a sanctifying influence in the home, not one that corrupts by creating tension and stress. The leader is always to be the shock absorber, not the shock emitter. He is to manage his home, thereby freeing her from being stressed out over things that are really not her responsibility. He will work with her as a partner, of course, by delegating responsibilities of agreed value to the marriage, family, and home. Her job is to implement the agreed-upon direction in the home, not to usurp his leadership role.

Verse 26 further states "*that He might sanctify her, having cleansed her by the washing of water with the word.*" When the husband minsters the Word of God, the Word acts as a cleansing element in her life. This does not mean the husband should be telling her what to do. Instead, he should be ministering the Word by praying with her, going over the Word of God with her, leading the home in studying the Scriptures, and seeking ways to implement God's Word together. This is what brings spiritual cleansing and sanctification. As "head" of the wife, the husband is in the overseer (or "headship") ministry, and there are several aspects of this that we will look at in greater detail later. The first and most important of

223

these elements is the ministry of prayer and making sure you have a prayer-filled home (note the corresponding passage on prayer in 1 Peter 3:7).

A second element pictured here in verse 26 is the ministry of the Word. By the ministry of the Word, the values for the home are set and implemented in obedience to God, thereby sanctifying, or setting apart, the home unto God. Without faith-obedience to the Word, the home is desecrated not consecrated. If desecration is the state of your home, repent now and seek your congregational leader for guidance on following God's Word in your home.

The husband's third ministry of faithful love is to present his wife: "*...that He might present to Himself the Assembly in all her glory, having no spot or wrinkle or any such thing; but that she would be holy and blameless*" (5:27 SN). This refers to Yeshua, when He brings us into glory. Representing Messiah's leadership in the home, the husband's work is to present his wife holy and blameless—that is, not to be blaming her or resenting her. "Holy" also means "to be set apart," just as *sanctification* does. She is to be treated as special, like the queen of the home that she is. Furthermore, the Scripture says you have the responsibility to present her as a result of your ministry to her. The Scripture states that what you sow is what you reap (Galatians 6:7). Here is the marital application of that concept: you get the wife you are investing in.

Joe told me that he no longer feels any love for his wife, Suzie. Upon further inquiry, he seemed to have confused love and lust. In truth, he only lusted for Suzie as a younger woman but didn't truly love her as a godly husband, and he really didn't understand what godly love meant. He apparently married Suzie under false pretenses, not understanding the love of Messiah for him and through him for his wife. Once Joe learned of God's sacrificial love for him and how that applied to his marriage, he repented of his false carnal values about marriage, was filled with the Spirit, and committed himself to faithfully love Suzie, as Messiah sacrificially loved him.

One day, you will have to face the Lord and give an account of your stewardship as a husband. According to Scripture, your wife is your ministry, just as the Assembly is Messiah's ministry. Hopefully you will be able to tell the Lord that you loved your wife—that you set her apart and treated her as special, and that you did not blame her or resent her. As husbands, we grow into this, although growth is slow. We want to be doing as Yeshua is doing, and present our wives as holy and blameless, better than we found them and more delightful than ever.

A man must be a Spirit-filled husband in order for this to be real; the flesh is stronger than we are and will naturally rebel against and resist the truth of God's Word. We must submit to the Holy Spirit and be Spirit filled so that we may carry out the work that God entrusted to us. Otherwise it becomes like the law, and the law only incites us to sin (Romans 7:7–8). Nevertheless, the Holy Spirit empowers us to carry out God's will.

His oneness in the maturity of love (5:28–31 SN)

So husbands ought also to love their own wives as their own bodies. He who loves his own wife loves himself; for no one ever hated his own flesh, but nourishes and cherishes it, just as Messiah also does the Assembly, because we are members of His body. For this reason a man shall leave his father and mother and shall be joined to his wife, and the two shall become one flesh.

In 5:31, Paul refers to Genesis 2:24 as the culmination of his teaching, to point toward our restoration to God's original design for marriage. In 5:28–30, Paul demonstrates that "marital oneness" is achieved by the husband loving his wife as himself.

The husband's obligation to love his wife as himself, 5:28a

The husband has a Messianic obligation. This passage begins with "*So.*" This word "*so*" refers us back to Messiah's love for the believing community. Messiah's ministry to us is our example for marriage in every way. As both our Creator and Covenanter, God in Messiah cares for His creation through His redemption of humanity. This Messianic redemption is promised to and through the seed of Abraham.[32] This is not an odious obligation to God, but is an obligation of love, like a parent caring for their desperately ill child. God loves us at our worst.[33] Because the woman was taken from the man, the husband has a leadership obligation for the wife that was produced from him. Though only seen perfectly in Yeshua, marital oneness requires personal integrity—as we say in Yiddish, *menschkiet*—being a person of godly character. As we "*grow in the grace and knowledge of our Lord,*"[34] and "*become conformed to the image of His Son,*"[35] we "*all attain to the unity of the faith, and of the knowledge of the Son of God, to a mature man, to the measure of the stature which belongs to the fullness of* [Messiah]."[36] Marital oneness obligates the husband to care for his wife as himself, even as Messiah is also obligated to our welfare by creation purpose and covenant promise.

The husband has a marriage obligation. The text uses the word *ought.* This word (*opheilo*) refers to having a debt to another.[37] To whom is the husband obligated?

---

32. "*In your seed all the nations of the earth shall be blessed*" (Genesis 22:18). So, the writer states in Hebrews 2:16, "*He does not give help to angels, but He gives help to the descendant* [seed] *of Abraham.*"
33. Romans 5:8 (SN): "*God demonstrates His love for us in that, while we were yet sinners, Messiah dies for us.*"
34. Second Peter 3:18.
35. Romans 8:29.
36. Ephesians 4:13.
37. This same word is used by the rabbis in the ancient Greek translation, the Septuagint, in Deuteronomy 15:2, as having a "debt" to a creditor. In Romans 15:27, Paul uses this word to say that the Gentile believers have a "debt of love" to the Jewish people for the blessings of Abraham that came through Israel to them in Messiah. And so, John writes in 1 John 2:6 that if we abide in

To his wife? Yes, the husband vowed (swore) to love his wife and have an overseeing concern for her, since she came initially from him and was presented to him by the Lord. No matter how you may see yourself in the marriage relationship, God sees the husband and wife as one, and treats you as one entity. That is why Yeshua, in His instruction about Messianic marriage matters,[38] reiterates the original design of Genesis 2:24.

The word *ought* speaks of responsibility and duty. If you do not love your wife as Messiah does, you are disobeying God and abandoning your duty and calling. Does the husband have an obligation to God? Yes, he has a stewardship from God to love his wife as God's gift. Just as leaders in the congregation will have to "*give an account*" for those God placed in their care (Hebrews 13:17), so too, the husband will be rewarded by God for the loving care shown to his wife. Grace makes no one a debtor, and we're not to pay God back for His grace and mercy. Instead, we are to pay it forward to others, especially to our spouse. As we were each obligated by our appreciation of our spouse to leave mom and dad, so this sacrificial duty in marriage obligates us to cleave unto our wives.[39]

As staying healthy for God's service is a personal obligation, so spiritual health is a marital obligation. Spiritual health obligates us to allow others—especially our wives—to love us, and also obligates each of us to love others—especially our wives. The unloving husband is the unhealthy believer. What ought the husband do? Be filled with the Spirit and love his wife as himself. Remember, the first fruit of the Spirit is love (Galatians 5:22).

How is marital oneness obligated, 5:28b–29b?

Marital oneness obligates the husband to care for wife so that there's healthy growth and warmth. Oneness reveals spiritual vitality. Oneness is a healthy spiritual condition.

Care for ourselves is rational. Paul states, "*He who loves his own wife loves himself*" (28b). Appropriate concern for ourselves indicates having a sound mind.[40] Marital oneness is sane, like taking care of ourselves. "Self-love" is a phrase that, perverted by sin, refers to selfishness. But as Scripture properly uses this idea, we should love ourselves as God loves us. This is a marital application of the second-greatest commandment to love our neighbor as ourselves.[41] No neighbor is closer to us than our spouse. But if we're to love ourselves (and our wives), then how does

---

Yeshua, we "*ought*" to walk as He did. Again, in 1 John 4:11: "*Beloved, if God so loved us, we also ought to love one another.*"

38. He says in Matthew 19:5, "*For this reason a man shall leave his father and mother and be joined to his wife, and the two shall become one flesh.*"

39. As discussed in Genesis 2:23–25 above.

40. Second Timothy 1:7. Biblically, sin is irrational, since "*the fear of the Lord is the beginning of wisdom*" (Psalm 111:10).

41. Leviticus 19:18.

God love us? He does not love us by encouraging self-indulgence or permitting a promiscuous lifestyle. Not at all! His love for us is a purifying love and not a corrupting love. God's love is selfless, not selfish, and it is 100 percent committed to our eternal welfare. His love was poured out into our hearts through the Holy Spirit when we trusted in Yeshua,[42] and this love motivates us to love and worship God, to glorify Him, and to thereby care about others, even the least of His brethren. This self-love is, ironically, selfless love that reveals the sacrifice of love through the Messiah. So, this sane, godly love for ourselves is revealed in our selfless love for our wives.

Cruelty to ourselves is irrational. Paul continues: "*For no one ever hated his own flesh*" (v. 29). By that he means that no sane person ever hated his own flesh. Paul is speaking in general terms here, for there are many people who loathe rather than love themselves. If you loathe and abuse yourself, your spouse doesn't stand a chance. There are plenty of people who deal with self-loathing. If you have an issue with this, you are encouraged to get counseling before you get married. If you're spiritually unhealthy, you cannot properly minister to your spouse. A form of spiritual disorder taught by false religion, called asceticism, includes severe self-discipline and avoidance of personal enjoyment with the idea that this will please God.[43] In truth, self-abuse is a sign of irrationality. As we are to love our neighbors as ourselves, so too, from God's perspective, our self-abuse directed outwardly becomes cruelty toward others.[44] The dysfunction of a society can be measured by the toleration of marital abuse in the home (adultery, pornography, drunkenness, illegal drug use, etc.), including divorce, which is the final abuse that kills the marriage. Godless societies, by definition, have no eternally objective means to measure or model a spiritually functional home, and can only declare as a "new normal" the growing dysfunction of the family through the overwhelming corruption to the society and home. As I write this, gay marriage is a new normal in the USA. Transgender curriculum is now taught to children in American schools.[45] Thus, spiritually healthy Messianic marriages are the redemptive hope and instrumental cure for an unhealthy society. Godly marital oneness is the living proof that you're spiritually healthy in Messiah.

Care for our wives is spiritual maturity. "*...but nourishes and cherishes it.*" Messianic marriages mature in oneness as husbands nurture and care for their own wives. What exactly does it mean to nourish and cherish my wife as myself? The first word, "nourishes" (*ektrepho*), does not mean "to feed," but "to nurture," or "to bring up to maturity." This same word is used in the Greek translation of the

---

42. Romans 5:5.
43. See Isaiah 58:1–8; Colossians 2:18–23; 1 Timothy 4:3, 8.
44. Proverbs 11:17: "*The merciful man does himself good, but the cruel man does himself harm.*" Ecclesiastes 4:5 "*The fool folds his hands and consumes his own flesh.*"
45. Thirty-nine states presently use a transgender curriculum. Margot Cleveland, "The Transgender Agenda Hits Kindergarten," *National Review*, September 4, 2017, nationalreview.com.

Tanakh for (*gadal*), "bringing up a child."[46] In the New Covenant, the word is only used again in Ephesians 6:4 to refer to nurturing or bringing up your children. Please realize the importance of the fact that this word is only used twice in the New Covenant and both times is for the man of the house, as husband and father in the home. The Spirit-filled husband is the nurturer and developer of the marriage and the home according to the original design. This word informs the husband that he is to commit himself to his spouse's blessed spiritual growth. It is in this way the husband himself grows in Messiah. That is, he grows through his intentional nurturing of his wife as He encourages his wife's growth through prayer for her and with her, as he daily studies the Scriptures to develop their home together according God's Word, as they are committed as a couple to a Messianic community that shares their spiritual values, and as they prayerfully share their faith with their neighbors. So a husband's nurturing ministry to his wife is a byproduct of his nurturing of himself.

The next word, "cherishes," literally means "to impart warmth," and it is used to speak of tenderly caring for others.[47] We're to "warm" our wives—that is, soften their hearts by our tender care for them. Stereotypically, husbands are fixers. If his wife has a problem, the husband tries to fix it. If he can, then it's a job well done; if he can't, it's frustration on his part. In marriage, not everything is easily fixed or fixable. This is especially true of the human soul. On this side of heaven, we have weaknesses that are divinely intended to prove His grace alone as our sufficiency.[48] When our wives go through circumstances that bring to the surface their feelings of inadequacy, their anxieties, and their human weaknesses, they need their husbands' loving acceptance and tender care.[49] Since some husbands may understandably find this contrary to their natural inclinations, this once more reminds them of the required Spirit-filled life that enables them to live out Messiah's love even through their husbandly weaknesses. By nourishing and cherishing (nurturing and caring) for their wives, Spirit-filled husbands care for themselves, while achieving marital oneness with their spouses.

Why is marital oneness obligated, 5:29c–30?

Paul writes in conclusion, "*...just as Messiah also does the Assembly, because we are members of His body.*" Often, people don't care about what they must do or how they must do it until they understand the why of a matter.

---

46. Job 31:18; Hosea 9:12; Isaiah 23:4.
47. This Greek word *thalpo* is used in the Greek Septuagint for the Hebrew word *chamam* in 1 Kings 1:2. It is used also in the New Covenant to mean "to tenderly care" (1 Thessalonians 2:7). It is used in Greek writings to mean "to soften by warmth," as in getting warm by a fire (*Thayer's Greek-English Lexicon*).
48. Second Corinthians 12:9.
49. This Greek word is also used in Deuteronomy 22:6 of the Septuagint for a mother bird "*sitting*," or brooding (*ravats*), on her young in the nest. Similarly, husbands need to gently care for their wives.

Marital oneness represents the fidelity of Messiah's model, 5:29b. Paul makes a comparison by using the phrase "*just as.*" Paul previously used "*just as*" in two verses that directly reflect upon his use of it here in 5:29. In Ephesians 5:2, we are taught that we are to walk in love "*just as*" Messiah sacrificially loved us. So too, in marriage, husbands are to love their wives just as Messiah sacrificially loved us (5:25). In both cases, the example to follow in love is the Messiah. So too, "*just as*" here refers to the direct correlation between the husband nourishing and cherishing his wife and Messiah doing the same for the Assembly. The Bible teaches that the Messianic marriage is the model that exactly represents Yeshua's love for us. For any husband, this can seem like an overwhelming responsibility, but that is why he must be Spirit-filled to live out the life and love of Yeshua in his marriage. The Messianic marriage testifies of His care for His people. A lack of marital oneness puts into doubt the valid testimony of Yeshua's fidelity to His people.

Marital oneness represents the unity of Messiah's members, 5:30, "*...because we are members of His body.*" If you are a member of His Body, this is revealed in your Messianic marriage unity. Present-tense membership in His Body reveals itself in the present-tense unity of your marriage. A lack of unity calls into question your membership in the Body. We do not properly function apart from being a member of His Body, just as a finger cannot function apart from the head. If a couple is unaware of this membership principle, they will not enjoy the marital oneness that is the spiritual norm for Messianic marriage. When coming to personal faith in Yeshua as Mashiach and Adonai, we unite spiritually with Him.[50] Spiritual union with Him is pictured as the Head and the Body. He is the Head of the Body and we are the various members of the Body.

Body-life is discussed extensively in Scripture.[51] Earlier in Ephesians Paul teaches: "*But speaking the truth in love, we are to grow up in all aspects into Him who is the head, even Messiah, from whom the whole body, being fitted and held together by what every joint supplies, according to the proper working of each individual part, causes the growth of the body for the building up of itself in love*" (Ephesians 4:15–16 sn). The principle here in the relationship between the whole Body of Messianic believers and the Messiah as the Head applies directly to the marriage for marital oneness. That principle is the Body's total dependence on the Head, and it is seen in the total interdependence of the members of the Body. Interdependence means "*being fitted and held together by what every joint supplies*"—that is, I need you, and you need me. We need each other to properly function in Messiah.

Interdependence also requires "*the proper working of each individual part.*" Through discipleship, we function as members of the Body. The undiscipled

---

50. John 15:2–6; Romans 6:3–5; 1 Corinthians 6:17; Ephesians 2:5–6; Philippians 3:10–11.
51. Romans 12:4–5; 1 Corinthians 10:17; 12:12–27; Ephesians 1:23; 2:16; 3:6; 4:4, 12; Colossians 1:18, 24; 2:19; 3:15.

believer is the dysfunctional member of the Body. Full growth only comes from total dependence on the Head and total interdependence upon the fellow members. A lack of interdependence on the fellow members reveals independence from the Head. Interdependence is how we grow in love. In the Messianic marriage the same principle applies. Each spouse must be totally dependent on Yeshua, the Head, and that will be seen in our total interdependence on each other. Where we are not interdependent with our spouse, we are independent from the Head. If this is the case, both must repent of their independence from Messiah and from their spouse and recommit in both areas. When a couple argues with each other about finances, you will find they're not dependent upon Yeshua for their resources. Where a couple can't agree on how to raise the children, you will find a lack of dependence upon Yeshua to parent the children on His behalf, "*because we are members of His Body.*" Our interdependent membership in His Body is the reason for marital oneness. Dependence on Him and interdependence on each other "*causes the growth of the* [marriage] *for the building up of itself in love*" (Ephesians 4:16). When we care for our wives, we are demonstrating that we are Spirit filled and in submission to the Head, which is Messiah.

His witness in the testimony of love (5:32–33)

This mystery is great; but I am speaking with reference to Messiah and the Assembly. Nevertheless, each individual among you also is to love his own wife even as himself, and the wife must see to it that she respects her husband.

When Paul says, "*This mystery is great,*" he is actually speaking of the great revealed truth[52] of Messiah and the Assembly. The whole point of Paul's discussion of Messianic marriage is that it is representative of Messiah and His people. This is the testimony and witness and why it is so important for married couples to represent Him well in marriage. Caring for one another is the picture of Messiah that we present to the rest of the world. In 5:33, Paul summarizes the Spirit-filled marriage, stating the mutual submission of the wife to her husband, and the husband's love for his wife "*as himself.*"

Take a good look at your marriage, for it is your testimony to your children and the community. If a husband is either cold or domineering towards his wife, it pictures his unbelief toward God. However, the God we serve loves people and humbly washes their feet. If a man wants to be respected and honored by his wife, he needs to respect and honor her. What he sows, he will reap. If he wants to be built up in the faith, then he needs to build up his wife. The testimony of the Spirit-filled husband is seen in his loving and caring for his wife. The testimony of the Spirit-filled wife is respecting and being responsive to her husband. In the

---

52. In the New Covenant, a *mystery* is a once-hidden, now-revealed truth (Romans 11:25, etc.).

Six • *The Spirit-Filled Life*

redeemed marriage, we see the partnership between husband and wife that God originally designed back in the garden, now lived out together by faith in Messiah.[53]

Some questions to help apply these teachings

1. In what ways are you complying with the Holy Spirit in your relationships? Is He grieved? Is He quenched? Are you obedient and dependent on Yeshua?

2. In what ways are you respectful of each other? In what areas are you tempted to be disrespectful or resent His initiative?

3. How have you demonstrated your love for your spouse as Yeshua loves you? In what areas are you less than sacrificial?

4. Do you harbor any unforgiveness toward your spouse? In what ways do you treat your spouse as special? How often do you minister the Word to your spouse?

5. As a husband, how have you developed the spiritual beauty of your wife? As a wife, how have you demonstrated your respect for your husband?

6. What are some ways that you nurture and cherish (show tenderness to) your spouse? How have you taken initiative to maintain the unity of your relationship?

7. In what ways does your relationship demonstrate publicly that the curse of Genesis 3:14–17 has been lifted?

---

53. For the application of the Spirit-filled life to the whole family in Ephesians 6:1–4, please refer to Appendix Eight.

CHAPTER SEVEN

Restored Leadership in the Family

Husband as Manager (1 Timothy 3:4–5)

Regarding the Messianic marriage, we left off in Ephesians considering the role of the husband and the father. We'll continue to see the redemptive return to the original design in Messiah as we consider the husband as a family manager in 1 Timothy 3:4–5. The values we are so accustomed to in society are very different from what the Bible teaches, and this is particularly true regarding the husband's leadership responsibilities in the home (and then in the congregation).

The context of 1 Timothy 3:1–7 refers to the qualifications for an overseer in the congregation, and one of the qualifiers is for the husband to be a caring leader in the home before he can be a leader in the congregation. We'll consider his management at home within the context of the larger portion, verses 1–7.

> *It is a trustworthy statement: if any man aspires to the office of overseer, it is a fine work he desires to do. An overseer, then, must be above reproach, the husband of one wife, temperate, prudent, respectable, hospitable, able to teach, not addicted to wine or pugnacious, but gentle, peaceable, free from the love of money. He must be one who manages his own household well, keeping his children under control with all dignity (but if a man does not know how to manage his own household, how will he take care of the Assembly of God?), and not a new convert, so that he will not become conceited and fall into the condemnation incurred by the devil. And he must have a good reputation with those outside the Assembly, so that he will not fall into reproach and the snare of the devil.* (First Timothy 3:1–7 SN)

Since Yeshua came to serve and not to be served, proper leadership for the husband is always servant-leadership. Yeshua said this in Matthew 20:28: *"Just as the Son of Man did not come to be served, but to serve, and to give His life a ransom for many."* Therefore, husbands and fathers are to serve and not be served. How different that value is from the rest of the world! To be successful servant-leaders, we need to follow the "ACE" model of servant-leadership, as outlined in 1 Timothy 3:1–7. This means:

- The servant-leader's **Ambition** (3:1): "*If any man aspires to the office of overseer, it is a fine work he desires to do.*" The man of God desires to serve for God. If you feel put upon (like having a distasteful obligation), then you're not ready to be God's servant in the home or in the congregation. First, a husband must embrace the calling.[1] You must have ambition to intentionally serve your marriage and family first, before leading elsewhere in the congregation.

- The servant-leader's **Character** (3:2–3): "*An overseer, then, must be above reproach, the husband of one wife, temperate, prudent, respectable, hospitable, able to teach, not addicted to wine or pugnacious, but gentle, peaceable, free from the love of money.*" A godly man has godly character—i.e., he is faithful to his wife, nurturing, kind, loving, etc. Falling short in these areas means he lacks maturity. Godly men desire their character to reflect the Messiah's in every way. These may not appear at first to be character qualities, especially "*the husband of one wife*" and "*able to teach.*" The phrase "*husband of one wife*" refers to faithfulness and loyalty—he's a one-woman man.[2] "*Able to teach*" doesn't refer to the skill of teaching as much as to the desire to help others grow.[3]

- The servant-leader's **Experience** (3:4–7): A three-fold experience is needed for a man to be a leader in the congregation (and to be a husband!):

    1. *His experience in the home* (3:4–5): He must be "*above reproach,*" faithful to his wife, godly in character, and a good manager of his own home.

---

1. Regarding the proper leadership attitudes, see also 1 Peter 5:1–4.
2. The phrase "*the husband of one wife*" has two very common interpretations: 1) not divorced and remarried—this view excludes any divorced person from a leadership role in the Assembly. 2) Married once only—not having more than one wife (either together or in sequence!). But Paul is speaking of a character quality. This quality is to be seen in both husbands and wives, as can be understood by reading 1 Timothy 5:9, "*A widow is to be put on the list only if she is not less than sixty years old, having been the wife of one man.*" Paul then says that younger widows should remarry (5:14). If their second husband dies, then haven't they been disqualified for congregational benevolence as the wife of two men, not just one? The phrase, "*husband of one wife*" (3:2) is the same grammatical form as "*wife of one man*" (5:9). Both verses are referring to the character quality of faithfulness and loyalty to one's spouse. He must be a one-woman man, and she must be a one-man woman. It is a character quality that Paul assumes we understand. Loyalty and faithfulness to one's spouse must exist in the marriage relationship before any consideration can be given to congregational roles. What, then, is marriage all about? It is sacrificial love, seen in the context of faithfulness and loyalty. Out of this essential principle we grow to be leaders in our homes and congregations.
3. The single Greek word (*didaktikos*) is translated with a phrase "apt to teach," as the word has no direct English equivalent. *Thayer's Lexicon* notes from Philo's usage: "the virtue which renders one teachable, docility." If a student desires to learn, we say he is teachable. But what do we call one who desires to help others learn—"studentable"? Thus, "apt to teach" refers to the character quality that seeks to help others grow.

2. *His experience in the faith* (3:6): He must not be a new believer—a novice in the faith. The Greek word is *neophutos*, "a new plant." In Leviticus 19:23–25, the fruit from a fruit tree was not for public consumption until the fifth year. Likewise, a man should be at least five years in the faith before being placed in leadership in the congregation (or the home!).

3. *His experience in the community* (3:7): He must have a good name and public testimony outside the congregation so as not to tarnish Messiah's testimony to those outside the faith.

This New Covenant section of Scripture, recognizing the fallen state of humanity from Satan's attack on the family in Genesis 3, warns potential leaders about such devilish tendencies (3:6–7).

Now that we have that overview of this section on the overseer (servant-leaders), we will examine the section on a potential leader's experience in the home. Does he oversee (manage) his home well?

Without visionary leadership the people perish![4] The redemptive purpose of marriage and family can be seen Malachi 4:6: "*He will restore the hearts of the fathers to their children and the hearts of the children to their fathers.*" The last living prophet in the Tanakh teaches that restoring lost humanity in Messiah will begin with the family, and fathers above all. That is why, in order to restore lost humanity, there must be restoration of the family. A redeemed Dad restored by grace is enabled by God to restore and redeem others, starting in his own home.

Even as we declare in the V'ahavtah, "*You shall teach them diligently to your sons* [children]," the redeemed father is expected to teach the Word of God to his family—not that he's required to have a teaching gift, but that he's "*able to teach*" his own children. The Hebrew word in Deuteronomy 6:7 for "diligently" (*shanan*) means "sharply, with the purpose of getting the point across." Whatever a father is doing, he is to teach the Word of God to his children. Of course, these words must be upon his own heart first (Deuteronomy 6:6).

Some may not think of fathers as leaders. However in the Bible, the father is called to lead in the home. We may think that one good mom is enough to rear up the children. In our society, single-parent homes are considered almost normative. Even though we commend the heroic single moms diligently raising their families, still this is not the ideal, according to both the Scriptures[5] and according to United States government! In a 2006 report, the U.S. Department of Health and Human Services stated: "Even from birth, children who have an involved father are more likely to be emotionally secure, be confident to explore their surroundings, and, as they grow older, have better social connections with peers. These children also

---

4. Proverbs 29:18.
5. Ephesians 6:4.

are less likely to get in trouble at home, school, or in the neighborhood."[6] Please note the phrase, "an involved father." Dad is not one who simply provides food for the table. He leads his family in all areas of his God-given stewardship. This is a matter of responsibility, not personality. So, where is a father to begin?

The first on the list is the home. In this regard we are to learn how to be become more effective in our redemptive love for our family. We will consider three principles:

1. We succeed when we recognize the stewardship, 3:4
2. We succeed when we receive the discipleship, 3:5a
3. We succeed when we provide the guardianship, 3:5b

We succeed when we recognize the stewardship (3:4)

He must be one who manages his own household well, keeping his children under control [subordination] *with all dignity.*

Notice the verb "*must*" in this verse. It means this is not optional! The blessings of God are provided only when the marriage follows the will and Word of God. Some may ask, "How come our marriage is not what it should be?" "What it should be" is what it "must" be! If God says, "you must," then your heart's prayerful response should be, "I must!" It is not a matter of having the personality to lead; it is a matter of accepting personal responsibility to lead. Regardless of a husband's personality, he must lead.

The Greek word *proistemi*, for the word "manages," literally means "to stand before," and it refers to stepping up and superintending all matters in the home.[7] In the context of this section, the overseer (*episkopos*) dad is the manager of the home. As manager, his main task is the spiritual life of the family. His primary concerns are prayer and applying the Word.[8] He makes sure there are enough resources (time and treasure) so that the primary matters can be emphasized in the family. The dad oversees the family (in partnership with his wife) to be sure that Yeshua is exalted in each of the hearts in their home.

Recognize the parameters: "His own household"
First, a father must understand he is called to manage his own household and not someone else's. In other words, he is called to a limited stewardship. He must learn the parameters of his household and learn to manage it well. He must learn to denounce sin in himself before renouncing it in others. He must learn that he

---

6. Jeffrey Rosenberg and W. Bradford Wilcox, "The Importance of Fathers in the Healthy Development of Children" (U.S. Department of Health and Human Services, 2006), p. 12, childwelfare.gov/pubPDFs/fatherhood.pdf.
7. Ephesians 5:24, "*in everything.*"
8. Acts 6:4.

cannot help others until he learns to be the leader in his own home; his position sometimes calls for uncomfortable decisions that don't go over well with the kids.

Recognize the priority: "His* [own] *children"
A father must perceive the priority of his stewardship as applying to his own children and must understand the limitations of that stewardship. A common misstep many fathers make is being involved in all sorts of activities outside the home but neglecting their own kids. Your own children must be your priority.

The father's designation for his own children: This verse also calls for children to be "*under control*," or in subordination. The word *subordination* means "to be in a proper order or position." Every child needs to know they have a place in the home and that Dad is the designator. Having a proper place in the home, kids develop security that this structure provides.

If you were to observe preschool children on the playground with no fence around it, you might notice that the kids stay very close to the building. This is because they are intimidated by the traffic nearby. When a fence is put up, they use every inch of the playground, because they now feel secure. Establishing boundaries doesn't limit kids—it gives them a sense of security, even if they test those boundaries regularly.

The father's dignity towards his own children: Your children need to see your dignity in the family. The Scripture says, "*Keeping his children under control with all dignity.*" That is, though some have thought that children must be disciplined into dignity, in fact, the father must demonstrate dignity while applying discipline to his own children. Leaders model the values they want to inculcate in others.[9] As we've noted, it is the father's responsibility to be the shock absorber and not the shock emitter. He is not to abuse his children by angrily beating the kid into submission. He's not to dominate, manipulate, or otherwise abuse his family. The father must maintain the dignity in the home while his is managing the home. This is the same intention we read of in Colossians 3:21, "*Fathers, do not exasperate your children, so that they will not lose heart,*" and Ephesians 6:4: "*Fathers, do not provoke your children to anger, but bring them up in the discipline and instruction of the Lord.*"[10]

Parenting must be pleasing to the Lord and represent Him in the home. The Bible places that responsibility on fathers to model and teach the values that they want their children to walk in. Their wives are the helpmates and assist in reinforcing the values set by the father. We want our children to be able to say, "My daddy is a safe place for me," because in a dangerous world, the home should be the safest place for the children. When they have trouble in the world, their home should be a refuge. When they have troubles in the rest of their lives with

---
9. This leadership principle is derived from Hebrews 13:7.
10. See Appendix Eight for more on Ephesians 6:4.

all other relationships, they should know that their family is always going to be there for them. I told both of my sons when they both moved out that, regardless what happens to them, I am their safety net. Even as adults, they still have to understand that their family is there for them.

We succeed when we receive the discipleship (3:5a)

But if a man does not know how to manage his own household...

Marital discipleship is a spiritually acquired skill: it's learned. Do you see the verb "*know how*"? This is used throughout the Scriptures in regard to knowing good from evil. When children do not know good from evil, it is because they are ignorant. However, there are many men who are ignorant about being husbands and fathers. They are not stupid people, but they were never taught the skills involved in being a good father and husband. They just do not understand their responsibilities and don't even know enough to ask. All children have differing personalities, and so, good interpersonal skills can be vital in raising godly children. That is why a father must learn the interpersonal skills needed to relate to his own children. Fathers need to be discipled in this area and must be teachable themselves. Otherwise, how will they teach their children?

To address the spiritual needs of engaged couples, I require several weeks of premarital counseling before I will officiate at their wedding. My premarital counseling often includes basic discipleship as well as reviewing what is written in this book. On several occasions, I have delayed couples from getting married because the man plainly did not know the first thing about being a responsible husband or father. He had no idea what spiritual responsibilities were expected from him, let alone how to handle those responsibilities well. He often does not realize that from the moment he says, "I do," he becomes the spiritual leader of that new home—ready or not! Far too often, husbands-to-be often need basic discipleship in the faith—they may not have a prayer life, may not be familiar with the Bible, may have little commitment to any faith community, and may never have shared their faith. It has also been my experience that far too many wives-to-be don't want to ask the challenging questions about his faith experience, because they don't want to risk encountering any "deal-breakers." They just want to get married and worry about spiritual matters later. Because of my requirement, some couples have found someone else to officiate for them who cares less about their spiritual condition. In one such premarital counseling situation, I recommended several more months of counseling (i.e., discipleship), because—as I frankly stated to them both—he was not prepared to be a spiritual leader. Rather than follow my advice, they found someone else to marry them. Six months later, the woman complained to me that her husband "never reads his Bible or prays." She sadly said, "He's not the spiritual leader he needs to be and that I want." And now there are major problems developing between the two of them, for he did "*not know how to manage his own household."* That is why premarital counseling is vital, and basic discipleship is necessary. For, *"Unless the* LORD *builds the house, they labor in vain who build it!"* (Psalm 127:1).

Far too many men foolishly think they don't need marital instruction, and they are therefore not at all teachable. Their arrogance exclaims, "No one has to tell me what to do! I know what I am doing. I know what I want in my home. You don't have to tell me anything." To such men, I say: "Maybe that is why everyone in the family is so unhappy."

The main point of this verse is that being a good husband and father, biblically speaking, is a learned behavior. Because it is a discipleship issue, the husband has to be taught these things. He needs to be trained by what the Scripture teaches and learn to rely on the Word of God when faced with challenging circumstances. *Marital discipleship is faithfully applied service: It's lived.* Some dads are so insecure by their limited parenting skills that they can become threatened by anything their child says or does—they just don't know how to manage their kids. One such dad considered every question a challenge to his leadership, and the child was just seven years old! This immature behavior stunts the growth of children, who must ask questions in order to grow. Dads must grow through these parenting moments and mature in Messiah. Once a husband and father learns the truth of Scripture, it must then be applied and lived out consistently.

Scripture must be learned before it can be lived, and Scripture is given to be lived and not just learned.[11] Learning that becomes living the truth is what makes you a successful parent in Messiah. Reading this book means very little unless the biblical principles being taught are applied in real time. Spiritual wisdom is the application of biblical knowledge. You are only wise when you live out what you have learned. Knowledge without implementation is vanity. Thus, as we have already said, Yeshua taught, *"If you know these things, you are blessed if you do them"* (John 13:17). His blessing is in our doing—that is, putting the truth of marriage and parenting into practice. Your marriage and family can only be blessed when you live by the truth that you have learned in proper discipleship.

Knowing right from wrong is education; doing what is right is execution. The latter is the hard part. If it is tough (and it always is), keep praying to keep loving your family. Remember, all that the Bible instructs us to do is only fulfilled when we're filled with the Holy Spirit. He poured out the love of God in our hearts, and His love fulfills all Torah.[12] When frustrated by your own limitations, yield to the Spirit to love your wife and family as you are called to do. We pray more and more because we know that we need His enablement through the Holy Spirit to complete our divine calling to live out God's image in our homes.

---

11. Leviticus 18:5.
12. *"For the whole Law* [Torah] *is fulfilled in one word, in the statement, 'You shall love your neighbor as yourself'"* (Galatians 5:14).

Relationships take time. Shabbat teaches that even our relationship with our heavenly Father takes time, and it is one the great reasons God gave Shabbat to us. This is why Yeshua worshipped in synagogue every Shabbat.[13] We too are to take time with Him so that we can develop our relationship with Him. The goal is to develop life that is oriented around Him with our family. And then in turn, we make the time with our families and speak of Him to our children, in our rising up and lying down, when we sit in our house and when we walk on the way.[14]

Only a properly discipled dad can properly disciple his children in the love and grace of God. If you haven't been discipled yourself, then get discipled to be the spiritual manager in your home. You can't give what you don't have!

We succeed when we provide the guardianship (3:5b SN)

How will he take care of the Assembly of God?

Managing at home is a form of guardianship. The verb "take care"[15] refers to the concept of guardianship. Do you believe that you are your brother's keeper? God thinks so! Therefore, the stewardship we have from God means that we are guardians of treasure. He highly values the Assembly, since he purchased it with His own blood.[16] We are to take care of His treasured people that God considers His beloved children (Ephesians 5:1; 1 John 3:2). Regardless of your opinion or the opinion of others, God thinks we are precious in His sight. This word for *"take care"* is used only three times in the Scriptures; the portion regarding the Good Samaritan contains the other two usages of this word: Luke 10:33–35: *"But a Samaritan, who was on a journey, came upon him; and when he saw him, he felt compassion, and came to him and bandaged up his wounds, pouring oil and wine on them; and he put him on his own beast, and brought him to an inn and took care of him. On the next day he took out two denarii and gave them to the innkeeper and said, 'Take care of him; and whatever more you spend, when I return I will repay you.'"*

Yeshua tells this story to illustrate what it means to love *"your neighbor as yourself."*[17] Whatever it takes, we are called to care for other people. While two uses of this word in the above story refer to sacrificial love, we see that the third use is to care for the Assembly in the same way we manage our families. Thus, to manage is to care. Caring for the family must precede caring for the congregation. Before you can be a leader in the congregation, where must a man first be a leader? In the home! We must grow as believers and mature in the matters of caring at home to prepare us for greater ministry elsewhere. This is because the

---

13. Luke 4:16, cf. Hebrews 10:25.
14. Deuteronomy 6:7.
15. *Epimeleomai* in the Greek.
16. Acts 20:28 SN: *"Be on guard for yourselves and for all the flock, among which the Holy Spirit has made you overseers, to shepherd the Assembly of God which He purchased with His own blood."*
17. Luke 10:25–37.

same principles and values that you apply to the family are the ones you apply to the community. There is only one God for both the home and the congregation. So too, there is only one value system for both the home and the congregation.

Managing the congregation is a form of guardianship. We will care for His children in the congregation if we learn how to take care of our children at home. If you do not care for your own children, then you should not be expected to care for anyone else's! I repeat: you must first be a caring leader in the home before you can be a caring leader in the community. As the enemy's attack began on a home, so the victory is first achieved in the home. The same set of values, the same responsibilities, the same standards, and the same love govern home and community. If you don't know how to show love at home, please don't try to do it at the congregation. We want leaders in the congregation who have learned how to represent Him in loving and caring for others, not those who are self-centered and domineering.

Why is it we have problems in families? We read, "*The goal of our instruction is love from a pure heart*" (1 Timothy 1:5). The problem in the home begins in the heart. The instruction must first be in your heart before it can be in your home. As in the V'ahavta, "*These words, which I am commanding you today, shall be on your heart and you shall teach them diligently to your sons and shall talk of them*" (Deuteronomy 6:6–7). Before you talk or teach God's words to your children, where must they first be, according to this verse? On your heart! You are expected to know the Word of God before you teach it. If God's instruction that produces love is not in your heart, then you have not that love for your home. Your family is shortchanged in what God wants for them through you, and you are disobedient before God because you are not fulfilling your stewardship or your calling. The undisciplined believer is a dysfunctional leader at home and in the congregation.

How does effective leadership occur at home? The heart that follows Yeshua is the heart that can lead others to Yeshua. When Yeshua has first place in your life, then your children will want to follow the One Dad follows. The heart that is Yeshua's home can bring His heart to their home.

The discipleship-inspired love of God from your heart is what your children need most of all. For, as God the Father so loved us that He gave His only begotten Son, so every father representing our heavenly Father is called to sacrificially love his children as well.

So, Dad, the first thing you must do for your family is for you to be restored in your heart to God. Rededicate your heart to the Lord. Then learn the "*know how*" and live out His truth to restore and redeem your home.

Messiah Yeshua died and was restored to life by the Father in order to restore you to eternal life with the Father. God desires restoration of all humanity to Himself. The starting point of all that is first in your heart, then in your marriage, then in your family, and then out to the community. This is God's plan to redeem lost humanity—it starts in the heart and the home. God gives us new life by His grace through your faith in Yeshua. That same grace through faith enables you to restore your home and even impact a corrupt society.

For some dads, a lot of water has gone under the bridge, and we are quite late in the game for some of these changes. I was teaching a seminar in New York on these matters. The head elder of the congregation came to me during one of the breaks and said, "I have been listening to you very carefully. It all makes a lot of sense. But what do I do now? All my children are adults. They act just like me when I was their age." I wasn't sure what he meant, so I asked him to explain. He sadly replied that when he was younger, he lived for his career. He didn't have time for his children, whom he expected his wife to raise. He thought that when they were grown they would understand. Now they have their careers. They live their lives for their professions in the same way he did, and they have no time for their families or their parents. He asked, "What do I do now, Sam?" I look at him and said, "You can always repent. Go to the Lord and acknowledge that you fumbled the ball. That you disregarded His stewardship for you—your family. Next you go to your wife and apologize to her because you placed more on her shoulders than God called her to carry. Apologize and ask for forgiveness. Pray with her about it. Then, go to each of your children, starting with the oldest, and apologize for forsaking them, for not giving them the time that God wanted them to have from you. Ask each of your children for forgiveness, but don't be discouraged, because some may not forgive you. At least you will have earned the right to speak into their lives about what is true and good from that point on."

That's what we do as humble, repentant people. We cannot change the past, but with repentance (and apologies), and a renewed commitment to what is right and true, we can earn the right to be heard. Regardless of our age, we can still be used of God to impact our family and community. His grace is sufficient for you. I encourage each of you to prayerfully repent and grow just a bit more in the calling we share: to live out the image of God, as we're empowered by the Holy Spirit to be His instrument of love and grace in this world.

Some questions to help apply these teachings

1. What character defects (i.e., areas of spiritual immaturity) keep you from leadership in the home? Name several ways you demonstrate stewardship over you home.

2. In what ways have you maintained your dignity in managing your home? Name several ways your family knows they have a place in the home.

3. Name some areas in which you had to learn to be a good manager at home. Name several sources that helped disciple you in these areas.

4. Can you name several areas that are still matters of prayer for you to be a mature, godly manager at home? Name several ways you have demonstrated guardianship (caring and helping) in your home.

5. Are you using this experience to help your congregation? Name several ways you are doing that.

CHAPTER EIGHT

The Triumphant Spouse in a Troubled Marriage

1 Peter 3

In the same way, you wives, be submissive to your own husbands so that even if any of them are disobedient to the word, they may be won without a word by the behavior of their wives, as they observe your chaste and respectful behavior. Your adornment must not be merely external—braiding the hair, and wearing gold jewelry, or putting on dresses; but let it be the hidden person of the heart, with the imperishable quality of a gentle and quiet spirit, which is precious in the sight of God. For in this way in former times the holy women also, who hoped in God, used to adorn themselves, being submissive to their own husbands; just as Sarah obeyed Abraham, calling him lord, and you have become her children if you do what is right without being frightened by any fear.
You husbands in the same way, live with your wives in an understanding way, as with someone weaker, since she is a woman; and show her honor as a fellow heir of the grace of life, so that your prayers will not be hindered. (First Peter 3:1–7)

The context of 1 Peter helps us to understand the application of the portion for our troubled marriages. Written to believers going through adversity and suffering, 1 Peter is divided into three sections:

First Peter 1:1–2:10, we are saved though suffering

First Peter 2:11–3:12, we are submitted through suffering

First Peter 3:13–5:14, we are sanctified through suffering

Saved, submitted, and sanctified is how we grow. Even as the plane flies higher when the winds are contrary, God puts us in contrary situations so that we might fly higher by grace. Only in adversity do we fully realize that it is not our personal sufficiency that secures us, but His grace alone. Adversity in marriage[1] is intended by God to lead Messianic believers to fly higher by His all-sufficient grace in our lives.

---

1. A vital word on adversity in marriage: where emotional suffering is occurring, I advise a separation with counseling until there can be a wholesome reconciliation. Where physical abuse is occurring, I advise that the abused spouse go immediately to a safe place, call the police, file assault charges, and have the abuser arrested. And then, only when the abuser offers sincere repentance, submission to professional counseling, and real-time evidence of a changed life, do I advise reconciliation, and that often limited and progressive as the abused spouse feels safe. None of the actions by the abused are to be retaliatory, but always motivated by a desire for redemption, reconciliation, and a restored Messianic home.

In many troubled marriages, one spouse may be living for the Lord while the other is not. In these cases, though both spouses say they are Messianic believers, it does not mean they are mature or even obedient to Messiah. First Peter 3:1–7 is placed in the Bible to address these matters of marital adversity and even spiritual suffering.

The point of this passage is that if either spouse is submitted to Messiah, they can still fulfill the image-of-God calling in their marriage, regardless of their spouse's spiritual condition. Your spiritual maturity is not dependent upon the spiritual condition of your spouse, but upon your responsiveness to God, regardless of your spouse's disobedient behavior.

The Submitted Wife, 1 Peter 3:1–6

How spiritually minded wives are to live with carnally minded husbands

***She's submitted in her marriage by her eternal reliance on her true Example* (3:1)**

In the same way, you wives, be submissive to your own husbands so that even if any of them are disobedient to the word, they may be won without a word by the behavior of their wives.

*Her reliance is "**in the same way**" as Messiah:* The believing wife can live a victorious life if she chooses to follow Messiah, even in her troubled marriage. The phrase "*disobedient to the word*" is also used in 1 Peter 2:8 for those that "*stumble*" over Messiah. That is, they are caused to stumble by Yeshua's life and teaching, for it directly conflicts with their own morality, lifestyle, and religious notions. In general, to be disobedient to the Word can refer to any attitude or behavior that is noncompliant with the Word's teaching about God's character and His instruction for our lives. In this regard, we must also remember that sin is not merely by commission (committing a prohibited deed), but also by omission (omitting a commanded deed). In other words, sin may have nothing to do with the husband's relationship with the wife, or how he acts around the house. Likewise, her ministry to her husband to win him back to a restored walk with the Lord may not impact her directly at all. Or it may impact her greatly, since her husband's wherewithal to minister and relate well to His wife is the byproduct of his relationship with the Lord.

In a worst-case scenario, with the husband committing nastiness toward his wife or omitting warmth from his treatment of his wife, how can the wife be victorious when married to a man who is disobedient to the Word? The answer is initially addressed in the first phrase of 1 Peter 3:1, "*In the same way, you wives…*" In the same way as what or whom? This phrase "*in the same way*" refers the wife back several verses to the instruction about Yeshua in 1 Peter 2:21 (SN): "*For you have been called for this purpose, since Messiah also suffered for you, leaving you an example for you to follow in His steps..."* In the same way that Yeshua exemplified suffering, so the wife is "*to follow in His steps.*" The word *example* in the original text[2] means "writing copy." Just as a child learns how to write by copying words carefully on paper, so we are to learn how to live by copying Him. He is our example and we are to follow in His footsteps. Only as we follow in His steps are we assured of His guidance in our life.

Therefore, the challenge for the wife is to trust God by following the example of Yeshua. In this way she will have a Yeshua-like victory in her marriage. Only His faithful example can victoriously guide the godly wife through these troubled marital waters. When Peter writes that she is to be submissive to her husband (3:1), she is to do so by following Yeshua.

Just as Yeshua endured suffering by remaining submissive in His calling to the disobedient authority of His day, the wife may be called upon to do the same. She will be looking to Messiah and living her life in the marriage as He lived His earthly life as our example. Some of us might understandably question this. If a husband is disobedient to the Word, his wife may be feeling chaffed and disappointed, even devastated. She may feel that her needs are not being addressed by him, nor does he even care about her. How is she to respond? Though the wife's circumstance is far different from that of the Messiah, "*in the same way*" indicates that the manner of her response to her difficult circumstance will follow Yeshua's response to His circumstance. He is her example of how to respond, interact with, and relate to her disobedient husband. Messiah's example is not that of a passive victim, but rather One who assertively trusts His Father through His suffering and does not respond in kind to those harming Him, even though it is in His power to do so. When He suffers, He submits to His calling as the Son of God. In the same way, a wife is called to assertively submit as a child of God in her calling ministry as a wife, and thereby testify of God's grace in Messiah as her sufficiency.

In being submissive to her husband, she is not to feel subjugated. Marriage, and indeed all meaningful personal relationships, are by consent. Therefore, she is to submit herself to her own husband by her willing consent. Her husband does not have the right to force her to submit (the Bible never teaches domination of a wife by her husband).[3] Just as Yeshua submitted to God in His calling by His consent,[4] so we are to consent to submit to God in our callings. Marriage, as we have mentioned before, is a calling through which we are to make a gracious difference in the life of our spouse. We are only fulfilled in our marital calling as we follow Messiah's example. Even though Yeshua was not married, the Bible teaches

---

2. *Friberg Greek Lexicon* on *hupogrammos*: "strictly writing copy for beginners; hence model, pattern, or figuratively an example, or guidelines."
3. On this point of consent, please review the previous study on Ephesians 5:22–24 and also Colossians 3:18 and Titus 2:5.
4. See John 10:18.

that He was "*tempted in all things as we are, yet without sin*" (Hebrews 4:15). In 1 Peter 2:22–24, Yeshua teaches us how to faithfully endure, depending on God's grace for strength.

*Her reliance has the goal to "***win him***," like Messiah:* Peter states that being submissive to your own husbands has a spiritual goal for the wife: "*So that even if any of them are disobedient to the word, they may be won.*" Your calling is to win your husband, thereby restoring him to fellowship with God. Being called as a spouse is somewhat like being called as a missionary to a foreign country where people may not respond pleasantly. Even so, a spouse is called to be a light in the darkness and must love the other with Messiah's own love as she follows His example. Your spouse may be an unbeliever, even though he said otherwise prior to the wedding. If he is an unbeliever, your calling is to win him to the Messianic faith.[5] Yeshua's suffering not only models how to respond to suffering in a godly fashion, but His faithful suffering was also the means of winning us.[6] This model is not just for our proper response to suffering, but, as with Yeshua, it is the means to win those who persecute us. Our godly responses are the witness that wins our persecutors—even our spouses.

The idea of winning another to obedience in Messiah is not just for unbelievers. A believer's disobedience to the Word may be due to spiritual immaturity. Matthew 18:15 says, "*If your brother sins, go and show him his fault in private; if he listens to you, you have won your brother.*" We are called to spiritually restore disobedient believers. This is also discussed in Galatians 6:1: "*Brethren, even if anyone is caught in any trespass, you who are spiritual, restore such a one in a spirit of gentleness; each one looking to yourself, so that you too will not be tempted.*" Here, "*anyone*" can refer to your spouse, as "*caught in any trespass*" can refer to any sort of disobedience to the Word. When the text states, "*you who are spiritual,*" it is to make sure you're not responding out of hurt or disappointment but from spiritual motives to restore him to a walk with the Lord. Being "*spiritual*" is revealed by your approach to your spouse "*in a spirit of gentleness,*" as gentleness is one of the fruits of the Spirit (Galatians 5:22–23). This gentle fruit is the spiritual result of abiding in Yeshua, who is the root of the Spirit. The Spirit-filled wife who has absorbed the teachings of the New Covenant is able to respond with gentleness that acts as a healing balm to the Messianic marriage.

Paul includes a caveat in the Galatians 6:1 instruction: "*...each one looking to yourself, so that you too will not be tempted.*" Be careful of being tempted to consider yourself better than the one who was caught in the trespass. We are all saved by grace, so none should look down on a weaker brother or husband. There, but for the grace of God, go any of us at any time. The wife's ministry to restore her disobedient husband is not to become an occasion of stumbling for her.

---

5. Paul describes winning the lost in 1 Corinthians 9:19–22.
6. First Peter 2:24–25.

Eight • The Triumphant Spouse in a Troubled Marriage

If your husband is in a weak spiritual state and not walking closely with the Lord, your job is to win him back to a right relationship with the Lord, not just to a right relationship with you! Remember, his right relationship with you—his wife—is the marital by-product of his right spiritual relationship with the Lord. If you are self-serving in this matter, your husband may see your supposed spirituality as a ploy to get your own needs met by religiously manipulating him. You want him to have a restored relationship with the Lord so that he can fulfill his own divine calling as a man of God and a godly husband, whether it benefits you or not.

*Her reliance is "**without a word**," like Messiah:* In 1 Peter 3:1, the means to win the disobedient husband is "*without a word by the behavior of their wives.*" What does "*without a word*" refer to—perhaps the silent treatment? Not at all! Once more, the explanation is in the previous instruction on the example of Messiah. Peter writes, "*…who committed no sin, nor was any deceit found in his mouth; and while being reviled, He did not revile in return; while suffering, He uttered no threats, but kept entrusting Himself to Him who judges righteously*" (1 Peter 2:22–23). "*Without a word*" is the application of Yeshua's example when He was suffering on the cross. Though suffering, He "*committed no sin*," for He did not deceive or revile or threaten those who were abusing and mocking Him. There may be some who would object to the direct application of Yeshua's sinless example to their lives, decrying, "Well, He was the Son of God after all. How could you possibly expect the same from me?" And perhaps with this objection in mind, they might justify their own sinful responses to being treated unjustly by a claim of being "only human." The amazing fact of the incarnation is that when Yeshua came in the flesh, He "*emptied Himself*" of all His divine prerogatives[7] and lived a mortal life walking by faith, dependent on grace, through all of His awful trials. Therefore, He is an example for us because He exemplified walking by faith, depending on grace. Sin may be measured in two ways: by what you do and by what you say. That Yeshua suffered without a word does not mean He did not say anything, for He spoke seven times from the cross, but always to edify those around Him and to give glory to God. He "*committed no sin*" in the form of misbehavior towards the professional Roman killers or the religious Jewish mockers, nor did He deceive.

In 1 Peter 2:22, Peter is quoting Isaiah 53:9, where the Hebrew word *mirmah* refers to treacherous, beguiling, deceptive, or misleading actions and words. *Mirmah* is used for Jacob when he deceives his father, Isaac, and steals his brother Esau's blessing (Genesis 27:35). The same meaning is carried by the Greek word for "deceive" (*dolos*)[8] from the rabbinical Septuagint translation of Isaiah 53:9. Yeshua did not use deception, though it was used against Him (Mark 14:1). Yeshua's followers were careful not to use any deceit regarding the Good News ministry,[9]

---

7. See Philippians 2:6–8 on this matter.
8. *Dolos* refers to bait for fish, meaning the use of "bait" words that draw others into deception.
9. Mark 7:21–22; 1 Thessalonians 2:3; 1 Peter 2:1; 3:10.

that is, they were not misleading in any way (e.g., "Believe in Yeshua and you'll be wealthy, problem-free, and popular"). The wife is not to use any deception towards her disobedient husband, in how she spends money and time, or with whom she is associating. Any use of deception makes her disobedient to the Word as well! Though she may feel justified to mislead in order to win him to Messiah, she must remember that the end does not justify the means. Human lies do not lead someone to the eternal truth.[10]

In Yeshua's ministry, that phrase *"without a word"* also refers to reviling words, though He was reviled by others.[11] To revile[12] means "to be reproached," "demeaned verbally," or "name-calling." The people were mocking Messiah even while He was dying. He could have mocked, threatened, and reviled in return, but He did not. Likewise, a wife is not to revile back when she is reviled. She must resist the very real temptation to snap back when being demeaned, disrespected, verbally assaulted, or emotionally hurt.

Peter continues by saying that besides not reviling in return, *"while suffering, He uttered no threats."* To endure revilement is a form of suffering, though the suffering paralleled with reviling in this verse also implies something more. Suffering[13] is the pain that results from the mistreatment. As He Himself forewarned His disciples, Yeshua's suffering included all that He endured from the false accusations by the religious leadership, to the beatings and crucifixion by the Roman soldiers, to being *"treated with contempt."*[14] His suffering while dying on a cross was the most agonizing death imaginable. Any threats[15] by Him could have brought eternal retaliation on His abusers. Instead He prays for those who abuse Him.[16] In His suffering we learn how to suffer redemptively—whether to unfair bosses (1 Peter 2:18–20) or to unbelieving husbands—always in innocence (1 Peter 3:17; 4:15) and according to the will of God (1 Peter 4:19).

Like Yeshua, we should not seek suffering. He prayed three times, *"If it is possible, let this cup* [of suffering] *pass from Me; yet not as I will, but as You will."*[17] Though we should not seek suffering or knowingly enter abusive relationships, in living righteously in an unrighteous world we will encounter diverse trials, and we will need to live faithfully through them all.

For the wife, the suffering may be the sting of her husband's insult, or the anxiety from feeling rejected in a loveless marriage. There are many women who are

---

10. First John 2:21: *"No lie is of the truth."*
11. John 9:28. The idea of 1 Peter 2:23 is that Yeshua was mocked as He suffered.
12. Greek: *loidoreo*, used for the Hebrew word for "quarrel" (*riv*) in Exodus 17:2; 21:18, etc.
13. Greek: *pascho*.
14. Mark 9:12; Matthew 16:21; Luke 9:22; 17:25.
15. To threaten (*apeileo*) expresses an intention to harm if a condition is not met, or to promise retaliation in kind.
16. Luke 23:34: *"Father, forgive them; for they do not know what they are doing."*
17. Matthew 26:39, 42, 44.

suffering great emotional distress while enduring what seems like a never-ending cycle of anguish and misery. But while suffering from being reviled and demeaned, a wife should not threaten her husband in response to her suffering.[18] In today's language, a wife could threaten to leave or threaten to divorce her husband. In her feeling of powerlessness, threats may seem her only defense against the bitterness and sorrow his insults produce. Yet the Bible teaches her not to do so. What did Yeshua do? He oriented His life around the Father, not the offender.

*Her reliance on the example of "**entrusting**" by Messiah:* First Peter 2:23 concludes by saying that Yeshua, *"kept entrusting Himself to Him who judges righteously."* Who is the *"Him"* referred to in this verse? God the Father! Despite what others were doing to or saying about Yeshua, there is One who always knows the full truth about the suffering servant. You are not what your spouse says about you, nor what you say about yourself when feeling helpless and powerless. If you heard it enough from your husband, you may have started to believe his lie! You are not who you say you are, but you are truly who God says you are, and you are His precious child.[19] So too with the Messiah. He is not what His mockers say about Him, but He is who His heavenly Father says about Him: *"This is My beloved Son, in whom I am well-pleased!"*—and His Father says it about Him twice![20] What did Yeshua do while being reviled and suffering? Yeshua *"kept entrusting Himself to Him."* The verb *entrusting* means "to hand over to another," and the form of the verb[21] means that Yeshua kept doing it! Yeshua was intentionally entrusting Himself to God over and over and over again. Why repeatedly? He needed to continue to give over to His Father for what He needed for each different assault. From when He was being falsely accused and wouldn't defend Himself,[22] to when the nails were being driven into his wrists and He prayed for His killers,[23] to when He gave words of assurance to the thief on the cross next to Him[24]—each time He would need a fresh enablement for every different situation He suffered. This exactly pictures the Spirit-filled life for every believer, for the Holy Spirit has to enable us for each and every different situation, as well as helping us persevere through the ongoing trials that we must endure in our callings.

In the same way, when your spouse hurts you, he does not spiritually know what he is doing. If he curses his spouse, he is really cursing the One she represents and the One who gave her to him. And even though he may foolishly feel

---

18. Regarding the advice at footnote 1 above in this chapter, when enduring emotional suffering or abuse, the abused party should not issue retaliatory threats, but redemptive action, which includes separation and even police action, but always, as noted, with an eye toward reconciliation and restoration of a God-honoring home.
19. First John 3:1.
20. Matthew 3:17; 17:5.
21. Greek: *paradidomi*, an indicative imperfect active verb.
22. Isaiah 53:7; Luke 23:9; Mark 14:60–61.
23. Luke 23:34.
24. Luke 23:43.

self-justified, he is hurting the one who is infinitely loved and valued by the Living God. When Saul was persecuting Messianic believers, Yeshua appeared and said to him, "*Saul, Saul, why are you persecuting Me?*" (Acts 9:4). What you do to the Body, you do the Head of the Body. What you do unto the least of His family, you do unto Him![25] Thus, in all of your afflictions, He too is afflicted![26] Even so, the discipled Messianic wife is to be purposely entrusting her life to the Father while it is still happening. So rather than focusing on the abuser, her attention should be focused on God, just as Yeshua focuses His attention on the Father during His hours of greatest need. This is where her Messianic discipleship may be most evidently seen. For in Messiah's example is her spiritual victory.

She's submitted in her external restraint on her possessions (3:1b–3)

They may be won without a word by the behavior of their wives.

The restrained life you live: behavior

The wife's behavior,[27] or conduct, reveals the lifestyle of the Messianic faith. This includes her attitudes as well as her actions. Rather than talk our husbands into the faith, the most effective means to win our loved ones is to model the life of Yeshua and the benefits of knowing Him. This is not only true for wives, but for all leaders. Your Messianic faith is best understood by others through how you live it out. Leaders are called not merely to teach but more importantly to model in their conduct the values they want others to follow.[28] Paul contrasts his former way of life as a persecutor of Messianic believers with his dramatically changed way of life as a follower of Yeshua.[29] He uses this same word (*anastrophe*) to say that we lay aside our "*former manner of life*" and by faith put on the new person and the lifestyle that reflects faith in Yeshua.[30] Faith in Yeshua changes your lifestyle from living according to your own values to living for Yeshua, as the divine witness of "*wisdom from above*" to your husband.[31] This word is also used often in 1 Peter: our lifestyle reflects the holiness of God (1:15) and stands in contrast to our inherited lifestyle (1:18) as a lifestyle characterized by "*good deeds*" (2:12). It is every believer's best witness in the world (3:15–16). So too for the witness of the wife at home (and for anyone else), this will prove to be her most effective testimony to her husband (and all others) of Messiah and the changed life she has in Him.

---

25. Matthew 25:40, 45.
26. Isaiah 63:9.
27. The Greek word (*anastrophe*) refers to the person's way of life.
28. Hebrews 13:7: "*Remember those who led you, who spoke the word of God to you; and considering the result of their conduct, imitate their faith.*"
29. Galatians 1:13ff.
30. Ephesians 4:22.
31. Jacob (James) 3:13–17.

Eight • The Triumphant Spouse in a Troubled Marriage

...as they observe your chaste and respectful behavior. (3:2)

The restrained wife he sees

Your internal faith is between you and God; your witness to others is external. Appearance does matter, because your witness is in what you live out. By appearance we mean a godly appearance that honors the Lord. The Scripture says that your husband is won not by words but by your behavior, or your conduct, as a wife. This means no rolling of the eyes, nagging, etc. Be yielded to the Lord, modeling the faith. You are being observed. Two observable adjectives describe your behavior: your behavior is "*chaste*" and "*respectful*."[32]

Your "*chaste*" behavior refers to a holy[33] lifestyle, which is a life set apart to God and not tainted by another's corruption. Since the husband's life is characterized as disobedient to the Word, the wife is expected to live the Spirit-filled life just so she can live a life pleasing to God without being spiritually impacted by her husband's ungodly influence. This Spirit-filled life is how Paul could maintain a godly lifestyle in prison, even as the wife may have her own "prison" ministry.[34] As set apart to God, the wife is called to be set apart to her husband as his wife, and the couple, though unequally yoked,[35] is seen as one by the Lord.[36] This holy life has many practical applications. If your husband asks you to do that which is explicitly contrary to the Word of God (e.g., cheat on your taxes, lie to others, public immorality, etc.), you must respectfully decline. Since the unbelieving husband is sanctified by the believing wife,[37] this is in your husband's best interests, though he may not be spiritually aware of it.[38] That the husband is sanctified by the believing wife means that the believing wife lives in a sphere of holiness (being set apart to God). Her husband is blessed by her godly influence in the home, even as Joseph was a blessing in the home of Potiphar, for the Lord was with him.[39] The Lord is with the wife and promises to never leave her nor forsake her[40] as well.

The believing wife is also to have "*respectful*" behavior towards her husband. The Greek word (*phobos*) refers to a profound respect for your husband's position. Remember that God is not a respecter of persons, but He is a respecter of

---

32. The noun *behavior* is repeated here in 3:2 and is modified by "*chaste*" and "*respectful*," thereby explaining what was meant in 2:1 as "*the behavior of their wives*."
33. Greek *hagios* is the word "holy."
34. There are numerous cases where the believing wife of an unbelieving husband could not tithe, attend worship services, and, in one extreme case, could not even have a Bible. And this is not even taking into consideration the horrors a believing wife would face in Muslim communities!
35. Second Corinthians 6:14.
36. Matthew 19:6.
37. First Corinthians 7:14.
38. First Corinthians 2:14: "*But a natural man does not accept the things of the Spirit of God, for they are foolishness to him; and he cannot understand them, because they are spiritually appraised.*"
39. Genesis 39:2–3.
40. Joshua 1:5, 9; Hebrews 13:5.

positions, since He has ordained the various positions of leadership for an orderly society.[41] As a Spirit-filled wife, she is called to be respectful of him as her husband, even if he is not being respectful of her.[42] When men feel disrespected, they feel attacked, and in their defensiveness they can be offensive to those that disrespect them. You are to always respect the position (husband) and pray for the person (who is disobedient to the Word), even though you may disagree with the policy (his ungodly ideas). Despite his fleshly attitudes and actions, you can and must respect the position, though he doesn't live up to his calling. When you give in to disrespect, revilement, or fear, these are telltale signs that you need to repent, go back to Messiah for cleansing, and be the forgiving, Spirit-filled person you are called by God to be. With this godly attitude in mind, you are being an accommodating, loving, respectful, and spiritually victorious wife.

> *Your adornment must not be merely external—braiding the hair, and wearing gold jewelry, or putting on dresses.* (3:3)

The restrained look others see: your attire

Peter[43] gives a caveat to the matter of a godly wife's appearance.[44] The phrase, "*Your adornment must not be merely external*" is a command[45] to stop acting this way. This doesn't mean that a wife (or any person) should be unclean[46] and improperly attired,[47] nor does it mean that there won't be biblical occasions for special attire, like a coronation, a festival,[48] or a wedding.[49] Peter is speaking of the matter of one's motive and reaction to their suffering, which can lower their godly priorities.[50] In this case, every time you feel the need to focus upon and emphasize your external appearance with fancy hairstyles, expensive jewelry, or eye-catching fashions, stop! The Scripture has great insight on the tendencies of people who are hurting—in this case, a hurting wife. When a wife is being mistreated and disrespected, quite often she may focus on her external appearance. This may be a way for her to feel good about herself by getting her mind off her husband's unkindness, or perhaps to physically attract her husband's attentions. In an even more despairing concern, she may do this to attract the attention of

---

41. See Appendix Seven for more on this matter of God-ordained authority in society.
42. Like stopping when a cop says stop, without regard for his personal character, but submitting to his position of authority.
43. Following the teaching of his Master, Yeshua the Messiah, in Matthew 6:25–33.
44. As does Paul in 1 Timothy 2:9.
45. The phrase (*esto oux*) is an imperative present active verb with the negative modifier. The Greek form means every time this situation occurs, stop doing it.
46. Second Samuel 19:24.
47. Proverbs 31:21–22, 25; Ecclesiastes 9:8; Luke 17:8; 1 Timothy 2:9.
48. Zechariah 3:4–5.
49. Ruth 3:3; Isaiah 61:10; Jeremiah 2:32; Psalm 45:13; Matthew 22:12.
50. "*Proper* [orderly] *clothing, modestly and discreetly...*" (1 Timothy 2:9).

other men (to vainly attempt to prove her husband as wrong) or to carnally prove she's still "got it." She may wish to passively but vindictively hurt her husband. In any case, to try and secure self-esteem by prioritizing and emphasizing external appearances will only reinforce her insecurities and fears.[51]

Your security as a person is only found in the Lord, for there is no condemnation in Messiah.[52] What a hurting wife (and all of us when we're hurting) needs to do is go to the Lord over and over as needed with the pain you are feeling and cast your cares upon Him.[53] Adonai is the true comforter of the suffering soul.[54]

She's submitted in her internal reverence as her priority (3:4–6)

The hidden is most precious (3:4)

> *...but let it be the hidden person of the heart, with the imperishable quality of a gentle and quiet spirit, which is precious in the sight of God.*

The real battle, for the wife, is within. First Peter 3:3–4 is one sentence in Greek, expressing the thought that the hurting wife's priority should not be external adornment before men (3:3) but an internal priority before God (3:4). When suffering, the "*hidden person of the heart*" is where God would have our attention as He develops our character, conforming us to Messiah, which is the plan of God for our lives,[55] regardless of whether or not you're married or to whom you're married. This hidden person of the heart is the real you! It is called "*hidden*,"[56] because your inner person is unseen to others and only seen by God. When the Scripture says that "*your life is hidden with Messiah in God*" (Colossians 3:3 SN), it refers to your hidden person of the heart that is hidden, secure, and unseen by others. On the outside, you may be getting older, but the hidden person of the heart is being renewed daily.[57] Though many do everything they can to catch their external persona reflected in the mirror in order to validate themselves, the hidden person of the heart is what God prioritizes, whether you do or not. When God works in your life—for comfort, holiness, and blessing—this is where He is at work. In other words, though you may be thinking, "I am angry, bitter, and hateful on the inside, but I am not telling anyone," God hears you loud and clear. Internal bitterness in the inner person of the heart undermines your testimony, for

---

51. This is not to say that she should give in to the opposite sinful reaction of despair, resulting in unclean and improper attire. Obedience to God's Word (such as 1 Timothy 2:9) will bring godly balance.
52. Romans 8:1.
53. First Peter 5:7.
54. Second Corinthians 1:3–5.
55. Romans 8:28–30.
56. Greek (*kruptos*) means secret. From it we get the English word *crypt*.
57. Second Corinthians 4:16.

Scripture teaches that in bitterness, you are falling short of God's grace for your life, resulting in a *"root of bitterness,"* to the defiling of many.[58] In this situation one must repent of one's disobedience and cast one's cares upon the Lord! God wants to develop in each of us a quiet spirit, not an angry heart. It is all about the hidden person of the heart, for women, and men as well.

Despite how our outer person may be decaying, the hidden person of the heart is *"imperishable"* (incorruptible).[59] Therefore, for faithful service, we will receive an imperishable crown (1 Corinthians 9:25) and in the resurrection will receive an imperishable body (1 Corinthians 15:52–54). The hidden person of the heart is imperishable, since we are *"born again"* of an imperishable seed (1 Peter 1:27). Created in the image of the *"incorruptible God"* (Romans 1:23), our hidden person of the heart is therefore incorruptible. When Scripture teaches that we have eternity in our hearts (Ecclesiastes 3:11), it refers to this eternal and imperishable part of you that desires after what is eternal and is never fully satisfied with that which is temporal. This is why it should be our priority before God, for it is His eternal priority for us.

This imperishable, hidden part of you is characterized by *"a gentle and quiet spirit."* As we mature in Messiah, we develop gentleness toward others and tranquility through our trials. This spiritual growth occurs as we trust the Lord when we're with others and when we go through our trials. Through it all, God's desire is to live out His love to loveless people in a loveless world. Yet, if we attempt to endure circumstances without trusting the Lord, those very same trials will make us bitter and not better. The difference is not our spouse or the circumstances, but whether or not we will trust the Lord through it all. For *"though I walk through the valley of the shadow of death, I fear no evil, for You are with me!"*[60] Yes, He is with you through it all, and He will never leave you nor forsake you.

This hidden person of the heart is most *"precious in the sight of God."* Is it equally precious to you? To God you are like a most precious pearl, for which He *"sold all that He had"* just to purchase you.[61] Remember, you are not a physical being with a spirit, but you are a spiritual being with a body. But do you value spiritual life more? If so, your marriage to your husband is your spiritual ministry to God as well—a ministry in which God has especially chosen you to represent His spiritual values in the home, to be His light in Messiah and to be His love gift to a man who desperately needs that, whether he knows it or not.

The question is going to be. . .does it matter to you? Our spouses observe our chaste and righteous behavior (our attitude). They are observing, just as God is observing. God is watching the heart. Ask yourself, "For whom am I showing off if not for God?" Who are you trying to kid?

---

58. Hebrews 12:15.
59. Greek (*aphthartos*) means "not subject to decay or death; immortal" (*Friberg Greek Lexicon*).
60. Psalm 23:4.
61. Matthew 13:46.

The hopeful is maturely submitted (3:5)

For in this way in former times the holy women also, who hoped in God, used to adorn themselves, being submissive to their own husbands.

"*For in this way*" refers to the spiritual adornment of the hidden person of the heart. "*In former times*" refers to the expanse of biblical history. This spiritual adornment of the hidden person of the heart always characterized "*the holy women.*" This refers to the women who lived for God, from repentant Eve, the matriarchs, Rahab the Harlot, the judge Deborah, Ruth the Moabitess, the widowed Abigail, through Miriam the mother of Messiah, all the way to the holy women of today. Yes, even you reading these very words are accounted along with all the holy women of history, whose lives were set apart hoping in God and who trusted in Yeshua, whether by the anticipation of faith before He came, or by the appropriation by faith since He came. These women lived differently from the world around them, for they hoped for what the world did not understand—let alone provide. Their hope in God was their inner adornment and was seen in their yieldedness to their own husbands. The word "adorn" in Greek is *kosmeo*, which means "to order," or "to arrange." They adorned themselves in that they ordered their lives to be harmonious to God's will—not merely making sure their wardrobe matched. You cannot both rely on God and rebel against your husband, the delegated authority that God established for the marriage. A life consecrated to the living God has confidence for living in God. As Yeshua, in His submission to Rome, bore the cross but always looked to God, so too wives "bear the cross" in submission to their husbands while hoping in God. Their submission to their husbands is the result of their holiness to God.

This adorning of the hidden person of the heart was how the holy women of old were submitted to their own husbands, just as each wife today is called to be. The text indicates that something acted upon them to submit to their husbands.[62] What could that be? The hidden person of the heart influenced their will to accept their husband's authority in their marriage. That is, their godly "*spirit*" ruled their (sometimes) hurting soul, with hurt feelings that might naturally motivate them to resist their husband's authority. Their godly spirit ruled over their troubled emotions. This defines the lifestyle of holy women who hope in God, including you.

The "*hidden person of the heart*" is manifestly sincere (3:6a)

...just as Sarah obeyed Abraham, calling him lord...

Of all the matriarchs, Sarah is especially highlighted as the example of the holy women who hoped in God. This may be because of the long and tumultuous

---

62. The Greek verb (*hupotasso*), meaning "being submissive," is a present passive participle, meaning that it was ongoing submission (present participle) by something that acted upon (passive) their will to submit.

marriage she had with Abraham. He denied her twice, he expected her to have a baby, he accepted Hagar as his second wife, and then she had to live with Ishmael threatening her son Isaac for a number of years. According to tradition, Sarah dropped dead after what Isaac was put through on Mount Moriah! The writer of Hebrews describes Sarah as a woman of faith who believed God for what she needed in order to have a child (Hebrews 11:11). She, along with Abraham, are considered "*the rock from which* [the Jewish people] *were hewn*," and she is to be looked to accordingly (Isaiah 51:1–2). Paul says that she pictures "*Jerusalem above*" (Galatians 4:21–27), and that God's "*word of promise*" was through her (Romans 9:9).

In our passage, Peter brings us to that time in Sarah's life when the hidden person of the heart was faithfully revealed before God. In Genesis 18, God and two angels come to the oaks of Mamre to have breakfast with Abraham,[63] and they reiterate to Abraham and inform Sarah that a year hence, Sarah will have a child. God asks Abraham, "*Where is Sarah your wife?*"[64] Abraham indicates that she is in the tent. God tells him that He will surely return to him "*at this time next year; and behold, Sarah your wife will have a son. And Sarah was listening at the tent door, which was behind him.*" When God mentions your name, you give ear to it. Sarah is listening to the conversation, though Abraham is unaware of her eavesdropping. But God knows this. Peter refers to her response upon hearing of this word of promise. Genesis 18:12 says, "*Sarah laughed to herself, saying, 'After I have become old, shall I have pleasure, my lord being old also?'*" She laughed "*to herself,*" which is literally "in her heart," but even during the "inside joke" she is enjoying, she calls Abraham "*lord,*" which is what Peter is referring to. This is the only place in the Bible where Sarah calls her husband "*lord.*" Despite thinking that having a child at their age is absurd, in her heart she still respects her husband and calls him "*lord*" (or "sir").

Can you imagine in your heart referring to your husband as sir or lord? Why would you? You would call him lord in your heart because you sincerely respect his position as husband, even if you "disagree with his policy." Hope in God is a heart matter; the hidden person of the heart is where we either believe or not. "*The fool has said in his heart, 'There is no God'*" (Psalm 14:1). Though a person's lips may praise God in the sanctuary, this person is a fool because the hidden person of the heart denies God in the practical issues of life.[65] Salvation is a heart issue.[66] We have a new heart[67] with new life,[68] and we look at everything and everyone

---

63. The fact that in Genesis 18:8 Abraham serves them milk and meat together is for another book.
64. Genesis 18:9.
65. Similarly, see Luke 12:45–48.
66. Romans 10:9–10.
67. Ezekiel 36:26–27; Romans 2:29; Colossians 2:11.
68. Romans 6:4.

Eight • The Triumphant Spouse in a Troubled Marriage

differently.[69] We now see our spouses differently; we now see our husbands differently; we see everything from God's perspective if we have a new life in the hidden person of the heart.

What's hindering the hidden person of the heart from hoping in God? (3:6b)

And you have become her children if you do what is right without being frightened by any fear.

Becoming Sarah's daughter, or "bat Sarah," is a term for becoming a "Jew by choice."[70] Peter uses it for a spiritual family trait of the hidden person of the heart. The family resemblance is seen when the wife of one disobedient to the Word faithfully chooses to "*do what is right.*" What is "*right*" is nurturing the hidden person of the heart to hope in God and live respectfully with your husband. God can use this behavior to win your husband to faith. Peter tells us that what hinders this right work of God through the wife is "*fear.*" The word *fear* is unusual,[71] meaning to be terrified. The wife is instructed that Sarah's daughters must not be frightened by any terror of her husband's response or by anyone else's intimidation. The choice for all people, husbands as well as wives, will be motivated by faith or hindered by fear. For every believer it is true: "*God has not given us a spirit of fear, but of power love and a sound mind.*"[72] If you are Spirit filled, you will not be hindered by fear. When you are Spirit filled, you have His power, love, and sound mind. When fear overwhelms you, you feel powerless, loveless, and not in your right mind.

What kind of fear might a wife have? "If I show him respect he will take advantage of me. If I don't treat him as he treats me, it will only reinforce his bad behavior." Because of fear, unforgiveness and anger arise in marriage—certainly in the heart, and often brimming over. Why? Because the heart is not yielded to God in this area, not submitted to God's calling upon the wife, and not Spirit filled with His power, love, and soundness of mind. By God's grace through faith in Yeshua, we win him without revilement, without resentment, without anger, but with respect for the position, even as we pray for the person and disagree with the policy. A wife's calling is fulfilled by following Messiah in her life, regardless of her husband's spiritual condition.

---

69. Second Corinthians 5:16.
70. "Why Jews By Choice are Sons of Abraham and Daughters of Sarah," *My Jewish Learning*, myjewishlearning.com.
71. This Greek word (*ptoesis*) is only used here in the New Covenant and in the Greek Septuagint translation of the Tanakh in Proverbs 3:25: "*Do not be afraid of sudden fear nor of the onslaught of the wicked when it comes.*"
72. Second Timothy 1:7, sn.

The Serving Husband: How Husbands Are to Live with Their Wives (3:7)

You husbands in the same way, live with your wives in an understanding way, as with someone weaker, since she is a woman; and show her honor as a fellow heir of the grace of life, so that your prayers will not be hindered.

Peter now addresses the man's side of the marital equation.

Live faithfully with your wife. The first phrase again says, "*in the same way,*" referring now to the husband. The Messiah is the example for both husband and wife when living with a spouse who is disobedient to the Word.[73] The husband has Messiah as his example of how to fulfill his calling as a husband, even when his wife is disrespectful to him or disobedient to the Word and not walking in the will of God herself. But can't he just force her to respect him? No! Some spiritually immature husbands have used their wives' faults as excuses for their own ungodliness. Two wrongs do not make a right! He is to minister to his disobedient wife by following in the steps of Messiah as his example. All attempts to bully, coerce, or manipulate his disobedient wife are contrary to God's calling upon the husband to live out the image of God in the home. Once more, the assumption is that the discipled husband is Spirit filled, wanting to live obedient to the Word of God and to the glory of God.

Husbands are to live with their disobedient wives in the same way as Messiah faithfully lived through His trials. If she reviles you, you are not to revile back. If her disrespect humiliates you, though you are suffering, do not threaten your wife. As with faithful wives, you are to win her "*without a word.*" Like Yeshua, who prayed for His killers while He suffered, you are to pray for her, "Father, forgive her for she knows not what she is doing." You are to be looking continually to the Lord, not to the lady. You are to be entrusting yourself constantly to Him who judges righteously. You are not to be distracted in your calling from God, which is to lay down your life for her, even as Messiah sacrificed Himself for the Assembly, and to love your wife as yourself,[74] which Yeshua did "*while we were yet sinners.*"[75] That is how husbands fulfill their divine calling, despite the wayward spiritual condition of their wives. That calling is what God planned from eternity past, and it is intended to conform you to the image of Messiah. Do not let fear hinder you in your calling, any more than the obedient wife should allow fear to hinder her in her calling. Do not fear what others might think of you. Husbands need to be concerned solely with what the Lord says. The faithful husband will one day hear Him say, "*Well done, good and faithful servant!*"[76] This, along with what follows, is what it means to be a faithful husband.

---

73. Paul also refers to the problem of an unbelieving wife in 1 Corinthians 7:12.
74. Refer again to Ephesians 5:25–32 above.
75. Romans 5:6–8.
76. Matthew 25:21, 23; Luke 19:17 (SN).

Eight • The Triumphant Spouse in a Troubled Marriage

Live intimately with your wife. "*Live with your wives in an understanding way.*" In the original, the phrase "*live with your wives*" implies an intimacy as opposed to an indifference.[77] The normal intimacy of the married life is assumed as the way the faithful husband will live with his disobedient wife. Despite her spiritual condition, she is still off limits to other men. He maintains a closeness and a warmth towards her.[78] How are husbands to live intimately with their wives? They are to live closely with them "*in an understanding way.*"[79]

Your goal is to get a PhD in your wife! You need to become an expert on who she is. Know what she likes in order to please her. Know what she does not like to avoid displeasing her. Don't push her buttons. Know what turns her off or what encourages her, and encourage her. Don't suggest those movies that upset her or distract her, etc. Don't do the kind of things that might be harmful, hurt her feelings, or endanger her. And certainly, don't go to improper places that are inappropriate for either of you. Avoid those acquaintances that might judge her for her spiritual disobedience. This may mean asking her questions, and talking to her about her interests (as long as it is not evidently contrary to God's Word). This is how God lives with you! He too loves you and cares about you, even on your bad days. Know her so you can be sensitive to "*live with your wives in an understanding way, as with someone weaker.*"

Sensitively care about her. The phrase "*as with someone weaker*" can sound like a disparaging and patronizing remark, but it's not. Please notice the "*as*" in the phrase. She is not weaker, but treat her as if she were weaker; treat her as precious. She may be bigger, stronger, or even smarter than you. That being the case, understand her and still treat her as a Ming vase—delicately, sweetly, and not roughly. Treat her gently, graciously, and lovingly. Remember, "*the spirit is willing, but the flesh is weak*" (Matthew 26:41). Living by her flesh may weaken her character and her ability to adjust to disappointment and difficulties. Yet, remember that this is how God loved us all in Messiah when we were helpless from our sinful flesh (Romans 5:6). Paul writes, "*To the weak I became weak, that I might win the weak*" (1 Corinthians 9:22). So too, husbands are to win their wives. It is very important to understand God's intention, which is His ministry to her through you.

Know her so you can be appreciative of her, "*since she is a woman.*"[80] Once more, stating that the husband should understand her as weaker "*since she is a woman*" may seem derogatory, but Peter's point is quite different. He is speaking about respectful appreciation. The husband should deeply appreciate his wife, for

---

77. "Live with" is the Greek word (*sunoikeo*), meaning "to dwell together," or "to cohabit," and implies intimacy, as seen in Genesis 20:3; Deuteronomy 22:13; 24:1; Isaiah 62:5.
78. *Warmth* is translated as "cherish" in Ephesians 5:29.
79. Literally "according to knowledge" (*kata gnosin*).
80. Literally, "the woman" (Greek: *to gunaikeios*) "belonging to woman" (*Friberg Greek Lexicon*) refers to a womanly matter, i.e., her femininity is being emphasized. Genesis 18:11; Deuteronomy 22:5; Esther 2:11, 17; Judith 12:15; Tobit 2:11.

in marrying him, she biblically consented to a subordinate role in the marriage. She could be president of a large company and make more money than the husband, but in marriage, since she is the woman, she consented to a subordinate role. Regardless of her abilities, skills, and the praise she may get in the world, she takes that subordinate role before her husband. So, live with her in understanding—that is, understand her great value, which she is submitting to your husbandly oversight. Understand her sensitivity as a consenting subordinate submitting to your leadership, and never take advantage of her, because she placed herself by consent into a submitted position to you. Treat her with gentleness and with great appreciation for the potential sacrifice to her dignity that having a husband may require. This is especially true when she is, at least in some way, disobedient to the Word. In her disobedience, she does not have the wherewithal through the Holy Spirit to forgive or understand God's grace for her and you, or what it means for her husband to have a sanctifying influence on the marriage and home. She may therefore go into deeper disobedience unless the husband sensitively, appreciatively, and sacrificially loves his wife as himself. Be respectful and sensitive not to stumble her in her role as your wife.

Know her so you can be respectful of her (3:7b)

And show her honor as a fellow heir of the grace of life.

The word translated here as "show" is better understood as "to grant or dispense."[81] You are granting her honor; she does not need to go after the honor in order to attain it. You are to freely give it to her. She does not have to earn it with great meals or having to be a Proverbs 31 wife. Simply because she is your wife you are to grant, show, and give her honor and value. We read in Hebrews 5:4, *"And no one takes the honor to himself."* It is unseemly for a person to speak highly of herself to gain honor. Honor is to be granted to her so she is not taken for granted!

In your attitude and mind, designate her as valuable and not as useless, then let your actions show your respect for that value. When Sarah was misjudged, Abraham received a thousand pieces of silver for any dishonor shown to her (Genesis 20:16). A story is told of a man who paid a dowry of seven cows for a woman to be his wife. No one had ever paid more than five cows before, and for an ordinary woman two or maybe three cows was average. When this woman heard of this high price and how her husband valued her, she took on a beauty from within that made her almost unrecognizable. He indeed had a seven-cow wife! What is your wife's value to you? You get what you pay for!

---

81. The Greek word (*aponemontes*) is literally "to dispense a portion" (*Thayer Greek English Lexicon*), and, along with the Greek word (*timen*), meaning "honor," or "value," the phrase means "to assign or impart honor, to show, give, or grant her honor or value."

Eight • The Triumphant Spouse in a Troubled Marriage

Honor her, and do not dishonor her, even if she is not having her best day. Show her honor because of her position as your wife. She is, by God's provision, your *ezer kenegdo*,[82] your counterpart, your helper and partner in the ministry of marriage. Whether she fully appreciates her calling or not, you do. Respect the position and pray for the person, even if you disagree with the policy. In your home, do you count your wife as a vessel unto honor or unto dishonor?

Husbands are to show their wives honor "*as*[83] *a fellow heir of the grace of life.*" Not only are husbands to grant their wives honor as their co-partners in the marriage ministry, but they are also to grant their wives honor as co-heirs in "*the grace of life.*" The "*grace of life*" refers to the grace that brings us eternal life.[84] By grace through faith in Yeshua, who is the "*life*,"[85] we receive that life, of which we are now stewards to minister to others, as well as to enjoy now and forever. The word translated "fellow-heir" is used three other times in the Bible, giving further insight on the co-heirs in marriage. Co-heirs share in the same blessings and the same suffering—as in Messiah,[86] so too as with the patriarchs.[87] This is understandable, since co-heirs are members together in the same family or Body;[88] and we share the joys and oys of finance, children, and aging. So, co-heirs in marriage are beneficiaries of the same blessings and the same suffering. This also means that if God is going to bless one of you, He is going bless both of you.[89] You are in partnership. How can husbands not grant honor to their wives, who are "joined at the hip" in their service as well as "joined at the heart" in their home?

Because of her position as wife, she is granted such honor, even though, in her disobedience, she may not be enjoying the grace of life. In Scripture, the remarkable matter is that the position can still do the work, even though the person in that position may not benefit from it personally! We read in John 11:49–52 that Caiaphas was High Priest, and though he was an enemy of Yeshua, he nonetheless prophesied beyond his own understanding—yet with divine accuracy—regarding the importance and impact of Messiah's substitutionary death. How can that

---

82. Genesis 2:18–23.
83. The Greek phrase *hos kai*, literally "as also," is used to mean "in the same way," or "just as" (Matthew 6:12; 20:14; 2 Timothy 3:9; Hebrews 3:2; 13:3, etc.). The phrase "as also" is used in English as an ellipsis, so that the preceding phrase is not repeated but understood.
84. Titus 3:7: "*So that being justified by His grace we would be made heirs according to the hope of eternal life.*" John's "*water of life*" that Yeshua shepherds us to (Revelation 7:17), which is acquired "*without cost*" (Revelation 21:6; 22:17), and which flows "*from the throne of God and of the Lamb,*" may be a glorious metaphor for Peter's "*grace of life.*"
85. John 1:4; 11:25; 14:6; Galatians 2:20; Colossians 3:4.
86. Romans 8:17 (SN): "*And if children, heirs also, heirs of God and fellow heirs with Messiah, if indeed we suffer with Him so that we may also be glorified with Him.*"
87. Hebrews 11:9: "*By faith he lived as an alien in the land of promise, as in a foreign land, dwelling in tents with Isaac and Jacob, fellow heirs of the same promise.*"
88. Ephesians 3:6 (SN): "*To be specific, that the Gentiles are fellow heirs and fellow members of the body, and fellow partakers of the promise in Yeshua the Messiah through the Good News.*"
89. As in Genesis 1:28.

be? God is not a respecter of persons, but He is a respecter of positions that He ordained. Even when Abraham is not living up to his position as husband, by denying Sarah as his wife, still God counts him as a prophet whose prayers will bring healing to the one he deceived.[90] So too, the disobedient wife (or husband) can still be a co-heir in the grace of life, of which she (or he) is not yet a beneficiary, for the believing spouse brings a sanctifying influence into the marriage and home. Since God sees them as one, their ministry for God proves that His grace is sufficient, for through their marital weakness, His power is made perfect. How can we not give Him great praise to the glory of His name! Admittedly, their effectiveness as a "grace couple" would be increased if both fully followed the Lord, which is why Scripture warns us not to be unequally yoked in marriage with an unbeliever.[91] Therefore, as a Messianic believer, be wise as you consider marriage. For those that are unequally yoked, you are nonetheless responsible to live for the Lord toward your wife, for you are fellow heirs of the grace of life.

Live prayerfully with your wife.

...so that your prayers will not be hindered.

In an earlier study, we mentioned that a husband, as overseer, is to manage well his own home before he can care for the Assembly of God. There are two primary ministries that the overseer ministry requires to be conducted in the home and the congregation to be a healthy family and a functional community. These two primary activities are prayer and teaching the Word.[92] We learned in Ephesians 5:26 that Spirit-filled, Messiah-like husbands are to minister to their wives as *"washing of water with the Word."* That is, the husband is called to minster the Word to his wife at home. The other primary ministry the husband has at home is the responsibility of prayer. The husband is to lead his wife and family in prayer. But here is the warning of Peter: if you do not communicate well with your wife you will not communicate well with your God, who gave her to you. You need to dwell with her with understanding and honor *"so that your prayers will not be hindered."* The word *hindered*[93] is "to cut up" a road, causing obstacles to block a path. Your hindered communion with your wife hinders your communion with your Lord, who gave her to you. Your spiritual walk with God and effective spiritual leadership in the home is hindered by not maintaining understanding and honoring relations with your spouse. Her disrespect of you does not determine

---

90. Genesis 20:7.
91. Second Corinthians 6:14.
92. See Exodus 18:19–20 and Acts 6:4.
93. The Greek (*egkopto*) means "strictly knock or cut into; hence hinder, impede, thwart"(*Friberg Greek Lexicon*). The meaning is "to prevent, hinder, or obstruct," as it is used in Romans 15:22: *"For this reason I have often been prevented from coming to you"*; Galatians 5:7: *"You were running well; who hindered you from obeying the truth?"*; 1 Thessalonians 2:18: *"For we wanted to come to you—I, Paul, more than once—and yet Satan hindered us."*

your behavior towards her. If you say you love God and hate your wife, you're a liar![94] As a faithful husband, you love God, and thereby also love your wife as yourself.

If you've had hindered prayers, repent to the Lord for anything in your life that may be causing your prayerlessness, including your relationship with your wife. Ask Him to help you, and review the section about being filled with the Spirit. Then talk to your wife about your relationship together. Listen carefully, get to understand your wife for who she is, and then honor her as your wife. Continue to follow Messiah and pray for your wife, to win her without a word. As the prayer leader in the home, do not give in to resentment, anger, and frustration, but rather, rely on the Lord, casting your cares upon Him, so that you might live the life you are called to live, as a victorious husband representing the image of God to your wife and family.

For either spouse, trusting in Messiah is the triumph in marriage. This is how we have victorious Messianic marriages. Even if your spouse is disobedient to the Word, you are to be more than a conqueror through Messiah who loved you. You can both fulfill your individual calling and be conformed to the image of Messiah representing and honoring God in all your ways as you follow Messiah through your marriage.

Some questions to help apply these teachings

1. In what ways does each of you show that you follow Messiah as your example?

2. Do you need to repent to your spouse for any word or deed that does not reflect Messiah's life?

3. If you're following Messiah, can you forgive your spouse from your heart—even if he/she doesn't repent? Can your spouse see your forgiving behavior?

4. Are you more committed to your external attire than your internal attitude? Describe the time spent on each. Is your hope in God or in your spouse's changed attitude and behavior? How does that show itself?

---

94. A marital paraphrase of 1 John 4:20.

5. In what ways does fearfulness impact your response to your spouse?

6. Do you respect your spouse's position as husband or wife, regardless of his or her behavior? Describe how this respect impacts your life.

7. How often do you pray together? If your spouse is unwilling to pray, how often do you pray for your spouse?

CHAPTER NINE

Divorce and Remarriage in the New Covenant

Messiah's Torah on Divorce and Remarriage

We have looked at the marriage foundation in Genesis 1 and 2, the marriage devastation in Genesis 3, the impact of that for the marriage regulations in the rest of the Tanakh, and the marriage restoration through Messiah's redemption. In spite of Yeshua's restoration of marriage to the original design, we find the plague of divorce throughout human society, in disobedience to Messiah's teaching. In light of the Messianic redemption, how do we approach the subject of divorce from a biblical point of view, that is, from Messiah's point of view? We will consider two portions in the Good News of Matthew, where Yeshua taught on divorce and remarriage.

Yeshua's Initial Instruction on Marriage and Divorce (Part 1)

Is your divorce causing adultery? Matthew 5:31–32

> *"It was said, 'Whoever sends his wife away, let him give her a certificate of divorce'; but I say to you that everyone who divorces his wife, except for the reason of unchastity, makes her commit adultery; and whoever marries a divorced woman commits adultery."*
> (Matthew 5:31–32)

The wrong reading of Moses results in divorce (5:31)

When Yeshua the Messiah is teaching on the righteousness of the Torah as recorded in Matthew 5, His intention is not merely to clarify the Torah's instructions. It is to bring Israel to the place of realizing that the Torah of Moses was intended to convict God's people of our utter sinfulness[1] and to show us our desperate need for God's grace and mercy in His atonement and the righteousness offered to all who would believe in Him.[2] Like a doctor showing a patient the X-ray of their cancerous tumor, Torah was to help with the reality therapy the patient needs in order to deal with the problem and live. In His teaching, Messiah challenges the traditional interpretations (i.e., spiritual "junk medicine") that mitigated the Torah's conviction of humanity's corrupted hearts before

---

1. Galatians 3:19.
2. Romans 10:4.

God. In Yeshua's divorce challenge, He restates what was probably an oft-quoted maxim on the traditional approach to divorce and remarriage: "*Whoever sends his wife away, let him give her a certificate of divorce.*" On the face of it, this may sound like a quote from Deuteronomy 24:1–4, but it is not. As we have studied,[3] Moses gave very detailed instructions on divorce and remarriage—instructions that, if they were followed, would greatly restrict divorces from taking place. But all that Moses taught was boiled down to the requirement of giving the woman "*a certificate of divorce*," and from the husband's perspective, his obligations were fulfilled. The result from this easy path to unbiblical divorces was women left with no recourse but to remarry to survive, while made ceremonially unclean from being dumped by their husbands.

Messiah has a very different perspective, though He agrees with Moses. Because of the hardness of the human heart, divorce was so rampant that God had to regulate the matter through Moses so that the woman would have some protection against malicious charges brought against her. That was Moses's teaching. Yeshua had to bring up the writ of divorce because, by the first century, Moses was so misinterpreted that divorce was rampant, as was the resulting immorality. One Rabbi said only for immorality should a divorce be granted. Another rabbi stated that it was for any cause that displeased him, even for "a bad meal."[4] If your community followed that reasoning, one could see how no-fault divorce would permeate and corrupt society. Messiah deals directly with the subject of divorce, not only in this portion of Scripture, but elsewhere.

This is the sinful consequence throughout Israel that Yeshua describes. "*But I say to you that everyone who divorces his wife, except for the reason of unchastity, makes her commit adultery.*" As we saw in Deuteronomy—that Yeshua reiterates—the responsibility for her ceremonially unclean condition is not on her, but on the husband, whose improper divorce from her caused her to remarry to survive. The man who then marries that woman is also held responsible, for an inappropriate divorce results in an adulterous remarriage. Divorce is a plague.

Though among believers the percentage for divorce is "around 33 percent," the divorce rate in American society is about 50 percent of all marriages.[5] Why is that? For the very same reasons. People are looking for self-satisfaction and not finding it in marriage, so they look elsewhere. The reason for divorce is the sinful human heart.

---

3. See above on the study of Deuteronomy 24:1–4.
4. Bavli, Gittin 90a, Mishnah. "Beth Shammai say: a man should not divorce his wife unless he has found her guilty of some unseemly conduct, as it says, because he hath found some unseemly thing in her. Beth Hillel, however, say [that he may divorce her] even if she has merely spoilt his food."
5. "Marriage and Divorce," *American Psychological Association*, apa.org. "Is the divorce rate among Christians truly the same as among non-Christians?" Got Questions, gotquestions.org.

Marriages can fall apart. Scripture does not promise that a marriage in the name of Messiah is guaranteed to stay together. But it does promise that if you both obey the Word of God, it will stay together. The reason divorces take place amongst believers, except for the reasons that Messiah gives and upon which Paul expands, is disobedience to God's Word. People want their own way. They cannot stand the unhappiness of their life. They believe their marriage was a mistake, regardless of how many times they stated that God brought them together. Couples give in to their impulses and go through divorce. Infidelity and immorality run rampant.

In Matthew 5:28, Yeshua states that adultery is so prevalent because if you lust after another person in your heart, you are committing adultery. The news media tells us that the greatest cause of divorces is infidelity.[6] Even if you do not act upon the lust in your heart, God sees lust as sin, though you may not. In a discussion with one unbelieving husband on the subject, he said he thought that desiring other women was the way God made him, and that there was nothing wrong with it. When I showed him in the Scripture that Yeshua calls it a sin, he responded that he didn't agree. So, I said, "How would your wife feel about your desire for other women?" He grew very quiet, realizing that his wife would think he was "stepping out on her" in that lustful moment. Many believe that if you don't get caught, it's like the cop (i.e., your wife) didn't see you speeding. However, from God's point of view this self-deception does not work that way. It is always wrong, and it's always a heart issue. If the heart is desirous for infidelity, immorality, adultery, or living for its own pleasures and satisfactions, divorce will eventually follow—in spirit, if not in fact. That is what is happening throughout America, and elsewhere.

Through the Internet, people easily find potential partners in adultery. The Academy of Matrimonial Lawyers noted that 56 percent of divorces involve one spouse having an affair after meeting someone on the Internet.[7] The Internet has provided greater opportunity for moral failure, for it gives us more convenient availability of sin and evil. Surveys show that "62 percent of high school seniors have had sexual intercourse."[8] Out-of-wedlock teen sex has become normal and commonplace, but in God's sight it is abnormal and evil. We may sing, "God bless America," but a highly immoral country must expect the judgment of God.

Scripture straightforwardly commands us that we shall not commit adultery.[9] In that commandment we see the sinful deed in focus, but Yeshua looks at the cause: lusting in your heart. It is not the deed, but the desire Yeshua wants to reveal

---

6. Shellie Warren, "10 Most Common Reasons for Divorce," *Marriage.com*, December 11, 2018, marriage.com.
7. "National Review: Getting Serious on Pornography," NPR, March 31, 2010, npr.org.
8. Kurt Conklin, "Adolescent Sexual Health and Behavior in the United States: Positive Trends and Areas in Need of Improvement," *Advocates for Youth*, February, 2012, advocatesforyouth.org.
9. Exodus 20:14; Matthew 5:27.

and heal. It is a heart issue. We must take responsibility for our hearts, and bring them to the Lord for His forgiveness and His empowerment by the Holy Spirit to live differently. That will safeguard our marriages if our heart is yielded to the Lord and not to our own passions and pleasures. But once more, this requires the Messianic believer to live the Spirit-filled life.[10]

The Messiah's correct analysis restricts divorce (5:32)

In Matthew 5:32, Messiah declares, *"But I say to you that everyone who divorces his wife, except for the reason of unchastity…"* Messiah graciously restricts the reason for divorce. In this matter, He says *"except for the reason of unchastity."* *Unchastity*, or in other translations, *sexual immorality*, in the original Greek is *porneia*, from which we get the word *pornography*. It is the Greek word the Septuagint translation used for "harlotry" (Hebrew: *zenunim*) in the Tanakh.[11] Yeshua is being gracious, for under the Torah of Moses, immorality by a wife was not a cause for her divorce; it was a cause for her death—it was a capital crime.[12]

In general, though, the idea of this sort of immorality was identified with unrepentant serial adultery, which may include desertion of the marriage and family. Adultery is a sin, and it certainly can lead to divorce, but it can also be the cause for forgiveness[13] if there is sincere repentance included in counseling.

Unbiblical divorces, however, bring about corruption beyond the divorce because we see that Yeshua stated, *"except for the reason."* There are many other reasons people will divorce: incompatibility, disrespect, emotional distance, etc. The Bible does not recognize those as valid reasons at all. Divorce sought on improper grounds leads to adultery, because the woman and man are basically left in a world where an improper divorce leads them to remarry others, multiplying the problems. God's work to redeem our divorce-plagued society starts with the marriage. When the marriage is unstable and fails, society is destabilized. This is because society is made up of relationships, and the key relationship is marriage.

Then what is the hope of society? Marriages that reflect the faithfulness of God and therefore last. The temptations of your heart need to be held back and restrained. How is that accomplished? What do you do when you have lust in your heart? You go to the Lord. How soon do you turn to the Lord? Immediately! Repentance is a good habit. You need to develop habits of going to the Lord in prayer whenever tempted. However, if you allow the corruption of your own heart to go on, it will bring corruption into your relationships, causing alienation in the marriage. This is because your heart relationship to your spouse is the actual relationship that your spouse was hoping for and depending on having with you.

---

10. Refer to the study on Ephesians 5:18–32.
11. Hosea 2:4; 4:11–12; 5:4; Nahum 3:4, etc.
12. Genesis 38:24; Leviticus 19:29; 20:10; Numbers 5:27; Deuteronomy 22:21–24; John 8:5.
13. Mark 3:28; John 8:3–11; 1 Corinthians 6:9–11; 1 John 1:7, 9.

Nine • *Divorce and Remarriage in the New Covenant*

Just as God wants your heart, so does your godly spouse. Otherwise, the marriage can become a superficial hypocrisy where there is no genuine sense of marital commitment and spousal devotion.

Yeshua said in Matthew 5:28 that the cause of the divorce problem is lusting in the heart. To put a fine point on the problem, Yeshua then states, "*If your right eye makes you stumble, tear it out and throw it from you; for it is better for you to lose one of the parts of your body, than for your whole body to be thrown into hell. If your right hand makes you stumble, cut it off and throw it from you; for it is better for you to lose one of the parts of your body, than for your whole body to go into hell*" (Matthew 5:29–30). Of course—get rid of the offending parts before going to hell. Messiah is emphasizing that the problem is not the eye and hand—for getting rid of them won't truly help. The problem is the heart, for the heart controls your eye and hand! The encouragement of Scripture is that God has a remedy for your corrupted heart: the grace of God in Yeshua that applies His forgiveness to your repentant heart when you go astray. In fact, when you come to Messiah for salvation, you spiritually receive a new, circumcised heart and God's own Spirit.[14]

Yeshua's Further Instruction on Marriage and Divorce (Part 2): The Permanence of Marriage. (Matthew 19:3–12)

The religious question about divorce (19:3 SN)

> *Some Pharisees came to Yeshua, testing Him and asking,*
> *"Is it lawful for a man to divorce his wife for any reason at all?"*

During a large-scale healing service (Matthew 19:1–2), certain Pharisees[15] tested Yeshua on questions about divorce (19:3). As previously noted, this subject was highly controversial in first-century Judea. But because of Yeshua's love for all people and His willingness to heal the worst of people (which the religious types thought was wrong[16]), the Pharisees sought ways to accuse Him of contradicting Moses, which would undermine His credentials as the Jewish Messiah. The true Messiah would have to fulfill Moses and not destroy the Torah of Moses.[17] Their question, "*Is it lawful for a man to divorce his wife for any reason at all?*" hinged on the cause for divorce: "*for any reason at all*," which was a popular view in that day.

---

14. Ezekiel 36:26–27; Romans 2:29; Colossians 2:11.
15. For a more complete understanding of the teaching of the Pharisees on divorce, read Bavli, Gittin 1–9.
16. To understand the religious attitude, see Luke 7:39.
17. Deuteronomy 18:15–19.

Yeshua's response: marriage is permanent (19:4–6)

Gender creation had the intention of marriage permanence (19:4)

And He answered and said, "Have you not read that He who created them from the beginning made them male and female..."

Yeshua's answer that marriage is permanent is first seen in God's intention of creating humanity with two genders—male and female—from Genesis 1:27. The very idea that God created humanity with gender distinctions indicated that they were to be united in marriage. There would be a permanent unity of relationship for the male and female, just as there is eternal unity in the Triune nature of God, in whose image we were created. Yeshua's reasoning was that if God did not intend marriage, He would have made us all the same gender with no need for marital bonding. If He wanted multiple wives for Adam, God could have created numerous females for the man. Or God could have made several genders with multiple marriage options. If God had intended divorce, He could have provided the woman to the man with term limits. But God did not. "*From the beginning*" God created them "*male and female*"—just two different genders that will reveal His special and permanent unity to all His creation.

Leaving parents had the intended result of marriage permanence (19:5)

"...and said, 'For this reason a man shall leave his father and his mother and be joined to his wife'..."

Yeshua quotes Genesis 2:24, refocusing Israel on God's original marriage intention of permanence. The man is meant to leave his parents. That living arrangement with his parents was not intended by God to be permanent. But as strong as that family's bond may have been, and as much as the man is later commanded to honor his father and his mother (Exodus 20:12), the man leaves his parents for one reason: to cleave to his wife. As noted in the study on Genesis 2:24, this matter of cleaving was intended by God to make them stick like glue. The family bond is not broken, but rather, transferred to the new home, where the man will maintain the family bond by his commitment to cleave to his wife as head of his new home.

Being "one flesh" reveals the intention of marriage permanence (19:5)

"'...and the two shall become one flesh'?"

Not only does the Messiah reiterate Genesis 2:24 for marriage, but this becomes the normative teaching of the *sh'lichim* (apostles) as well. Paul makes Genesis 2:24 the renewed reality of the restored marriage in Messiah in Ephesians 5:31–32. Paul states that the Spirit-joined relationship between the husband and wife reveals the mystery of the Messiah and the Assembly! The importance of this marital cleaving principle as seen in marital unity is profoundly presented by Paul in 1 Corinthians 6:16–17 *"Or do you not know that the one who joins himself to a prostitute is one body with her? For He says, 'The two shall become one flesh.' But the one who joins himself to the Lord is one spirit with Him."* The permanence of marriage reflects upon the unity between the believer and the Lord Himself! If you have prenups for your marriage, that reflects on your lack of assurance of eternal salvation as well. For, the One who promised, *"I will never desert you, nor will I ever forsake you"* (Joshua 1:5; Hebrews 12:5), reveals His faithfulness to His creation through marriage by declaring that *"the two shall become one flesh."* As you are one with Adonai in Messiah, so the Messianic marriage is one in Yeshua as well.

God seeing them as "one" reveals His intention of marriage permanence (19:6a)

"So they are no longer two, but one flesh."

According to the declaration of Yeshua, though they are a couple (indicating two), they are actually *"one flesh"* in God's sight, if not their own. Yeshua took *"one flesh"* in the most literal way. To the Messiah, there wasn't a figurative, poetic, or romantic interpretation for that Scripture, but simply and literally, they were *"one flesh"*—period. Yeshua declared this literal interpretation to religious leaders, who already knew the Genesis Scripture, because their traditional interpretation that contradicted God's intention was wrong. They could not possibly see the couple as one flesh if they could dare discuss the divorce of a marriage *"for any reason at all."* Since opposites attract, a couple may understandably see themselves as distinct individuals. They might act as if they are two different people with two different value systems, two different interests, and two different lives to be lived—with separate vacations, separate bank accounts, and separate lives. But this dual perspective would be spiritually wrong. Once you marry, God treats you as a unity.

If you are not one with your spouse, you are being double-minded and are unable to move forward on your spiritual calling, which assumes single-mindedness. Scripture informs us that the double-minded man *"ought not to expect that he will receive anything from the Lord, being a double-minded man, unstable in all his ways"* (James 1:7–8). As we saw in 1 Peter 3:7, God does not answer those prayers, for His blessing is not just for him or for her, but for *"them."*[18] Marital blessedness requires the couple to be of one mind.[19] The marriage remains unhealthy as long the husband and wife view themselves as two ships slowly passing each other in one very long night. The Messianic marriage becomes a healthy relationship when they act in accordance with what God says and how He treats them—as one flesh.

---

18. See Genesis 1:28. For those that are married to a spouse who is *"disobedient to the Word,"* see the chapter on 1 Peter 3:1–7.
19. As does Israel's blessedness (1 Chronicles 12:38) and the Messianic congregation's blessedness as well (Acts 1:14; 2:46; 15:25; Romans 12:16; 15:5; 1 Corinthians 1:10; Philippians 1:27; 2:2).

In your marriage, you are seen by God as one flesh. Therefore, you must act as a unique unity in Messiah. God expects both people to be just as open and honest with each other as you are honest with yourself. Your marriage must be a safe harbor for each other, that your family can be a safe place for the children. The children's security results from the parents' unity. Your Messianic marital oneness and unity reveal God's wholesome testimony to the surrounding community.

God's warning assumes marriage permanence (19:6b)

"What therefore God has joined together, let no man separate."

Yeshua then states a warning to the religious leaders and to all of us: *"What therefore God has joined together, let no man separate."* The immediate question for the Messianic couple (and others) to consider is, Has God joined the couple together? Did you once vow in the Lord to be married? Did you have a rabbi, priest, or minister officiate at your wedding? Then, despite your present feelings and thoughts to the contrary, you were and are joined together by God.[20] To consider divorce is therefore to consider rebellion against God. Your consideration to divorce your spouse is a denial of God's Word on the matter, and defies His revealed will for your life. To consider a divorce is to be in spiritual despair, for you're not walking in the Spirit, but in your flesh. To consider divorce, you are already not living for the Lord, for you are not seeing your marriage as a ministry to address each other's needs. To consider divorce is to misunderstand your marriage as a way to meet your own felt needs, which your spouse is ill prepared to do, since God alone both understands your real needs and meets them in Messiah. Only in Yeshua are you each "*complete*" (Colossians 2:10) and your marriage divinely meaningful to each another.

We should also ask, who does Yeshua mean when He says, "*let no man separate*"? Evidently, "*no man*" includes those who are married to each other, but also the religious leaders who raised the question to Yeshua initially, as well as the community that permits or even encourages divorce. As the divorce capital of the world, it is no wonder that Las Vegas is also called "sin city." Anyone involved in unbiblical divorces[21] is going against the clear teaching of Yeshua: what God joined, don't separate. Don't encourage the divorce, don't assist in the divorce, and don't validate the divorce. Do not act against God, for "*The fear of the LORD is the beginning of wisdom*" (Psalm 111:10).

When a couple agrees to divorce, they have spiritually turned their back on what God wants for their life as well as their marriage. Even though they may

---

20. For those present believers who were married in a secular ceremony, you may want to renew your vows or make biblically godly vows and dedicate your married lives to the Lord for His blessings upon your home.
21. The stipulations for divorce that Yeshua has set (Matthew 5:32) and will repeat (Matthew 19:9) only include unrepentant adultery, infidelity, and immorality.

still be religiously involved in some house of worship, they are spiritually separated from God (Isaiah 59:1–2). That said, divorce is not the unforgiveable sin. We can all do awful things, but we each need to recognize our misdeeds as wrong and sincerely repent of our sins against God and our now-former spouse. This acknowledgement of your sin in the divorce (especially as the initiator), with sincere repentance, restores you to a wholesome relationship with the Lord.[22]

Like all biblical injunctions, biblical marriage instructions can be disobeyed. If you break this injunction because it does not suit your interests any longer, then anything God has instructed is now likewise open to your ongoing, self-serving, rebellious disobedience. We are immature and carnal when we are uncommitted to God's will that does not fit into our personal plans. Like all of God's truth, we are only as mature as we are consistently committed to God's will and His Word, above our own agenda for our personal happiness. Happiness is the fruit of holiness.

The religious rejoinder to Yeshua (19:7)

> *They said to Him, "Why then did Moses command to give her a certificate of divorce and send her away?"*

The Sadducees represented the priesthood that handled matters at the temple in Jerusalem, where, until its destruction in AD 70, the bloody sacrifices were offered. The Sadducees accepted as authoritative only the first five books of Moses. At that time, the Pharisees were considered the Bible teachers for the Jewish people. They were the ones who taught the Scripture in the synagogues, and they considered their own interpretations authoritative.[23] Yeshua's response contradicted their own interpretation, which to them meant that Yeshua was in contradiction to Moses. They therefore ask Him, "*Why then did Moses command to give her a certificate of divorce and send her away?*" In their response, they thought they were protecting Moses from Yeshua's contradiction of their interpretation of Moses. When they said, "*Why then did Moses command,*" they were referring to the teaching of Moses on divorce from Deuteronomy 24:1–4.[24] They interpreted Moses to mean that when their wives displeased them, they were commanded to divorce them, giving them a writ of divorce and sending those wives away.

---

22. "*If we confess our sins, He is faithful and righteous to forgive us our sins and to cleanse us from all unrighteousness…*[for] *the blood of Yeshua His Son cleanses us from all sin*" (1 John 1:9, 7 SN).
23. Bavli, Berachoth 20a, Shabbat 94b, Eiruvin 37b, etc.
24. Moses did not command divorce, which they admit in Mark 10:4. All other references to divorce in the Torah of Moses (Leviticus 21:7, 14; Deuteronomy 22:19, 29) merely recognize its existence, but there is no command to divorce. In Deuteronomy 24:1–4, the only command is a prohibition about certain remarriage matters.

Yeshua's clarification of the concern of Moses (19:8 SN)

> *Yeshua said to them, "Moses permitted you to divorce your wives because of your hard hearts, but from the beginning it was not this way."*

Yeshua's response to these religious leaders contradicts their words and disproves their teaching. The Pharisees said, *"Why then did Moses command?"* Yeshua says, *"Moses permitted."* There is no command from Moses or anyone else to divorce your wife! They wrongly interpreted Moses to command divorce if a man is unhappy with his spouse. Yeshua's rejoinder clarifies Moses: Moses's instruction was merely a concession because of the rampant sinfulness of society, and that concession was out of concern for the wife and not for the "unhappy" husband.[25]

Yeshua gives the reason for the Mosaic regulation: *"Because of your hard hearts."*[26] The hardness of heart both resists the will of God and is indifferent to human suffering, even in a marriage. The concession Moses made was because of human sinfulness, that is, hardness of heart. In a marriage relationship where both are living in disobedience to the Word, there is incessant chafing, insults, disrespect, and hurt feelings. In this case, hardness of heart may be a self-serving protection to make the wounded less vulnerable to their spouse's attack and to protect their shredded self-respect and belittled self-esteem. This strategy for survival is wrong. Attempting to be unoffended keeps us from being merciful, forgiving, and prayerful for the other. You are commanded to *"love your enemies,... bless those who curse you, pray for those who mistreat you"* (Luke 6:27–28). But, rather than prioritize obeying the Word of God, we prioritize protecting ourselves.

Then too, there are some spouses with their own agendas, values, and goals that are indifferent to their spouses' needs. They may place their career above family time and their indulgences (gambling, alcohol, travel, etc.) above their family's needs. That too is hardness of heart. But there is Good News! In the Tanakh we read God's promise: *"I will remove the heart of stone from your flesh and give you a heart of flesh"* (Ezekiel 36:26). Ezekiel was anticipating the Messiah, for Yeshua authoritatively interpreted the prophet's promise of a new heart and spirit as our

---

25. When the wife traveled to a different area, she had to have accepted rabbinical signatures (Bavli, Gittin 2a, chapter I) as well as other requirements (two witnesses, etc., Gittin 2b).

26. Hardness of heart is a person's stubborn resistance to God and His Word (Ezekiel 3:7). The rebellious heart becomes hardened because of sin, for God made it so the work of sin is a hardening agent on the human heart. Because God has so ordered His universe, it can therefore be stated as well that God hardens the sinner's heart. But God does not harden the seeking heart, so that the hardness will be seen purely as a result of the transgressor's sin. As with Pharaoh, the hardened heart resists the will of God (Exodus 7:13–14, etc.) and dooms the sinner to disaster (Proverbs 28:14; Romans 2:5; Ephesians 4:18). For Messianic believers, a hardened heart can be a stronghold (2 Corinthians 10:4) that doesn't learn, respond to, or obey the truth of God's Word (Mark 6:52; 8:17; 16:14; Hebrews 3:8, 15; 4:7). On a social level, the hardened heart ignores the needy (Deuteronomy 15:7), and—as in Matthew 19:8—even the needy wife. But hardness of heart grieves the Lord (Mark 3:5).

great need to be "*born again*" in Him. When you come to faith in the Lord you are born again. What was stony and dead is now made alive in Messiah.[27] The old stony-hearted person has died, but some of the mental habits, survival tactics, and emotional triggers may still remain. These you must now outgrow as you mature in the truth of God's Word, to understand how to develop that new heart and walk in the Holy Spirit. "*Every plant which My heavenly Father did not plant shall be uprooted*" (Matthew 15:13), that you may be conformed to the image of Messiah in all ways.

The point Messiah is making to the Pharisees and to us is that this Mosaic concession to our hardness of heart is no longer a valid cause for divorce. In Messiah, we have a new heart. Yeshua closed the loophole, for He says, "*but from the beginning it was not this way.*" Yeshua, in His redemptive work, gives us a new heart to bring us back to the original design of Genesis 1 and 2. The corrupted motives of the human heart have been restored, enabling us to live out the creation calling of the image of God as individuals and through our Messianic marriages.

Think about the regulations of Moses. As Moses recognized, his Torah could not heal the heart.[28] His regulations applied a bandage to the wound. But now, Messiah has come and has healed our hearts.[29] Once the wound is healed, the bandage is no longer required. Yeshua's finished work no longer requires Moses's regulation nor concession as to marriage.

Divorce certificate is exceptional to God's will (19:9)

> "*And I say to you, whoever divorces his wife, except for immorality, and marries another woman commits adultery.*"

Messiah reiterates His instruction of Matthew 5:32. But here He declares it to the religious leaders based on His own authority. Thus, to disregard His one exception for divorce is to defy His authority over marriage. Remember, the laws of the land may permit what God has forbidden. Yet, "*We must obey God rather than men*" (Acts 5:29). If you say you are a believer in Yeshua and have initiated an improper divorce, you must recognize that you are not following Him as His disciple. Your disobedience to His Word makes your life unblessed, for Yeshua taught, "*If you know these things, you are blessed if you do them*" (John 13:17). The blessing is in the doing, for Torah was given, not merely to be learned, but to be lived (Leviticus 18:5). You must repent and be cleansed in Messiah's atonement to walk closely with the Lord and enjoy the blessings of His fellowship. Beware of attempting to live for the Lord without repenting of sin. God is not stupid and will not be

---

27. "*But God, being rich in mercy, because of His great love with which He loved us, even when we were dead in our transgressions, made us alive together with Messiah (by grace you have been saved)*" (Ephesians 2:4–5 SN).
28. Deuteronomy 29:4.
29. Isaiah 53:5.

mocked! Do not just draw the target around the rotten arrow and claim a bull's eye. No, you have missed the mark, and must repent. Once more, if you have had an improper divorce—that is a divorce apart from Yeshua's one exception—as a Messianic believer you are to acknowledge your sinful disobedience and rebellion and repent. Turn from that whole way of selfish thinking and behaviors.

Are you also remarried after being improperly divorced? You don't give up that marriage, but you must repent of how you got there. It is like a baby born out of wedlock; you repent of how you sinfully conceived, but not of the baby. No baby is a mistake; they are each a *"gift of the Lord"* (Psalm 127:3). But you must repent of the immorality that led you to having a child out of wedlock. And so it is the same principle regarding an improper remarriage. Repent of the sinful attitudes that led to an improper remarriage, but then live for the Lord in that marriage. Admittedly, you may have been undisciplined in the faith and ignorant of the biblical instruction about marriage, divorce, and remarriage. Understood. But sins of ignorance are still sins and need repentance as well. With true repentance and restoration to the Lord, you can be restored to God's service in your Messianic marriage with greater maturity. Be aware that an unrepentant person cannot be in Messiah's service, let alone a teacher of God's Word.

Yeshua has clearly taught that marriage is permanent. The unbelieving religious leaders would disregard Messiah's instruction. But how do you think His disciples responded?

The unmarried state is a special calling (19:10–12)

Permanence makes unmarried life preferable (19:10)

> *The disciples said to Him, "If the relationship of the man with his wife is like this, it is better not to marry."*

Yeshua's own disciples were shocked at His teaching on the permanence of marriage. Prior to receiving the empowering Holy Spirit in Acts 2, they thought permanent marriage was impossible. From their point of view, adultery was a death sentence, but Yeshua made marriage a life sentence! They realized that being permanently married is mission impossible for the natural man. As natural men, it seemed foolish for them to try,[30] and the unmarried life seemed a better option. Since marriage is so highly regarded in the Scriptures, they may have been hoping that Yeshua would back off from the idea of marital permanence and have a more reasonable position.

---

30. First Corinthians 2:14: *"But a natural man does not accept the things of the Spirit of God, for they are foolishness to him; and he cannot understand them, because they are spiritually appraised."*

Nine • Divorce and Remarriage in the New Covenant

The unmarried life is better, but it's not for everyone (19:11–12)

> *But He said to them, "Not all men can accept this statement, but only those to whom it has been given. For there are eunuchs who were born that way from their mother's womb; and there are eunuchs who were made eunuchs by men; and there are also eunuchs who made themselves eunuchs for the sake of the kingdom of heaven. He who is able to accept this, let him accept it."*

The Messiah may have shocked the disciples even more, for He actually agreed that it is better not to marry! But the unmarried life is not for everyone, "*only those to whom it has been given.*" It is given as a gift—the gift of celibacy, or restraint.[31] The Lord's gift of restraint eliminates the need to marry or be driven to immorality by unchecked desires. Most people have not received such a gift, and so they cannot "*accept this*" either. In this day and age, though a percentage of believers is in one form of unmarried state or another, marriage is the normal status for most people. Marriage is the norm, both for the purposes of God, and for the physical bodies we presently have. The Messianic marriage presently represents God's love to His creation, and keeps us from immoralities.[32] In our resurrected physical bodies this will not be the case, for in the resurrection, there will not be marriage,[33] but more like the eunuch, or celibate state. Do not see this as a defective spiritual life but merely a celibate one. Being a sexual being is not necessary to being a godly person. In fact, with the gift, celibacy is intended to lead to single-minded devotion to the Lord.[34]

Yeshua gives three options for the eunuch state (19:12)

> *"For there are eunuchs who were born that way from their mother's womb; and there are eunuchs who were made eunuchs by men; and there are also eunuchs who made themselves eunuchs for the sake of the kingdom of heaven. He who is able to accept this, let him accept it."*

1. Eunuchs by birth: *"For there are eunuchs who were born that way from their mother's womb."*

A eunuch born that way from their mother's womb is one who cannot have sex. The person who has no sexual desires because he was born that way naturally leads a celibate life.

---

31. In the next chapter on 1 Corinthians 7:7–8, we will explore Paul's teachings on this gift.
32. First Corinthians 7:2.
33. "*For in the resurrection they neither marry nor are given in marriage, but are like angels in heaven*" (Matthew 22:30).
34. First Corinthians 7:32-35.

2. Eunuchs by men: *"And there are eunuchs who were made eunuchs by men."*

In many countries with harems, the men who served around the harem were castrated. All of the harem guards were eunuchs so they would not cheat with the king's wives. Eunuchs (Hebrew: *sarisim*) served in Ahab and Jezebel's Israeli court (2 Kings 9:32). Isaiah prophesied that, as a judgment, Judean men would be taken to Babylon to become eunuchs (2 Kings 20:18; Isaiah 39:7). We read of eunuchs in the Persian court of Queen Esther (Esther 2:15; 4:4–5, etc.). Like all other eunuchs (Deuteronomy 23:1), the Ethiopian eunuch could not enter the temple to have his biblical questions answered. But once more by grace, God promises that the faithful eunuch will have a high status in God's kingdom (Isaiah 56:3–5).

3. Eunuchs by choice: *"And there are also eunuchs who made themselves eunuchs for the sake of the kingdom of heaven."*

What does that mean? It does not mean mutilating yourself; that is improper. This refers to eunuchs who have taken an oath of celibacy. Who has taken this oath? All unmarried people who follow the Lord. Widows that do not remarry, teenagers, and divorced individuals who remain single are to take a vow of celibacy. They are trusting God for His gift of restraint. They thereby "*made themselves eunuchs for the sake of the kingdom of heaven.*" That is, they have made this vow of celibacy so that they may serve the King in undistracted service for His kingdom.

As believers, all unmarried people are called to be celibate. If God later calls them to marriage, then God has changed their calling. We are to live holy unto the Lord in either calling. Look to Messiah, for His grace is your sufficiency. If you abide in Him, you will bear much fruit, and He will give you what you need to live for Him. He can give you the grace you need to remain married or to remain single, and to fulfill your creation calling to live out the image of God.

Some questions to help apply these teachings

1. How often do you think about divorce? Does it lead to further prayer or further alienation from your spouse?

2. How often do you think about adultery (lust in the heart)? Does it lead to repentance or distraction from the Lord? Have you ever threatened divorce? In front of the kids? Have you repented? In front of the kids?

3. Have you divorced on non-biblical grounds? How did you justify it? Have you repented?

Nine • Divorce and Remarriage in the New Covenant

4. Though you were divorced on non-biblical grounds, did you remarry? How did you justify it? Have you repented? Have you improperly married a divorced person? How did you justify it? Have you repented?

5. What is your view on divorce now?

6. How often do you experience hardness of heart toward your spouse?

7. Are you committed to the permanence of marriage? How have you demonstrated this?

8. If you are single, are you committed to celibacy? How have you demonstrated this commitment?

CHAPTER TEN

Faithful Wisdom for the Marriage Condition

1 Corinthians 7

In considering the Messianic marriage matters in 1 Corinthians 7, it is helpful for us to understand its place in the whole letter, for a text out of context becomes a pretext for any subtext. In this first letter to the Corinthians, Paul is seeking to develop the believers in Messiah. The letter is in two parts: chapters 1–6, and chapters 7–16. The theme of chapters 1–6 is noted in 1:11: "*I have been informed concerning you,*" regarding the Messianic witness in our identity. The theme of chapters 7–16 is noted in 7:1: "*Now concerning the things about which you wrote,*" regarding the Messianic wisdom in our liberty. Paul wants the Corinthians to gain wisdom for marriage in Messianic liberty so that they can grow in Yeshua. Their abuse of their liberty had given them a bad reputation. Maturely handling their liberty will provide a godly testimony about Messiah, and Paul begins a discussion of that liberty with Messianic marriage matters.

The immediate context for 1 Corinthians 7 regards the principle of faithfulness for our spiritual unity in Messiah, and how it excludes faithless immorality (1 Corinthians 6:15–20). As the result of this principle, chapter 7 teaches the practice of faithfulness—that is, how our marital unity in Messiah expresses itself in faithful duty.

Chapter 7 itself is broken into two portions: first about the wisdom to remain faithful in our marital condition (7:1–24), and secondly about the wisdom regarding faithfulness on other marital questions (7:25–40). The main principle for 7:1–24 is "*Only, as the Lord has assigned to each one, as God has called each, in this manner let him walk*" (1 Corinthians 7:17, 24). This means that you should live faithfully in your calling by the Lord regardless of the circumstances or condition in which you were saved. As a universal principle, it is first applied to the condition of marriage (7:1–16), and then to the condition of circumcision (7:18–20), and then to the condition of slavery (7:21–24).

Therefore, the questions in this chapter are about how the Corinthians can live faithfully in the married condition. By Paul's answers, it seems that some who raised these concerns found it quite difficult to remain godly while married. Paul's responses assure them that marriage is not their problem, as long as selfishness is not their lifestyle.

The Marriage Condition of Spouses, 2 Corinthians 7:1–16

In this section Paul is treating marriage as a voluntary condition, that is, we're at liberty to enter marriage or not. As in the remainder of this letter, Paul understands our liberty in Messiah as a means to fulfill our calling, not a means to fulfill our comforts, conveniences, or cultural preferences. Those who use their liberty to enter marriage are to see their Messianic marriage as a means to fulfill their divine calling, not as a hindrance to their calling.

The normal marriage condition (7:1–6)

In these six verses, Paul will speak of the marriage condition as a normal aspect of faithful living, but faithfulness assumes selfless duty on the part of both spouses. In each verse Paul presents another marriage principle intended to mature us in faithful living through our marriage relationship.

It's a condition of purity (7:1)

> *Now concerning the things about which you wrote,*
> *it is good for a man not to touch a woman.*

This application of "touching" is already taught in Scripture regarding intimacy as part of the marriage relationship. The reason Paul mentions this at the outset is that there were two groups in the congregation. One was made up of those who were immoral (see 1 Corinthians 6:15–20). The others leaned towards asceticism, believing that all physical pleasures diminished their spirituality. They thought marriage pleasures, etc., were a distracting, if not ungodly, pursuit. The Bible does not teach this. Consensual intimacy in marriage is encouraged in Scripture as a blessing from God.[1]

Part of the condition of purity is "*not to touch a woman.*" Does that mean we cannot hold hands? This does not mean the same thing to all people. When a man touches a woman, they can get excited and distracted. When women have their hands held they feel there is a commitment.[2] There are some who say it does not mean anything, but this would be going too far. There is a measure of commitment when you are publicly holding hands. Be that as it may, "*touch*" as Paul uses it is a Hebrew euphemism for sexual contact.[3] Therefore, the question they raised is really about whether or not it is good for a man to have sexual contact with a woman. As noted above, this question comes from those who think all physical pleasure is contrary to spiritual life.

---

1. See Appendix Six.
2. In a popular song from the early 1980s, Toni Basil sang: "Oh Mickey, what a pity you don't understand; you take me by the heart, when you take me by the hand."
3. Genesis 20:6; Ruth 2:9; Proverbs 6:29.

It's a condition of morality (7:2)

*But because of immoralities, each man is to have his own wife,
and each woman is to have her own husband.*

Both men and women can be sexually immoral. Unless God has gifted them for a celibate life, they will face the pressures and temptations of sexual immorality. Because of the way we are genetically designed, sexually healthy individuals are to have one spouse. This is revealed from the beginning, even before sin: "*For this reason a man shall leave his father and his mother, and be joined to his wife; and they shall become one flesh*" (Genesis 2:24). The Scriptures encourage sexual intimacy in marriage: "*Let your fountain be blessed, and rejoice in the wife of your youth*" (Proverbs 5:18). This is part of being a healthy married person. As you become older, it is not always the same thing for every couple; you need to be mindful of each other's needs and have discussions about these matters. Many people think that Messianic faith is prudish. There may be some denominations that lend themselves to this, but the Bible is not prudish at all; it just limits sex to marriage.

It's a condition of responsibility (7:3)

*The husband must fulfill his duty to his wife,
and likewise also the wife to her husband.*

The point this verse brings out is that people have sexual needs. Your spouse has needs, and you have a responsibility to recognize and address those needs. In some cases, you might be unable to meet those needs. Some people may have physical or other personal problems that prevent them from meeting the needs of their spouse, but those problems do not preclude lovingly addressing those needs. In any case, recognize that the calling in marriage is to have that intimacy with your spouse. Each individual has the same responsibility toward the other. Both are to be caring for the other's personal needs.

This duty comes from Torah. "*When a man takes a new wife, he shall not go out with the army nor be charged with any duty; he shall be free at home one year and shall give happiness to his wife whom he has taken*" (Deuteronomy 24:5). The couple needs to get their marriage life oriented properly. Scripture indicates that this is a duty more important than military duty. For society to be stable, there have to be stable marriages.

The problem in a godless society is tied to the problem of unbiblical marriages and relationships. A lack of intimacy in our relationships leads to alienation in society. That is why it is so important to have wholesome, healthy families and marriages, especially because this is the hope of society. This is how God is going to change our society and restore humanity through our restored Messianic marriages.

A restored marriage is going to be intimate as a responsibility of love towards each other. It is a responsibility and mutual duty towards each other.[4]

It's a condition of authority (7:4)

The wife does not have authority over her own body, but the husband does; and likewise also the husband does not have authority over his own body, but the wife does.

This means we are not to resist each other. We are to be submitted to one another in love. In Ephesians chapter 5, we saw this in a different light. There we saw that the woman is to submit to the husband's spiritual authority, while the husband is to be sacrificial for his wife's spiritual growth. However, in this instance, the submission applies to intimacy in the marriage relationship. This means excuses are not to be used to avoid being intimate. Why? Because by making untrue excuses, you are lying to the Holy Spirit and resisting God, who called you to such a marital responsibility. It is your marital calling from God, and when you resist your calling you are actually rebelling against God. Therefore, you not only have to apologize to your spouse, but repent to your Lord about this matter.

This is a growing responsibility we have towards our spouse as we grow together in the Lord. In today's autonomous society, men and women assume control of their own bodies, and no one, including God, has the right to tell them what to do with their own bodies. Because the Corinthians understood their freedom in Messiah, those who were immoral were saying, "Anything goes." Paul quotes the Corinthians: "*Food is for the stomach and the stomach is for food, but God will do away with both of them*" (1 Corinthians 6:13). This statement refers to having an open sex life. They thought, "It has nothing to do with the spiritual life, it is just a physical thing—just like eating. My stomach is for food and food is for my stomach. No big deal." Notice how Paul responds: "*But God will do away with both of them.*" Scripture addresses this idolatry of autonomy: "*Yet the body is not for immorality, but for the Lord, and the Lord is for the body*" (1 Corinthians 6:13). When you think that you have the right to have such libertine ideas, you are unaware of the bad habits you are developing and the bondage you will be putting yourself into. The body is not for immorality, but for the Lord, and the Lord is for the body. Understand that your body is God's business, not just your responsibility. You belong to the Lord, but He has given your body to your spouse. It is not for your personal pleasure but for your marital responsibility. This is why Paul concludes the whole section on immorality with the fact that you have been bought with a price. You are not your own. "*Or do you not know that your body is a temple of the Holy Spirit who is in you, whom you have from God, and that you*

---

4. For more on sex for older married couples, refer to Michael Castleman, "The Real Sex Lives of Men Over 65," March 31, 2017, *Psychology Today*, psychologytoday.com.

are not your own? For you have been bought with a price: therefore glorify God in your body" (1 Corinthians 6:19–20). And this exhortation leads directly into this chapter on marriage.

Glorifying God in our bodies brings us to the marriage relationship, where your body has actually been delegated to someone besides yourself—to your spouse in the intimacy of the marriage relationship. The marriage condition is one of released authority regarding your own body.

To the questioning ascetics (people who thought that physical pleasures were tainted, improper, and should not be performed by godly people), Paul tells them to "*stop depriving one another*." In other words, stop using spiritual life as an excuse not to have intimacy with your spouse. God has called us in the marriage relationship to testify of His faithfulness, that He will not withhold any good thing from us. How dare we withhold anything from our spouse! We have to understand that the way Scripture looks at marriage may be very different from anything you have been told or seen in your family or in the media.

It's a condition of maturity (7:5)

> *Stop depriving one another, except by agreement for a time, so that you may devote yourselves to prayer, and come together again so that Satan will not tempt you because of your lack of self-control.*

Scripture tells us to "*stop depriving one another*," but then gives an exception: "*except by agreement for a time*." The reason for this is so both spouses can reorient themselves around the Lord as they devote themselves to prayer. They are then to come back together, so "*Satan will not tempt you because of your lack of self-control*." This time of separation is permitted, if it is by mutual agreement—and only for a limited time, after which there is a reunion for the couple. This indicates that at times, couples need prayer and fasting for which, by agreement, you would abstain from sexual intimacy. This was normal in the Tanakh. When we came to Mt. Sinai, the people were told to fast from sexual intimacy in order to prepare themselves for God.[5] Paul is referring to this sort of spiritual and personal consecration to God. Such a set-aside time reflects marital maturity on these issues.[6]

---

5. Exodus 19:15: "*He said to the people, 'Be ready for the third day; do not go near a woman.'*" Also see 1 Samuel 21:4; Joel 2:16; Zechariah 7:3.
6. Since there is a time permitted for separation in a marriage, this can be applied to periods of hostility in the marriage when we need to be counseled, by agreement of both parties, and separated for a time, in order that there may be a reorientation around the Lord. When there is estrangement going on in the marriage, it is because of an alienation from God. The two are not walking with the Lord together, and it becomes necessary for them to reorient themselves through counseling.

It's a condition of leniency (7:6)

> *But this I say by way of concession, not of command.*

This is a "*concession*" to be used if needed. Therefore, we are to have leniency and compassion towards each other if there is a need for a separation for prayer and fasting. In other words, it is not to be used as an excuse to live apart, take separate vacations, or create other unnecessary absences from the marriage relationship.

The unnecessary marriage condition (7:7–9)

In this paragraph, Paul describes the marriage condition as unnecessary, as long as there is sexual self-discipline among both men and women.

Being unmarried is a spiritual gift (7:7)

> *Yet I wish that all men were even as I myself am. However, each man has his own gift from God, one in this manner, and another in that.*

Paul identifies himself with the unmarried; therefore, he has a gift of celibacy. Being unmarried is a spiritual gift. All unmarried people should pray that they have this gift from God. Why? The spiritual calling of God requires the spiritual gifts of God. The gifts of the Holy Spirit enable you to fulfill the calling that God has for you, single or married. You cannot fulfill your calling without God's gifts through the Holy Spirit.[7] Those gifts are His enablement and empowerment for the work He has called you to accomplish. Therefore, if you are going to get married, both are to trust that He has enabled them both for the marriage calling. If are you called to remain single, then trust you have been gifted in that regard.

These gifts are a grace from God, exercised as we are filled with the Spirit.[8] We all have God's grace in different aspects, but need to understand it from this point of view.

Being unmarried is a singular good (7:8)

> *But I say to the unmarried and to widows that it is good for them if they remain even as I.*

When you study through this chapter, you see that the "*unmarried*" are not just virgins or widows. Paul uses the term for those who were married but are not presently married because of divorce, separation, etc. These people living the single life he encourages by saying that "*it is good for them if they remain even as I.*" "*Unmarried*" contrasts with the married (1 Corinthians 7:32–33; 4 Maccabees 16:9), the widows (7:8), and the virgins (7:34). Thus, "*unmarried*" refers to the

---

7. For further study on the gifts of the Spirit, see the author's instruction on 1 Corinthians 12–14 at https://vimeo.com/180946149.
8. For the Spirit-filled life, refer above to the study on Ephesians 5:18–33.

divorced (7:11). The unmarried (7:8) by reason of divorce (7:11) may not remarry any other person (7:11–12), but the widow may marry (7:39), or the virgin (7:34).

We may deduce that Paul was a widower or divorced. He is evidently unmarried,[9] though it would have been unseemly if not impossible for Paul to be an unmarried rabbi in traditional Judaism. Paul's wife may have left him when he came to faith. In any case, the issue is that being unmarried is a good thing in the sight of God, not a bad thing. It is certainly a good state to be in if you are gifted for it, even though there may be social or family pressure put on the individual to be married.

Single people can find themselves under this extreme pressure, as if there were something wrong with them. This pressure can cause those with the gift and enablement to be single to instead get married. They may actually diminish their calling by being married, and now they must ask the Lord for gifts for a marriage calling. This may happen because you are divided in your interests between pleasing the Lord and pleasing your family.

What should we do with this teaching? Share it with your children. "*Train up a child in the way he should go,*"[10] which is not always marriage. Do not let them think that you will guilt trip them or pressure them to get married. Let them know that being single is a calling. Of course, while they are single, they are to be celibate. This is a good thing, so don't make it a bad thing.

Singles are not less blessed than married people, for all blessings are in Messiah.[11] We should therefore appreciate Paul's point, and in our teaching, we should make certain we are focusing on the same godly values.

Can one lead in a congregation as a single person? Though the norm is married leaders,[12] we must remember that Yeshua, Paul, Timothy, and Barnabas were all unmarried. The maturity for Messiah's service is not limited to those who are married. Though marriage is a norm in most societies, being single is "good" in the Lord.

Being unmarried must be self-governed (7:9)

> *But if they do not have self-control, let them marry;*
> *for it is better to marry than to burn with passion.*

People should marry young so that they can grow up together and be faithful. In our society today, children are given sexual outlets that are ungodly and improper. Internet porn is a plague upon the nation. Because hormones are raging, teens

---

9. First Corinthians 9:5.
10. Proverbs 22:6.
11. Ephesians 1:3.
12. "*If a man does not know how to manage his own household, how will he take care of the Assembly of God?*" (1 Timothy 3:5 SN).

may think these improper and immoral outlets are natural. No, the proper outlet provided by God is marriage. Children should be trained in the truth that being single is fine, but only if you have self-control. Otherwise, you need to be looking for a spouse and praying for one, seeking God's guidance in that regard.

Self-control,[13] or self-governing, as the Greek word is used elsewhere, is a prerequisite for godliness,[14] spiritual leadership,[15] and is an expression of God's character as a fruit of the Spirit.[16] Scripture tells us that the fruit of the Spirit is love, joy, peace, patience, kindness, goodness, faithfulness, gentleness, and self-control. Self-control is a fruit, not the root, of the Spirit. The root of the Spirit is faith in Yeshua, and we are to abide in Messiah, casting our cares on Him and depending on Him. The consequence, by-product, or result of that faith is the fruit of the Spirit that you will produce for whatever the circumstance, as the Spirit may lead.

Whatever you are experiencing, God has the enablement for you to live a godly and faithful life if you will only look to Yeshua and trust in Him. Self-control is not only a gift but it's also a fruit. If you think you do not have the gift of singleness in the time before the Lord provides you with a spouse, you need to ask the Lord to help you develop the fruit of self-control. Otherwise, you will be living an unfaithful life, which can lead to bad habits and encumbrances, not just a sinful lifestyle.

Scripture tells us that every athlete who competes exercises self-control.[17] Competitive swimmers shave every hair from their bodies in order to remove every encumbrance. Athletes demonstrate self-control in every aspect of nourishment, rest, and activity. All Messianic believers must likewise exercise self-control in order to be faithful to the calling God has given, whether single or married.

There are marriages where husbands and/or wives do not have self-control, and because of this they are undisciplined and either impatient or unfocused on the Lord. They may actually find immoral outlets in order to fulfill their lusts. This is totally wrong and requires repentance and a recommitment to the Lord.

Godly habits need to be developed, and over time will be developed if you look to the Lord and follow Him. If you do not, then you likely already have bad habits. Lack of self-control is a problem regardless of whether you are single or married. You need to develop the fruit of the Spirit, that you might actually be a faithful person, regardless of your calling.

---

13. Self-control (*egkrateuomai*) is needed in various circumstances of life. Paul uses it in the area of athletics (1 Corinthians 9:25) as an illustration of the spiritual life, as well as for marriage.
14. Second Peter 1:6.
15. Titus 1:8.
16. Galatians 5:23.
17. First Corinthians 9:25.

The abnormal marriage condition (7:10–16)

Now that Paul has addressed the marriage condition as normal (7:1–6), yet unnecessary (7:7–9), he now addresses the abnormal marriage condition of seeking divorce (7:10–16). Though divorce may have become normalized in our spiritually wayward society, it is abnormal in the sight of God and should be such in the eyes of every Messianic believer. God hates divorce (Malachi 2:16), and it is contrary to His intention for humanity.

It's abnormal to divorce a believing spouse (7:10–11)

No one should leave their spouse (7:10)

> *But to the married I give instructions, not I, but the Lord, that the wife should not leave her husband.*

The instructions Paul provides, he says, are from the Lord. Yeshua taught on this subject in chapters 5 and 19 of Matthew.[18] Here Paul is reiterating and applying Yeshua's instructions to the Corinthians' concerns. These are instructions specifically for those already in a married condition. Paul states that the wife (or husband) "*should not leave*" their spouse. It is not a command—"must not leave"—but it is written as a very strong exhortation not to leave. Why is that? Marriage is by consent. And though it is not God's will that there be divorce, there may be extenuating circumstances that make the marriage unhealthy for the wife or husband.[19] This is said without endorsing a divorce for anything but the exceptional grounds that Messiah permitted.[20]

But if you do leave (7:11)

> *(But if she does leave, she must remain unmarried, or else be reconciled to her husband), and that the husband should not divorce his wife.*

If a believing wife or husband does leave their spouse, their options are extremely limited. The one who leaves the marriage (i.e., initiates the divorce) must remain unmarried. They cannot remarry anyone else. They are going to have to remain single for life. That is their option, because divorce and remarriage is not God's will. Yeshua says that the initiator of divorce who remarries another person is committing adultery.[21] It is quite possible that if people didn't think they could just simply remarry the next best person who came along, they might learn how to work out their relationship with their present spouse. They may foolishly think there is opportunity through divorce to improve their marital options—perhaps

---

18. Also in Mark 10.
19. It could be forms of emotional or psychological abuse of various degrees, etc.
20. "*Immorality*," that is, unrepentant infidelity (Matthew 5:32 and Matthew 19:9).
21. Matthew 5:32 and 19:9.

finding someone a little younger, richer, more spiritual, etc. But in so doing, they are further spiritually destabilizing themselves. They are part of the problem, further destabilizing society. So, if the believer understands that divorce is not God's will but still refuses to stay married, then his or her first option is to not remarry, but remain single for life.[22]

There is a second option, and that is to "*be reconciled to*" the spouse. As long as there has not been a remarriage, this is a viable possibility. Perhaps during the time of separation from each other, she or he could clear their heads, reorient spiritually to think straight and understand God's will for their lives, and repent. They can reconcile with their spouse. This is a form of repentance that God will bless.

These are the only two options provided in the Scriptures for a believer who initiates a divorce from their spouse.

It's abnormal to divorce an unbelieving spouse (7:12–16)

The problem of leaving a marriage to a believer has been addressed from the teaching of Yeshua. But now the question arises: What about if you're married to an unbeliever? Is divorce permitted in that situation?

It is normal to stay with them (7:12–13)

> *But to the rest I say, not the Lord, that if any brother has a wife who is an unbeliever, and she consents to live with him, he must not divorce her. And a woman who has an unbelieving husband, and he consents to live with her, she must not send her husband away.*

Paul is giving his authoritative apostolic counsel on a matter that Yeshua did not address. In Jewish societies, there were no believers marrying unbelievers, since all Jews were considered believers by the traditional Jewish community. If you married a pagan, you were outside of Jewish society, and your marriage was not considered a marriage by the Jewish community. One who married a pagan did so to leave the Jewish community and its biblical basis on marriage.[23] This is why Yeshua never taught on this subject.

However, once Paul proclaimed the Good News to the non-Jewish communities of Asia, Asia Minor, and Europe, the issues of marriage and morality were entirely different than what was the norm in the Jewish communities.[24] Once people came to faith in Messiah, they would be instructed to marry only a believer,

---

22. There is the vague possibility that after the death of their ex-spouse, they could remarry, if they attempted to reconcile earlier. That and many other matters in these difficult situations would be left up to the congregation's leadership to judge.
23. Though, as studied in Matthew 5:31–32 and 19:3–9, it was misinterpreted by tradition.
24. In 1 Corinthians 5:1, Paul had to rebuke a believing elder who was sleeping with his step-mother!

since the Scriptures forbid marrying an unbeliever.[25] But many people coming to faith who were already married now found themselves married to an unbelieving spouse. Their questions to Paul on the subject may have reflected their concern that their spouse would now be an encumbrance to their spiritual walk, or that being married to an unbeliever may be displeasing to the Lord.[26] As for all Messianic believers considering marriage, they should pray for a spouse who will spiritually encourage them, pray with them, help raise their children in the Lord, and have a home that will glorify Yeshua. In this situation, these new believers needed to be told what to do with their unbelieving spouse.

They were not to initiate a divorce from their unbelieving spouse, as long as the unbelieving spouse consented to remain. Since it is abnormal to divorce and is normal to stay together, they were to remain in the condition in which they were called (7:17). The believing spouse will of course differ on many matters of life, but that is not a biblical cause for initiating divorce. Once more, to desire divorce without biblical grounds, you are being self-serving and spiritually rebellious to God. Marriages that are not the best of marriages are still better for the kids than a divorced home. Don't fool yourself. You need to obey God's Word, for even in this married condition, His grace is still your sufficiency to fulfill your calling and your life. As elsewhere,[27] when you are married to someone who is "*disobedient to the Word*" (1 Peter 3:1)—and a non-believing spouse is that—you still have a calling to fulfill, as Paul is about to point out.

It is normal to sanctify them (7:14)

> *For the unbelieving husband is sanctified through his wife, and the unbelieving wife is sanctified through her believing husband; for otherwise your children are unclean, but now they are holy.*

This verse does not mean that when a believer marries an unbeliever, the unbeliever is automatically saved. The word *sanctified* means "set apart," or placed in a sphere of influence produced by the presence of the Spirit-filled spouse. This is not the perfect sanctification that all believers in Messiah receive upon faith in Him.[28] Instead, the unbelieving spouse has an opportunity to see the sanctified life in the daily life of their believing spouse.[29] Though they are still unbelievers,

---

25. Second Corinthians 6:14, etc.
26. We find the problem of intermarriage in Ezra 10 and Nehemiah 13 among the returnees to Judah, and we see the counsel to put away their pagan wives. In those cases, they were believers that broke Torah and married pagan wives and were not raising their children in the biblical faith (as implied by Nehemiah 13:23–24). Paul's counsel differs from Ezra and Nehemiah's since Paul was not in Judea with Jewish returnees that had broken Torah and married outside the faith. Paul counseled those who were already married to unbelievers and were subsequently saved.
27. Review the study on 1 Peter 3:1–7.
28. Hebrews 10:14.
29. First Peter 3:1–3.

they are under the influence of godliness. The children are likewise set apart and have an opportunity to be raised in godliness and then be perfectly set apart by coming to personal faith in Yeshua.

This is the marital calling for the spouse who now believes in Yeshua the Messiah. If your spouse is disobedient to the Word, you must not divorce. Instead, you are fulfilling your unexpected marriage calling.

And if the non-believer leaves? (7:15)

> *Yet if the unbelieving one leaves, let him leave; the brother or the sister is not under bondage in such cases, but God has called us to peace.*

What this means is that if the unbelieving spouse wants to initiate divorce, then the believer is to permit the unbeliever to leave the marriage (and the home). In this instance, the believing spouse "*is not under bondage*"—that is, marriage is not a slave condition, but a consensual relationship. Neither the believer nor the unbeliever is bound to remain married. The believer is not to initiate the divorce. But the unbeliever, who is by definition disobedient to the Word, would not be bound to biblical teaching without faith in its Author. The believing spouse is not to fight the unbeliever's departure from the marriage, because marriage is by consent. If you merely manipulate your unbelieving spouse to get them to stay married to you, you are actually voiding the entire concept of consensual marriage, and you are disobedient to the Word.[30]

If the believer does not initiate the divorce but is a victim of the divorce, he or she is not in bondage and is therefore free in the same way that the believing widow is free and not "*bound.*"[31] You must have clear understanding of who initiated the divorce and who is the victim.

It is normal to save them (7:16)

> *For how do you know, O wife, whether you will save your husband? Or how do you know, O husband, whether you will save your wife?*

Paul puts a fine point on why the believing spouse should not divorce the unbelieving spouse: you may be God's providential means for the unbeliever's salvation. If you are married to an unbeliever, then you are a "missionary" reaching out in love to the lost. Your calling from God is to be a sanctifying influence for the sake of the Good News so that, hopefully, that unbelieving spouse will come to faith. That is the desire of the faithful heart, which will minister accordingly. The believing spouse is to be praying constantly for the unbelieving spouse, desiring their salvation and being very patient.

---

30. First Peter 3:1–7.
31. First Corinthians 7:39–40.

The believer who divorces their unbelieving spouse is to either remain single or be reunited with them. However, if the unbeliever divorces the believer, the believer is not bound in this matter. As you study this, you will see that if you are married to an unbeliever, the normal thing is to seek their salvation, not divorce. If they are believers who are disobedient to the Word and not walking with the Lord, the normal thing is to seek to restore them in the faith.[32]

The Principle of the Marriage Condition, 1 Corinthians 7:17–24 (SN)

Only, as the Lord has assigned to each one, as God has called each, in this manner let him walk. And so I direct in all the assemblies.

Paul says, "*As the Lord has assigned to each one*," meaning, if you are single you should remain single (pray to be gifted for this, or pray to develop the fruit of self-control). If you are not gifted for singleness and you know it, then you may certainly marry. This is why the next three verses (18–20) teach us that Gentile believers are not to get circumcised. Circumcision is the unchangeable Jewish condition that is limited to those with a Jewish parent. This restriction is not upon the Gentile believer because they already have all they need in the Messiah. The circumcision of the heart is all that is required of a Gentile believer to be part of the Messianic community. The reason that Jewish believing boys still need to become circumcised has to do with their testimony to God's faithfulness in Yeshua. Both Jewish and Gentile believers are already fully complete in the Messiah by faith in Him, but the testimony that Yeshua is God's fulfillment of the promises to the Jewish people is why Paul circumcised Timothy in Acts 16:1–3. Yeshua completes the Jewish testimony, of which circumcision is one part.

The same principle applies to the changeable miserable condition of the slave in 7:21–24. God's grace is sufficient for anyone to fulfill their divine calling of living out the image of God and representing Him in the world, even in a miserable slave status. If one can gain freedom, that is better, but they remain Yeshua's servant even in their freed status, just as they remain Yeshua's freed person in their slave status.

Whatever your circumstance, you are complete in Messiah and your social condition is not your personal fulfillment or failure, but your spiritual opportunity in Yeshua. Marriage is not for your personal fulfillment. It is a ministry. Your fulfillment is that you live for the Lord in your marriage ministry, or single state, as also in every other area of life, if utilized for Messiah and the Good News.

---

32. Galatians 6:1.

Marriage Wisdom: Weighing Your Options, 1 Corinthians 7:25–40

Now concerning virgins I have no command of the Lord, but I give an opinion as one who by the mercy of the Lord is trustworthy....

"*Now concerning*" refers to other marriage-related matters the Corinthians asked Paul about, which he includes as an addendum on the topic of virgins and widows.

Paul's wise advice for virgins (7:25–38)

Yeshua gave no specific teaching on virgins, at least not regarding what the Corinthians were asking Paul. Since these are matters that call for wisdom, Paul will give his trustworthy opinion[33] (7:25). An apostolic opinion is helpful in secondary matters of faith, where the outcome might be a judgment call by anyone.[34]

Wisdom in distressing times (7:25–28)

Distressing times can result from economic downturns, catastrophic disasters, or just being overwhelmed by life.[35] In 7:27, Paul reapplies the principle of remaining in the condition in which you were called. During distressful times, don't seek (note the imperative) divorce, even if there are grounds. If able to be single and pure, don't seek (imperative again) marriage. Wait until life stabilizes. In premarital counseling, we assess whether or not the couple has stability before getting married—emotional stability, financial stability,[36] etc.[37] If not, wait until you can stabilize your lives before changing your status. Marriages are difficult enough without trying to build them upon an unstable foundation.

Wisdom in shortened times (7:29–31)

Paul says, "*The time has been shortened*," for we are living in the "*last days*,"[38] and the Lord's return could be at any time. Paul counsels young people to reprioritize their understanding about life. Marriage is part of the form of this world; a "marriage made in heaven" doesn't carry over to heaven. Since we live for His return and have a priority of the Good News, rethink the matters of marriage. As your marriage can serve His Good News and His return, it may thereby have a last-days purpose. Rethink your priorities, for "*those who use the world*" should be "*as though they did not make full use of it; for the form of this world is passing away*" (1 Corinthians 7:31). We need to be living to leave.

---

33. The Greek word for "opinion" (*gnome*) refers to giving a judgment on matters (1 Corinthians 1:10), that is, a thought-through decision, as in Acts 20:3. Elsewhere it is translated "purpose" (Revelation 17:13, 17).
34. For a fuller discussion on primary and secondary matters, refer to the author's book *Developing Healthy Messianic Congregations*, pp. 42–48.
35. Psalm 25:17; Proverbs 17:17; Zephaniah 1:15; Matthew 18:7; Luke 21:23.
36. Proverbs 24:27: "*Prepare your work outside and make it ready for yourself in the field; afterwards, then, build your house.*"
37. On finances in general, refer to the author's book *Messianic Wisdom*, pp. 175–186.
38. Acts 2:17; 2 Timothy 3:1; James 5:3; 2 Peter 3:3.

Ten • *Faithful Wisdom for the Marriage Condition*

Wisdom for devoted times (7:32–35)

Paul's concern for those who seek marriage is for their victorious life in the Lord. Marriage necessarily divides our focus from undivided devotion to the Lord to caring for our spouse as well. Couples must spend alone time together and build their relationship with each other to continue to grow in the Lord. But be ready for a new reprioritizing to live as a spouse for God through the Messianic marriage. It's hard enough to be single-minded when single; as a married person, the couple must be single-minded together!

Wisdom in aging times (7:36–38)

"*Past her youth*" (v. 36) would be someone past their prime.[39] The final phrase of verse 36 is the command:[40] "*Let her* [them] *marry!*" and do not be distressed regarding the matter (v. 37). If engaged, don't forestall too long. Make up your mind to marry, or not. If you're the father, don't keep your child from marrying. Consider her needs in the matter, not yours. But if there is no proper man for her to marry, you may hold your ground. Be convinced in your own mind. Verse 38 tells us that being married or single is a choice between what is good and what is better!

Wise advice for widows (7:39–40)

If a believing widow or widower desires to remarry, that is permitted, but they must only marry a Messianic believer, so the union is "*only in the Lord.*" Marriage is "until death do us part." Marriage is optional; whom you marry is not. Loneliness can be a great incentive to fill one's empty days with a marriage companion. Understood. But pray for God's person for you, for he or she must be a believer in Messiah.

The widow or widower is happier remaining single. This is Paul's mature opinion, as the *Ruach* (Spirit) is inclining his considerations for the spiritual welfare of the individual. Paul is an apostle of Messiah; his command is God's command on primary matters;[41] his advice is God's advice on secondary matters. So, you're complete in Messiah, single or married!

---

39. "Prime" (*huperakmos*) literally means "beyond the bloom, overripe."
40. It is in the imperative present plural form (*gameitosan*).
41. First Corinthians 14:37.

Some questions to help apply these teachings

1. Have you repented of premarital sex? Have you apologized to the partner involved?

2. Does your spouse understand your needs for intimacy? Do you understand your spouse's need for intimacy? Have you surrendered your body to your spouse's authority? Has your spouse surrendered to you?

3. How often have you neglected the duty of intimacy? Are there certain occasions that cause you to resist this duty?

4. How often do you find yourself depriving your spouse of intimacy? How often are you deprived? Have you prayed together about this?

5. Have you taken opportunity for devoting yourself and reorienting yourself around the Lord? Has your spouse? Has it been by mutual agreement?

6. Are there times that you lack self-control? And for your spouse as well? What do you do at those times to seek His help?

7. Have you repented of thoughts of, desires for, and past divorce?

8. Please take the time to pray that you will stay, sanctify, and (if need be) even save your spouse.

Remember your Messianic married condition is not your fulfillment, but rather, it is your spiritual opportunity for wholehearted service and dynamic testimony.

Ten • Faithful Wisdom for the Marriage Condition

APPENDICES

APPENDIX ONE

The Order of Human Creation

Genesis 1:1–25: the creation of the universe in anticipation of humanity (1:1, a summary statement).

Genesis 1:26: the proposal for humanity.

Genesis 2:2–22: the creation of male (2:7) and female (2:18–22). The third day: vegetation, reiterated in 2:5–6. The first command is 2:16. The creation of land animals on the sixth day, referred to in 2:19.

Genesis 1:27: summary result of the creation of humanity.

Genesis 2:23–25: the ordained relationship of the man and woman.

Genesis 1:28–29: the provision and purpose for humanity. The five further commands in 1:28 detail humanity's calling to rule creation as God's representative.

Genesis 2:1–3: the seventh-day Shabbat at the completion of human creation for fellowship of God and humanity.

Genesis 3:1: that first Sabbath? There is no notice in Genesis 2 that the seventh day ended.

APPENDIX TWO

The Provisions of the Edenic Covenant: Genesis 1:26–2:25; Hosea 6:7

First, man is created in God's image, 1:26.

Second, man is created in God's likeness, 1:26.

Third, God blesses humanity, 1:28.

Fourth, man is to be fruitful, 1:28.

Fifth, man is to multiply, 1:28.

Sixth, man is to fill the earth, 1:28.

Seventh, man is to subdue the earth, 1:28.

Eighth, man is to rule over the earth, 1:28.

Ninth, man's diet is vegan, 1:29–30; 2:16.

Tenth, man works in the garden, 2:15.

Eleventh, man is forbidden to eat of one tree, 2:17.

Twelfth, penalty for disobedience is death, 2:17.

Thirteenth, man names the animals, 2:19–21.

Fourteenth, man is to lead a unified home, 2:22–25.

APPENDIX THREE

Birthright

The rights of the firstborn (Deuteronomy 21:17), the birthright of honored leadership, priestly service in the family, and double portion of inheritance, can be changed.

The birthright can be sold, as with Esau selling his birthright to Jacob for a bowl of beans (Genesis 25:33–34). The birthright can be lost, as with Reuben, who lost his birthright to Joseph (1 Chronicles 5:1–2).

Prior to the giving of the Torah (Deuteronomy 21:15 –17), the birthright can be sovereignly determined by the father, as Jacob does by putting the younger Ephraim before the older Manasseh (Genesis 48:14–20; affirmed by God in Jeremiah 31:9). God sovereignly makes Israel His firstborn among the nations (Exodus 4:22–23).

Humanity's birthright as God's representative and ruler over the world was lost as well. It was apparently lost to Satan, who seems to vaunt the matter (Matthew 4:8). This enemy is therefore called *"the ruler of this world"* (John 12:31; 14:30; 16:11), *"the prince of the power of the air"* (Ephesians 2:2), and even *"the god of this world"* (2 Corinthians 4:4; not because he is actually god, but that he is worshipped by those in the world as their god: Isaiah 14:9–15; 1 Corinthians 10:20; 2 Thessalonians 2:4; Revelation 13:8, 12, 15; 14:9–11; 16:2), and so *"the whole world lies in the power of the evil one"* (1 John 5:19).

So God did by making the Levites the priestly tribe in exchange for the firstborn in each family (Numbers 3:12–50).

God did this also in making the greater Son of David *"My firstborn, the highest of the kings of the earth"* (Psalm 89:27).

So the Messiah, as the Firstborn over all authority, is seen as the goal of humanity, and so we're conformed to the image of the Son (not the Father, Romans 8:29: *"...conformed to the image of His Son, so that He would be the firstborn among many brethren"*). As to our eternal hope, not even death removes what we have in the Messiah, since He is also head of the body—the Assembly—*"and He is the beginning, the firstborn from the dead, so that He Himself will come to have first place in everything"* (Colossians 1:18; Revelation 1:5). Yeshua will receive glory from the angels at His second coming: *"And when He again brings the firstborn into the world, He says, 'And let all the angels of*

God worship him" (Hebrews 1:6). To His honor, heaven will declare that all the redeemed are the *"general assembly and congregation of the firstborn who are enrolled in heaven"* (Hebrews 12:23 SN).

As the Firstborn, He is over all creation, which regains the lost estate of Adam and Eve on behalf of all humanity: *"He is the image of the invisible God, the firstborn of all creation"* (Colossians 1:15). Through His incarnation, He defeated Satan in the very tests where humanity was tested and failed in the garden (Genesis 3:1–6). By His resurrection from the dead, Yeshua removed the chief tools of Satan, the fear of death, by which the devil enslaved humanity to do his evil will (Hebrews 2:14–15; Soncino Zohar, Bereshith, Section 1, page 113b–114a). But, praise the Lord, *"The Son of God appeared for this purpose, to destroy the works of the devil"* (1 John 3:8). In Messiah, the Firstborn, we are freed from the fear of death, the bondage of the enemy, and the judgment upon all those who follow *"the father of lies"* (John 8:44). And now, praise the Lord, we are, in Messiah, inheritors of the kingdom (Jeremiah 3:19; Matthew 25:34; Luke 6:20; 12:32; Acts 1:6; 2 Thessalonians 1:5; Hebrews 12:28; James 2:5; 2 Peter 1:11; Revelation 1:6), and so *"the humble will inherit the land!"* (Psalm 37:11; Matthew 5:5; Romans 4:13).

APPENDIX FOUR

Comparisons between Adam and Messiah

Biblically, Adam is a picture of sinful failure: Job 31:33: *"Have I covered my transgressions like Adam, by hiding my iniquity in my bosom."* Hosea 6:7: *"But like Adam they have transgressed the covenant; there they have dealt treacherously against Me."*

Like a photo's negative is the opposite of the positive picture, so Adam is a negative, of which Messiah is the positive, for Messiah was victorious over sin for our sake.

Adam negatively pictures that the positive gracious impact of Messiah is universal: In Romans, Adam *"is a type of Him who was to come"* (Romans 5:14). Romans 5:15 (SN): *"But the free gift is not like the transgression. For if by the transgression of the one the many died, much more did the grace of God and the gift by the grace of the one Man, Yeshua the Messiah, abound to the many!"* As Adam impacted all humanity, so Messiah's work impacted all humanity. Where Adam's impact was his sin that ruined humanity, the Messiah's impact is His righteousness that redeems humanity.

Adam negatively pictured the positive hopeful instrumentality of Messiah. The same comparison is made in 1 Corinthians 15:20–22 (SN): *"Now Messiah has been raised from the dead, the first fruits of those who are asleep. For since by a man came death, by a man also came the resurrection of the dead. For as in Adam all die, so also in Messiah all will be made alive."*

Adam negatively pictures the positive, heavenly image of Messiah, for on a more positive note, as to resurrection life, we have 1 Corinthians 15:42–49: *"So also is the resurrection of the dead. It is sown a perishable body, it is raised an imperishable body; it is sown in dishonor, it is raised in glory; it is sown in weakness, it is raised in power; it is sown a natural body, it is raised a spiritual body. If there is a natural body, there is also a spiritual body. So also it is written, 'The first man, Adam, became a living soul.' The last Adam became a life-giving spirit. However, the spiritual is not first, but the natural; then the spiritual. The first man is from the earth, earthy; the second man is from heaven. As is the earthy, so also are those who are earthy; and as is the heavenly, so also are those who are heavenly. Just as we have borne the image of the earthy, we will also bear the image of the heavenly."*

Adam's pre-sin innocence pictures Messiah our righteousness, whose purpose was not to be merely a singular servant, but who knew that His death would produce much fruit. John 12:24: *"Truly, truly, I say to you, unless a grain of wheat falls into the earth and dies, it remains alone; but if it dies, it bears much fruit."* 1 Corinthians 15:36: *"You fool! That which you sow does not come to life unless it dies."*

As Adam would bring forth life from his side (Eve in Hebrew is *Chavah*, or "life"), so too out from Messiah's side, His death would bring forth life. John 19:34: *"But one of the soldiers pierced His side with a spear, and immediately blood and water came out."* (This *"blood and water"* reflects on another typical picture in Scripture. Pictured in Torah, leprosy was cleansed by blood and water (Leviticus 14:52). First John 5:6 (SN): *"This is the One who came by water and blood, Yeshua the Messiah; not with the water only, but with the water and with the blood. And the Spirit bears witness, because the Spirit is the truth."*

This comparison of Adam's negative to Messiah's positive is also recognized in the rabbinical writings:

Midrash Rabbah Genesis 12:6. "R. Berekiah said in the name of R. Samuel b. Nahman: Though these things were created in their fulness, yet when Adam sinned they were spoiled, and they will not again return to their perfection until the son of Perez [viz. Messiah] comes."

Midrash Rabbah Exodus 30:3. "When God created His world, there was no Angel of Death in the world, and on this account is (*toledoth*) spelt fully; but as soon as Adam and Eve sinned, God made defective all the 'toledoth' mentioned in the Bible. But when Perez arose, his 'generations' were spelt fully again, because from him Messiah would arise, and in his days God would cause death to be swallowed up, as it says, He will swallow up death for ever (Isaiah 25:8)."

Midrash Rabbah Leviticus 15:1. "The King-Messiah will not come until all the souls which it was originally the divine intention to create shall have come to an end, namely, those spoken of in the book of Adam, the first man, of which it is said, This is the book of the generation of Adam (Genesis. V, 1)." (Also found in Midrash Rabbah Ecclesiastes 1:12).

Midrash Rabbah Number 13:12. "Six, corresponding to the six things which were taken from Adam and which are to be restored through the son of Nahshon, that is, the Messiah. The following are the things that were taken from Adam: His lustre, his life [immortality], his stature, the fruit of the earth, the fruit of the tree, and the lights."

Soncino Zohar, Bereshith, Section 1, Page 113b–114a. "R. Simeon then wept and said: 'Woe to the world which has been lured after this one. For from the day that the evil serpent, having enticed Adam, obtained dominion over man and over the world, he has ever been at work seducing people from the right path, nor will the world cease to suffer from his machinations until the Messiah shall come, when the Holy One will raise to life those who sleep in the dust in accordance with the verse, "He will swallow up death for ever, etc." (Is. XXV, 8), and the verse, "And I will cause the unclean spirit to pass out of the land" (Zech. XIII, 2).' Meanwhile Satan dominates this world and snatches up the souls of the sons of men."

APPENDIX FIVE

Be Fruitful: Reproduce a Godly Seed in the Image of God!

God created the world to be self-sustaining, and therefore every living thing was given the ability to reproduce *"after their kind."*[1] God's ultimate purpose in creation was for man and woman together to reproduce godly seed, that is, offspring in the image of God. Marriage is intended not only to include physical children, but also spiritual children (godly seed[2]) to impact humanity. Adam was called to see his children (physical and spiritual) developing in the image of God and relating well to God and each other. And so are we. You are not limited to your physical ability to procreate; all believers have the potential to make "spiritual children," as commanded in the garden, as well as in Yeshua's Great Commission. So, *"go therefore and make disciples of all the nations."*

Only our interdependence would fulfill the will of God.

Interdependence is a hard concept to grasp, because our sinful lives resist dependence on God. This is recognized as patriotism in most nations, as well as in American society, where we pride ourselves on independence—as in, "Give me liberty, or give me death." So, too, various states express their independent spirit with their state mottos: Kentucky, Unbridled Spirit. New Hampshire, Live Free or Die. Texas, Don't Mess with Texas. However, we are created to be interdependent. This is the fullness of life. Those who wish to have a fulfilled life on their own do not know what it truly means. A fulfilled life is one that represents God well. Since God is love, you will be fulfilled when you love and when you are loved. This is understood because you have been created for this very thing, to care about others and to be cared for. This is what it means to be created in the image of God.

Interdependence is the basis of society and community

The marriage relationship is the very cornerstone of the congregation and society. Ephesians 4:15–16 (SN) says, *"But speaking the truth in love, we are to grow up in all aspects into Him who is the head, even Messiah, from whom the whole body, being fitted and held together by what every joint supplies, according to the proper working of each individual part, causes the growth of the body for the building up of itself in love."*

Ephesians 4:15–16 pictures our unity in Messiah as a corporate entity, but it pictures marriage as well. The *"proper working"* is discipleship, training, and teaching. The *"proper working"* of each individual part causes the growth. This is how the sovereign God has organized all of it. Growth is by full dependence on Messiah and is revealed by the full interdependence of the Body. He is the head, and we are all called to orient our lives around Him. The proper working of those parts causes *"the growth of the body for the building up of itself in love."* Commitment to one another and interdependence cause the marriage relationship, as well as the Body of Messiah, to grow.

Thus, called to community, it is not good for anyone to be alone. We need to be reaching out to and caring for others; this is the biblical model that reveals the image of God.

---

1. Genesis 1:11–12, 21.
2. Malachi 2:15: *"Did the One not make her with a remnant of Ruach? Then what is the One seeking? Offspring of God!"* (TLV)

APPENDIX SIX

Sex in Scripture

Proper sex according to Scripture
1. To disciple offspring together: Malachi 2:13–16 (Genesis 1:28; 30:22–23; 49:25; Deuteronomy 25:5; Psalm 127:3–5)
2. To demonstrate unity with each other: Genesis 2:24–25 (1 Corinthians 6:15–17; Ephesians 5:31–32)
3. To delight in each other: Proverbs 5:15–20 (Song of Solomon 7:1–10; Proverbs 9:17; Song of Solomon 4:12, 15; Ecclesiastes 9:9 [the Hebrew word here for "portion," or "reward," is *cheleq*, as in Numbers 18:20])
4. To be dutiful to each other: 1 Corinthians 7:2–5

Improper sex according to Scripture
1. Fornication (sex before marriage), is contrary to "*the will of God*" (1 Thessalonians 4:3). Flee it! (1 Corinthians 6:18).
2. Masturbation
    - Deuteronomy 23:10, as a ceremonial uncleanness, "*a nocturnal emission*" is a misdemeanor while away from home (and brings uncleanness until evening; see also Leviticus 15:16–17).
    - Genesis 38:8–10, as willful disobedience, it's a felony for breaking the law of love (and brings capital punishment by HaShem).
3. Adultery
    - Exodus 20:14, one of the top ten, but see number ten, 20:17—it's motivated by coveting. It is a felony, Leviticus 20:10.
    - Matthew 5:27–28, adultery is a heart issue, as also in Matthew 15:19. We need to control our thought life, 2 Corinthians 10:5. It is part of covetousness and/or anger issues.
4. Improper divorce
    - Matthew 5:31–32, for any cause other than "*unchastity*," which is seen as either improper marriage or unrepentant adultery in desertion.
    - Matthew 5:21–48, this is part of a pattern of sin: the sin of anger (heart murder), 5:21–26; this leads to adultery, 5:27–30; this leads to the sin of improper divorce, 5:31–32; this leads to the sin of false vows, 5:33–37; this leads to the sin of revenge, 5:38–42; this leads to the sin of hate and lovelessness, 5:43–48.

APPENDIX SEVEN

Functional Subordination in Society

The Five Biblical Levels of Delegated Authority from God
1. Government leaders to citizens: 1 Samuel 24:6; Romans 13:1–2; 1 Peter 2:13
2. Employers to employees: Psalm 123:2; 1 Peter 2:18; Ephesians 6:5
3. Congregational elders to the congregants: Deuteronomy 18:18–19; Jeremiah 7:25–26; Hebrews 13:17
4. Husband to wife: Genesis 3:16; 1 Corinthians 11:2–3, Ephesians 5:22
5. Parents to children: Exodus 20:12, Ephesians 6:1–3

APPENDIX EIGHT

The Spirit-Filled Family, Ephesians 6:1–4

Children, obey your parents in the Lord, for this is right. Honor your father and mother (which is the first commandment with a promise), so that it may be well with you, and that you may live long on the earth. Fathers, do not provoke your children to anger, but bring them up in the discipline and instruction of the Lord.

Having discussed the Spirit-filled community (Ephesians 5:18–21) as built on the foundation of the Spirit-filled marriage (Ephesians 5:22–33), Paul makes the application of the Spirit-filled life to the family (Ephesians 6:1–4).

The Spirit-filled children (6:1–3)
The Spirit-filled life is an assumed norm for all believers, regardless of age, including the children in the Spirit-filled home.

The command for Spirit-filled children (6:1)
The command for children to obey their parents is that the son or daughter is to obey both mom and dad. As parents are not to play favorites, so the children are not to obey favorites, since both parents are provided by the same God. While my two adult sons will always be my dear children, I expect their honor of the dad and mom, but I rarely ask them to obey me, for two reasons. First, being raised in my home, they have been discipled in our primary Messianic values, so their obedience is to the values we share in Messiah. As adults, I respect their ability to make their own decisions, and to live with consequences. This is how they will continue to mature. But while living at home through their teen years, they were expected to obey their parents "*in the Lord.*" Anything contrary to the Lord, I'd expect them not to obey, from me or anyone else, for they are to "*obey God rather than men*" (Acts 5:29). If I or their mother were to ask them to do what is contrary to reason, I also taught them to respectfully ask why, because I wanted them to understand the reason behind any

request (or command) from their parents, or from any in authority over them. But proper obedience to their parents, who are obedient to the Lord, is expected by Him, *"for this is right"* (i.e., righteous). A righteous child is obedient in the Lord and is the evidence of the Spirit-filled life.

The honor by Spirit-filled children (6:2)
Paul reiterates the command found in both Exodus 20:12 and Deuteronomy 5:16. Parents are to be honored in the Lord by their children, not because of unusual or heroic actions by the parents, but because of the God-ordained position of parents. God is not a respecter of persons, but He is a respecter of positions, and so should we be as well, and this includes our children. Honoring parents honors the God who provided the parents, even as parents should deeply appreciate their children since He also provided the children to the parents (Psalm 127:3).

As the first command accompanied with promise, Paul is in fact referring to the first promise for the child, since the second command not to worship idols also has a promise attached (*"mercy to a thousand generations"* [SN]). As the first authority that the child will have to submit to, this is key for the people of God to have a land that is at peace and not in rebellion, for the rebellious attitude begins in the home with the child's dishonor of the parents.

The promise for Spirit-filled children (6:3)
The promise assures a good and long life. This is certainly true, but with notable exceptions. The calling and length of our life is in the hands of God. Yeshua, as the perfect Child, had a life that lasted only thirty-three years and ended with great pain and suffering on our behalf. But the promise is one that is in general to be counted upon, though a particular calling may require the fulfillment of the promise in the world to come, not here.

The Spirit-filled dad (6:4)
The Spirit-filled husband is now to serve as the Spirit-filled father. As we mature, we more and more represent the heavenly Father. That said, there are instructions to the Dad that, if obeyed, will enable the dad to grow to be a father who will encourage the child to follow the heavenly Father as well. This verse is addressed to fathers, not mothers or parents.

As the children are commanded to obey their parents, the father is commanded not to provoke his children. To "provoke" (*parorgizo*) is to exasperate and merely seek to anger your child. This is often a problem where the dad is unwilling to be pleased with the child's earnest efforts to obey their parents, and this will frustrate the child and can lead to disobedience and even rebellion. The word is used throughout the Tanakh regarding provoking God to anger through idolatry (Deuteronomy 4:25; 31:29; 32:21; Psalm 78:58; Jeremiah 7:18). In the same way, dads must be careful of making an idol of sports, A+ grades, bullying, or any other personal preferences that are a carnal substitute for the love of God toward your child. Those who so provoke their children to anger are not filled with the Spirit but may suffer from anger issues or frustrations of their own unfulfilled dreams that they are forcing upon their kids. The Spirit-filled dad is not perfect but always repents whenever he acts carnally towards his kids.

Rather than provoking your kids to anger, dads are instead to *"bring them up in the discipline and instruction of the Lord."* As noted in Ephesians 5:29, to *"bring them up"* (*ektrepho*) is "to nurture."

This is a reiteration of the father's calling to be a spiritual leader in the home, and especially regarding the children. Parents work as partners in the grace of life, but the husband's responsibility as the family's spiritual leader is re-emphasized in his role as the dad. This means that, though he may delegate the discipline and instruction to his wife while he is away, he is nonetheless responsible for the spiritual development of the children in his home.

There are two words that explain in what way the dad is to spiritually bring up his children: "*in the discipline and instruction of the Lord.*"

Discipline is normal for all disciples, and the dad is developing home-grown disciples. The Greek word (*paideia*) reflects upon the same structured instruction that was expected throughout the Tanakh (Proverbs 3:11; Isaiah 50:4–5, etc.). This discipline is the discipleship training expected for all disciples in the New Covenant, including the father (2 Timothy 3:16; Hebrews 12:5, 7, 8, 11). As the word means "training," it pictures a good coach that teaches each player on the team how to precisely handle responsibility, but then has the player perform the same skill over and over again. Training makes a skill into a successful habit. In many sports, the right habits can make the difference between a team's success or defeat. By the end of the game, all the players are exhausted, but the players with the best habits will be able to perform effectively nonetheless.

So too for the spiritual disciplines. Our kids need to pray, whether they have time or not, be kind when treated unkindly, and trust the Lord through all the trials of life. Every other godly habit will reveal the difference between believers who are easily defeated and disciples who are more than conquerors in Messiah.

The other word, "instruction" (*nouthesia*), can be translated as "admonition" since it refers to ethical and corrective instruction for our spiritual well-being in both belief and behavior. This is often an illustrative warning (1 Corinthians 10:11)—an example of what not to do. It is also a warning that there are consequences to inappropriate behavior (Titus 3:10). Yes, there are consequences to both doing what is right and doing what is wrong. Children need to know that they are to "*refuse evil and choose good*" (Isaiah 7:15) before they can enjoy either greater liberty or greater responsibility in the home. Since this teaching is "*in the Lord*," we cannot expect society to reinforce it, let alone teach it to our children. This is the responsibility of the dad, within the wholesome atmosphere of the family that practices these biblical values, and with the reinforcement of the Messianic community to which the family is committed.

APPENDIX NINE: A WEDDING OUTLINE

Earlier meetings

Wedding rehearsal: date: _____ time: _____ where: _____

Decoration and chuppah teams: coordinator: _____ time: _____

Pictures? Time: _____ Where: _____

Pre-wedding signing of license: time: _____ where: _____

Before Wedding Ceremony
- 45 minutes before wedding ceremony: ushers take their places
- 30 minutes before wedding ceremony: rabbi signs marriage license and prays with the couple.
- 15 minutes before wedding ceremony: wedding coordinator gathers and organizes wedding party at assigned spot to prepare for processional, and checks that they have the rings.

Processional
- A. Processional music _____
- B. Rabbi (and Cantor) proceeds down aisle
- C. Groom proceeds down aisle
- D. Maids, matron of honor, etc. proceed down aisle (names): _____
   _____
- E. Bride (and dad) proceed down aisle (name): _____
- F. Processional music ends.

Service
- A. Blessing of the Lord _____
- B. Blessing over the Cup, Prayer of Praise, Sharing of Cup _____
- C. Berakhot _____
- D. General Charge (sermon) on marriage _____
- E. Personal charges (the "I dos") Do you want to write your own vows? _____
- F. Rings exchanged ("With this ring I thee wed") _____
- G. Declaration of marriage ("By the authority…") _____
- H. Aaronic Benediction (in English): _____
- I. Breaking the glass ("You may kiss your Bride.") _____
- J. Introduction of the couple: _____

Recessional: music _____

Receiving line (if so, where): _____

Reception Coordinator _____
- A. Music: _____
   _____
- B. Food: _____
   _____
- C. Other activities _____
   _____

APPENDIX TEN: KETUBAH WORDS

On the _____ of the week, the _____ day of the month of _____ , corresponding to the secular date _____ here at _____ in _____ , I, _____ , son of _____ , from the family _____ _____ said to you: be my wife according to the faith of Israel. And I, _____ _____ , daughter of _____ , from the family _____ _____ , said to you: be my husband, according to the faith of Israel.

By Messiah's grace, I betroth you to me forever; I betroth you to me in righteousness and justice, in love and compassion, I betroth you to me in everlasting faithfulness. I shall treasure you, nourish you, support you, and respect you as Jewish men have devoted themselves to their wives with integrity. By the power of *Ruach HaKodesh* I will be your loving spouse, as you are mine. Set me as a seal upon your heart, like a seal upon your hand, for love is stronger than death: it is the flame of God. And I will cherish you, honor you, uphold, and sustain you in all truth and sincerity. I will respect you and the Divine image within you. I shall treasure you, nourish you, support you, and respect you as Jewish women have devoted themselves to their husbands with integrity. We promise to try to be ever open to one another while cherishing each other's uniqueness; to comfort and challenge each other through life's sorrow and joy; to share our intuition and insight with one another. We also pledge to establish a home open to the spiritual potential in all life.

A home wherein the flow of the seasons and the passages of life are celebrated through the symbols of our biblical heritage. A home filled with reverence for learning, loving, and generosity. A home wherein ancient melody, candles, and prayer sanctify the table. Therefore have I said to you: By this ring be sanctified to me, according to the faith of Israel. ALL THIS IS SPOKEN AND DONE.

This marriage has been authorized also by the civil authorities of _____ _____ . It is valid and binding.

APPENDIX ELEVEN: KIDDUSH

The Torah refers to two requirements concerning Shabbat: to keep it and to remember it (*shamar* and *zakhar*). According to tradition, we remember the Shabbat through the Kiddush.

Kiddush means sanctification—the separation of Shabbat from the rest of the week. Blessings, *berakhot*, is from *berek*, "knee." We must yield ourselves to Him for blessings!

The text of the Friday night Kiddush begins with a passage from Genesis 1:31b–2:3, as a testimony to God's creation of the world and cessation of work on the seventh day.

And there was evening and there was morning, the sixth day. Thus the heavens and the earth were completed, and all their hosts. By the seventh day God completed His work which He had done, and He rested on the seventh day from all His work which He had done. Then God blessed the seventh day and sanctified it, because in it He rested from all His work which God had created and made.

A day with no end!

In honor of Messiah Yeshua I will say the blessing over the bread and then the blessing over the cup: Barukh Attah HaShem, Eloheinu, Melekh ha-olam, hamotzi lechem min ha'arets. Barukh Attah HaShem, Eloheinu Melekh ha-olam, borei p'ri hagafen.

Blessed art Thou, O Lord our God, King of the universe, who brings forth bread from the earth (Amen). Blessed art Thou, O Lord our God, King of the universe, Creator of the fruit of the vine (Amen).

Blessed art Thou, O Lord our God, King of the universe, Who sanctified us with His commandments, and hoped for us, and with love and intent invested us with His sacred Sabbath, as a memorial to the deed of Creation. It is the first amongst the holy festivals, commemorating the exodus from Egypt. For, You chose us and sanctified us out of all nations, and with love and intent You invested us with Your Holy Sabbath.

Blessed are You, Sanctifier of the Sabbath (Amen).

The blessings remind us of His person and His sacrifice.

His person is the Bread of Life that gives life to us and nourishes our soul. May He who is the Bread of Life be our daily bread. He is the new wine of the Spirit for our soul. He turned water into wine, to tell us that in Him the ceremonial cleansing has become true cleansing and the life of joy in Him!

His sacrifice is two-fold: the bread is His Body that was payment for our sins in His death; the cup is His blood by which we are truly cleansed, so that HaShem not only forgives but can thereby forget!

APPENDIX TWELVE: MESSIANIC JEWISH HANUKKAH CANDLE-LIGHTING CEREMONY

(Traditional) Blessed art Thou, O Lord our God, King of the universe, Who has sanctified us with Thy commandments and commanded us to light Hanukkah lights. Barukh Attah Adonai Eloheinu, Melekh ha-olam, asher kid'shanu b'mitzvotav v'tzivanu l'hadlik ner shel Hanukkah.

(Messianic version) Blessed art Thou, O Lord our God, King of the universe, Who has given us holidays, customs, and times of happiness, to increase the knowledge of God and to build us up in our most holy faith. Barukh Attah Adonai Eloheinu, Melekh ha-olam, asher natan lanu chagim, minhagim, umoadim l'simcha, l'hagdil et da'at Adonai, v'livnot otanu b'emunah kidoshah v'na'alah.

Blessed art Thou, O Lord our God, King of the universe, Who performed miracles for our fathers in those days at this season. Barukh Attah Adonai Eloheinu, Melekh ha-olam, she'asah nisim la avoteinu bayamim hahem bazman hazeh.

On the first night you can add:

Blessed art Thou, O Lord our God, King of the universe, Who has granted us life and sustained us and permitted us to reach this season. Barukh Attah Adonai Eloheinu, Melekh ha-olam, shehecheyanu, v'kimanu, v'higianu laz'man hazeh.

Shamash (Servant) Candle (which lights all the others)

Messiah Yeshua stated in Mark 10:44–45: "*Whoever wishes to be first among you shall be slave of all. For even the Son of Man did not come to be served, but to serve, and to give His life a ransom for many.*"

First Candle

Genesis 1:3–4 describes the creation of the first light: "*God said, 'Let there be light'; and there was light. And God saw that the light was good; and God separated the light from the darkness.*"

Second Candle

Exodus 13:21–22 reveals that God is the source of Israel's light: "*The Lord was going before them in a pillar of cloud by day to lead them on the way, and in a pillar of fire by night to give them light, that they might travel by day and by night. He did not take away the pillar of cloud by day, nor the pillar of fire by night, from before the people.*"

Third Candle

King David reminds us that God Himself is the source of our own individual light: "*The Lord is my light and my salvation; whom shall I fear? The Lord is the defense of my life; whom shall I dread?*" (Psalm 27:1). "*For You light my lamp; the Lord my God illumines my darkness*" (Psalm 18:28).

Fourth Candle

Psalm 119:105 and Psalm 119:130 describe the light that comes from God's Word: "*Your word is a lamp to my feet and a light to my path…. The unfolding of Your words gives light; it gives understanding to the simple.*"

Fifth Candle

Messiah Yeshua is the greatest light of all: "*In Him was life, and the life was the Light of men. The Light shines in the darkness, and the darkness did not comprehend it*" (John 1:4–5). As Messiah Yeshua was in the Temple in Jerusalem watching the illuminating lights, He declared: "*I am the Light of the world; he who follows Me will not walk in the darkness, but will have the Light of life*" (John 8:12). Aged Simeon was promised by the Lord that he would not die until he saw Israel's Messiah. When he saw Yeshua as an infant in the Temple, he knew that this One was the light of Israel and the Nations. Simeon declared: "*My eyes have seen Your salvation, which You have prepared in the presence of all peoples, a Light of revelation to the Gentiles, and the glory of Your people Israel*" (Luke 2:30–32).

"*For God, who said, 'Light shall shine out of darkness,' is the One who has shone in our hearts to give the Light of the knowledge of the glory of God in the face of Messiah*" (2 Corinthians 4:6 SN).

Sixth Candle

After we come to know Messiah, we are to be His reflection of light for the world. King Messiah tells us in Matthew 5:14–16: "*You are the light of the world. A city set on a hill cannot be hidden; nor does anyone light a lamp and put it under a basket, but on the lampstand, and it gives light to all who are in the house. Let your light shine before men in such a way that they may see your good works, and glorify your Father who is in heaven.*"

Seventh Candle

The prophet Isaiah speaks of the future glory of a restored Israel in Isaiah 60:1, 3: *"Arise, shine; for your light has come, and the glory of the LORD has risen upon you.... Nations will come to your light, and kings to the brightness of your rising."*

Eighth Candle

Revelation 21:22–27 give us a description of our glorious eternal dwelling place in the New Jerusalem: *"I saw no temple in it, for the Lord God the Almighty and the Lamb are its temple. And the city has no need of the sun or of the moon to shine upon it, for the glory of God has illumined it, and its lamp is the Lamb. The nations will walk by its light, and the kings of the earth will bring their glory into it. In the daytime (for there will be no night there) its gates will never be closed; and they will bring the glory and the honor of the nations into it; and nothing unclean, and no one who practices abomination and lying, shall ever come into it, but only those whose names are written in the Lamb's book of life."*

APPENDIX THIRTEEN: MEZUZAH PRAYER

Before affixing the mezuzah to the doorpost, the following blessing should be recited:

Barukh Attah Adonai Eloheinu, Melekh ha-olam, asher kid'shanu b'mitzvotav v'tzivanu al lik'boa mezuzah. Blessed art Thou, O Lord our God, King of the universe, who has sanctified us with His commandments and commanded us to affix a mezuzah.

The mezuzah should then be affixed to the upper third of the doorpost on the right side as one enters the house or room. If the doorpost is wide enough to permit, the mezuzah should be tilted with the upper part slanting inward toward the house or room. The mezuzah is both a witness to all who pass by the house that this home is under the authority of the Word of God, and a reminder to the family that Messiah, the living Word of God (John 1:1, 14), is Lord of their home.

APPENDIX FOURTEEN: PREMARITAL DISCUSSION GUIDE

I. Personal History

1. When you were a child growing up, what was the warmest place in your home? What made it so warm?

2. What is your favorite memory of a time alone with your father?

3. What is your favorite memory of a time alone with your mother?

4. What fun things do you remember that your family did together when you were a child?

5. How did you spend your leisure time as a child?

   a. During elementary years

   b. During junior high years

   c. During senior high years

   d. During college years

   e. How do your leisure activities differ today?

6. What responsibilities and chores did you have to do regularly as a child in your home? How do you feel about these today?

7. What special privileges did you "have to be old enough" for (e.g., driving, riding a bike, bedtime, etc.).

8. When did you sneak your first cigarette, can of beer, or "naughty" book?

9. How did you feel about it at the time?

10. With whom would you go to talk and share your personal concerns?

11. Which parent could you communicate with the easiest? Why that parent instead of the other?

12. Who was your favorite teacher from your school days? What made this teacher more special than any other?

13. What was the happiest time of your childhood?

14. What was the unhappiest time of your childhood?

15. How did you feel about yourself at these times?

16. When were you first kissed or did you first kiss someone? Describe briefly what you felt at that time.

17. When did you first rebel against your parents or other authority figures?

18. When did you first consciously choose some value on your own?

19. Describe what events or feelings drew you to your salvation experience.

20. List ten adjectives that apply to or describe what God the Father is like.

21. Describe the meal that your family always enjoyed the most. What was or is your favorite food that your mother always fixed for you?

22. What are your family's holiday traditions (what you always do together)?

    a. Christmas/ Hanukkah

    b. Thanksgiving

    c. Passover/Easter

    d. High Holidays

    e. Other

23. How will you feel if you have to miss the next family holiday at your home?

24. How do you expect your mate to be like (or unlike) your parents?

25. What habits are you going to have to change before you will be a good roommate for your mate?

26. What things could your roommate do that would really irritate you?

27. What have you and previous roommates argued about the most?

28. What did your parents expect of you in terms of your money and the use of it?

29. How much allowance were you given? What did you have to do to earn it?

30. These questions probably have raised several questions you have wanted to ask your mate. (Perhaps you have been fearful of asking them in the past.) List below three or more questions you would like for your mate to answer.

_____
_____
_____
_____
_____

APPENDIX FIFTEEN: PREMARITAL DISCUSSION GUIDE

II. Marital Roles

1. What should the role of the husband be, in your opinion?

2. What should the role of the wife be, in your opinion?

3. Using the letters "W" for wife and "H" for husband, designate the following jobs, chores, or roles as to which spouse you believe should most often do it. Use a "B" when you think both should handle it:

___ Wash dishes
___ Shop for groceries
___ Balance checkbook

__ Discipline children
__ Mow yard
__ Care for car (gas, oil, repairs)
__ Take out trash
__ Wash clothes
__ Vacuum
__ Fold clothes
__ Initiate sex
__ Shine shoes
__ Change babies' diapers
__ Clean bathroom
__ Fix meals
__ Clean flower beds
__ Ironing
__ Attend PTA (and school functions)
__ Take children to doctor
__ Shop for clothes
__ Take children to barber or beauty shop
__ Determine use of savings
__ Manage budget
__ Handle problems with neighbors
__ Mopping
__ Cook out of doors
__ Decide whose parents to visit at holidays
__ Choose place of worship
__ Train the kids spiritually

4. How do you feel about both spouses working outside of the home?

5. What was your mother's role in your home?

6. What was your father's role in your home?

7. How did you feel about their respective roles?

8. What chores or jobs around the house do you dislike doing the most?

9. What was expected of you as a child? (List items from question #3 that you had to do as a child.)

10. How much money can your spouse spend without checking with you?

11. How much money can you spend without checking with your spouse?

12. How do you feel decisions should be reached as to who will do what in your marriage?

13. How have all of the discussion in our culture about feminism and the changing roles of men and women affected you personally?

14. How do you feel about separate vacations?

15. Define briefly what the term *submit* (Ephesians 5:22) means to you.

16. Define briefly what the term *head* (Ephesians 5:22–25) means to you.

17. How many hours a day do you watch TV_____, are you on the Internet _____, on email _____, and on the phone with friends _____?

APPENDIX SIXTEEN: PREMARITAL DISCUSSION GUIDE

III. Sexuality

1. What is your earliest sexual memory? How old were you?

2. What is your earliest awareness of sexual differences between male and female?

3. What feelings do you associate with these early memories?

4. How did you learn the "facts of life"? How old were you?

5. What feelings do you associate with this early knowledge?

6. As your awareness and feelings of your own sexuality grew during childhood, did you share your feelings with an adult? Why or why not? With whom did you share your feelings?

7. When did you first notice that you began to mature physically and sexually?

8. How did you feel about it?

9. Did you share these feelings with anyone? Who?

10. What information did your parents give you about sexuality?

11. What books have you read that have proved helpful in educating you sexually?

12. When did you have your first "date"? How old were you?

13. What feelings do you associate with this memory today?

14. What traumatic sexual experiences have you had in your life?

15. How do you feel about these today?

16. What are your thoughts on the subject of abortion?

17. What types of birth control are you aware of?

18. What types would be your first and second choice?

Appendices

19. What are your thoughts or ideas about homosexuality? Have you ever had a homosexual experience? How old were you? What are your feelings today about these experiences?

20. What are your thoughts or ideas about masturbation? Have you ever had a problem with a habit of masturbation? When? Have you ever had a problem with a habit of reading pornography? When? How have you dealt with these habits?

21. What are your thoughts concerning sex before marriage? Have you had relations with ___ one; ___ a few; ___ several; ___ many sexual partners?

22. How much do you think marital partners should know about each other's previous sexual experience? Can you forgive your spouse for similar premarital experiences? Can you forgive yourself for your past experiences?

23. What fears or doubts do you have about your wedding night or your ability to perform sexually in marriage?

24. What thoughts or ideas do you have in your fantasies concerning sexual activities?

25. These questions have possibly made you curious about other sexual activities or have raised additional questions you would like to ask your mate. List five or more questions or topics of interest below that you would like to discuss in addition to the ones above.

_____
_____
_____
_____
_____

APPENDIX SEVENTEEN: PREMARITAL DISCUSSION GUIDE

IV. Financial Profile

In the space provided, predict what your finances will be like after you are married.

Current Outstanding Debts:

Description	Total Amount	Monthly Amount
Wife's Debts:		
1.		
2.		
3.		
4.		
5.		
Husband's Debts:		
1.		
2.		
3.		
4.		
5.		
	Total:	Total:

Predicted Monthly Income:

Wife's salary (take-home pay) per month:

Husband's salary (take-home pay) per month:

Additional monthly income (stocks, investments, interest, etc.):

Total per month:

Predicted Monthly Expenditures:

House payments or rent:

Auto payments and maintenance:

Utilities (gas, electricity, water):

Telephone:

Food and household items:

Recreation and entertainment:

Medical and dental:

Savings and investments:

Insurance:

Miscellaneous:

Tithe:

Personal allowances:
Other:
Total per month:

Questions to ask yourself:

1. Can any of the debts be eliminated before the wedding?

2. Can you cut any of your expected expenditures?

3. How much in savings do you each have now?

4. How do you plan to pay for the wedding?

5. How do you plan to pay for the honeymoon?

6. What medical-hospitalization insurance will you both have after the wedding?

7. How much life insurance will you each have?

8. Do you each have a will?

Questions you want to ask your counselor about finance:
_____
_____
_____
_____

APPENDIX EIGHTEEN: BRIEF (MESSIANIC) SEDER AT HOME[3]

Blessing over the Candles: B'rekhot ha-Ner

Barukh Attah Adonai Eloheinu, Melekh ha-olam, asher kid'shanu b'Yeshua ha-Mashiach, Or ha-olam u'vish'mo l'hadlik ner shel Pesach. Blessed art Thou, O Lord our God, King of the universe, Who has sanctified us through faith in Yeshua the Messiah, the Light of the world, and in His Name we kindle the Passover Lights.

1. *First Cup*: Sanctification. *"I will bring you out from under the burdens of the Egyptians"* (Exodus 6:6).

Bless and drink the First Cup.

Barukh Attah Adonai Eloheinu, Melekh ha-olam, borei p'ri ha-gafen. Blessed art Thou, O Lord our God, King of the universe, Who creates the fruit of the vine.

Urchatz. Washing of hands

Karpas. Dipping the parsley into the salt water

Barukh Attah Adonai Eloheinu, Melekh ha-olam, borei p'ri ha-adamah. Blessed art Thou, O Lord our God, King of the universe, Who creates the fruit of the earth.

Echad. Unity (middle matzah is removed and broken)

2. *Second Cup*: Plagues, or judgments. *"I will deliver you from their bondage"* (Exodus 6:6).

Matzah. Blessing over the bread: "This is the bread of our affliction."

Barukh Attah Adonai Eloheinu, Melekh ha-olam, ha-motzi lechem min ha-arets. Blessed art Thou, O Lord our God, King of the universe, Who brings forth bread from the earth.

Maror. Dipping bitter herbs

Barukh Attah Adonai Eloheinu, Melekh ha-olam, asher kid'shanu b'mits'votav v'tsivanu ahl akhilat maror. Blessed art Thou, O Lord our God, King of the universe, Who sanctified us with His commandments and commanded us to eat bitter herbs.

Charoseth. Eating charoseth (with bitter herbs, optional)

Haggigah. Egg displayed

Reciting the four questions, response, and Passover story

Remembering the ten plagues: Wrath poured out:

    Blood, Frogs, Vermin, Flies, Pestilence,

    Boils, Hail, Locusts, Darkness, Slaying of the firstborn

Zeroah. Shankbone of the Lamb

Dayenu. It would have been enough/Our God is sufficient!

Bless and drink Second Cup.

Shulchan Orech. Meal is eaten!

---

3. For a fuller explanation and to conduct a full Messianic Seder, see the author's book *The Messianic Passover Haggadah*, which can be acquired at the Word of Messiah Ministries website bookstore, wordofmessiahbookstore.com/.

3. *Third Cup*: Redemption. "*I will also redeem you with an outstretched arm and with great judgments*" (Exodus 6:6).
Afikomen. Partaking of the broken matzah, repeating prayer over bread
Redemption. Bless and drink third cup, repeating prayer over cup.

4. *Fourth Cup*: *Hallel* ("Praise"), or Elijah's Cup, "*I will take you for My people*" (Exodus 6:7).
Elijah sought.
Hallel. Bless and drink fourth cup, repeating prayer over cup.

APPENDIX NINETEEN: TORAH BLESSINGS

Before the Reading of the Torah:

Bar'khu et Adonai ha-m'vorakh!

Barukh Adonai ha-m'vorakh l'olam va'ed!

Barukh Attah, Adonai Eloheinu, Melekh ha-olam, asher bachar banu mikkol ha-amim v'natan lanu et Torato. Barukh Attah, Adonai, notein ha-Torah.

Praise Adonai, to whom our praise is due! Praised be Adonai, to whom our praise is due, now and forever! Blessed is Adonai our God, Ruler of the universe, who has chosen us from all peoples by giving us God's Torah. Blessed is Adonai, Giver of the Torah.

After the Reading of the Torah:

Barukh Attah, Adonai Eloheinu, Melekh ha-olam, asher natan lanu Torat emet v'chayei olam nata b'tokheinu. Barukh Attah, Adonai, notein ha-Torah.

Blessed are You, Adonai, our God, Ruler of the universe, for giving us a Torah of truth and implanting within us eternal life.

Blessed are You, Adonai, Giver of the Torah!

APPENDIX TWENTY: WEDDING SYMBOLS

Chuppah (Hebrew for "covering")

Traditionally symbolizes marriage canopy, symbolizing new home, fragility, and protection.

In ancient times, the marriage was consummated in the groom's chuppah, or tent. Today its use is symbolic. The couple stands under the marriage canopy, representing their new home. Ceremonies using the chuppah invoke home or protection. Some say that the canopy represents security, and the open sides represent hospitality. Talmud tells us that the chuppah also represents divine light. Just as the chuppah covers the bridal couple, so His light surrounds all of creation. It is the light of wisdom and the root of all existence. Of course, Yeshua is the Light of the world (John 8:12).

In Scripture, the sun is symbolized *"as a bridegroom coming out of his chamber"* ("chamber" is *chuppah* in Psalm 19:5). The chuppah further symbolizes the marriage joy, as in, *"the bride out of her bridal chamber"* (Joel 2:16). In the future Messianic kingdom, the chuppah will symbolize heavenly protection over redeemed Israel. Isaiah 4:5: *"Then the LORD will create over the whole area of Mount Zion and over her assemblies a cloud by day, even smoke, and the brightness of a flaming fire by night; for over all the glory will be a canopy."* In heaven, Messiah will spread His protection over us, His Bride (Revelation 7:15: *"They are before the throne of God…and He who sits on the throne will spread His tabernacle over them."*)

Candles

Traditionally symbolizes joy, spirit, soul.

On Shabbat and holidays, candles are lit to symbolize the light of the Sabbath. Mashiach is symbolized as the Light of *olam ha-zeh* ("the present world": John 8:12) and will be the light of *olam ha-ba* ("the world to come": Isaiah 60:19–20; Revelation 21:23). His light *"enlightens every man"* and brings into the marriage the Light of life (John 1:4–9).

Challah (braided egg bread)

Traditionally reminiscent of bread eaten by priests in the temple, manna, and sustenance eaten on Shabbat and holidays. As bread is called the *"staff"* of life (Psalm 105:16), Scripture declares that Yeshua the Messiah is for all who believe in Him *"the Bread of Life"* (John 6:35).

Circle

Traditionally symbolizes wholeness, completion.

A round wedding ring symbolizes the circle of marriage. Traditionally, the bride circles the groom seven times under the chuppah (in some cases, three times). The never-ending life is pictured in marriage—that eternal life we have in relationship to Messiah (Ephesians 5:31–32).

Glass (breaking of)

Traditionally symbolizes destruction, protection.

A glass is traditionally shattered at the conclusion of a wedding ceremony. It is said to symbolize our grief at the destruction of the temple, the fragility of relationships, and the warding off of demons. Sometimes people save the shattered glass and make something decorative out of it. This too is a beautiful reminder of our Messiah, who was broken for us (Luke 22:19: *"And when He had taken some bread and given thanks, He broke it and gave it to them, saying, 'This is My body which is given for you; do this in remembrance of Me.'"*) In His brokenness, He broke down the diving wall between people (Ephesians 2:14: *"For He Himself is our peace, who made both groups into one and broke down the barrier of the dividing wall"*). In marriage as well, the brokenness of selfish pride can provide the humility that demonstrates loving concern for our spouse (Psalm 51:17: *"The sacrifices of God are a broken spirit; A broken and a contrite heart, O God, You will not despise"*). And then something beautiful can be made as a reminder of God's healing power (Psalm 147:3: *"He heals the brokenhearted and binds up their wounds"*).

Ketubah (Hebrew for "writing"; pl. *ketubot*), Jewish wedding contract

Traditionally, the *ketubah* protected the wife in marriage by spelling out the husband's obligations to her and guaranteeing her a financial settlement in case of divorce. Throughout the ages, *ketubot* have been illuminated and calligraphed and are also significant as Jewish art. Today, all manner of egalitarian *ketubot* are written. Some dispense with the financial and legal aspects, focusing more on the emotional and spiritual sides of the relationship.

Other *ketubot* maintain the rabbis' concerns with the practical, but define mutual obligations for husband and wife. Biblically, the Torah was a *ketubah* that the Lord made with Israel (Ezekiel 16:8; Isaiah 54:5–6). Then the Lord promised and provided a B'rit Chadashah (New Covenant) as a ketubah that Messiah would establish for Israel and all who believe in Him (Jeremiah 31:31–34; Hosea 2:18–23; Luke 22:20; Hebrews 8:8–13).

Kiddushin (Hebrew for "set apart" and "sanctify"; or *erusin*, Hebrew for "betrothal")

This refers to the first part of the traditional wedding service, in which the groom acquires the bride by giving her a small token, usually a ring, and declares that she is betrothed to him according to Scripture. Today, many couples exchange rings. Thus Messiah paid the "dowry" price in His atonement and thus redeemed the bride (1 Corinthians 6:14–20; 2 Corinthians 11:2). This idea of "kiddush"—that is, to be set apart, sanctified, and treated as special—is the picture of Messiah's treatment of His Bride, the believers in Him: "*so that He might sanctify her*" (Ephesians 5:26).

Nissuin (nuptials; Hebrew for "lifting")

This is the second part of the wedding ceremony, during which the seven blessings are read. The final book of Scripture, Revelation, has Messiah's seven blessings for His bride (Revelation 1:3, 14:13, 16:15, 19:9, 20:6, 22:7, 22:14). Indeed, all the blessings of heaven for our marriages and our lives are found in Messiah Yeshua (Ephesians 1:3).

Kippah (Hebrew for "covering"); Yarmulke (Yiddish)

Traditionally symbolizes fear/awe of heaven, humility.

The kippah is a small cap, traditionally worn by men, symbolizing humility before God. In the Torah of Moses, all priests wore caps (Exodus 28:40; 29:9; 39:28; Leviticus 8:13). This reverence for God is what is to typify each person in Messiah (1 Peter 3:15 [SN]: "*But sanctify Messiah as Lord in your hearts, always being ready to give to everyone who asks you the reason for the hope that is in you, with gentleness and reverence*"). In reverence for God, we trust in the atonement/covering (*kippurah*) of Messiah.

Tallit (prayer shawl)

Traditionally symbolizes commandments, God's sheltering presence.

A tallit is a four-cornered garment to which ritual fringes (*tzitzit*) are affixed (Numbers 15:38–39). The knots in the fringes represent the name of God and remind us of God's commandments. The tallit can also be drawn about oneself or around the bride and groom to symbolize divine protection (see Ruth 3:9). The *tzitzit* on Messiah's clothing spoke of His accessibility to people as the way to God's presence and comfort (Matthew 14:36; Zechariah 8:23). In Messiah as our tallit, we have His protection forever (Romans 8:1).

White

Traditionally symbolizes purity.

The wedding couple traditionally wears white, symbolic of purity. In the B'rit Chadashah (the New Covenant), Messiah provides His Bride (symbolizing believers in Him) with the white wedding garment, which, as it is stated, symbolizes righteous deeds (Revelation 7:9, 19:7–8, 21:2, 9). This will be the color of Messiah's garments in the kingdom (Matthew 17:2).

Wine

Traditionally symbolizes joy.

Nearly everything in Judaism is sanctified over a cup of wine—Shabbat, holidays, a marriage, and a *brit* (circumcision), to name a few. Grape juice can always be used instead of wine. In the B'rit Chadashah (the New Covenant), Messiah's first miracle is to turn water into wine at a wedding. The water was taken from the household's ceremonial *mikveh* water (used for ceremonial cleansing), symbolizing that in Him there is not merely ceremonial cleansing but true spiritual cleansing that brings with it the joy of life (John 2:6–10).

APPENDIX TWENTY-ONE: TRADITIONAL JEWISH WEDDING VOWS

There is no actual exchange of vows in a traditional Jewish ceremony; the covenant is said to be implicit in the ritual. Ceremony structure varies within the Orthodox, Conservative, and Reform synagogues, and also among individual rabbis. The marriage vow is customarily sealed when the groom places a ring on his bride's finger and says: "Behold, you are consecrated to me with this ring according to the laws of Moses and Israel."

However, today many Jewish couples opt for double-ring ceremonies, so the bride may also recite the traditional ring words, or a modified version. The traditional Seven Blessings, or Sheva B'rachot, are also an integral part of Jewish ceremonies; often relatives and friends of the couple's choosing recite them. And because many Jewish couples today do want to exchange spoken vows, they are now included in many Reform and Conservative ceremonies.

Reform

"Do you, _____ , take _____ to be your wife/husband, promising to cherish and protect her/him, whether in good fortune or in adversity, and to seek together with her/him a life hallowed by the faith of Israel?"

Conservative

"Do you, _____ , take _____ to be your lawfully wedded wife/husband, to love, to honor, and to cherish?"

Other Jewish vows:

"With this ring, you are made holy to me, for I love you as my soul. You are now my wife."

"With this ring, you are made holy to me, for I love you as my soul. You are now my husband."

In Messianic weddings it is customary to honor Yeshua the Messiah in the vows and throughout the wedding ceremony. The officiating rabbi should be able to assist the couple in this matter.

ABOUT THE AUTHOR

I was born on a snowy winter day, January 2, 1948, in Queens, New York. Both my father and mother were hard-working people. My dad was involved with the Furniture Workers Union after the loss of the family furniture business during the Depression. Growing up in my neighborhood, Middle Village, in the late 40's and early 50's meant growing up Jewish. With a synagogue on every block, the choices seemed endless. Where we attended, however, depended mostly on whom we were getting along with during any given High Holy Day season.

Religious

I received a normal Jewish upbringing, and was eventually Bar Mitzvahed according to orthodoxy. This both pleased and relieved my family, because even at such a young age I tended to resist religion.

You see, I had questions. There were a number of Auschwitz survivors in my neighborhood—the numbers on their arms were a constant argument for me against God's existence. "How could there be a God, much less a 'God of Israel,' that would allow such atrocities to be perpetrated against people, especially the Jewish people?" One night when I was nine years old, I put God to the test: "Okay, if you're there, have a penny appear under my pillow," I demanded. I figured I wasn't being greedy—anyone can come up with a penny, right? So the next morning, when there was no penny under my pillow, I concluded there was no God over my head either.

After my Bar Mitzvah, the pressure was off for me to attend synagogue. My parents were no longer responsible for my spiritual commitments or failures, as I was now considered an adult. So I gave up any participation in religion, which I'd only done to honor my family.

Rebellious

My teenage years were spent removing any residual effects of religiosity. I actually took great pride in talking my friends out of going to services, whether church or synagogue. I got involved in petty crime and local mischief, and the police would occasionally show up at the door, raising suspicions among our neighbors. So I became, I'm now sorry to say, a source of disappointment to my family.

Following my stint in Vietnam, where I developed a fondness for both using and selling drugs, I lived in various scenic locales of California. At first I traveled around and lived in an old green Econoline van that I called "Wire and Whimsy," because that was what held it together. It was sort of a "rolling party," though we were lucky if it rolled at all, since an elderly van requires one to be more of a mechanic than poet. I broke down in Eureka, California, and got a job there at the Snug

Saloon. It was a bar for hippies, fishermen, and lumberjacks that not only provided entertainment in the form of nightly brawls, but gave me a place to crash until the van was fixed.

It was here that I met my first Christians, who were genuine believers in Messiah. Around closing time, they would come in to give the drunks a place to sleep, which was fine with me since I had to do something with them anyway. But these were trouble-making Christians: they would take the opportunity to talk about Jesus to whomever was still on their feet! It turns out that talking about Jesus in a saloon is really bad for business, so I'd throw out these zealots, with or without the drunks. Nothing personal, but business is business.

One night one of these Christians tried to tell me how much I "needed the Lord." "You'll never be truly happy until you come to faith in Jesus," she said. Just to show her how "happy" I was, I laughed at her and said, "I have so much religion of my own that I'm not even using, what would I want with any of yours?!" I went on to say some rather creative and colorful but not very flattering things. But something happened. I was not totally aware of it then, but a spiritual seed was planted.

Circumstances changed very quickly after that. The saloon changed hands, the house I was living in burned down, but the van was running somewhat, so I figured it was time to move on.

Back in San Francisco I shared a flat with about a dozen other "denizens of the dark"—all involved in one illegal activity or another, generally drug-oriented. It was during that time that I met a Jew who believed in Jesus. He was "witnessing" with some people where I "did business." Sort of a place where angels fear to tread. When he told me he was Jewish, I genuinely felt sorry for him. I figured his mother must have dressed him wrong growing up or something. This had to be the dumbest Jew I ever met, for if there's one thing a Jew should know, it is that Jews do not believe in Jesus. Period. When he invited me to a Bible study, I could only mock, "Thursday night? Sorry, that's my night to sleep in, but if I come down with insomnia I'll be sure to drop by."

The strange thing is, the night of that study I decided on a whim to go, just to laugh at the believers. While I was there someone showed me a portion from the Hebrew Prophets, Isaiah 53. I read it. I couldn't believe my eyes. It spoke of one who would die for the sins of my people, but yet not stay dead! Nothing is supposed to be this clear, especially not the Bible!

I figured spiritual matters were supposed to be vague, and you could interpret what it meant "for you." There isn't supposed to be objective evidence. Sneaky Christians, acting so sincere and Jewish—they must have taken part of their New Testament and stuck it in "my side of the Bible!" They were confusing me with the facts! I pretended not to be interested. When they said they'd pray for me and wrote my name in their Bibles, I could only sarcastically laugh and go back to the little world I was familiar with and comfortable in.

Things began to change, though. Over the next several months, the more I tried to disprove what they were saying, the more intrigued I became with Jesus. I even tried studying the occult and what is now called "New Age" religion, taking courses at the Metaphysical Institute of San Francisco. But the more I searched for truth in all the wrong places, the more I came back to considering this Jesus.

About the Author

Redeemed

On the evening of January 10, 1972, I became convinced of the spiritual reality of evil. Until then I figured there was no objective right and wrong; "spiritual power" was simply what you made of it. It was then that I realized that drugs were opening me up to the spiritual realm—but to the wrong spirit! I saw a spiritual battle for my soul, which I was losing, and I was thoroughly convinced that I needed a Savior. I needed Jesus.

Though I didn't know all the right words to say, I asked Jesus to save me. And He did. When I prayed that simple prayer the Spirit of God came down upon me with power. I was cleansed, forgiven, and I experienced a peace that I had never known before: a peace that passes all understanding.

I woke the next morning and I knew in my heart one thing: Jesus is Lord. I don't know how I knew that, but I did. I also knew I could not live where I was living or the way I was living, but what was I to do? I thought surely I had to be the only real Jew who had ever done this before. After a few dead ends I remembered the Bible study I had attended months before, and thought, "Maybe they know what to do?"

As I called them up I was sure they would never remember me, so I explained who I was, then finally blurted out, "Jesus saved me last night—what do I do now?" The other end of the phone sounded like the Hallelujah Chorus. They hadn't forgotten, but had been praying for me every day! Though I hadn't believed in prayer, they believed that there is a God who does answer prayer. So if you're praying for someone, don't stop. The Lord does answer prayer!

I soon started studying the Scriptures, growing in Messiah, and learning to share Him with others. There were many more blessings to follow. I went off to Bible college, and soon after, I met and married my wife Miriam. The Lord called me to bring the Good News to my people—something I've attempted to do for the past thirty-plus years. Some of that will have to wait to be told at another time, but this is my story, and I'm sticking to it!

Other Books by Sam Nadler:

Messianic Discipleship (available in English, Hebrew, Russian, Amharic)

Messianic Wisdom

Messianic Foundations

The Messianic Answer Book

Messiah in the Feasts of Israel

The Book of Ruth: Hope Fulfilled in the Redeemer's Grace

The Book of Jonah: Finding & Following the Will of God

Developing Health Messianic Congregations

Pamphlets:

"Even You Can Share the Jewish Messiah"

"S.W.A.T. 'Street Witnessing and Training'"

Made in the USA
Lexington, KY
19 November 2019